A SPRINGTIME AFFAIR

Gilly runs her own B&B business from her much-loved family home, which she doesn't want to part with — at any price. But that's before she meets handsome estate agent Leo, and soon she begins to wonder whether selling up might not be such a bad idea after all. Meanwhile, Gilly's daughter, Helena, has a budding romance of her own. A talented weaver, she's becoming very close to her new landlord, Jago, who's offered to help her at an upcoming craft fair. It's what friends do, and they are just friends. Aren't they? With spring in full bloom, Helena and Gilly begin to ask themselves the same question: might their new loves lead to happily ever after?

KATIE FFORDE

◆

A
SPRINGTIME
AFFAIR

Complete and Unabridged

CHARNWOOD
Leicester

First published in Great Britain in 2020 by
Century
London

First Charnwood Edition
published 2020
by arrangement with
Century
Penguin Random House UK
London

A catalogue record for this book is available
from the British Library.

ISBN 978–1–4448–4621–8

Published by
Ulverscroft Limited
Anstey, Leicestershire

Set by Words & Graphics Ltd.
Anstey, Leicestershire
Printed and bound in Great Britain by
T. J. International Ltd., Padstow, Cornwall

This book is printed on acid-free paper

Acknowledgements

As always, a lot of people helped me with the research for this book, they were generous with their time and told me all I thought I needed to know. And as always, I will have made mistakes and got it wrong. It is not their fault! It is entirely mine.

Among the many, are two wonderful weavers, Cyndy Graham, who has a thatched cottage in Donegal, with sensational views, and Nick Ozanne, the creator of Leto and Ariadne. They both produce beautiful and very different items and were both very kind to me.

I heard about super recognisers from James Wilks, whose wife, Emma Wilks, is one. The moment I heard about this, I knew I had to put it in my book.

Andy Rhoton, with her husband, Bill, used to run what must have been the best Bed and Breakfast in the country. Thank you, Andy, for all your in-put. (And funny stories — not in the book.)

I happen to have the very best publishing team there is (in my far from humble opinion). They include Selina Walker, inspirational, supportive and full of brilliant ideas, who turns my words into a readable book. Cassandra Di Bello, who sadly now lives in Australia. (No connection, I'm sure!) Ajebowale Roberts who has taken up

Cass's role with equal efficiency and kindness.

Thanks also go to the wonderful sales team, Laura Garrod, Rachel Campbell, Mat Watterson, Claire Simmonds and Sasha Cox. Not forgetting the magicians that are the marketing team, Sarah Ridley and Natalia Cacciatore, or the artists who create my covers, Ceara Elliot for art direction and Jacqueline Bisset for illustrations. And the people who get the books out on time and looking fabulous, Linda Hodgson and Helen Wynn-Smith. Last but not least, brilliant Katie Sheldrake, and as always my much loved friend Charlotte Bush in publicity.

My copyeditor, Richenda Todd, who stops the clangers (there are always clangers!) and makes me look like I know what I'm writing about. So grateful!

And to Bill Hamilton, officially best agent ever, my staff and stay.

Never forgetting my family, who are now more than emotional supporters. I love you and I'm truly grateful to you.

To Briony Wilson-Fforde, Heidi Fforde and Anastasia Fforde, my girls, whose friendship and support I value so much. Thank you!

To Briony Wilson-Fforde, Heidi Fforde and Anastasia Fforde, my girls, whose friendship and support I value so much. Thank you!

1

Helena was not happy. She had nearly finished weaving a throw in quite a complicated pattern only to be interrupted by a knock at the door. But as she had an idea who was knocking, she didn't feel she could ignore it. So, retying the scarf that was holding her hair back from her face, she got up from her loom, went to the door and opened it.

'Yes?' she said to the man standing there.

He was surprisingly large and dressed in jeans, rugby shirt and what Helena thought of as builders' boots. He was covered in dust and was smiling ruefully, possibly to make himself seem unthreatening.

'I'm terribly sorry to disturb you,' he said, pushing his dusty blond hair out of his eyes, 'but I have an animal emergency. I need someone a bit smaller than me.' He cast his eyes rapidly up and down her. 'And you're a lot smaller. You'd be perfect.' His smile was crooked and had a tinge of anxiety which made him hard to resist.

'Would you care to elaborate?' Helena was an animal lover but she needed some details before committing herself. He might want help with a flock of angry geese, for example, in which case she was not the best person to ask.

'It's a kitten. It's my sister's and Zuleika, the mother, is getting desperate. I'm keeping her in the house because if she gets in where her kitten

1

is, she might well make everything a whole lot worse.'

'Then let's go,' said Helena, and shut her door behind her, not worrying about locking it. Her studio had been part of a barn that was near the farmhouse, which her landlord had just moved into, and it was all part of the same property, so it wasn't exactly far.

'I'm so grateful,' said the man as they set off. 'I probably spent rather too long trying to sort it out myself but I'm just too huge.' He stopped. 'By the way, I'm Jago, Jago Pen — '

'I know who you are,' said Helena. 'Your name is on the lease of my studio.'

'So it is,' he said and set off again. 'Come on. Let's get that kitten out of bother.'

It didn't take them long to cross the courtyard to what would one day be a very lovely house. It had a rather 'cobbled together' look about it: a small original house had had bits added on to it over the centuries at a time when no one worried too much if a Georgian section would look odd next to a bit built in far earlier times. But the years had blurred the edges and it was now charming. It belonged to Jago Pengelly, Helena's landlord, but although he had owned it for over six months, he had only just started working on it. His presence indicated her notice was up; he was about to turn her out of her studio, which was where she not only did her weaving but also lived. She really wanted to hate him but her sense of fair play made it difficult: six months' notice was more than generous and if she had concentrated more she would probably have

2

found alternative accommodation for her and her loom by now.

'We need to go round the back,' Jago said.

Disappointed that she wasn't going to get a look inside Jago's house, Helena followed him to where he was standing in front of a huge pile of soil and rock. He was looking anxious.

'There was slippage. I wouldn't have started with the digger if I'd known Zuleika and the kitten were anywhere near while I was working. I thought Zulie was shut in but she must have slipped out after me and the kitten followed.'

'Where is the kitten?' asked Helena.

'Behind there.' They were at the back of the house now and he indicated a huge pile of soil and stone.

'Oh my God. Can't you just climb up and get her?'

'Not without dislodging more rubble, which could bury her, poor little thing.'

'So how can I help? The same thing could happen if I climbed up.'

'There's a window in the house that opens on to the bit behind the slippage. Come inside, I'll show you.'

The inside of the house was pretty much a building site, but Helena hardly had time to be disappointed and she hurried behind Jago to the back of the house.

'There.' He pointed to a window. 'If you look through there and down you'll see the kitten.'

And there it was, absolutely tiny, its little mouth opening pinkly in what was obviously a persistent cry. It was on a much lower level than where they were standing.

'There's no way through from the cellar,' Jago went on. 'I've been through every possible solution, and this is the only one. We have to get a ladder out of this window and you have to climb down and bring the kitten up. Maybe in a bucket?'

Helena swallowed as she contemplated her task. Refusing wasn't an option but she felt perspiration prick along her hairline at the prospect of a ladder and a small space. She wiped her hands down the side of her jeans. 'OK, let's do it.'

Jago went to fetch a ladder while Helena did some deep breathing which was somewhat disturbed by the sound of an anguished mother cat — Zuleika — trying to escape from behind a door. The yowling and the scratching was agonising to hear.

'Right,' Jago said cheerily, carrying an extending ladder, unaware of Helena's misgivings. 'I'll try not to squash the kitten when I put the ladder down.'

'Is there room for me as well as the ladder?'

'Check for yourself.' He was struggling to manoeuvre the ladder and was obviously surprised by her question.

Helena didn't move until the ladder was in place and then she didn't bother to look — knowing wouldn't help. 'OK!' she said brightly. 'I'm going down!'

Getting out of the window wasn't straightforward. It involved balancing on the window ledge as she was too short to just swing her leg over to the ladder, which wasn't quite long enough to reach Helena's level.

'I could get a taller ladder,' Jago offered after a bit of undignified heaving on Helena's part and shoving from him.

'It's all right,' she said, panting slightly, 'my foot's on the top rung now.'

'Before you go down, take this.' Jago handed her a flexible plastic trug with a rope tied to the handle. 'Put her in this and I can haul her up. Then all you need to concentrate on is getting up the ladder.'

He made it sound so easy, thought Helena. It *was* easy — a few steps down, scoop up the kitten, put her in the bucket and then back up the ladder and away, out of the coffin-shaped space and back into the house. Piece of cake.

Physically it was easy, she told herself, trying to forget her fear of confined spaces. But trying to forget her fear brought it to the forefront of her mind. Her foot slipped on the muddy ladder and suddenly she was nearly stepping on the kitten. The space was too narrow for her to move in.

Jago, leaning out of the window, saw the problem. 'I'll have to withdraw the ladder,' he said. 'There's not room for it and you down there. Stand on one leg until I get it out of the way. Then I'll pass down the bucket.'

Helena closed her eyes and breathed deeply while he hauled up the ladder. When she opened her eyes again she was face-to-face with a pile of earth. She could smell it and felt as though she could taste it too. It was like a vertical grave, she thought, and started to sweat.

'There's not much room down here,' she said, to herself as much as to Jago. 'We'll have to do without the bucket. I need to turn sideways.'

She edged her feet to make a bit more room and sent another heap of earth tumbling down. For a moment she didn't dare look to see if the kitten was all right; then she heard a tiny squeak. Nausea, more sweating and a fear of fainting told her she hadn't got long; if she collapsed down here she'd squash the kitten and it would take forever to get her out, especially if more soil fell on top of her. She gulped, reached down and snatched round her ankles until she found the kitten, grabbed it and stuffed it down her top. 'Ladder!' she called shakily, knowing she might vomit, hyperventilate, cry or all three at any moment.

The kitten tried to escape from her cleavage, but she clamped her hand over its head, hoping she wouldn't suffocate it while trying to save it.

At last the ladder came down and by climbing on to the pile of earth she made room for it. Then she stepped on it and climbed up.

Jago caught her when she got to the top and hauled her through the window, supporting her when she almost landed on the floor. He kicked a chair under her and she collapsed on to it.

'Were you suffering from claustrophobia just now?' he asked.

Helena nodded.

'You should have said! I'm so sorry! If I'd known, I'd have found someone else to help. Come into the kitchen and I'll get you some brandy.'

He put his arm round her and half carried her. She still had her hand round the kitten under her top, who was now struggling. When they got to the kitchen she fished it out. 'Here, she's getting claustrophobia now.'

He took the wriggling bundle and guided Helena to a scarred and paint-splattered table. 'Sit down while I reunite this ball of mischief with her mother.'

In the few moments he was gone she recovered a little and looked around her. She had longed to get a look inside this house and now was her chance to at least see the kitchen. She would have preferred not to be in a state of shock and covered with mud when she did it, though.

It was large and had windows at both ends and at first glance seemed to be several kitchens joined together. Helena realised that although the principle of adding bits together was the same in here as it was outside, the effect wasn't as pleasing. It was obviously a work in progress.

Jago reappeared with a bottle of brandy. 'I feel terrible. It never occurred to me you'd feel claustrophobic. You really should have told me.'

'I hoped I'd grown out of it,' said Helena, feeling a bit foolish.

He frowned and shook his head but she couldn't tell if she was the one he was annoyed with, or himself. 'I'll put the kettle on too. It's what people do when they don't know how to be really helpful.'

'A cup of tea would be quite helpful, and I'd actually prefer it to brandy right now, if you don't mind.' She watched him make the tea. 'You haven't exactly got all mod cons in here yet, I notice.'

He laughed. 'This room at least has leccy and running water, which is a bit scarce everywhere else, so as far as I'm concerned this is full-on luxury.'

'How do you manage without electricity?' Helena asked, her interest in her surroundings growing.

'Torches. And I have a big industrial light that's plugged in elsewhere. That works.' He laughed again. 'Everyone I know thinks I'm mad to live on site but I'm trying to do this whole thing as cheaply as possible. Why waste money renting?'

Helena shrugged and sipped her tea.

'Now, how can Zuleika and I repay you for being so noble and overcoming your claustrophobia to rescue her kitten?'

'I suppose letting me stay in my studio for another three months isn't an option?'

Jago frowned and bit his lip, but then smiled and shook his head. His crooked, quirky smile lit up his grimy, unshaven face like an industrial light in a house without electricity. 'What about another cup of tea and sandwich instead?'

Helena shrugged and smiled back. 'If that's all that's on offer, it is about lunchtime, I suppose. But I'm a bit muddy to eat.'

'One day there'll be a wet room with a waterfall shower head. Currently it's a bucket and a sponge, taking me back to my car-washing days.'

'I'll just go back to my studio then, but thank you for the offer.' She started to stand up but he was up before her.

'Go back and shower but, please, come and eat the sandwich afterwards. Or I'll just feel terrible.'

Helena considered telling him how terrible it was knowing one was about to become homeless, and, more importantly in her case, studio-less. While she could always stay with her mother, her large loom could not — it took up far more space than she did. But what was the point? 'OK.'

'So, what can I make you? Cheese and ham on sourdough with salad, mustard and mayonnaise? I could toast the bread — might be nice?'

'Hold the mustard,' she said, 'and toast the bread and it sounds like the perfect sarnie.'

'It may not be perfect, but it will be good, I promise,' he said. 'Don't be too long!'

★   ★   ★

Helena's hair was still wet and knotty when she returned. She had put it into a rough plait and tied the end round with wool as it took so long to dry properly. She hadn't put on any make-up, because, as she would report to Amy later, she wasn't going to dress up for a man when she didn't want a man. She did, however, want a sandwich.

She could see that Jago had done a bit of tidying in the kitchen while she'd been in the shower. There were fewer power tools on the work surfaces and there was now a board on the worktop on which he was assembling ingredients.

After watching him cut a gherkin into wafer-thin slices she said, 'Do you mind if I ask you why you seem to have several different styles of units in here? You've got a Shaker and a very modern alongside some interestingly retro orange knotty pine. What look are you going for?'

He laughed. 'The orange knotty pine, of course! No, actually, I've just put in here bits of kitchen that no one else wants. People are always ripping out kitchens and starting again. I can often repurpose the good stuff but there's always a bit left over which is what I get to keep. I'll do something to make it all look a bit more sensible eventually — when I get round to it.' The toast popped out of a very old-looking toaster that had a pattern of poppies and wheat ears on it. 'My sister gives me all her cast-off toasters but I've kept this one. It's old but it always works.'

He assembled two sandwiches so efficiently that she guessed he had worked in a sandwich shop at one time. He put mustard on one sandwich and put the other on a plate which he handed to her.

'Now, eat that and tell me it's not worth rescuing a kitten for!'

'Are you still sure I couldn't swap it for an extra three months?' Helena asked, suddenly ravenous at the sight of the sandwich.

He sighed. 'Quite sure. I was pushing it when I gave you six months when I first bought the property. But your studio, and the one next to it — '

'Amy's,' said Helena.

10

'That's right. The two together are going to become a two-bedroom cottage for a family. They've been waiting to move into it for ages. I really do want to get on to it and that means I have to have you out.'

'So what about your own house? Couldn't you spend your time on that, and leave me and Amy alone?'

He shook his head. 'I only work on my house between working on proper jobs.'

'So my studio's not going to be a holiday home?' Helena and Amy, neighbours and old friends, had spent a lot of time raging that their studios were likely to be turned into holiday lets or second homes.

Jago shook his head. 'Nope. All my projects are for families who want homes. Or — to be fair — single people as well. But they have to have a commitment to the area. Now please start — I'm longing to know if you like it.'

Helena felt a bit nonplussed as she took a bite of sandwich. She needed time to process this. All property developers were evil, everyone knew that. Why was this one not conforming to type? 'Oh God!' she said after a couple of chews. 'This sandwich really is delicious!'

'Told you!' Jago bit into his own version. 'I haven't lost it. I used to work in a sandwich bar.'

'I guessed as much.'

'Would you like a beer with that?'

Helena shook her head. 'No thanks. Another cup of tea would be great though.' She might have to go and see her mother anyway when she'd finished her throw, just to pass on all the details she'd discovered about the man who was making her homeless. She didn't ever drink and drive. It was such a shame Amy was away — she'd find it even more fascinating.

She sipped her tea when it came and carried on eating. Eventually, when she wiped her mouth with the back of her hand in case there were traces of mayonnaise around it, she said, 'What's the kitten's name?'

'Dobson,' said Jago.

'Oh? Like the book?'

'That's right.' His expression became more intense, as if she suddenly interested him. 'Not many people would have made that connection.'

Helena shrugged. 'My mum told me about it. *Zuleika Dobson*, I mean. Zuleika was one of the names she thought of for me. She likes literary associations.' She looked at her watch. 'I'd better get back. I was in the middle of finishing a throw when you knocked on my door.' She paused. 'It was a really great sandwich.'

He smiled, his teeth white in his generally sandcoloured face. 'I'm glad you enjoyed it.'

★ ★ ★

As Helena walked back to her studio and her work she wondered whether, if Amy had been asked to rescue the kitten, her friend would have managed to get more out of Jago in return than a sandwich. Amy was good at getting what she wanted from men and would have said Helena didn't have enough practice.

As Helena worked, throwing the shuttle back

12

and forth in a way she always felt helped her think more clearly, she calculated how many more blankets and throws she would have to do to have sufficient product for the next big wool show. World of Wool was in late May and it was now the first week of April — she should be able to make enough. Woolly World, as she liked to call it, was more important than most shows, because as well as the general public other weavers would be there to see her specifically. Her weaving guru, Julia Coombes, whom she always thought of when she was weaving, had said good things about her and she owed it to her to produce good work. Julia had always been such an inspiration to her.

And she'd have to have lots of different things to show. Rectangular shapes — blankets, shawls and throws — on their own wouldn't cut it; she'd also need plenty of fine woven fabric that could be made into waistcoats, jackets or even handbags.

Feeling a bit despondent and unexpectedly tired she decided it was probably delayed shock and that she should go and see her mother and tell her all about having to climb down a ladder into an enclosed space to rescue a kitten. She had been slightly tempted to text Amy but Amy would somehow manage to turn the conversation on to her favourite theme: getting Helena to try a dating app. Her mother would give her tea, cake and sympathy — much more what she wanted right now.

2

Helena never went up the drive to her old childhood home without thinking how lovely it was. And, now it was a very upmarket Cotswolds bed and breakfast, Fairacres was even lovelier than it had been when she was a child. The garden, which had been a bit rambly and overgrown, was much neater now it had to have 'kerb appeal'. But the atmosphere of homely comfort was still the first and lasting impression. High-end it might be, but it was supremely welcoming.

She drove round to the back of the house, leaving the sweeping drive for any guests who might be arriving. She went in through the back door and found her mother in the kitchen. A cooling tray with fingers of shortbread on it stood on the table, obviously just out of the oven. 'Hi, Mum! Baking again? I've chosen my moment well.'

Gilly laughed. 'There are some broken ones you can eat.'

'Can't give the guests broken biscuits,' said Helena, picking up two shards of shortbread, still warm. 'These are so good! No wonder I had to move out! You'd have had to remove the doors to extract me, I'd have been so fat.'

Gilly moved the kettle across to the hot part of the range. 'It's nice to see someone eat. The last time I offered Cressida a biscuit she looked as if

14

I'd handed her a dog turd on a doily.'

Helena assessed her mother's mood. Personally, she was always up for a bitch about her sister-in-law but her mother was generally more loyal. Gilly didn't seem to want to go on about her son's model-like wife, or 'waif' as Helena privately — and guiltily — called her. 'Why did you mention her?' she said, taking another crumbling mouthful and sitting down.

'She's just phoned. She wants us to go to them for Sunday lunch. That's nice, isn't it?'

Helena thought her mother sounded rather desperate, so she nodded in what she hoped was a neutral way. 'It's been a while. We can take sandwiches in the car for afterwards.'

Her mother laughed. 'Helena! I know she's not exactly a lavish hostess but you never leave the house hungry.'

'I'm sure we get exactly the right amount of calories required for a light lunch and there's always plenty of delicious kale to fill up on. But we never leave thinking, that was a lovely meal, do we?' Helena had given up trying not to let her feelings for her sister-in-law show. 'Whenever I see Cressida — the sky will fall in if anyone called her 'Cress' — with her over-toned arms and perfect fake tan, I want to tell her to put on a cardi and eat a scone!

'But, Mum! I have news — sort of.'

'Really darling? Shall I make tea? Did you have lunch?'

'Yes please to tea,' said Helena, anticipating her mother's excitement. 'But no to lunch. I had an enormous ham and cheese sandwich on

15

toasted sourdough and it was delicious!'

When Gilly had put the kettle on she sat down opposite Helena. 'So tell me your news?'

A huge fluffy ginger cat, apparently just as keen for information, landed on Helena's lap like a furcovered sandbag. Automatically, Helena started stroking it. 'Well, I had to rescue a kitten from a very narrow space, with a ladder, for my landlord. A kitten about a tenth the size of you, Ulysses.'

'But darling! You're claustrophobic!' Gilly moved the shortbread out of reach of cat hairs.

'I know! I was sort of hoping I'd grown out of it, but it was like a grave down there, surrounded by soil. It was heaped up and could have smothered the kitten and me at any moment.' Thinking back to being in that space made Helena feel shaky all over again. She broke off a bit of a biscuit that was quite good enough to go into the guest bedrooms.

Gilly frowned. 'This is the landlord that is imminently going to make you homeless?'

'Yes. I've only got the one landlord. And I could hardly not rescue the kitten, could I?'

'That was so brave.'

This was exactly the response she was looking for. 'It was difficult! But Jago — the landlord — was far too big to get into the space.'

Gilly had pulled her chair a bit nearer to Helena's. 'Surely he could have found someone else?'

'There was no time. The heap of rubble could have collapsed at any moment. It wouldn't take much to squash a kitten.'

16

'Don't!' said Gilly, getting up to make the tea. 'Do you want brandy? Or Rescue Remedy?'

'I've already declined the offer of brandy,' said Helena. 'But Rescue Remedy might be good.'

Helena thought she heard her mother mutter, 'Same thing really,' as she went to find the bottle.

★ ★ ★

After Gilly had waved off her daughter, who was bearing a plastic box of bolognese sauce as well as quite a lot of shortbread, she went to find her phone so she could make an appointment. While she had told Helena about their lunch date with her brother and sister-in-law, she hadn't told her that Cressida had added, 'We've got an exciting plan we want to share with you,' when she'd issued the invitation. Gilly had an idea she knew what this plan was, and she wanted to prepare before the visit. Hence the appointment with her accountant.

William Davies had been her accountant for seven years. He had advised her when she was setting up her bed and breakfast business and had been a supportive presence ever since. She'd had him recommended to her by a friend who felt that Sebastian, her ex-husband, who was using an old school friend 'mates rates' solicitor to arrange his divorce, was far too advantaged. Putting Gilly in touch with William Davies was her attempt to level the playing field somewhat.

★ ★ ★

17

The following morning in William's office, Gilly took the chair offered to her and sat down opposite him. She smiled, aware she was pleased to see him. 'How are you?'

William sat back down behind his desk, having risen as she was shown in. 'Well, thank you. And you? Mandy will bring us some tea in a moment.'

Gilly nodded. She'd left a tin of home-made shortbread at the front desk as usual. The tea which was brought, unasked, every time she visited, was part of the thank you from Mandy and her colleagues. While they waited she contemplated the fact — not for the first time — that William had very good hair. It was greying in an attractive way and there was lots of it.

'So,' William said when the tea had arrived, 'what can I do for you?'

'I'm wondering if there's any way I can raise some money from my house without actually selling it.'

'Why?'

It sounded like an intrusive question but Gilly knew it wasn't. William was her accountant, after all, and well used to the demands on the Bank of Mum made on her by her son, though very rarely by Helena.

'I've been invited to lunch on Sunday. Cressida has 'an exciting plan' and, to be honest, if they didn't need my money I doubt she'd have mentioned it. On the phone, anyway.'

William nodded slowly. 'Do you have any idea how much?'

Gilly shook her head. 'Not really, but I imagine as it's a lunch, and they've invited Helena too, it must be quite a lot or they wouldn't feel the need to involve her.'

'I see.'

Gilly felt that William managed to express quite a lot of disapproval with those two short words. He wasn't even frowning. She went on. 'It's Helena I'd like to help, if I can. She's being evicted quite soon and she's found it hard to find new premises, as she needs quite a large space. Her friend Amy — also a weaver but who uses small looms — doesn't have the same trouble and has already found somewhere.'

William nodded. Gilly ploughed on. 'I wondered if I could let Helena have the ground-floor bedroom as a studio? She hasn't asked me, of course, she never asks me for money, but if I end up giving her brother. something I have to do something for her too, to make it fair.'

William didn't reply immediately, giving Gilly the impression he was preparing to give bad news. 'To be honest, Mrs Claire, if you gave up that room you'd stop being profitable. The other rooms give you enough money to pay for the upkeep of the house but it's the extra room that makes the profit. And it's your only room with disabled access and going on your TripAdvisor ratings, people do really love it.'

'You've looked me up on TripAdvisor?' Gilly was surprised and a little bit indignant.

William nodded. 'I did my research.' He went on: 'You had to spend quite a lot of money converting the bathroom for wheelchair access. Even if Helena paid you rent it wouldn't cover the lost income.'

The trouble with her accountant, Gilly thought, was that he was nearly always right. And at that particular moment she couldn't think of a time when he'd been wrong. She examined the large ring she wore on her wedding finger. She'd bought it herself as a symbol of her independence when she was finally free of her ex-husband.

'I can't believe you looked me up on Trip-Advisor,' she said to give herself time to think. She sighed. 'And you don't think there's any way I can raise capital on my house? Equity release? Something?'

'I don't think that's really for you. You do have to pay back the money — or your children will after you die — and really, you're a bit young for equity release. If the money was for you I might feel differently about it. But think how hard you had to fight to keep your house, the house left to you by your parents. You shouldn't have to compromise that.'

'OK, so what about me selling? I could downsize?'

'You could, of course you could. But that would mean giving up your business and you're so good at it I can't believe you don't enjoy it. TripAdvisor,' he added, before she could argue. 'Your reviews. I don't think you want to sell.'

Gilly felt a bit stubborn. 'Maybe I'm tired of running a B & B?'

'If you are, then you should sell, but are you really? You're a comparatively young woman. Do you want to retire? Or maybe travel? Have an adult 'gap year'? Do something else with your life?'

20

'You were supposed to be talking me out of selling, not offering alternative lifestyles,' Gilly said, and then realised she'd sounded a bit grumpy.

'I'm pressing you because I know you love your B & B, your home, and that TripAdvisor tells me it's one of the best places to stay in the area.'

'If you think that flattery . . . ' But Gilly didn't finish her sentence. She knew he would see the smile that she'd couldn't suppress. She *was* one of the best B & Bs in the area and no, she wasn't remotely ready to downsize and retire.

'I'm not flattering you, Mrs Claire, I'm telling you the facts as I see them. Of course, it's your decision.'

'But you think I should say no to any requests for money?'

He smiled. 'I think you should try very hard to say no, but I do realise how difficult that is for you. You have a very kind heart.'

He had told her before that she was the only client who felt obliged to bring shortbread for the staff and she knew that as an accountant he didn't see having a kind heart in quite the same way as, for example, a vicar would. 'Well, I will try to stand firm,' she said at last.

'Good. But while you're here, I wonder if I could take advantage of your kind heart and consult you about a party I'm organizing for the eightieth birthday of one of my aunts.'

'Oh?'

'I was wondering if you knew anything about January Barn. Would it be suitable for a family

21

party, with lots of the family being quite elderly?'

'Oh yes. I quite often have people who are going to events there and they all say it's lovely.'

'Which brings me to the second thing I want to ask you. Could I rent all the rooms in your B & B?'

Gilly was a bit taken aback. 'Of course you can, but it rather depends on when your party is. I may have bookings already.' She smiled apologetically. 'I do get bookings quite far in advance. I know I should have my diary on my phone but although Helena explained how to do it I kept forgetting to update it. And frankly, it's quite nice to have a bit of time to reflect sometimes.'

William nodded. 'It's quite soon, I'm afraid — this month. January Barn have had a wedding cancelled and haven't yet filled the spot. They were quite keen on having a less labour-intensive event although obviously one not quite as lucrative.'

Gilly got up. 'Why don't you email me the dates and I'll get back to you? I'd love to have your family to stay.' Already she was considering passing on any bookings she might have to her friend nearby whose B & B was nearly as good as her own.

'And I know they'd love staying with you,' he said. 'It would be for my aunts and some cousins. I'm very fond of them.'

'Of course I'd be happy to give you a special rate as your family will be taking all the rooms,' said Gilly.

'As your accountant I shouldn't let you do that,' he said firmly, but Gilly could see a twinkle in his eye he couldn't quite suppress.

She felt a rush of warmth towards this kind man who wanted to do something nice for his elderly relatives. 'But as your friend I think you have to let me charge what I think appropriate.'

He laughed. 'I'm glad you think of yourself as my friend, Mrs Claire.'

'I do, and I think it's high time you called me Gilly.'

'And you must call me William.'

Gilly smiled and got up. 'I must go. Thank you so much for your advice and get those dates to me as soon as you can.'

He got up too and walked her to the door where she stopped, pointing to the wall. 'I've never mentioned it before, but I really love those photographs. Seeing the hills covered in frost with the sunshine just catching them, the river looking magnificent, they're really beautiful.'

'Do you like them? I took them from my glider.'

'Glider? You have a glider?'

He nodded and opened the door.

That's a bit of a surprise, thought Gilly as she left.

3

Helena's best friend Amy called on her the following evening. Helena had sent her a text — *Met our new landlord Jago Pengelly* — but hadn't gone into detail. She knew she couldn't cheat Amy by being brief. While Helena wasn't interested in him as a possible date, Amy probably would be.

'So?' said Amy, putting the wine down on Helena's tiny worktop and finding a couple of glasses, knowing exactly which cupboard to look in. 'What's he like?'

'He's a gentleman-builder,' said Helena. She liked to be able to categorise people. A snappy two-word 'type' and they were filed away into a part of her mind she didn't often visit.

'So, good-looking?' Amy handed Helena a glass of wine and came to sit next to her on the sofa bed.

Helena thought. 'Not amazingly so, but quite attractive, I suppose.' She paused. 'I'm trying to think how you'd see him.'

'And you're not going after him yourself?' It was obvious Amy knew what the answer was but she could never resist trying to bring Helena round to her way of thinking.

'No, I'm focusing on my career, finding somewhere to relocate to, and getting enough stuff for Woolly World,' said Helena carefully, as if to a small child who hadn't heard this many times before. 'Those are my priorities.'

'And you can't multitask? I care about my career too, but I can manage to run a few dating apps.'

'Come on, Ames! I'm willing to share everything I know about someone you may well fancy. Just get off my case!' She took a sip from the glass Amy handed to her.

'You need to sort out your trust issues. Just because your father was a snake, it doesn't mean all men are,' said Amy, sitting down next to Helena.

'I'm sure I'll know the right man when I've got time to focus on it but just now I'm concentrating on my work. I have explained this about a million times, but having met a new man, I thought I'd pass him on to someone who might be interested. You.'

'OK,' said Amy, pulling one of Helena's handwoven throws over herself. The mezzanine of Helena's studio had been made into a tiny flat, but although it was now April and not actually that cold outside, it wasn't ever very cosy. 'About how tall is he?'

'Tall, big, bigger than me, anyway. Which is why he needed me to rescue the kitten.'

'You are quite small, Hels,' said Amy, sizing her up. 'He wouldn't need to be huge to be bigger than you.'

'All right, he looks as if he could play rugby.'

'What? He has a cauliflower ear?' Amy appeared put off by this thought.

'No.' Helena pictured Jago's ears. 'Nothing odd about them.'

'You should be able to tell me all about him, with your spooky superpowers,' said Amy.

Helena was a super-recogniser, which meant she had a photographic memory for people even if she'd only glimpsed them. While Amy knew about this, she was a bit sceptical.

'I could pick him out in a crowd but it's my powers of description that are failing me now.' She thought about him. 'He has a small scar above his eyebrow and his hair has a sort of straw-like quality. Not that it's like straw exactly, but it's the colour really.' Thinking about him, Helena realised she felt a bit warm towards him. While she was perfectly capable of having men as friends and liking them, with Jago she felt the stirrings of attraction which was rare.

'Voice?' prompted Amy as Helena had stopped trying to describe him.

'A nice voice. No noticeable accent.'

'Eyes?'

'Yes, he definitely has eyes.'

'Agh! Colour?'

'Not easy to define. Bluey-greeny, or maybe greeny-bluey.'

'Nothing else you can tell me about him?'

Helena shrugged. 'To be honest I was mostly dealing with my claustrophobia.'

Amy looked at her. 'Helena! What on earth have you been doing?'

'Earth does come into it, as it happens.' And Helena related the story of how she'd had to rescue the kitten. 'So we know he's definitely an animal lover.'

Amy was less impressed. 'Yes, but does he want

kids? Some people prefer animals to children.'

'Strangely, we didn't get on to whether or not he wanted children. He does know I don't take sugar in my tea, though,' said Helena, not bothering to hide her sarcasm. 'Nor does he.'

'Ah!' said Amy triumphantly. 'Something in common!'

Helena sighed. 'But seriously, I think he is a nice guy. He's making our space into affordable housing and says that's what he's most interested in. You should definitely get to know him.'

'I will,' said Amy. 'If you're leaving this diamond on the beach.'

'He's all yours. Now tell me about the workshop. Was it OK doing it on your own? I am sorry I couldn't come and do it with you.'

'It's fine. I know you had to work. And it was OK although it is better doing it as a couple. People aren't left waiting for help for so long.' She twiddled the fringe on the throw. 'Tell me more about this Jago Pengelly. Is that Welsh, do you think?'

'Cornish, I imagine, though I'm not sure. Amy, why don't you pop over and ask him?'

'He won't be there now,' said Amy. 'It's nearly nine o'clock in the evening. Builders don't work that late.'

'He's living on site! Which is why he was able to look after his sister's cat and her kitten. Though I think they've gone back now. I saw him putting a loaded cat basket into his pickup.'

Amy had lost interest in the cats. 'But is the house fit to live in? It doesn't look like it.'

'He's tough. Pop over and borrow a cup of

sugar or something, although maybe make it quinoa as we know he doesn't take sugar.' Her friend looked doubtful. 'Or take him some of Mum's shortbread. Everyone loves that.'

Now Amy frowned at Helena with her head on one side. 'You know, I'm beginning to get why you don't go in for dating. You have no idea about normal behaviour.'

Helena shrugged, feeling vindicated but hiding it.

'But tomorrow,' Amy went on. 'I'm going over as soon as I decently can. So, how's your mum?'

Everyone loved Gilly because she was always baking and had been fairly relaxed when they were growing up. 'She's OK, I think,' said Helena. 'We've had a summons to Sunday lunch with stick-woman and my brother.'

'You're very unkind about Cressida,' said Amy, who'd met her. 'She's perfectly nice.'

'I know there's nothing major wrong with her but I'd like her better if she wasn't quite so obsessed with running and healthy eating. She's aggressively skinny' — Helena held up her hand — 'which is fine! But she wants everyone else to be too.'

'I don't think you can be aggressively skinny.'

Helena raised her eyebrows. 'Spend a little time with her and you'll know that isn't true.'

'But Gilly gets on OK with her?'

'You know Mum, she gets on with everyone even though Mum is definitely a feeder and Cressida thinks everyone should live on green-sludge smoothies.'

'I stayed in a B & B when I was away,' said

Amy. 'It was so not up to Gilly's standards!'

Helena laughed. 'She is obsessed. She has *Four in a Bed* on series record and is always looking for obscure places to dust. I keep telling her she should go on that programme.'

'She takes such pride in Fairacres, doesn't she? And when you stay with someone who doesn't, you do notice.' Amy had been an early guinea pig for Gilly when she was testing her bedrooms for comfort.

'She's lucky she loves baking,' said Helena, 'so the home-made biscuits she puts in every room are a pleasure for her to make.'

'And the top-quality bed linen makes such a difference!' said Amy. 'So luxurious.'

Helena grew serious for a moment. 'She had all that before she opened. She told me it was how she comforted herself when Dad was being so horrible. She bought bed linen.'

'That was a truly awful time for you all,' said Amy.

'But you and your mum were so supportive.'

Amy smiled. 'I remember my mother panicking after she'd invited you over to stay. Gilly's such a brilliant cook and she thought Gilly would hate everything my mum cooked.'

'She wouldn't have cared!' said Helena. 'And your parents have a very deft hand with the corkscrew and that really helped.'

'She's done so well since the divorce,' said Amy. 'You must be proud of her.'

'I am! And I'm going to make sure my brother and his wife don't take advantage of all her hard work.'

'You don't think they're going to try, do you?' Amy was horrified.

Helena shrugged. 'Why else invite us both to Sunday lunch? I think Mum knows more than she's telling me because she's afraid I'll go ballistic at the thought.'

Amy shook her head. 'Well, keep me informed. I'd love to think badly of a green-smoothie addict.'

4

'Shall I drive?' said Helena. It was Sunday morning, and Helena had parked her car outside Fairacres and gone inside to pick up her mother. 'Then you can have a glass of wine?'

'A whole glass? I don't think so. That would be more units than would be healthy,' said Gilly, looking around to check everything was locked. 'Cressida always wants everyone to be healthy.'

'Mum! It's so unlike you to say something like that. I love it when you find your inner bitch.'

Gilly laughed. 'I'm always quite relieved to discover I have one, I must say. Now, have I got everything?'

'I'm not sure Cressida appreciates home baking, Mum,' said Helena, eyeing the collection of Tupperware her mother had in her basket.

'I know she doesn't, but Martin does and he takes it into work. He tells Cressida that it's to give to his colleagues, but I know he eats it too.'

'But don't you think she breathalyses him to detect the consumption of carbs and sugar when he gets home?'

'Probably. Mostly I take biscuits so Issi has something she can eat when she gets home from school. I don't think that little girl actually gets enough calories. It's all cucumber and carrots and the odd seed. But I expect you're right, I shouldn't be her enabler — '

Helena giggled. 'To home-made shortbread.

31

Oh, what a wicked granny you are!'

Helena spent the journey wondering if she should mention her suspicions about her sister-in-law's motives behind inviting them both to lunch to see if Gilly confessed to thinking the same thing. But she knew her mother didn't like it when she said unpleasant things about Cressida and so didn't want to do it unless it was really justified.

She parked outside the sleekly modern house, which had a steep drive that didn't encourage visiting vehicles. Helena and her mother sat in the car for a few seconds, bracing themselves. 'I hope you're wrapped up warm,' said Gilly eventually.

'Mum! It's April!'

'Only just! And that house is always cold, but Cressida is always warm. It's the running.'

Helena shuddered. Her sister-in-law's addiction to running always unsettled her. 'Let's go in.'

*　*　*

Martin, her brother, greeted her with a hug and a 'Hey, Sis.'

His wife, who was tall as well as thin, was dressed in black. Her hair was pulled back into a very tidy ponytail and she was wearing silver jewellery. Her make-up was pale and either didn't include lipstick or she was using one the same shade as her foundation.

Her welcome was a bit more gushing than her husband's. She smiled at Helena and kissed Gilly on both cheeks and patted her shoulder. The little girl, Ismene, who was five years old and serious, said, 'Good morning, Grandma and Helena.'

Helena winced for her mother. Gilly was a devoted grandmother but she hated being called Grandma. However, in spite of her expressing her dislike of it when Ismene was tiny, Cressida had insisted this was how she was to be addressed. Cressida was big on proper names.

'So, come along in,' said Martin, ushering them through to the sitting room.

Although the room was cold, there was no fire in the super-modern fireplace. But even if the underfloor heating had been on, it would always be chilly. Helena felt it was something about the decor, which was white and mauve with black accents.

The look that Cressida gave Helena's feet was clear — she wanted Helena to take off her shoes. Helena ignored the message. She was cold enough even though she had put on a warm cardigan before coming and she couldn't cope with just socks. She wouldn't have objected to being asked to remove her shoes had she been offered fluffy slippers to replace them but there was nothing fluffy in this house. She noticed that Cressida hadn't given her mother the silent 'take off your shoes' message. Just for a moment Helena wished that one of them had stepped in dog poo.

'Sherry, Martin!' ordered Cressida crisply.

Helena refused sherry but noted that the fact it was offered meant it wasn't just an ordinary lunch. She noticed her mother accepting, obviously needing alcoholic support.

'Well, this is nice!' said Gilly, halfway through her tiny glass. 'When were we all together last?'

'Christmas?' suggested Helena. 'Ismene has grown, anyway. Hey?' She crouched down to address the little girl directly. 'When you grow out of your shoes can I have them? They are so cool!'

Ismene frowned. 'Don't be silly, Aunt Helena, your feet are much bigger than mine.'

Helena looked down at her trainers. 'Oh, so they are. What a shame.'

'Ma,' said Martin. 'We want to ask you something.'

'Wait until after lunch, Martin!' said Cressida. 'We discussed this!'

'Maybe we'd better have lunch then, if it's ready,' said Gilly.

'Have another glass of sherry first, Ma,' said Martin.

'Although lunch is ready,' said Cressida. 'It's only soup and salad.'

'I'd love another sherry, Martin,' said Gilly.

Helena wished she could join her. She knew that technically she may well be able to drink a small amount and still be safe to drive but she would never take the risk.

Gilly seemed to get through her second glass of sherry fairly quickly and they were ushered into the icy dining room with amazing views and a glass table. The surface of it was so cold that Helena was reluctant to let her wrists touch it. Perhaps the tabletop was a deliberate ploy to encourage good table manners. Cressida was very keen on table manners.

They started with a thin soup that may well have been hot when it left the saucepan but by the time it had been poured into enormous, icy plates, it was tepid. It also had no apparent seasoning. But still it was bound to be healthy and meant Helena could have a full-fat sausage roll or, indeed, almost anything else to compensate afterwards.

'Did you know,' said Cressida, 'that you can lose weight just by not eating after seven o'clock at night and not having breakfast until nine o'clock. It's not as good as doing twenty-four hour fasting, in my opinion, but you may find it helpful.' She smiled at Helena as if she'd just asked her how Cressida kept her lovely figure, which she hadn't.

'I'm so glad it works for you, Cressida,' said Helena sweetly, 'but although you've tried before, I'm not interested in diets that make me think about food all the time. In fact, I'm not interested in diets at all. I'm perfectly happy with my shape.'

Cressida shrugged. 'I was only trying to be helpful.'

'We know,' said Gilly, patting her daughter-in-law's hand. 'And you do always look so lean and fit, it obviously works.'

'Personally, I'm only interested in diets that have Greggs' sausage rolls on them,' said Helena. Aware that everyone, including her five-year-old niece, was looking at her in horror, she went on: 'I just mean, if I want a sausage roll I'm going to have one.'

35

'No wonder you're a bit — ' Cressida began.

'Porky?' suggested Martin.

'I am not porky!' said Helena.

'Children!' said Gilly. 'Helly, Martin was only teasing. Don't rise to it.'

Martin grinned. 'If you eat pork, you'll be porky.'

'Anyway!' said Cressida, getting up. 'Let's move on. I'll get the salad.'

The salad was colourful and quite tasty with its 'squeeze of lemon juice instead of an oily dressing', as Cressida proudly announced. It wasn't very filling though and Helena wondered if she could raid the box of shortbread when she helped clear up. She could do it while Cressida — or Martin — went to get more dirty plates from the table. But she lost hope in this plan when she realised how few plates there were for five people.

Cressida put a fruit bowl on the table. 'We never have puddings in the middle of the day. But do help yourselves.'

Helena took an orange and pulled her side plate in front of her. 'I love oranges,' she said, 'but would you really class them as pudding?'

'There's a lot of sugar in fruit,' said Cressida, 'which is why I limit it.'

Gilly didn't speak but Helena noticed her press her lips together and then take a breath to say something. 'So, what's your 'exciting plan', Cressida?' she said, making the inverted commas audible.

Cressida laughed. 'Oh! I was going to wait until we were sharing a nice cup of tea, later. I've got some new organic herb tea that is a super detox.'

'Let's hear about it now,' said Gilly, her words and expression jolly, her feelings obviously less so.

'Better get your tablet,' said Martin, who hadn't said a lot up until now except to goad his sister.

Cressida came back to the table and sat down next to Gilly, pulling her chair in close. She laughed again. 'You may not know this, but I have a terrible Rightmove habit!' she tinkled.

'Really?' said Gilly, obviously genuinely surprised.

'Yes!' said Cressida. 'And I've found something really rather exciting. Let me find it for you.'

Helena got up, determined she wasn't going to miss out on any excitement going. Besides, the sooner the plan had been shared the sooner they could go home.

'Look!' said Cressida. 'Isn't it to die for?'

Revealed on Cressida's favourite website — one which Helena was quite fond of too — was indeed a lovely property.

It was a mansion, with seven bedrooms, four reception rooms and multiple bathrooms. There was a tennis court and lovely grounds. There was even an outdoor swimming pool and accompanying pool house. Unsurprisingly, it was very expensive.

'But you could never afford this, could you?' asked Gilly, looking at her son, who had a very good job but surely not good enough to support

37

the sort of mortgage they'd need to buy this enormous house.

'And look!' said Cressida, ignoring this question. 'It has a granny annexe!' She clicked along to the picture.

Helena leaned in. She peered at the double bedroom (double doors on to the garden), kitchenette, and living room which was big enough for a three-piece suite if the furniture was arranged more or less sideways. There was a huge television on the wall. 'Hmm,' she said, 'I wouldn't care to put my granny in there. If I had one.'

'You could let it,' said Gilly. 'Airbnb, or just bed and breakfast. Would you want to do that?'

Cressida looked annoyed and disappointed. 'Well, no, we wouldn't want to do that. We'd want you to live in it, Gilly.'

'Me? Why?' Gilly sounded confused.

'It would be so handy. You could see so much more of Ismene than you usually do,' explained Cressida. 'You're always saying you don't see enough of her.'

'That is true, Grandma,' said Ismene. She was a solemn, truthful child. Helena liked her but found her a little unnerving.

'But you already live quite near,' said Gilly, 'I don't see why you moving would make me see more of Issi — Ismene,' she corrected herself quickly.

'Cress wants to go back to work full time,' said Martin.

'Then you'd need this space for a nanny,' said Gilly quickly. 'But I still don't see how you'd afford this house.' She smiled at Cressida.

'Unless you've been offered a really well-paid job, which of course you so deserve and could obviously do.'

While Helena was privately vomiting at her mother's obvious sucking-up to Cressida, she did wonder if there was a hidden message in her flattering words.

'Ah!' said Cressida. 'Although I have got a job offer with a very good package, this is where we come to our exciting plan!'

'Which is?' said Gilly.

Helena recognised a hint of steel in her mother's gentle enquiry.

Some of Cressida's confidence left her. 'Gilly, we think it's time you thought about downsizing. Although you're amazing for your age, you're not getting any younger.'

'Not even you are doing that, Cressida,' said Helena.

'My age?' said Gilly, her tone a combination of bemused and affronted. 'I'm still in my fifties! Surely I don't have to be thinking about my age yet!'

'The bed and breakfast is a lot of hard work,' persisted Cressida. 'You often say so.'

'But Mum loves her B & B!' said Helena. 'Are you suggesting she gives it up? And even if you are, there's no reason why she should move into a granny annexe.' Helena was aware she was being disingenuous; she knew what was coming but she wanted Cressida and her brother to say it.

'It's about repurposing her property,' said Cressida.

'What?' said Helena, no longer bothering to sound polite. 'I do wish you'd speak in plain English sometimes!'

'That is English,' said Ismene. She was looking confused now.

'It is English, darling,' said Gilly, 'but the meaning isn't exactly clear.'

'What exactly do you mean by 'repurposing'?' said Helena. 'Do you mean convert it into executive second homes?'

'No, of course not!' snapped Martin. 'Get off your hobby horse, Hels.'

'We would never suggest doing anything to your lovely home!' said Cressida. 'But you are sitting on a lot of very valuable real estate and if you sold it, you could help Helena buy somewhere to do her weaving and we could buy our new house and you could live with us!'

Helena suddenly felt sick. Surely Cressida wasn't suggesting that her mother sold the family home, the house she had struggled so hard to keep after her divorce, so Martin and Cressida could go and live in a mansion? Keeping her rage under control made her sweat slightly. She helped herself to a glass of water. 'I'm not sure Mum would like that,' she said.

'I was reading an article in the paper just the other day about how baby boomers are sitting on millions of pounds' worth of property and their children are struggling to get on to the property ladder,' said Cressida.

'But you are on the property ladder,' said Gilly.

'And Mum helped you get there!' said Helena.

Cressida gave her a withering look. 'Five thousand isn't exactly a deposit, Helena. Not these days.'

Helena saw the hurt flash across her mother's face. Giving her children five thousand pounds at that particular time had been a real struggle. She'd had to give so much to her ex-husband to stop him forcing her to sell the family home there had been hardly anything left over. 'It was worth a lot more then,' Helena said. She'd only discovered afterwards how hard it had been for Gilly or she wouldn't have accepted the money.

'Anyway,' said Cressida, looking a little uncomfortable. 'We just wanted to share our plan with you, and offer you a home with us for your — older years.'

Gilly took a breath. 'Had I been in my eighties or nineties I'd probably have been grateful,' she said.

'But we need the money now, Mum,' said Martin, 'not when you're dead.'

'Martin!' Cressida snapped. 'There's no need to talk like that.'

Helena cleared her throat. She felt if she stayed any longer she was likely to say something that would cause a permanent family rift. 'You've given Mum a lot to think about, but now I think perhaps I'd better get the poor old dear home.' An exchanged glance told her that Gilly knew she was being sarcastic.

Gilly got to her feet. 'Yes, I need to think about what you've said.'

Cressida stood up too, evidently happy to get her guests out of the house. 'But don't leave it

41

too long. That to-die-for house won't stay on the market forever!'

It was only by clamping her jaws together and murmuring her goodbyes through clenched teeth that Helena got out of there without being rude to anyone.

'Would you believe it!' she said, as soon as she and Gilly were in the car and had driven a few yards away from the house. 'God! I know that woman is a viper but the cheek of it! Just suggesting you should sell your house so they can buy that stately home is iniquitous!'

'You don't think I should go for it, then?' said Gilly.

Helena braked and pulled into the side of the road. 'You are joking?'

'Yes of course!' said Gilly. 'Now let's get home and have something proper to eat.'

★　★　★

But after Helena had finally gone home, Gilly was thoughtful. Like Helena she was outraged at the suggestion that in her mid-fifties she was in need of sheltered accommodation at her son's house, while giving up her own life to become a nanny — presumably without being paid. But she was the owner of quite a valuable property and while Martin and Cressida didn't need to live in a seven-bedroomed mansion, Helena could certainly do with some money to buy a studio. Helena had spent the five thousand she'd received at the same time as Martin on a loom and other equipment. It would be wrong to

42

dismiss the idea without giving it some thought. What she needed was someone she could discuss it with, someone with her interests at heart. Of course she wouldn't go and live with Cressida and Martin but maybe it was time to downsize?

43

5

It was still light when Helena dropped her home
and Gilly had noticed that the signs outside the
house were a little mud-spattered so she decided
to go out and wash them, as well as tidying up a
bit in the garden. First impressions were so
important. Helena might tease her about being
obsessed with *Four in a Bed* with its critical bed
and breakfast owners, staying in each other's
businesses and peeling back every layer of
bedding and standing on chairs to find dirt on
the chandelier, but attention to detail was very
important. Besides, she wanted to think, and she
thought better if physically occupied.

But half an hour later the light was seriously
beginning to fade and Gilly was about to go
inside when she heard a car pull up in the road
behind her.

'Excuse me!' said a voice.

She turned round and saw a large, smart car
and a man with silver hair and a nice smile
leaning across so he could speak to her through
the passenger window.

'Can I help?' she asked, glad she had make-up
on from having been out for lunch and that her
hair was reasonably OK for the same reason.

'I wonder if you can,' said the man, whose
voice was as pleasant as the rest of him. 'I'm
looking for this address.' He stopped the engine,
got out of the car and came round so he could

talk to Gilly properly. He was holding a bit of paper.

Gilly took the offered paper and considered it for a moment. 'Well, you're not far but you've come up the wrong way from the crossroads at the bottom of the hill.'

She gave him instructions about how to find his destination and he smiled again. 'Thank you so much. The satnav wasn't co-operating today. I'm only going to the house to do a valuation.'

'Valuation?' said Gilly, her attention caught.

He nodded. 'Yes. I'm doing a valuation for a friend.' He didn't seem in any particular hurry to get going. 'Here's my card.'

Gilly took it and read it. There was his name, Leo Simmons, and a string of letters afterwards, none of which meant anything to Gilly. 'So do you do valuations as your job?'

'Not exclusively but it's part of what I do.' He paused. 'Why do you ask?'

'It's just . . . Oh, nothing.' She stopped and realised he was waiting. 'I think I ought to get my house valued,' said Gilly quickly, before she could change her mind.

'It's never a bad thing,' said Leo quietly, 'although I can see you're not quite happy about it. Knowledge is power, after all.'

'It is! I'll make an appointment,' said Gilly, holding his card tightly and getting mud on it.

'I tell you what, unless you're busy later, why don't I do this house up the road and then come back and do yours?'

'Excellent idea,' said Gilly. Then I can't back out, she added to herself. Knowledge was indeed power and having her own valuation done meant Cressida couldn't start telling her how much valuable real estate she was sitting on.

'Brilliant. I'll be round in about an hour.'

Which gave Gilly an hour to give the house another tidy in his honour.

Gilly kept everywhere open to the public immaculate, which included the kitchen. But her own bedroom would have put any teenage girl's to shame — in fact, she thought, it could belong to very untidy teenage twins. But as with so many occupations, running a B & B had an element of smoke and mirrors about it and making a room, even her own, look good in a very short time wasn't much of a challenge to Gilly.

The first thing she did was take the duvet off the bed. Then every item of clothing that wasn't dirty (in which case it went in the capacious laundry basket) was laid on the bed. Floordrobe became bed-drobe. When she was satisfied there was nothing else lying about she laid the duvet carefully over the top. A few scatter cushions, artfully placed, and the room was instantly tidy.

The en-suite bathroom took a little longer but she had time to refresh her make-up before she hid it all away in the cupboard behind the mirror. Leo wouldn't need to open the cupboard to value the house and if he looked like doing so, she'd stop him.

As she reapplied her foundation she wondered if it would look as if she fancied him if she appeared too made-up. But no, she decided, she always made sure she was looking her best when she knew guests were due — it was only

46

professional. This was a professional visit and she should prepare for it. Although she couldn't help reflecting that he was a very attractive man and while she had seen many attractive men since her divorce this was the first one that made her feel just a little bit fluttery.

The thought made her happy.

★ ★ ★

'Well, this is a lovely house,' said Leo Simmons, having arrived back an hour later, as arranged. He was in the large hall, looking around. 'But I imagine running a bed and breakfast is very hard work.'

Gilly smiled warmly at him. Not everyone understood that there was work involved. Many people thought it was just showing people to their perfect rooms and frying up a few freshly laid eggs. They didn't realise the effort making those rooms perfect required.

'It is a labour of love but I do love it, so that's OK. I'll show you the B & B bit first and then the rest of it. I have six bedrooms, one of them wheelchair friendly. We'll start there.'

'This is a very good size,' said Leo, writing down the measurements in his book as they went into the downstairs bedroom. 'French doors on to the garden. Large en suite.'

'It was the morning room in the old days, when I was a little girl living here with my parents,' said Gilly. 'But it makes a lovely bedroom.'

'So this was your family home?'

She nodded. 'It was. It was a struggle to keep it when my husband left.'

'What, bills and things?'

'That, but mostly because he wanted half of it, which would have meant selling.'

'So how — ' Leo stopped, obviously not wanting to pry.

'There was quite a bit of land which I could sell. There was an orchard which was a bit heartbreaking to lose, but the other bit went as a building plot so I could pay off my husband and turn the house into a bed and breakfast.' She smiled at the memory of those early days. 'At first it was something I had to do to keep my family home but I soon found out I loved it. I love the people — they're all so interesting. Not even the boring ones are completely boring; they all have something about them that's fascinating.'

They ended up in the kitchen, which was large — some would say cluttered — and Gilly's favourite room. 'And here we have the heart of the home,' said Gilly. 'And it really is.'

Ulysses got up from where he was sleeping in front of the range and walked over to them. He sniffed at Leo's trousers. 'You're a fat chap, aren't you?' said Leo.

'His name is Ulysses,' said Gilly.

But Leo was still measuring. 'It's a good size, certainly,' he said, referring to the kitchen, not the cat. 'Range cookers are always popular.'

'Helena — that's my daughter — said that one cost the same as a small cottage. I'm not sure what part of the country you'd have to be in to

48

get a cottage for that price, but it was very expensive.' Gilly paused. 'But it's in use all the time. I do evening meals as well as bed and breakfast.'

'No island?'

'No,' she said. 'I prefer a kitchen table that you can move if necessary. Once an island, always an island, and it would annoy me if I had to keep walking round it.'

'To be honest, if you did sell, whoever bought it would probably rip out the kitchen and start again,' said Leo, not unsympathetically. 'I like the mix of free-standing and fitted units myself but people are very into sleek white cupboards with invisible catches.'

'I've never been a fan of integral dishwashers and things. I like a fridge to look like a fridge!'

'Some of the modern kitchens I see, it all looks like a fridge,' said Leo.

'I wouldn't be without my dresser,' said Gilly, looking at the huge old bit of furniture that her father had had built in when he and his wife first bought the house. It took up an entire wall and swallowed up a vast amount of crockery, dozens of mugs and jugs that hung on the hooks that edged each shelf and a fair amount of clutter that was stuffed into the cupboards. It was her work of art and she loved it as if it was a family pet. Just the thought of having to live without it made Gilly shudder. It would never fit in that granny annexe her daughter-in-law had been so keen for her to live in.

Gilly cleared her throat. The tour had taken quite a long time, there was a lot of house and it seemed natural, now, to add, 'Would you like a glass of wine?'

Leo smiled and shook his head. 'Driving. But I'd love a cup of tea and maybe a piece of the shortbread you put in every room.'

'There's always plenty of that,' said Gilly. 'Let's go through to the conservatory and look at the view,' she said, putting two mugs and a plate of biscuits on a tray.

He took the tray from her hands. 'Lead the way,' he said.

Gilly had the very short time it took them to go from one room to another to work out why she found these words so very sexy.

6

Helena got back from taking her mother home in a state of repressed anger. She'd been keeping a lid on her outrage all day and now she nearly scraped the side of her car when she pulled up outside her home.

Jago was in the yard and came over. 'Everything all right?' he said as she got out of the car.

'Fine thanks. I didn't hit anything,' said Helena.

'Forgive me but you said that as if you wished you had hit something — or someone.'

In spite of herself Helena laughed. 'Very perceptive of you. I am in a bit of a strop.'

He regarded her for a few moments as if debating the wisdom of his next words. 'Would you like to come and have a glass of wine and tell me about it? I can no longer offer you a cat to cuddle. Zuleika and her kitten have gone back to my sister.'

'I saw them leaving, but even without them, that's a very tempting idea. Especially if you've got a fire going. I've spent the day in a glass house — not a heated one.'

'With people you don't awfully care for, I can tell. Wait till you've had half a glass of wine and then you can really let rip about them.'

Helena went into her own house first, to use the loo and check on her hair. Cressida always made her wish she'd spent hours coaxing it into fat curls that ended on her shoulder, like the woman who helped Lord Sugar on *The Apprentice*. Only Helena never quite had the time or inclination. Now, as it was a mess, she put it in a loose plait and went across to Jago's. The thought of wine, a fire and a good old grump about her sister-in-law was calling to her.

'If you pull your chair right up to the fire you feel some heat and, more importantly, overlook the fact you're sitting in a building site,' said Jago. 'One day it'll be my 'des res' but now — well, you can see how it is.'

'Oh, this is lovely!' said Helena. 'I didn't think you'd actually have a fire, it being April and all.'

'April is the coldest month,' he misquoted, handing her a very large glass of red wine. 'And I always have lots of wood that needs burning. You start on that' — he indicated the wine — 'I'll bring in some bread and cheese. You don't have to join me but I'm starving.'

'I'm hungry too. And I've got shortbread we can have for pudding.'

'Shortbread?'

'My mother makes it as a reflex action. She has a B & B and puts it in the guest rooms. She gives any that are left over to any passing person and it's often me. I'll get it later.' For now all she wanted was to sink into the extremely shabby, exquisitely comfortable armchair, sip her wine and look into the flames.

When they had both eaten quite a lot of the sourdough loaf and selection of cheeses with strange-sounding names that he produced, along with another glass of wine, Jago said, 'So tell me.'

Helena sighed the sigh of the replete person

52

who never stayed angry for long. 'It's my sister-in-law.'

'Yes?'

'She seems to want my mother to sell her house so she and my brother can buy a mansion with seven bedrooms and a horrid granny flat. My mother would live in the granny flat and look after their child.' She paused. 'Mind you, me and Mum both feel that Issi — short for Ismene, but we're not allowed to shorten it — is a bit thin and could benefit from Mum's cooking.'

Jago considered. 'People who call their child Ismene could be capable of anything.'

Helena checked to see if he was teasing and while he was twinkling a bit, his look was basically sympathetic. 'My worry is that Mum will actually do it. She says she won't but she's a bit soft; I can't totally rely on her to stand firm.'

'When you say soft, you mean stupid?'

'No! I mean soft-hearted, too kind. I promise you, she can't pass a homeless person without giving them money and she never comes back from London without at least ten copies of the *Big Issue*.' She paused. 'If she gets lost, which she does all the time, she asks a *Big Issue* seller and gives them a tenner for their trouble.'

'Oh, that is kind-hearted.'

'And I don't mind that, or the fact that she cries at almost anything she sees on telly — I can't even go with her to the cinema — but it's the worry that when Cressida suggests she's being selfish, keeping her big house when they could do with most of its value, guilt will make her say: 'Yes, that's true, here you go, darling.''

53

'Did your sister-in-law suggest that?'

'No, but she will, and Mum will cave in. And she had to work so hard to keep the house after the divorce.'

Explaining what happened — her mother selling the orchard and land for a building plot, something that caused such heartache at the time when no one knew who might buy it and what kind of a property her mother might find next to hers — Helena took another glass of wine, and she knew she would probably wake with a hangover.

'So what did happen?' asked Jago, putting down the bottle. 'Who bought it?'

'Actually a lovely couple who built a kit house but it looks really nice and they get on well so it all worked out. But poor Mum was beside herself. She had to have hypnotherapy to get through it.'

'And did that work?'

'Brilliantly.' Helena paused and started to get up out of her chair. 'Thank you so much for the wine and the moan, not to mention the bread and cheese, but I should get back. I have so much work to get through while I still have a space to do it in.'

'You promised me shortbread. You know builders live on biscuits.'

'Oh! I'd forgotten. I'll pop back and get it. It's still in the car. I usually have to give it away because if I ate all Mum gives me I'd be fat as a pig.' She laughed. 'I'll tell Amy I gave it to you and she'll be pleased. Mum too.'

'Why's that?'

'Because they'll think I'm flirting with you, showing normal human behaviour in the presence of a single male. Mind you, we never found out if you are or not.'

'I am,' he said quickly. 'Very single.'

Helena looked at him with a narrow gaze, suddenly aware of how attractive he was.

'I'm just a man who has no time for romance.' He said it as if he had no wish to elaborate.

'Well, there's something we have in common! Why is it people find it so difficult to accept that one can be perfectly normal but not want to spend time looking for a life partner!' Helena realised she was just a little bit drunk and her filters were down but she didn't stop. 'I don't want to spend my time on dating apps! I want to be weaving, not swiping left or right, saying yes or no to someone I've never met who is bound to be boring. My friends seem to think that I should see every man under seventy as a potential partner.'

He seemed amused. 'Under seventy? Your friends are tough. I wouldn't have thought you should look at anyone over about forty myself. Because — how old are you?'

'Twenty-seven.'

'Well, make that under thirty-five unless you fancy older men.'

She couldn't help laughing. 'I don't fancy any kind of man — well, I don't mean that exactly; I do fancy men sometimes but I don't want to do anything about it. Not just now. I've got too much on.'

'That's exactly how I feel. I can appreciate a

pretty girl or a lovely woman but I'm not going to ask her out. I haven't time to maintain a relationship. And, like houses, they need maintaining.'

'And you're too busy maintaining your property empire,' said Helena and then hoped it didn't look as if she was having a dig.

'I am! Being a slum landlord is very hard work!'

She laughed. 'I wouldn't describe you as a slum landlord.'

'I'm flattered.' He considered for a moment. 'Here's an idea. Supposing we have an arrangement where if one of us needs a partner to go to anything, or wants to get a matchmaker off our backs — Lord, how I hate matchmakers — we can use the other person, say we're an item.'

Helena exhaled slowly. 'I don't actually hate my matchmaker. Amy is my best friend and my mother doesn't matchmake often, she just sighs and clamps her lips shut if any of my friends has a baby. I'm not sure it would work.'

'Why?'

'I've been determinedly single for so long. I'm not sure anyone would believe it. It's so hard to make a living as a craftsperson, I haven't had time to look for a partner as well.'

'They don't have to believe we've fallen in love. But if you took me along to something that had Amy or your mum at it, for example, you could just say it's early days when they ask if we're an item — '

'And they will ask,' said Helena. 'They will explode.'

'Of course my mates would tell me I was punching.'

'What?'

'Above my weight,' he explained. 'But I'll just shrug in a casual way and say, 'If you've got it, you've got it.' I'll channel Joey in *Friends*.'

'That's a brilliant plan. And I'll get the shortbread immediately!' said Helena. 'Joey eats everything!'

'Actually, hang on a minute. I've just had an idea. Somewhere you might be able to put your loom for — say — at least another six months.'

'Well, that's amazing!'

'It might not be that amazing. The room needs an awful lot doing to it to make it useable and I can't do the work.'

'So . . . '

'You'll have to do it.'

'Listen, mate, I like DIY as much as the next girl, but I'm not a builder.'

He laughed. 'You don't need to be a builder.' He hesitated. 'Would you like me to show it to you now? It's not far.'

Helena suddenly felt very tired and regretted drinking so much wine. 'Actually, I don't think now is a good time. I'm a bit drunk and I'd probably say yes to something I'll think is a really bad idea in the morning.'

He laughed. 'I'll come with you to your car and get the shortbread. And I'll knock on your door tomorrow and arrange a time to see the building.'

★ ★ ★

57

When Helena was in bed, reading a couple of pages of her book, she realised she'd spent the nicest evening with a man that she had for a long time. She had resolved to give Amy a little lecture on the benefit of platonic friendships when she stopped herself. Much better to stick to Jago's plan of letting everyone think they were together. Then Amy would stop going on about her trying to find a boyfriend. She could say she had one and Jago would back her up. She felt very satisfied, not to say smug. Helena was glad now that Amy, after her brave words about checking Jago out, had confessed to her that she actually had her eye on someone else just at the moment and so wouldn't mind Helena claiming Jago. Everyone would be happy! She even fancied Jago a bit, which would make the whole charade a bit more realistic. Result!

★ ★ ★

It was about ten when Jago turned up the following day. He was holding the empty shortbread tin.

'I can't believe you've eaten it all already!' Helena said when she saw him.

'No, although it was absolutely delicious. I put what I didn't eat into another box. I popped over to arrange a time to go and see this building.'

Aware that he was busy and it was very kind of him to try to find her somewhere for her loom, Helena said, 'When is good for you?'

'Now, actually. I could start another job but then I'm due over at another part of my vast

58

empire.' His tone was expressionless and it made Helena smile.

'I could do now too. Just let me get a jacket. It's still not warm, is it?'

A few minutes later she swung herself up into his pickup.

'It's not far, we could walk really, but we're both busy,' he said. 'It's an old barn I'm converting. But it's not a priority — haven't currently got the cash to do it up.'

'I'm never sure about barn conversions,' said Helena. 'How on earth do you heat them? They'll never be cosy with the heat going straight up to the rafters, which would get dusty and be hell to clean.'

He laughed. 'You're probably right about the rafters, but underfloor heating solves the other problem. This'll have a wood burner as well. For the look of it really. When I've finished, it'll be energy neutral, more or less.'

'Oh, very green!'

'I try to be. I hope to sell this one for loads of money and then I can reinvest in some more affordable housing.'

'Very philanthropic,' she said, but more seriously this time.

'I try to be,' he repeated.

Helena glanced across at him and caught him looking suddenly very serious. There was a glint of real determination in his expression. She looked out of the window quickly. There was something behind the jolly-builder exterior of Jago she didn't want to disturb.

He pulled back a large sliding door to a substantial barn. It was empty of agricultural trappings but although there was a wooden floor and staircase, indicating where the bedrooms would be, the rest was still as it had been when it had been a working building.

'So you see, it's a work in progress,' he said. 'You could put your loom in here in return for a bit of lime mortaring.' He indicated the huge gable end of the barn.

'Just a bit. Can't you plaster it?'

'I could but people love a bit of exposed stone and I'm building to sell here.'

'I think too much exposed stone makes it look like a prison,' said Helena, aware she might be doing herself out of a work space.

'I like to give buyers a certain amount of choice. I'd need to point it anyway. Those gaps in the stone need filling, whatever the final finish is.'

'It's a big space!'

'Too big?' he asked. 'I've got industrial heaters you can use if you feel cold.'

'Summer is on its way — they tell us — and if I could just be in here until I've done enough work for my big exhibition that would be great.'

'Presumably it takes a while to set the loom up?'

She nodded. 'It does. But as I insisted on having a large loom instead of just the small ones that Amy has, I have to pay the price. I can do much bigger stuff on a large loom.'

'I haven't met Amy yet. I've been remiss as a landlord.'

She laughed. 'We must make a plan so we can get together. If I don't do it, she will! And when she's met you, we can tell her, and for the moment her only, that we're an item. I can't wait to see her reaction!'

Helena couldn't help feeling relieved that she had seen Jago before Amy had. Whoever Amy had her sights on just this minute may well have not got a look in had she seen Jago.

7

'Mrs Claire? It's Leo Simmons, the house valuer.'

Gilly wouldn't have admitted to anyone how excited she was to hear Leo's voice at the other end of her landline, a couple of days after he had valued the house — and not because she was desperate to know the value.

'Gilly, please. Hello, Leo.'

He laughed softly. 'Hello, Gilly. I've rung to tell you how much your house is worth.'

'Go on then. I'm keen to know.'

'Well, I hope you're sitting down.'

'Goodness,' she said when he had told her. She'd thought she had a rough idea of how much her house was worth; this was quite a lot more.

'Don't make any hasty decisions,' said Leo, 'but if you do decide to sell, I'd be delighted to advise you. While I'm not really an estate agent — more a property consultant — there are a lot of charlatan estate agents out there and I could help you stay out of their clutches.'

'I'll definitely consult you if I decide to sell.' She paused. 'So, how much do I owe you for the valuation? And where and how do I pay?' She wasn't sure if you did pay for valuations but thought she'd better make sure.

'Nothing. I did it as a favour.'

'You can't! You don't even know me — I mean — before. I insist on paying.' Gilly hated getting things for nothing.

'I can, because I have a favour to ask you in return.'

'Oh, well, that is a bit different. What can I do for you?'

He didn't speak immediately. 'It's a bit awkward and you might think it terribly forward besides being very short notice . . .'

'What is it?' Gilly was on tenterhooks.

'I was forced to buy two tickets for Music at Gainsborough tomorrow night. Do you have a clue what I'm talking about?'

Gilly laughed, feeling relaxed and very happy. 'Of course! I've been a couple of times. It's our local Glyndebourne, only they have it in a barn. It's a shame it's so early in the year but apparently they have it then because the singers are cheaper to hire or something. The gardens at Gainsborough House would be such a perfect setting for opera. Then it really would be like Glyndebourne.'

'But it's only extracts, isn't it? Being new to the area I don't know what to expect. Will you come with me? You're probably going already — it's such short notice,' he repeated.

'I'd be delighted to come with you, but as a pleasure, not a favour.'

'Tell you what, you bring the picnic and we'll call it quits. But let me do the wine. It's a hobby of mine.'

'Then I'll do the food. It's a hobby of mine.'

A second later she wished she hadn't said that. Food definitely was a hobby of hers and ideas for a sumptuous picnic were already going round in her head but she didn't want him to expect too much.

'That's wonderful! I'll ring you tomorrow when I've worked out the details. I'll arrange a cab so I can enjoy the wine.' He sounded very pleased. 'This is so kind of you,' he said.

'It's so kind of you to invite me!'

'To be honest, I don't know any other attractive women in the area I could ask, so I'm thrilled you said yes.'

Gilly laughed. 'I think I'd better end the call now,' she said. 'Ring me when you know the details.'

She went round the house in a haze of happiness, wishing she had someone she could tell about this rather surprising conversation. She didn't want to tell Helena because she didn't want to have to explain that she'd had the house valued. She would go mad with rage at her brother and sister-in-law. No, she just wanted to enjoy the anticipation. Going to a big local event with an attractive man was a real ego boost. She was going to savour every second of the event, and the run-up to it.

But Gilly's joy was marred by the burden of knowing how much her house was worth. While it was lovely in some ways, was it fair of her to sit on a property valuable enough to give both her children sizeable amounts of cash and leave enough for her to buy a little cottage somewhere? Probably not.

She was researching high-end picnic options when her son rang her. 'Martin? Is everything all right?'

'Mum! Does there always have to be something the matter? I just rang for a chat. That's OK, isn't it?'

'It's very OK, darling, it's just very unheard of. You're always so busy!'

'Yes, well, we have plans to change that. We've decided we need to reassess our lives. We just don't get enough time together as a family.'

'Oh, darling, that's wonderful! Little Issi — I mean Ismene — won't be little for long; they grow up so fast. You don't want to have missed it. Either of you.'

'I'm so glad you agree, Mum. So you're thinking about our suggestion? You need to cut down on the hours you work too.'

'Running my own B & B is hardly the same as a high-powered, full-time job!'

'It is very hard work. You're always saying so.'

'Yes, it is hard work but I do love it.'

'You could love it just as much if you did it a bit less.'

Gilly was aware that she was breathing too quickly. She knew what Martin meant and it was making her anxious. 'Sorry, I'm not with you. I could cut down on the number of rooms I let but then I wouldn't have a profitable business. Then it would just be the work without the money.'

'What we're suggesting is that if you sold Fairacres, and we bought the house we showed you online, you could run a couple of the extra rooms as B & B rooms and the extra income would mean me and Cress could work less intensively.'

Remembering what the hypnotherapist had

told her after her divorce, Gilly did some measured breathing, making sure the outward breath lasted longer than the inward. 'So you're suggesting that I do the work and you get the money?'

'Mum! Don't go all mercenary on me! If you sold your house you wouldn't need the money.'

'I think I would, darling, because all the money would go into buying your house.' This wasn't quite true. If Leo's valuation was correct, there'd be quite a bit left but she wasn't inclined, just at this moment, to share this with her son.

He hesitated. 'I'm sure not all of it. It must be a very valuable property.'

'It was your childhood home, Martin,' Gilly said. 'It's not just 'real estate'.'

'I know,' he said soothingly, 'but everything has its time, Mum, and we don't need a childhood home any more. We need homes for now, when we're grown up. And Helena needs somewhere for her loom.'

'I'm not saying I won't think about selling, darling, but I won't be running a B & B in your house.' Gilly was very particular about how she treated her guests and presented the rooms and she wasn't going to risk Cressida telling her how to do it differently. And she would.

'Fair enough!' said Martin, not quite getting it. 'It wouldn't be a deal-breaker. You could still come to live with us!' he said generously.

'Or I could buy a little cottage somewhere, then you wouldn't need a house with a granny annexe. Which would be much cheaper.'

'Oh, but we need you on site — for Ismene.

You know you'd love that!'

'I've said I'll think about it,' said Gilly. 'And that will have to do for now.'

But she was so enraged by his suggested plan that she had to have a cup of tea and one of the shortbread biscuits she continually made for other people, but never ate herself.

She was certain she was right not to tell Helena she'd had Fairacres valued — she might let slip about Martin's call and then Helena might ring her brother and rant at him. They'd always got on well as children but since he'd married Cressida and Helena had stopped being the baby sister, relations were sometimes strained. Far better that Gilly should think things through on her own and make her own decision.

She decided to make sausage rolls for the picnic but didn't go as far as making her own puff pastry. She mixed caramelised onions into the sausage meat though, which was a lovely addition. Then she made smoked salmon Scotch eggs before focusing on some little fruit tarts using her own frozen raspberries. While she baked she didn't let herself think about selling her house, she just focused on providing the perfect picnic for two. Helena would have said she was providing for twenty-two, but baking kept anxiety away and she was good at it.

★ ★ ★

Leo collected her the next evening in a limousine. He looked extremely handsome in a dinner jacket and Gilly was very glad she was wearing a rather expensive full-length coat to go over her favourite dress. She felt dressed up but not overdressed, and, most importantly, a pashmina meant she wouldn't be cold.

'You look sensational!' he said when he'd taken the picnic hamper from her and kissed her cheek.

'You look pretty smart yourself,' she said, trying not to hyperventilate. She hadn't felt like this about a man since she'd first met her ex-husband, Sebastian. It was lucky she was no longer in her twenties and was now very sensible, she thought.

'It's so kind of you to come.' He sat down in the back seat next to her.

'The pleasure is all mine, really,' said Gilly. 'I had fun making the picnic.'

'If I'd done it, it would have been sandwiches from M&S followed by one of those tubs of brownies or fudge bites or whatever they are.'

'Which I happen to love!' said Gilly.

'Next time,' he said. 'But I'm looking forward to what you've brought with you.'

'We are going for the cultural experience!' said Gilly, laughing. She realised she was completely giddy with excitement and what could quite possibly be lust. Whatever it was, it was lovely and she was going to enjoy every second.

★   ★   ★

'I can't believe that apart from everything else, you are a sensational cook,' said Leo a few hours later, on his second smoked salmon Scotch egg.

He had found a delightful place for them to eat in the garden room of the main house, with views over the lake and the woodlands beyond. 'I'm not sensational,' Gilly replied, trying not to giggle, having had two glasses of champagne. 'I just have a knack with pastry.'

'I'm not eating pastry,' said Leo, 'so you must be sensational.'

Gilly looked at him over her glass, trying to think of something sensible to say. 'It's time for the second half of the performance,' she said eventually.

'Really? Do we have to go? Couldn't we just stay here and eat this delicious food and get drunk? After all, neither of us has to drive, and how often can one say that?'

'Not very often but I'm afraid we do have to see the second half. There are quite a lot of people I know here and if we didn't reappear there would be talk.' Privately Gilly was thrilled at possibly being the subject of gossip and speculation. Currently she was known as a good woman and while she didn't want to be a bad one, it was fun to challenge people's ideas about who she really was. She felt her reputation was rather dull.

Leo put the picnic hamper in a safe place and they walked back together into the main barn. Gilly was just settling herself in, wondering if she needed her pashmina or not, when she caught someone waving at her.

It was Amy's mother. Although not as close friends as their daughters were, she'd known Michelle since the girls were at school together.

Now Michelle was raising her eyebrows, smiling and looking at Leo. There was no chance Gilly could pretend that she and Leo were just sitting next to each other by chance.

If it had been any of her other friends she'd have been thrilled to be seen with such an attractive man at her side. But Michelle would tell her daughter Amy, and Amy would tell Helena faster than the speed of thought. What would Helena have to say about her mother going to the opera with a man like Leo? The first thing she would want to know is where did Gilly meet him. And if Gilly told her, Helena would want to know the details and if Gilly told her about getting her house valued, Helena would be outraged.

She took a breath. She didn't have to worry about that until tomorrow. She looked up at Leo and caught him smiling down at her. Her stomach flipped. She was thrilled that her stomach could still do that. She'd sort of assumed that it was an ability one lost with age, like being able to do the splits.

This thought amused her so much she almost laughed out loud. Leo caught her expression and gave her a very wry look.

This was worth any amount of interrogation from Helena tomorrow, she decided.

★   ★   ★

Gilly felt incredibly like a teenager on the way home. She sat in the back of the car with Leo wishing she lived a lot further away than she did.

70

He picked up her hand and looked at it. 'You have lovely hands,' he said.

Gilly used to be proud of her hands but felt that work and the passing years had spoiled them. She managed not to argue with him though and was proud of herself. 'Thank you.'

Then they were outside her house and the driver was taking her up the drive to her front door.

Leo got out, ran round the car and opened the door for her. He ushered her up to the door. 'Thank you so much for a lovely evening,' he said, stealing her line. 'I do hope we can do something like it again.'

'I'd like that very much,' said Gilly, suddenly desperately shy. 'I've had such a nice time. Thank you so much.'

He kissed her lightly on both cheeks. 'I'll be in touch. Soon.'

8

From the moment Amy had arrived to pick Helena up for a weaving workshop, Helena could tell that Amy had gossip. She didn't say anything on the journey and Helena decided not to give her friend the gratification and ask her.

When they'd arrived at the venue and done most of the setting-up, Helena caved in.

'So why are you looking so pleased with yourself?' she asked, ostensibly checking the list of names she had in front of her. 'You're looking amazingly smug and you obviously have big news.'

'I have such brilliant gossip you will not believe it! And it's really nice gossip too, nothing nasty.'

'So, tell me?'

'Not sure we've got time now. Everyone's pretty much here. But afterwards, deffo.'

Helena considered that Amy's use of rather old-fashioned slang was one of the many things she loved about her. Her habit of leaving you hanging was less endearing. But Amy had a point, people were ready to start and they should crack on.

★　★　★

'So,' said Amy when the session was over and they were driving back to Helena's, 'my mum

72

saw yours yesterday evening.'

'Who? My mum?'

'That's what I said!'

'If that's the gossip, it's very lame.'

'It's all about the context! She saw her at that posh opera thing.'

'Well, that's nice. I didn't know she was going.' Still not proper gossip.

'With a man! Not just any man, a gorgeous one. Mum said he was a silver fox!'

'Oh.' Helena felt put out and a bit worried about her mother. 'Why didn't she tell me she was going? How did she even dress herself without my going over her wardrobe?'

Amy understood there was more to this than Helena's objection to not being consulted and shrugged her shoulders. 'She's a free agent. She can go out with whoever she likes without asking permission.'

'No she can't!' said Helena, knowing she was being unreasonable. 'Supposing she gets carried off by a conman? A 'silver fox', you say? That doesn't sound like he's trustworthy, does it?'

'No, but it sounds like he's hot. And being hot doesn't make you a bad person. I should know!' Amy pointed to herself and made a face. 'Seriously, Helly, I thought you'd be delighted, your mother meeting someone. She's been on her own long enough.'

Helena sighed. 'I'm delighted if he's nice, but you know Mum, she's vulnerable. She can be taken in by anyone.'

'I don't think you give her enough credit. She must have to judge character every day with her

73

business. Think how she's made your old house into a B & B that's so good it's practically a boutique hotel. You can't do that if you're an idiot.'

'I know,' said Helena, feeling chastened but not reassured. 'But I worry about her and men. She made such a bad choice when she picked my father, I'm not sure she can make good decisions about them.'

'This may not be an actual thing. They may just have gone to the opera together and never see each other again.' It was Amy's turn to sigh. 'You know what men are like.'

Helena did relax a bit now. 'True.'

'I wouldn't have told you if I thought you'd worry about it. I just thought you'd be pleased Gilly had had a night out with a good-looking man.' She paused. 'Why don't you give her a call? Not to tell her off, obvs, but to congratulate her. Say you'd heard and you're a bit jel.'

Helena laughed properly now. 'She won't believe I'm jealous! But, on the subject of men, have you met our gorgeous landlord yet?' Helena realised that she hadn't thought of him as gorgeous before and now she'd described him as such Amy would get overexcited.

'No, I didn't go in the end as I had someone else in my sights — I told you. But you didn't describe him as gorgeous — I might have called round anyway.'

Helena shrugged.

'So have you done anything about him?' Amy went on, firing up all her regular arguments. 'You need to get in there! You can't just stand back

74

and hope that he'll do something, he won't! Men are totally lazy when it comes to women.'

'Probably because if most women are like you, men have them crawling all over them. They don't have to make an effort.'

'And women do!' Amy was very clear on this point.

Helena was very tempted to say something about her and Jago, but she held back. It might rebound on her. So instead she said, 'Well, my mother obviously doesn't seem to have to make much of an effort. I'd have known if she'd had her eye on this silver fox.'

'Give her a call,' Amy repeated. 'But don't tell her off!'

'As if!' said Helena, although she took the warning to heart. She would be very casual, as if she wasn't remotely worried about who her mother went out with.

★   ★   ★

She waited until early afternoon, when her mother was likely to be at her desk sorting out her diary, before she rang.

'Hi, Mum! What's this about you being seen with a silver fox!' Helena hoped she sounded sufficiently light-hearted. 'Did you have a good time?' she added.

'Amy told you?' Gilly laughed. 'I didn't think it would take Michelle long to tell on me.'

'To be fair, I think she was more impressed than disapproving.' Helena managed to hesitate for a tenth of a second before going on. 'So who

75

was he and how did you meet him?'

'Honestly, darling, anyone would think I was an underage convent girl, not a middle-aged woman, quite old enough to be in a public place with a member of the opposite sex.'

Helena's laugh sounded a bit false, even to her. 'Sorry! I'm just curious.'

There was a pause. Helena could picture her mother, who by now would be playing Spider patience on her computer, something she always did while on the phone unless it was a business call. Therefore a hesitation on Gilly's part didn't always mean she was thinking of what to say — she could just be working out a move with her game. 'Are you still there, Mum? Or have you got a tricky patience to get out?'

Gilly laughed again.

Honestly, Helena thought, her mother could almost be accused of being giddy. 'So? I can't decide if you're holding out on me or wondering if you'll have to start your game again, for the hundredth time.'

'Of course I'm not holding out on you. His name is Leo Simmons. I have only just met him and he had a spare ticket for the opera at Gainsborough House and asked me if I'd go. He's new to the area and doesn't know many people. I was just helping him out.'

'And did you bring the picnic?'

'I did! You know how I love making picnics.'

'Were there leftovers?'

'There were but I'm afraid I left them in the car with Leo. He was so appreciative.'

'I'll forgive you if you promise to arrange for

76

me to meet him,' said Helena, feeling she was winning. 'Just a casual Sunday lunch would do. You could invite Martin and Cress.'

'Then it would look as if he was having to meet all the family because we were going out properly which would be a bit much considering we're not.'

'Just invite me, then,' said Helena, determined to meet her mother's silver fox.

'That would look worse! Really, Helly, you are being a bit unreasonable.'

'You know me, I'll go to any lengths to get one of your Sunday lunches.' She paused. 'I know! Why don't I bring someone?'

'Who? Amy? That would look very normal, I must say! I go out with him once and then five minutes later make him come to Sunday lunch with two giggling schoolgirls.'

'We don't giggle any more, Mum! At least, not all that often. And besides, I don't mean Amy. I mean a man.' Jago would do well out of the invite. Her mother's Sunday lunches were famous locally.

'A man? You? Good Lord!'

'Just a friend, Mum, just like your friend!' Helena was sowing the seeds carefully, not letting it look as if she and Jago were anything more than friends just yet.

'OK,' said Gilly. 'I'll see what I can do.'

★ ★ ★

Gilly continued to sit at her desk, playing Spider, when an email appeared at the top right-hand corner of her computer and drifted into her in-box. Maybe inviting Leo to Sunday lunch would be easier than she'd thought.

She clicked on his email, unable to stop smiling with delight.

9

'It's kind of you to come with me,' said Helena to Jago as she drove them to Fairacres the following Sunday. 'It'll stop my mum thinking I'm checking out her boyfriend, which I totally am.'

'We all need to take time off to have lunch,' said Jago easily. 'Although neither of us are very good at that.'

'We have deadlines,' said Helena. 'And I promise the food will be good. If you can put up with a certain amount of probing and we stick to our 'just good friends, trying it out', things like that, it should be fine.'

Jago shrugged. 'Some people would think I was mad not to claim you as my girlfriend properly.'

'Sweet of you to say so,' said Helena, convinced he was just being gallant. 'But those who know me would think it was crazy if I was treating us seriously as a couple so soon.' She paused. 'It's a slight shame that my brother and his wife are going to be there. Although my niece is good fun, in a strange way. We had lunch with them only last week and, frankly, I prefer the gaps between family meals with them to be bigger.'

'What's wrong with your brother and his wife, then?'

'My sister-in-law, Cressida, doesn't really

79

approve of food. She'd rather have a smoothie full of supplements than a proper meal. She disapproves of my mother's old-fashioned methods that mean her roast potatoes are the best.'

'What about your mum's Yorkshire puddings?'

Helena took a breath. 'I feel so disloyal saying this but, just sometimes, they aren't so good. Everything else will be stunning. Two puddings afterwards at least. And lots of fabulous gravy. Sometimes I make the Yorkies for her.'

Jago didn't speak for a few moments. 'OK, I'm still on board for this. I can cope with a little bun instead of a Yorkshire pudding.'

Helena laughed. 'It sounds as if you've experienced those.'

'Many times.'

★　★　★

Gilly wished Leo hadn't been so keen to come to her early and help. She found it slightly difficult to talk to people and cook — unless it was breakfast when she was so practised. But his enthusiasm for her company was flattering. He obviously wanted the lunch to go well as much as she did. Now, she was whisking her gravy, wondering if there was enough and, as always, deciding there wasn't.

'There's always a point with gravy,' she said to Leo, who was pulling corks out of the bottles of wine that he'd brought, 'when it tastes perfect, but wouldn't give people more than a teaspoon each. You have to steel yourself to possibly ruin it

80

when you add things to make it enough.'

'Wouldn't it be better to have a teaspoon of perfect gravy than a lot of substandard stuff?'

Gilly was horrified. 'My gravy is never substandard and not enough gravy is the most depressing thing. I'm going to get out my 'Mother's little helpers'.'

'Which are?'

'Soy sauce, Madeira, Bisto, they all have their place.' She really wanted him out of her kitchen. 'Leo, I know I don't know you very well, but do I know you well enough to ask you to set the table? Everything you need should be in the sideboard in the dining room?'

'Of course, anything I can do to help.'

Gilly turned on her fan oven. Most of the meal was being cooked by her large range but she wanted control for her Yorkshire puddings. She was always a bit nervous about them but with Cressida coming, she really wanted them to be right. Although it should have been Leo she was keen to impress she trusted him not to be critical about them. The beef was superb, resting under layers of tea towels. The potatoes were perfect, the roasted carrots buttery and sweet. The broccoli and were all ready to steam. All she needed now was a couple of trays of nicely risen Yorkshire puddings. Ismene, her only grandchild, loved Yorkshire puddings. She wanted them right for her especially.

While she sorted through the cutlery fresh from the dishwasher — Leo would find a lot of things missing in the sideboard drawers — she thought about the enormous bundle of narcissi

81

Leo had brought. They were so perfect. Much nicer than lilies or something more exotic and there were so many of them! She never liked flowers out of season and he obviously felt the same. It was all going so well. They'd been out for dinner the previous evening and it had made her so fluttery and excited.

★ ★ ★

'Shall we introduce ourselves?' suggested Leo as everyone arrived at once.

'Good idea,' said the tall man who'd arrived with Helena.

At first sight, Gilly liked him. He was relaxed and easy, not particularly smartly dressed — unlike Leo who was wearing an immaculate suit and silk tie — but he was friendly and managed to make conversation with Martin, which could be difficult.

'I can't believe you drink sherry,' said Cressida, who was nursing fizzy water with a sprig of thyme in it. 'It's an older person's drink.'

'I like sherry,' said Helena, sounding defiant. 'And I think it's coming back into fashion.'

'Who cares about fashion?' said Jago. 'You either like something or you don't.'

'So that's why you're wearing clothes out of the eighties?' Cressida asked, but in a way that didn't quite qualify as being rude.

Jago gave her a very charming smile. 'That's it exactly.'

'Oh, look! Here's Uly!' said Ismene, leaving her mother's side and going towards the cat.

'Don't touch him!' said her mother sharply. 'You'll get covered with hairs.'

Gilly noticed that Leo had stepped away from the cat as well but cat hairs would be hard to get off those elegant trousers. She clapped her hands and Ulysses, taking offence, stalked out of the room.

'Maybe you could top up everyone's glasses for me, Leo?' said Gilly into the silence. 'I've just got to put the green veg on.'

As she hurried back to the kitchen, wishing she could stay there, Gilly hoped that the cat would stay out of the way and that Jago and Cressida wouldn't get touchy with each other. Helena was being a bit odd although she was saying all the right things. Probably hungry, she thought. She'd have gone without breakfast to save herself for a big lunch. As a child she was always grumpy if her blood sugar level dipped.

Gilly came back into the drawing room and sensed that two glasses of sherry hadn't been enough to lighten the atmosphere. 'Let's go and eat,' she said. The veg should be cooked by the time everyone had sat down. Overcooked, possibly.

'Would you like me to carve?' suggested Leo instantly.

'Thank you!' said Gilly. She really preferred to carve herself but with everything else that needed to be organised, letting him do it freed her up for other things.

Helena followed her mother into the kitchen. 'Terrific Yorkshires,' she said admiringly, taking the dish from Gilly so she could take them through. 'Well done, Mum!'

'I did them in the fan oven,' said Gilly. 'But I'm relieved they turned out so well.'

'Wanting to impress the new boyfriend, then?' Helena said this in a joking way but something about her worried her mother. She was being perfectly polite but she didn't have her usual sparkle.

'Well, you know me. I like things to be perfect.' Gilly paused, shifting her grasp on the potatoes. 'Everything OK with you?'

'Yes!' said Helena vehemently. 'I've practically got a boyfriend, too!'

'Lovely!' said Gilly, trying to match her daughter's enthusiasm.

'So, how did you two meet?' asked Helena when all the initial passing things round the table and Gilly getting up to fetch the horseradish had been got over. She was looking at her mother.

'Didn't Leo value the house for you?' asked Cressida, her fork loaded with broccoli.

Gilly felt herself blush and hoped Helena would think it was a hot flush. 'Er . . . yes.'

'And I was able to give it a very good value,' said Leo, sounding satisfied with a job well done.

'I didn't know you were going to have the house valued,' said Helena bleakly.

'Well, of course she would, if she's thinking of selling it,' said Cressida, looking at Helena as if she were two sandwiches short of a picnic.

'I hope you're not selling,' said Jago. 'This is such a beautiful family house.'

'You can't expect Gilly never to downsize because you like her house!' said Cressida.

84

Jago looked quizzically at Cressida. 'I was just saying . . . '

'Mummy, can I have a roast potato?' asked Ismene.

'Just one,' said Cressida. 'All those bad fats and carbs. Not healthy.'

'Oh, come on, Cress!' said Helena. 'It's Sunday lunch. Let Issi have a roast potato and a Yorkshire pudding!'

'I have!' said Cressida, glaring at Helena.

Gilly's heart sank. Just when she needed her family to behave, when they had strangers among them, Helena got irritable with Cressida. She found herself sending Leo a desperate look.

'So, what do you do, Jago?' asked Leo, responding to Gilly's silent appeal.

'I'm a builder,' said Jago cheerfully.

'He's my landlord,' said Helena. 'Only not for much longer. I have to move out very soon.'

'That doesn't sound very friendly,' said Leo.

'Darling,' said Gilly, putting her hand across so she could touch Helena's. 'You could always have the ground-floor bedroom if you need it. In spite of what my accountant said,' she added, not meaning to say it out loud.

Leo looked at her. 'Oh, accountants. They're always stuffy and boring,' he said. 'Take no notice of him.'

'I always take notice of mine,' said Jago. 'He keeps me out of trouble.'

'So, Jago,' said Gilly, keen to take control of the conversation. 'Tell us about your building work?' Only after the words were out of her mouth did she realise it might be hard for

85

someone to talk about being a bricklayer, or whatever. Sometimes she wished she wasn't so middle-class.

'I mostly do conversions,' said Jago. 'I buy big old dilapidated houses and turn them into flats.'

'Creating second homes for Londoners, no doubt,' said Cressida.

'Actually,' said Helena, 'Jago creates homes for first-time buyers who can't afford much.'

'Can you afford to be so philanthropic?' said Leo.

'Yes,' said Jago, smiling calmly.

Gilly felt a bit put off by that remark from Leo. But when she looked at him he caught her gaze and smiled in a way that made her melt inside. 'Who's for seconds?'

'Oh, yes please,' said Jago. 'This is the best Sunday lunch I think I've ever had.'

Gilly's heart swelled a little. She loved feeding people and she loved Jago for being so enthusiastic. Although she knew she mustn't become too fond of him. He and Helena may well not get together properly. It was far too early for her to look on him as a second son.

'Yeah,' said Martin, 'your gravy is great and for once your Yorkshires have risen properly.'

'Thank you for your kind words, both of you,' said Gilly. 'Although Jago's words are quite a lot kinder than yours, Martin dear.'

'Mum! I am your son! You shouldn't expect compliments!'

'I think she should,' said Jago, 'when her cooking is as good as this.'

'Shall I help clear away?' asked Cressida, just

86

as Gilly was about to see if she could persuade anyone to have another potato or another sliver of meat.

Helena leaped to her feet. 'Don't bother, Cressida, I know where everything goes.'

'So do I!' said Cressida, sounding a bit surprised.

'I'll help too,' said Leo.

Gilly got to the kitchen first, hoping to field the huge number of dishes that were about to fill it. It was a magnificent kitchen and she loved it but it was slightly short of work surface. 'Why don't you go back into the dining room and see if everyone's got wine?' Gilly said to Leo. 'Cressida, will Ismene have pudding? Or would you rather she had cheese? Or some grapes?'

'Grapes are full of sugar. I can't believe you still think they're suitable food for a child,' said Cressida.

'Well, go away anyway,' said Gilly, feeling fairly calm about this admonishment. 'I'm assuming you won't want chocolate, then? I have some of the ninety per cent cocoa solids you're so fond of.'

Cressida managed a smile. 'Then I do want it! Unlike ordinary chocolate I count it as a health food.'

Gilly took a bar from the cupboard and handed it to her daughter-in-law with a smile that even Cressida would realise meant 'please leave my kitchen'. Now Gilly could find out what was up with Helena.

'Everything OK, love?' asked Gilly as Helena rinsed the plates and loaded the dishwasher while she retrieved one pudding from the range and another from the fridge.

'Oh yes, fine!' said Helena. 'Actually Jago has found me somewhere for my loom so that's one less thing to worry about.'

'He's such a nice man!' said Gilly, which was code for 'tell me all the details of your relationship'.

'He is! Although of course we're only really friends at the moment.' Helena found a tablet for the dishwasher and switched it on.

'Although it might lead to something else?'

'You never know!' said Helena with a teasing smile.

'Starting off as friends is always a good thing — even if it doesn't develop into something more,' she added quickly, seeing that Helena was going to protest about it being 'early days' and 'too soon to tell'. But as she said it, Gilly wondered if she and Leo were just friends? She thought not — not from her point of view anyway.

'What else have you got to worry about?' said Gilly, wishing Helena would just tell her why she was being twitchy.

'Oh, you know! All the work I need to do before World of Wool. Nothing you can help with, Mum.' She looked around the kitchen. 'Are we having cheese first and then pudding? Or what?'

'Both at the same time,' said Gilly. 'I can never decide which is better so it's easier to let people decide for themselves.' She smiled at her daughter. 'I like your Jago's appetite!'

Helena laughed. 'I knew you would! I didn't say anything to him but if I had wanted him to make an extra good impression I'd have told him to accept second helpings of everything.'

'Why didn't you tell him?'

Helena shrugged. 'Didn't think I'd need to!' She paused, possibly searching for the right thing to say. 'Mum, you know I like to clear up a bit before I go? But today I need to get off fairly speedily. Will you be OK? Will Leo help?'

'I'm glad you like him,' said Gilly, although she knew that Helena hadn't said that.

She wasn't entirely surprised that Helena was ambivalent about Leo, which was why she hadn't really wanted to introduce him so soon. Leo was the first man she'd gone out with since her divorce. It was bound to be a shock for Helena. Cressida and Martin seemed quite relaxed about it, but it was different for them, she supposed. Martin had left home, more or less, before the divorce. He'd had a couple of years working abroad before he came home and went to university. He hadn't seen her pain in quite the same way that Helena had. She sighed. Maybe it was asking too much for Helena to like any new man she might meet as much as she did. But perhaps Leo would grow on her.

10

'So, if you don't mind my asking,' said Jago, 'what's the matter?' He had a collection of foil-wrapped parcels on his lap, given to him by Gilly as he got into the car.

Helena slowed down a little. 'Sorry. I'm just a bit upset.'

'I can see that, but why? Leo was OK, wasn't he? Not my type, obviously but — '

Helena had been fighting with herself from almost the first moment they had arrived at her mother's house. 'Do you mind if I tell you why I don't like him?' Jago's quickness to pick up on her feelings encouraged her to confide in him.

'Of course not. I don't think he's ever going to be my best friend.'

'Why do you say that?' asked Helena sharply.

Jago shrugged. 'As I said, not my type. So why don't you like him? He seemed to be pretty much a ladies' man.'

'Maybe I should wait until we get home. It's a bit weird.'

'So? Your place or mine? I quite fancy having the third portion of pudding your mother gave me. Her pastry is amazing.'

'Yours — mine — I don't care really.'

'Let's go to mine,' said Jago.

Ten minutes later, Jago had settled Helena down with a mug of tea — having offered her wine and been refused — and pulled the sofa round so it caught the sunshine. Then, having put both portions of different sorts of pudding on to the same plate, he said, 'Spill.'

Helena sipped her tea, wondering where to start. 'It does mean telling you something rather weird about me.'

'Which is?'

'Do you know what a super-recogniser is?' she asked, desperately hoping for an affirmative.

'Nope, never heard of it.'

Helena exhaled. She hated having to explain this unusual ability: she felt it made her sound a bit strange. 'You obviously don't read enough crime fiction. It means I can recognise faces, even if I've only glanced at them, and remember them, even years afterwards. Or even if I see them at a funny angle.'

'Oh. That is a bit weird. But useful at parties,' he added solemnly.

She laughed. 'Very useful at parties but it has its downsides and this is one of them.'

'What is?'

'Recognising that the man my mum has started to go out with, and obviously is already quite into, is the man who nearly got her and me killed years ago.'

Jago sighed now. 'That is awkward. What were the circumstances?'

'He was driving a car towards us on the wrong side of the road, far too fast. If Mum hadn't reacted so quickly he'd have crashed into us and we'd both have been killed.'

Jago didn't speak for quite some time. 'Are you sure?'

91

Helena bit her lip. 'I've had the whole of lunch to think and rethink and I can't make the answer different. If I could I would. Yes, I am sure.'

'And he was driving too fast?'

'For a motorway, no, but for the country lane we were on, definitely. If Mum hadn't pulled out of his way into the ditch, really quickly, we'd have met head on. He didn't stop although he'd obviously seen us. He just drove on.'

'That's outrageous.'

Helena drank some more tea. 'We don't know why he was driving so fast. He may have had a sick child on the back seat, or a dying dog.'

'It's possible, I suppose. A bit unlikely.'

'I agree, it's not really likely. I'm just trying to find excuses for him.'

'Oh God, Helena! I don't know what to say.'

'And nor do I! Not to my mum, anyway. If I say anything it's going to look as if I don't want Mum to have a boyfriend, or any fun or anything nice like that.'

'But she knows about your — superpower?'

'Of course, but I still can't call her or turn up and tell her Leo was the man driving the car that time. Or maybe I should?' She paused. 'Tell me honestly, how did you feel about Leo before I told you all this?'

Jago didn't rush to answer. 'Like I said, I don't think we'd ever be soulmates.' He paused again, for an agonisingly long time. 'I'm not sure I entirely trust him.'

'Weirdly that makes me feel a bit better,' said Helena. 'I couldn't trust him the moment I saw him but I had to give him the benefit of the doubt. Just in case. I mean — Mum's not likely to find many men she likes at this time in her life, is she? I know she's not old or anything, but the chances of me finding someone are slim, and not all the men I meet are married. It must be much harder at her age.'

'Could you talk to your brother about this?'

Helena shook her head. 'I wish I could. But Martin's never really approved of my super-power, as you called it. He can't deny I have it, but I think he's a bit jealous. Besides, he has an agenda.'

'Which is?'

'He and Cressida want Mum to sell her house and share out the money so they can buy a fancypants house with a granny annexe that Mum could live in and so look after Issi, and the massive garden, for nothing.' It all came out in one anxious breath.

Jago frowned. 'Oh. I don't think your mother would like that, would she? Unless she absolutely loves gardening.'

'She quite likes it but wouldn't want to do it day in, day out.'

'So what has this to do with Leo?'

It was a reasonable question. 'He's something to do with property and, as you heard, he valued Mum's house. She must have asked him to. She will have got him round because Martin and Cress guilt-tripped her into it.' She sighed. 'Maybe I'm paranoid, but I got the impression they knew him already.'

Jago considered this. 'Are you sure you won't have a glass of wine? I definitely want one and I

93

don't want to drink on my own.'

'In which case I will.' She smiled. 'I really appreciate having you to talk to about all this. I'd have talked to Amy but she hasn't met Leo and she would probably just see him as a good-looking older man, perfect for my mum. And if I said anything against him she'd just think I was jealous, or that I wanted to be the only one with a presentable boyfriend.'

He grinned. 'Glad to know you think I'm presentable.'

'Obviously I'm bigging you up a bit for friendship's sake,' said Helena, smiling back at him. 'Were you going to get wine?'

'I was and I am.' A few minutes later he handed her a large glass of red. 'I hope you like it.'

'What we have to wonder is would Leo like this wine? He's obviously a bit of an expert,' said Helena.

'I don't actually care if he likes it or not. But I want you to have something you like. Then we have to find a solution to your problem.'

'Oh, that's delicious!' said Helena, having taken a sip. She was finding Jago very easy to talk to and the wine would make him even more so. 'I'm not sure we can find a solution. It happened such a long time ago.'

'I have some contacts that might make it possible. Can you give me the details of the road, the day, and the time of your near miss?'

'Yes I can.'

'Well, that is amazing! Do your superpowers mean you remember dates as well?'

'Not the super-recogniser one, no, but the

other one.' She paused for effect, enjoying the fascination in his expression.

'You have two?'

'I kept a diary so we know the date and we can work out the road because of where we were going.' She felt very smug. Being a super-recogniser was interesting and rare but it was a God-given talent. Keeping a diary meant effort.

'So why did you keep a diary? Or is it something all girls do?'

'I did it because the recognising thing made me different at school and I was bullied a bit. It's why I don't tell everyone — anyone really — unless I have to. The diary was my friend. I had Amy, of course, but I put more in my diary than I told her.'

He nodded. 'After all, you couldn't expect Amy to care what the date was when you went — '

' — to visit my bro at university,' she finished.

He got up and fetched the bottle of wine. When he had topped up their glasses he said, 'Why don't you give me all the info and let me see what I can find out?'

It took Helena a few moments to grasp what he was offering but much longer to think what to reply. 'The thing is, Jago, I'm not used to other people dealing with my problems.'

'I wouldn't be dealing with it, I'd just be getting information for you.'

'But you're so busy — '

'And so are you. As I said, I have contacts — people I met under rather strange circum-stances — that could make things quicker for me.'

95

'That sounds incredibly shady!'

'Well, it's a bit shady but not incredibly. And not morally wrong, I promise.'

Although she was tempted, Helena still wasn't sure. 'The thing is, I've told you more than I've told anyone else — '

'Because I was the first friend on hand. I know you don't know me that well but I promise you can trust me. And I'd like to get this sorted out. I think your mum is wonderful and I'd love to help her. Wouldn't it be great if Leo was carrying a heart to a transplant patient which was why he had to drive so fast?'

She couldn't help smiling. 'I don't think they send vital body parts across the country in Beemers.'

He returned her smile. 'OK, that's a long shot but there could be a good reason — a benign reason — for his speeding and I'd really like to find it out for you.'

Helena rubbed her eyes to help her think and then remembered she'd put make-up on. 'Damn,' she muttered. 'Now I look like a clown.'

'The joy of being with a friend is that you don't have to care what you look like,' said Jago.

Helena wasn't sure how to take this. He was right, of course, but somehow it did matter what she looked like. But it was too late now. 'OK, Jago,' she said, 'I'll take you up on your kind offer. And I'm really, really grateful.'

She liked Jago a lot and couldn't help feeling it was almost a shame he was just a friend.

11

Gilly was having trouble sleeping. She would fall asleep but then, about half an hour later, wake up and, having lost all her sleepiness, lie there for hours. What she was most annoyed about was that she would spend the time thinking about Leo. She told herself she was far too old to lose sleep over a man, particularly one who was very attentive. He emailed or texted almost every day.

It would have been easier if she could have talked about it to someone, but somehow she couldn't. Her oldest friend was no longer local and it all felt so silly and girlish she didn't feel she could talk about it on the phone. She also couldn't forget that Helena had been a bit funny about him at lunch. She didn't know why but her daughter wasn't happy about her mother falling in love. Admittedly it was all quite fast but that was how these things happened! Surely Helena knew that?

When she could drag her mind away from how wonderful Leo was she forced herself to think about whether she should seriously consider downsizing, giving up her B & B and releasing some capital for her children. Of course it was the sensible thing to do. It was now that Martin and Helena needed money, not in thirty years' time when she was dead. And if Fairacres was worth what Leo said it was, she could buy a nice

97

little cottage and Helena would have enough to buy a studio, and Martin and Cressida could buy something a bit bigger.

What she was certain of was that she was too young to live in a granny annexe. She didn't even like the expression! While she loved being a grandmother and looked forward to being one again (although Martin and Cressida were convinced one child was enough), she hated all the names given by society to grandmothers. She found them patronising.

And could she give up her B & B just now? It was extremely hard work, especially when you went to the pains she went to, to make everything as perfect as it could be. But give it up? Probably not.

She sighed and turned her pillow over again and put some more lavender oil on it. Then she turned on the radio and turned it off again. She needed to work out what was happening with her daughter.

But at least Helena seemed perky in herself, which was lovely. Although when Helena had rung to say thank you for lunch and Gilly had asked about Jago, Helena hadn't given anything away. She'd just said, 'Oh he's fine! Still going on about your cooking!'

The answer Gilly had been looking for was 'I think I'm in love!' and then maybe she could have admitted that perhaps she was too.

She finally drifted off trying to work out if Jago was the one for Helena. The fact that her 'I'm staying single' daughter was even going out with someone was surely a bonus. She was still arguing with herself about why she felt Helena needed a man when sleep claimed her.

* * *

A few mornings later she was waiting for William, her accountant, to collect his old ladies. They'd been to their party and come back, later than planned, the previous evening, and, Gilly hoped, had a good night's sleep. Gilly picked up the tray of tea and coffee she was serving them while they waited and took it through to the conservatory. William's aunts had been hugely appreciative guests and she had loved having them.

'Darling!' said the lead aunt, whose name was Daphne and who set the tone for the party. 'You are so kind! We are such demanding old biddies with our various breakfast requirements and yet you never hesitated to cater to our whims, however unreasonable! Even when Doris and the others had to leave so early.'

It hadn't seemed that early to Gilly. 'If only all my guests were like you!' she said, setting down the tray. 'Looking after you has been such fun.'

'It's your attention to detail that makes this place so special,' Daphne went on. 'Fresh flowers in the rooms — '

'Only a couple of sprigs from the garden,' said Gilly, dismissing the praise.

'I really like having fresh milk to put in my tea in the room,' said Mary, Daphne's sister. 'And a good selection of herb teas, and more than just a couple of teabags, too.'

99

'As for the shortbread,' said Miriam, who may have been a sister-in-law — Gilly had lost track. 'Delicious!'

'I loved the lavender oil by the bed,' said Mary. 'Not sure if it made any difference to how I slept but it smelt lovely.'

'You were supposed to sprinkle it on your pillow,' said Miriam. 'I loved it!'

'And the breakfast,' said Daphne. 'I'm very fussy and I had nothing to complain about. Hot plates — '

'So important,' her sister Mary agreed.

'Proper butter in a dish and not those little packets I find so difficult to open.' Miriam gestured with her hands. Her fingers sported many rings but Gilly noticed they were showing signs of arthritis.

'And home-made marmalade!' said Daphne.

'I have to confess I don't make it myself,' said Gilly, embarrassed by this fulsome praise. 'I buy it from the WI market.'

'Well, someone made it at home,' said Daphne, no less enthusiastic. 'And again, not in those horrid sachets.'

'Ah! Here's William,' said Mary as he came in through the open front door. 'William? We've had such a lovely stay with Gilly. Thank you so much for recommending such a wonderful B & B.'

'She's looked after us brilliantly!' said Daphne. 'We had hot chocolate when we got back after the party — '

'With a little something in it!' added Mary.

'I'm not sure you should tell me all this,' said William. 'I'm Gilly's accountant, remember. Can these things be cost-effective?' He gave Gilly a smile that made her wish he smiled more often. He was really quite good-looking, she noticed, now she had a chance to look at him. Thick hair in a man in his fifties was rare.

'It might get me repeat custom,' she said, glancing round at the group. 'And then it would be like advertising, which is a legitimate business expense.'

William laughed. 'In which case — '

'Don't you dare cramp her style,' said Miriam with emphasis. 'It's a marvellous place to stay and I think we should all come again. What do you think, girls?'

'Marvellous idea!' said Daphne. 'We could go on trips out in the area.'

Gilly had thought about doing this for a while so she nodded. 'I could arrange a minibus,' she said. 'And send someone with you — or even go myself.'

'Now my client is in the tour business,' said William, raising his eyebrows in mock horror. 'I think I'd better relieve you of my female relations before you end up running a home for wayward pensioners. If I can persuade them to leave, that is.'

There was a lot of laughter, friendly insults and goodwill involved in loading Gilly's guests into the car while she held sticks and handbags and cheered from the sidelines. But at last they were in, buckled up and away. Gilly waved them off and went back inside.

'Hello, you,' said Leo, who was waiting in the hall. He had come in the back entrance, avoiding the farewells at the front. He kissed Gilly's cheek.

Gilly found herself beaming. She was delighted to see him and for some reason pleased he hadn't clashed with William's old ladies. 'Come and let me make you a cup of coffee. You can drink it while I clear up breakfast.'

'While you're obviously brilliant with dotty old women, I don't think you should have to run around after them like you do.'

Gilly paused. While William's female relations were eccentric she wouldn't have described them as dotty. They were very sharp and on the ball and even if they weren't, she'd have enjoyed caring for them.

'I like it. I even liked getting up at six so I could send them home with packets of home-made shortbread. There's some left,' she added.

She insisted on getting the dishwasher filled before she'd go with Leo to the conservatory to drink the coffee she had made. She didn't really want more coffee but she did want to spend time with Leo.

'I think it's time you retired,' he said as she handed him coffee and a plate of biscuits.

'Why?' said Gilly, smiling at his joke. 'What would I do with myself if I didn't have my guests? I'd only get up to mischief.'

'You could get up to mischief with me,' he said. 'I want to take you to Vienna.'

'Vienna!' said Gilly.

'I think Paris and Venice are rather overdone, don't you? I don't want to take you to a romantic cliché.'

Gilly was taken aback. The thought of being

102

taken to Bognor Regis by Leo would have seemed romantic. 'It sounds wonderful.'

It did. Already she was imagining a gorgeous little boutique hotel, going to amazing world-class restaurants, chauffeured limousines. The number of bedrooms involved was for contemplation in private. It wasn't that she hadn't thought about sleeping with Leo, but her imagination had never got her from being fully clothed to being naked in his arms. She just didn't see how it could happen, at her age.

'But we can't go if you're still running a B & B.'

'I do go on holiday . . . ' she protested.

'But presumably it takes planning?'

'Of course, but it must be the same for you, surely?'

Leo nodded. 'Some, of course, but I can work from anywhere. It's not the same as being a bed and breakfast landlady.'

Gilly had a sudden vision of herself standing at the door of a boarding house in some desolate seaside town, her arms folded, her expression grim. Her excitement about his invitation dimmed a little. 'Well, no.'

He smiled and put his hand on her knee. She felt it all over her body.

'Did you get Martin's email?' he asked.

'What? How did you know he'd sent me an email?'

'He copied me in. He realised you didn't really like the house they showed you before so he's found somewhere else. It's got a proper granny annexe.'

103

Gilly swallowed. 'I'm not sure I'm ready to live anywhere with the word 'granny' in it. I'm still a working woman.'

His laugh was very sexy. 'That makes you sound like you're on the streets, if I may say such a thing.' Then he rubbed her knee. 'Now I've offended you. I'm sorry. Let's look at this house, shall we?'

As Gilly went to find her laptop she realised Leo and Martin must have met before they all had lunch together, and wondered where that was, and why they hadn't mentioned it. Was it something to do with Martin and Cressida wanting to move? But then she decided it wasn't important.

'OK,' she said, having joined Leo at the partially cleared breakfast table. 'Let's have a look at this house.'

It was over-modernised, Gilly felt, but it would suit Martin and Cressida. 'So I am supposed to sell my house so Martin and Cressida can buy this?' She tried very hard to keep her voice neutral.

'The joy of this one is, you could build in the garden,' said Leo, 'and so add to the value of the property. It could house staff or be rented . . . ' He paused.

'When I die?' said Gilly, suddenly feeling very old. Looking at the price of the property Martin had been so keen to show her meant he was expecting a good chunk of money from the sale of Fairacres.

'Maybe you wouldn't want to move in there? Maybe you could just have it as a fallback position.'

'Sorry? I'm not quite following.' Leo was implying she wouldn't need to live there, so where did he think she could live instead? In his house? However she might feel about him, it was far too soon for her to think about cohabiting.

'We can talk about it later,' he said easily. 'Now you get your diary up on your laptop and we can find a weekend when we can go to Vienna — a long weekend. It's a fascinating city.'

At that moment Gilly regretted her failure to fully master using the diary function on her laptop and relying on an old-fashioned desk diary for her B & B bookings. She realised it made her look ancient, as if she couldn't grasp new technology. She could, but she was a bit lazy about it, Helena always said.

Leo didn't comment when she carne back with her diary. Ulysses followed her into the room and jumped on the sofa between them. 'So,' she said, 'when were you thinking of?'

'June's a lovely month,' he said, pushing the cat on to the floor.

'Yes,' said Gilly, knowing it was also a busy one for her. She flicked through to June. There was a booking for every single weekend. 'July?' she suggested, hoping there'd be a vacant weekend in it.

'I can't understand why you're booked up so early,' said Leo, sounding a bit cross, possibly because the cat had jumped up again and was heading for his lap. 'It's only April!'

'These clients have been coming for years,' explained Gilly, setting Ulysses gently on to the floor. 'They like to book well ahead to make sure of getting their favourite rooms.'

'Well, could you ask them to rebook so they all come on the same weekend and you have a weekend free?'

'Not really,' said Gilly. 'They've been coming on those weekends for years and there wouldn't be room for them all at the same time.' She realised she was repeating herself. 'The weeks are freer. Why don't we go midweek?'

'I can't go midweek. I work.'

'September is a lovely month,' said Gilly, dismissing the thought that she worked too at the same time as she fielded her cat who seemed determined to get on Leo's lap. 'Let me pencil in some dates for us to go away then.' She quickly did so.

'I'm sorry to be so impatient,' Leo said. 'I just want to take you away. If you sold this house and retired, you'd be freer.' He got up from his chair and swiped at the cat hairs that had landed on him in spite of Gilly's efforts to protect him.

Gilly laughed and realised it had sounded rather brittle. 'That would be a rather drastic way of solving the problem,' she said. 'And it would take a lot longer than until September for it to be accomplished.'

'I could expedite it. I'd have a buyer for this house in a flash. In fact, I've got someone — ' He stopped abruptly, possibly noticing Gilly's reaction.

'No need,' she said crisply. 'I don't want to move.'

'Don't be too hasty to reject the idea. Think of the advantages. You'd be freeing up capital for

106

your children, just when they need it most.'

'I promise I'll think about it,' she went on. 'Would you like more coffee?' She got up, desperate to stop this horrible conversation. 'I'll make some.'

She was on her way back to the conservatory to check that Leo did actually want more coffee when the doorbell jangled. The old-fashioned bell was one of the things her clients particularly enjoyed and she opened the door with a smile. It was William.

'I'm so sorry to trouble you, but Aunt Miriam thinks she left her hearing-aid batteries in the bedside drawer . . .'

'Oh, easily done, I'm sure. I'll pop up and look.'

'I could go,' said William.

'It's no trouble — I know which room Miriam was in. I thought I'd checked all the rooms before they left but I may have missed the bedside drawer.'

Gilly found the batteries and came back down the stairs. She paused. Leo had joined William in the hall and just for a second she had the impression that the two men were facing up to each other. Then as she arrived in the hall one of them moved but the tension still seemed to be there.

'I was just saying what a valuable property this is,' said Leo. 'The market in this area is surprisingly buoyant. It's a good time to sell.'

No one spoke for a few seconds — Gilly didn't know what to say. Then William looked up at her and smiled very slightly.

107

'Only if the owner wants to sell,' he said firmly. 'And I don't think Gilly does.'

At first Gilly thought Leo was going to argüe but he didn't. But after William had gone, hearing-aid batteries safely in his pocket, Leo turned to Gilly.

'Does your accountant always call you by your Christian name? You must visit him a lot, which rather implies things aren't really working on a financial level. I can't help thinking you'd be better off getting out of the B & B business and having a bit more spare time.'

'I've got spare time now,' Gilly said, although she hadn't finished clearing the dining room or got the second load into the dishwasher, and then there were the beds to strip.

'Sadly, I haven't. But it's been lovely to see you, Gilly.' He kissed the top of her head. 'But now I must go and have a good look at that house of Martin's. I'll text you a time when I can take you out for lunch.'

'Us boarding-house landladies always have time for lunch,' said Gilly with a laugh, hoping he'd join in.

But he didn't.

12

Helena and Jago were making good progress on repointing the wall of the barn where Helena hoped to put her loom. They were up separate ladders on separate scaffolding towers putting lime mortar between tiny stone bricks. They'd been doing it for a couple of hours.

'It's kind of you to do this when you said you hadn't got time,' said Helena.

'It was, but now I'm stiff and cold and want to stop,' Jago replied. 'Shall we call it a day?'

'I feel I should press on but if you're fed up you could go and make us some tea?'

'OK. I have a few phone calls to catch up on. If you don't mind carrying on on your own?'

'Of course not. Hand me up the radio so I can choose my channel and I'll be fine.'

Helena found something on Radio 4 to listen to — she needed talking not music if she was going to be doing something fairly mindless on her own — and carried on. Eventually she'd done everything she could without moving the scaffolding and climbed down. She was ready to call it a day now too and, having sorted out her equipment, went to find Jago.

'Oh? Are you knocking off?' he said. 'I was just coming in with tea and snacks.'

'I've done all I could reach. It's just your corner now.' She pulled out a chair and plonked

109

herself down at the table. 'How soon can I move my loom in?'

'If you don't mind being in a bit of a building site, whenever. The wall will have to be plastered. You'll see that I took what you said about it looking like a prison to heart.' He paused. 'And the plaster will have to dry, before I can think about decorating. But that will take ages. If you don't mind a bit of work going on around you, we can put it in next week.'

'I don't mind and its partly my fault.' Helena took a piece of cheese on toast. 'This is lovely!'

'You deserve something nice. You've been working hard.'

'Purely for my own ends,' said Helena. She smiled, and then was embarrassed in case he read more than just heartfelt gratitude into the smile. 'It's going to be a wonderful space for a loom. Those huge doors looking out into the courtyard will make it magical in summer.'

She sighed happily. One of the joys of getting to know Jago so well while they pointed his wall together was that he now knew how to make her perfect cup of tea. 'Although of course when you have a buyer for it I'll have to find yet another home for my loom.'

He smiled. 'I'm sure I can help you sort something out.'

'Property developer that you are — you've always got some barn or other to do up.' She patted his hand to make sure he knew she wasn't having a go at him. He *was* a property developer but definitely one of the good guys.

He put his hand on top of hers. 'Shall we call

the cheese on toast a starter? Shall I cook you supper? Nothing fancy. Only with what I happen to have in the fridge and the cupboard, of course.'

'I'll go and get what I've got in my fridge. There's some chorizo and some lovely little tomatoes.'

'Excellent!'

On the way back to her studio Helena found herself thinking about her mother and Leo. He had escorted her to lovely places and her mother seemed to really like him. But would he make her happy in the long term? She'd feel a lot less worried when she'd found out why he'd been driving so fast that day, when he'd nearly killed her and her mother.

She wasn't going to ask Jago what he'd managed to discover though, not tonight. Tonight she was just going to have a nice meal and a couple of glasses of wine with a man who threatened to become more than just a good friend in her heart. Which was fine, as long as no one ever found out about the heart bit.

★ ★ ★

Gilly was a bit taken aback by how quickly William's aunts got their act together to arrange their minicoach tour. She had hardly had time to change the sheets on their beds before Daphne was on the phone looking for dates.

'We can come next weekend, if you could have us,' Daphne said. 'And have supper with you, too.'

Gilly looked at the diary and decided she could do that if she moved the one booking she had to her bed-and-breakfast friend.

'Um — I wouldn't be able to cook dinner if I was showing you the sights. Maybe — '

'Yes, you would!' said Daphne, not to be gainsaid. 'Just do a casserole and put it in the range cooker. You could serve it with rice. I find that packet rice you put in the microwave very easy.'

Gilly couldn't help smiling. Daphne was obviously one of those people who was used to getting their own way. 'Well, it couldn't be an extensive tour of the Cotswolds . . . '

'We wouldn't want that. We're too old for too much culture. So we can come? Oh,' Daphne added, 'and we think William should drive. And we need a minibus so we have plenty of room. Now that's sorted, I must go. See you soon!'

The moment Daphne had said goodbye Gilly rang William.

'William!' she said as soon as she was through. 'I think Daphne is being a bit unreasonable!'

'Only a bit? She must be on some new medication.'

Gilly laughed. 'Seriously! She wants you to drive a minibus round the country for her and the rest of the gang.' She paused, distracted. 'Is there a collective noun for aunts, do you think?'

'I think in this case it would be a Daphne of aunts,' said William. 'But don't worry, she did warn me and I'm perfectly happy to do it.'

'I'd drive them myself only I'm not entirely sure I'd be up to it.'

'Also, I don't think you could be a proper tour guide if you were wrestling a large vehicle down small lanes, while wrangling that crew of reprobates. I certainly couldn't do both.'

'That is really sweet of you. Your Daphne of aunts don't know how lucky they are having a nephew like you.'

'I think they do,' said William. 'And to be fair, only two of them are my actual aunts.'

'Well, they want dinner afterwards so I do hope you'll join us. In fact, I'll channel my inner Daphne and insist that you do.'

'But will you want to cook dinner after being with them all day? Wouldn't you rather I booked us all in at the George?'

'Oh no. Daphne told me that I could do a casserole and that microwave rice is very easy, so not a problem at all.'

William laughed. 'In which case, I'd be delighted to accept. You will charge them a handsome amount, won't you?'

Gilly didn't answer. She hadn't had a chance to work out how much to charge but her fondness for the ladies would have made her lenient.

Possibly knowing her better than she realised he went on, 'I insist that you do! And you can't hide anything from me, you know.'

Gilly laughed. 'Oh, OK! I know my dinners are the 'added extra' that boosts my profit.'

'My work has not been in vain. See you on Saturday.'

13

The following Saturday the Daphne of aunts arrived a quarter of an hour before they were expected. They had booked a driver to collect them all from their various houses and, in spite of a traffic hold-up on the M4, had got to Fairacres in far less than the time they had allowed. Fortunately, Gilly was aware of Daphne's passion for punctuality (which in her case meant being early).

'How lovely to see you all!' she said. 'Do invite your driver in for a cup of coffee — '

'Euphemism for a pee,' said Daphne.

'But also for coffee,' Gilly persisted. 'I expect he needs some after that long journey.'

'Euphemism for he needs caffeine after driving a rabble of batty old ladies,' said Daphne.

Gilly laughed. Daphne could have been a mind reader. 'That too. I'll go and get him. You come in anyway. I'm all ready. We just have to wait for William. He's picking up the minibus.'

★ ★ ★

When everyone was installed in the minibus, sticks and walking aids to hand, Gilly turned round from her seat in the front next to William. 'I feel like a proper tour guide. If I start holding up a rolled-up umbrella, talk me down gently.'

'You carry on, darling,' said Daphne. 'We are

as eager to follow you as a playground full of children after an ice-cream van.'

'That's a rather energetic analogy,' said Mary, more thoughtfully. 'But I like it.'

'If everyone's strapped in,' said William, 'we can go.'

Their first visit was to a little church which was not only historic but quite near a garden centre. Everyone loved a garden centre, especially one that had a huge outlet section.

Gilly had chosen the church for its history — it was a plague church, built a little way away from the village, but also because it wasn't huge — it wouldn't tire the old ladies too much.

'Don't come in with us,' said Daphne firmly. 'If you do we'll feel obliged to look at everything and contribute generously to the upkeep of the building. You stay here and keep William company.'

'I was looking forward to coming in,' objected William. 'I like old churches.'

'So do I,' said Gilly. 'I picked this one particularly because it has high ratings on TripAdvisor.'

'TripAdvisor!' said Daphne, turning away from the minibus. 'Pah!'

'I do feel like that about TripAdvisor myself, sometimes,' Gilly confided when she and William had got everyone safely into the church. 'Shall we defy Daphne and go in?'

'We could, but on second thoughts it might also be nice to go back to the minibus and sit quietly.' He took her arm and they set off back in blissful silence.

Gilly and William sat in the minibus and said

115

nothing until the ladies returned. It was indeed peaceful. As she and William assisted the aunts back into the minibus the thought flicked through her mind that being with Leo was always exciting. He liked to talk and talked well. Perhaps that was why she found him so attractive. Being with William was quite a different experience. She found herself enjoying the contrast.

As she predicted (only to herself) the ladies loved the garden centre and came back to the minibus laden with carrier bags.

'We've all bought these super-comfy shoes,' declared Daphne. 'Mine are bright pink.'

'It's one of the joys of growing old,' said Mary, having displayed her blue pair, 'that you don't care what you look like.' She paused. 'I don't mean that exactly, but if it's a choice between comfort and glamour I choose comfort every time.'

Gilly thought about this. Before she'd met Leo she'd have put herself in the comfort camp without hesitation. But would she let him see her in shoes like that? She doubted it. He was a man who appreciated elegant footwear — something resembling a gym shoe in dayglo colours would not meet his approval. Gilly appreciated lovely shoes too, but only if they were comfortable and, sadly, either she'd been unlucky or it wasn't possible to have elegance and comfort at the same time.

'Obviously you're far too young to have to make those choices,' said Daphne, mind-reading again. 'But I don't think anyone can look appealing if they're in uncomfortable shoes.'

116

'But can they look appealing if they're wearing shoes like miniature bumper cars?' said Gilly, without really thinking.

William laughed. 'Of course!'

'So what did you buy?' asked Miriam, possibly sensing that Gilly needed a change of subject. 'From the garden centre?'

'Oh! Plants!' said Gilly. 'A silver thyme, a lemon thyme and another plain culinary one.'

'You can never have enough thyme,' said William.

Gilly made a face at him. 'I get through a lot of it and they all do taste different. And talking of time, we should move on. Our lunchtime appointment is in . . . ' She looked at her watch. 'Fifteen minutes and it's about twenty-five minutes away.'

'Drive, William!' said Daphne. 'Drive like the wind!'

William exhaled and shook his head. 'Let's go.'

Lunch was very jolly. Gilly and William were not permitted to pay for theirs in spite of their protests. 'It's as if we're children and you're taking us out for a treat,' said Gilly.

'And we are!' Miriam said. 'So you must let us buy you lemonade and ice cream.'

'In my day we sat in the car outside pubs for hours, sharing packets of crisps,' said Mary. 'It wouldn't be allowed nowadays.'

'A bottle of warm Coke if we were lucky,' said Daphne. 'I hated Coke. I suppose because I only ever had it warm.'

'This sparkling water is lovely and cold,' said Gilly.

117

Daphne laughed. 'You can have wine later. Now let's have a look at the menu.'

★ ★ ★

Gilly had planned a short walk to a monument for after lunch but when she turned round to declare they had arrived she saw that everyone was asleep, mouths open, faintly snoring.

'Oh,' she said to William. 'We might as well have a nap too, then, I suppose.'

'Are you feeling drowsy? If not we could go and see the monument? Have a bit of a walk?'

'Actually some fresh air would be good.'

He got out of the minibus quickly and was there to take her arm as she got out. She was confused. Had he just got into the habit of helping people, given he'd been doing it all morning? Or was he quite old-fashioned?

He kept hold of her arm as the path was muddy. 'I'm quite glad our party didn't get out here now,' she said. 'They might have slipped and hurt themselves.'

'And they would have brought a lot of mud into the bus, too,' said William. 'So now I don't have to clean up after them. Come on.'

He continued to hold her arm as they walked and Gilly found it surprisingly pleasant. He let her go when he reached the viewpoint.

'Wow, look at that,' said Gilly. 'This view is why I thought the ladies would like the monument.'

'It is spectacular,' William agreed. 'Fantastic to glide over.'

118

'I'm not sure I'd ever be brave enough to go gliding. I'm not great at small planes.'

'I took Daphne up once. She loved it, although she didn't expect to. It was a few years ago though, when she was more mobile.' He chuckled. 'Getting her into the glider was interesting but worth it.'

'She's jolly brave,' said Gilly, 'a proper feisty woman.'

'Definitely on the eccentric spectrum but that's a good thing. She, Mary and Miriam have a lot of fun.'

'Sometimes I wonder if I have enough fun,' said Gilly, thinking about what Leo had been saying a few days earlier. 'Maybe I should sell up.'

'And spend your children's inheritance on foreign travel and cruises? I can't quite see you doing that,' said William, looking down at her.

'But maybe I ought to! I don't mean I ought to spend the money on travel and things — I like travel but I don't have a huge desire to go round the world. I mean maybe I should release the money from my house and give it to them now. Am I being selfish hanging on to it, do you think?'

'To be honest, speaking as your accountant who has a bit of liberty in these matters, I think your children are being a bit selfish suggesting you should sell up when you're so young.'

'I'm not young — '

'Very young to retire, unless you hate what you do in which case I think everyone should retire at thirty-five.'

She laughed. 'And then do nothing? Or do something they love?'

'Do something they love, definitely.'

'Do you love being an accountant?' she asked.

'I do find a lot of satisfaction in it, yes. I like working with people.'

'But aren't you mostly working with figures?'

'Yes, but the figures are attached to people. I get to know people's lives from how they spend or save, take risks or keep their money safe at all costs. It's fascinating.' He paused for a minute, looking at the land. 'I don't think you'd do so well at your B & B if you didn't love it.'

She nodded. 'Like you, it's the people I love. They all bring their stories; I see snippets of their lives and I enjoy making them happy. It's why I like doing evening meals for them. It's a service they need so I offer it. Value added.'

'So don't sell.'

'But my children need the money!'

'I never thought I'd say this but there's a difference between *need* and *want*. Your children may want your money but they don't need it.'

Gilly laughed reluctantly. 'You're right in Martin's case. He doesn't need to live in a mansion with a granny annexe — they've got a very nice house already.'

'Which you helped them pay for,' he said.

'I can't hide anything from my accountant!' said Gilly, laughing properly now. 'But Helena does need it.'

'Does she? Wouldn't she rather sort out her own problems?'

'Probably, but I'm not sure she can.' As a mother she'd never got over the 'wanting to make everything all right for her children' phase,

120

even when they were adults. 'What about equity release?'

He shook his head. 'If you really want to do something, you should come in and we'll look at all the options but really I think you should leave everything as it is for now. It's too big a decision to make in a hurry.' He paused. 'Or because someone else suggested you should.'

★ ★ ★

After they'd got back from their tour, tired but happy, William stayed for dinner, dealt with the wine and was generally useful. Gilly reflected that her ex-husband, Sebastian, had never been useful like that. He always claimed he didn't know where anything went and it was true. Gilly felt he could have taken the trouble to find out where things went. But it was a policy with him: he prided himself on not helping around the house as he was the one who put food on the table, as if that exonerated him from doing anything else. Sebastian had never changed a nappy in his life. Not part of his job description.

Now here was William filling the dishwasher and finding where the glasses were by looking and asking.

'You are being amazing,' said Gilly after he'd managed to locate some very pretty pudding plates she didn't use very often but thought the ladies would appreciate. 'You could have just played host in the dining room.'

'It's a pleasure to hide out in here doing things. If I'd stayed in the dining room my aunts

121

would have started dropping heavy hints in stage whispers about my asking you out.'

'Goodness me!' said Gilly, hugely taken aback.

'Matchmaking is what aunts like to do best. They've been on at me for years — well since about six months after Annabel died at any rate,' he went on cheerfully. 'But don't worry, they haven't managed to make me do anything I didn't want to yet.'

'Good,' said Gilly, not sure how to take this. It was the first time he'd mentioned his wife since she'd known him although she did know she had died tragically young.

'They've already told me what a good cook you are, how pretty you are and how you'd make me a wonderful wife.'

'Oh, William, I am sorry!'

'Don't be. It's all true and anyway, I told you I always make my own decisions.'

Gilly didn't know what to say so she smiled and put a tray full of lemon syllabub into his hands.

★　★　★

It was Sunday morning and Helena was about to round up a couple of friends to help her and Jago move her loom into the newly pointed barn when he looked through the open door of her studio.

'Have you got a minute?' he asked.

His expression was serious, which was unusual for him. 'I hope you're not going to tell me you can't help me move my loom,' said Helena, frantically thinking who she could call on instead.

'No.'

'So why are you looking like you've got bad news?' Then she remembered. 'You've got bad news.'

'I'm afraid so.'

'Should I make coffee?'

'Probably. Or maybe something stronger like a turmeric latte.'

She forced a smile. 'Fresh out of latte. I'll put the kettle on.'

* * *

'So?' asked Helena. They both had drinks and were settled in her little sitting room. 'Tell me all. Is he an axe murderer?'

He laughed. 'If he is, no one's caught him at it, but Leo Simmons is not a nice person.'

'Where was he off to the day he nearly killed me and Mum?'

'I didn't manage to find out but I did discover he appeared in court a few days later facing a charge of embezzlement.'

'And did he get off?' asked Helena.

'He got seven years but of course didn't serve anything like that. He's not someone you'd want your mother involved with though.' Jago sipped his coffee. 'Do you want all the stuff I printed out? Or would you rather not know the details? There's a charge of dangerous driving in the mix.'

'Oh God! Although I suppose that shouldn't come as a surprise.' Helena bit her lip. 'Just tell

123

me what you think I need to know. I may have to give Mum all the stuff though. This is horrible, Jago! It's going to break her heart!'

'Better now than later, I suppose, when it may be *too* late.' He went on to tell her of shady property deals, offshore accounts, even dodgy funeral plans. 'So when will you tell her?'

Helena sighed and didn't answer for a little while. 'Part of me wants to run over to Fairacres now but the other half wants her to stay being happy for as long as possible.'

'Why don't we get your loom moved now and then you can decide? If she's upset you won't want to leave her and this old girl' — he patted the loom fondly as if it were a horse — 'needs to go to its new home.'

'Just the two of us?' asked Helena.

'I think we can manage.'

Although it took longer than Helena had hoped, they did get the loom moved. But by the time she'd bought fish and chips for them both it was too late to go and see her mother.

Helena had appreciated the distraction. The loom had to be partly dismantled to move it and while she was taking photos of how various intimate bits of it looked before it was taken apart, she wasn't thinking about the shattering information she felt obliged to tell Gilly.

She had wondered briefly if she actually needed to tell her but soon realised she couldn't risk a man she saw as practically a murderer becoming permanently attached to her mother. And Jago had been quite sure he felt her mother should be warned.

She decided to invite herself for lunch. It would give them plenty of time to talk. She didn't want to drop a bombshell and run, much as she might have liked to.

14

Gilly was a bit surprised when Helena rang to say she wanted to come for soup and a sandwich. Helena had told her she'd moved the loom and Gilly would have thought she'd want to get it set up so she could press on with some work. But as Gilly had a butternut squash to hand she set about making soup. Pre-roasted with chilli oil and made creamy with coconut milk, it was Helena's favourite.

As she hacked at the squash and made cheese scones to accompany the soup, Gilly wondered what was on her daughter's mind. She couldn't help remembering that she'd been a bit twitchy at the Sunday lunch when she'd brought Jago to meet her. Since then she'd seemed fine, although Gilly realised she hadn't seen much of her. They'd been in regular contact and with Helena helping to get the barn ready for her loom and trying to get as much done for her wool fair, all had seemed normal.

Maybe the poor girl just wanted some of her mum's soup, Gilly concluded, giving it a stir and tasting it. Not everything everyone did had an ulterior motive.

'Hi, Mummy!' said Helena quietly as she let herself in through the back door and Gilly's heart sank. Helena hadn't called her 'Mummy' since she was in primary school: there was definitely something wrong.

'What's up?' said Gilly. She watched as her daughter tried to pretend there wasn't anything but she'd always been an awful liar.

'Let's have lunch first,' said Helena, taking a cheese scone from the cooling rack and breaking off a bit. 'I'm starving!'

'OK,' said Gilly, 'but promise me it's nothing health-related, or something really ghastly.'

'Nothing health-related,' Helena said quickly. 'Let's have lunch.'

Gilly found bowls, plates and knives and put them on the table. The butter was already there. 'Do you want a sandwich or will the scones do?'

'They're my favourite! Of course they'll do.'

Gilly relaxed a bit. But as Helena sipped the soup Gilly noticed she was only nibbling her scone and was spending quite a lot of time fiddling with her knife, slicing off slivers of butter; she wasn't actually eating much.

'What's wrong, darling?' Gilly said. 'I wish you'd tell me. Have you broken up with Jago?'

Helena put down her spoon. 'Jago and I are just friends, Mum.'

'So what is it?' Seeing the anguish on her daughter's face was killing her.

'Mum, it's about Leo.'

'Leo?' This was the last thing Gilly would have thought of. 'What about him?'

'It's not easy to say.'

'Oh, please, Helly! Just tell me! If it's not health-related what on earth can it be?' The thought that Leo might turn out to be married with a family did now cross her mind. 'Is he married?'

127

'OK, Mum. Do you remember that time we were going to visit Martin at uni and there was a car on the wrong side of the road, coming at us full pelt, and you had to swerve into the ditch to stop us getting killed?'

Gilly thought, then nodded. 'Yes. It was terrifying. And afterwards I never thought I'd get the car out of the ditch.'

'Leo was driving the car.'

'What do you mean? How can you possibly know?' Then Gilly began to realise what had happened. 'You recognised him?'

'As soon as I saw him, when we all had lunch. I got a very good look at him at the time of the accident.'

Gilly had never known Helena to be wrong about things like this. If she said someone was whoever she said it was, it was them. One hundred per cent. 'So why wait until now to tell me?'

'Because I wanted to find out more about it. He may well have been taking a sick child to hospital.'

'We would have seen if there'd been a child in the back of the car.'

'Not if it was lying down! Or it might have been an animal he was taking to the vet?'

Gilly's head was spinning. What a horrible coincidence! A coincidence that it had been Leo driving — one she would never have known about if it wasn't for her daughter's uncanny ability. They'd always joked about her having a superpower but its effect was far from super now. She felt sick. 'But how would anyone be able to find out anything like that! It's not possible!'

Helena nodded. 'You're right. But my friend did find out other things about him, things you ought to know too.'

'Gossip, in other words!' Gilly was cross now and glad to be. It was so much better than being devastated.

'No, not gossip. Facts that can be proved.'

Gilly realised that Helena was as upset as she was but she still wanted to kill the messenger. 'Like what?'

'He did time in prison for embezzlement.'

'Well, that's not murder, is it? And he's served his sentence. Does he have to be treated as a criminal for the rest of his life?' Gilly got up from the table and started flinging things in the dishwasher in a way that she knew meant she'd have to reload it later but not caring. She was shocked and angry and wanted to make a lot of noise.

'Mum! I'm not telling you what you should do with the information, but when I found out I couldn't not tell you.'

'But why were you even looking?'

'You know why.' Helena was very quiet, possibly a bit tearful now, but Gilly didn't care.

'Because of your stupid 'thing',' said Gilly. 'Why can't you find out something nice with it from time to time!'

Helena got up. 'I'm going now. I'm really sorry to have upset you. And if Leo is the love of your life I'll learn to get on with him.'

Helena went to Gilly as if to embrace her but Gilly kept her arms by her side, refusing a hug from her daughter for possibly the first time in her life.

'I'll ring you,' Helena said and walked out of the kitchen, leaving the soup still steaming.

⋆ ⋆ ⋆

Tears were pouring down Helena's face as she drove back to her studio. She felt as awful as she could feel given that nobody had died. Jago came across when he saw her getting out of her car.

'Not go well?' he said, taking in Helena's tear-streaked face and tragic expression.

'As badly as it could have gone, given that we didn't actually come to blows. I was as tactful as I could be but Mum was just devastated. I could have tipped a barrel of water over her and she'd have been less shocked. Honestly, Jago, I think I've made a terrible mistake telling her. I should have just kept it all to myself. She'll never want to speak to me again.'

Jago came forward and took her into his arms, pressing her face into his old Guernsey jumper. It was dusty, a bit smelly and scratched her face. She didn't ever want to move away.

'Look, it seems terrible now but you and your mum love each other. You'll be friends again in no time. It's just the shock of it. When she gets used to the idea of it all she'll think about it and realise you only did it for the best.'

'I know,' Helena told his jumper. 'But I've shattered her dreams, and for what? If she loves him, she's going to stay with him. It's just me she'll hate.'

130

'Come into the house and have a cup of tea,' said Jago.

'You're busy. You haven't time for tea.' Reluctantly Helena let go of Jago's jumper; she'd been unaware of clutching it.

'If I haven't got time to give a friend a cuppa when they're in a state we might as well give up. Come on.'

He put his arm round Helena's shoulders and took her into the house.

'I'm so sorry to cry all over you like that,' said Helena, sitting down at the kitchen table. 'I hope I haven't got snot on your jumper.'

'My jumper would be honoured and besides, it's had far worse. Fish guts being one example.'

'Oh, yuck!' Helena had stopped sniffing now and felt bizarrely better for her cry.

'I know!' he said. 'I had a job on a fishing boat one summer and I kind of liked the uniform so I kept it.'

Helena nodded, not knowing what to say.

'Now,' he went on, pushing a mug of tea towards her. 'Tell me what Gilly said?'

When Helena had finished, he said, 'So you didn't even eat your soup? 'You must be hungry.'

'Not really. I've lost my appetite. The tea is good though. I should go, anyway.'

'I expect you want to finish sorting out your loom.'

'Yes, but I've also got a room to look at, for me to live in, for when I have to move out of my studio. It's in a shared house at the top of town. Not huge and quite expensive for what it is, but OK.'

'I'm probably way out of order here, but why don't you live with me? There's a room at the end of this house that is finished, near the bathroom, and I'd let you have it for nothing. Because you're a mate,' he added, possibly aware she was about to protest.

'But if I say I've moved in with you, everyone will think we're a major item and not 'it's early days yet, who knows how it will turn out'.'

'Just tell them you want to stay close to your loom and not share a house at the top of town?'

Helena nodded. 'That could work.'

He laughed. 'I do love the way you've defined our relationship, by the way.'

'I've got it!' said Helena. 'If I pay rent, it makes perfect sense. Then they can think what they like.' She studied him. 'Are you sure? You see enough of me as it is.'

'I could never see enough of you,' he said and then added, 'Joking!'

Negotiating a rent that was satisfactory to both of them took a little while. Helena wanted to pay Jago what she would have paid for a room anywhere else; Jago insisted that anywhere else would be more comfortable if less convenient. Eventually they reached a compromise that they could both live with.

When they had moved Helena's things over to her new room she said, 'Now I'm going to cook you supper to thank you for taking me in. But it has to be chilli as it's my signature dish. I didn't inherit my mother's cooking skills, I'm afraid, but my chilli is good.'

'You don't have to — ' Jago began.

132

'Yes I do!' said Helena quickly. 'It's what I'd do if I wanted to get on with my new house-mates. No reason why you should miss out just because we're friends.'

133

15

The moment she was on her own, Gilly stopped being furious and became devastated again. She didn't know what to do with herself or what to do with the information Helena had given her. It was like a bomb, only there was no handy bomb-disposal unit she could call. She'd never known Helena to be wrong about anyone when she'd recognised them. But there was always a first time!

She put the kettle on for tea but then didn't fancy any. She cleared up the soup and scones and wanted to cry for being so horrible to Helena. But she didn't feel ready to apologise to her. Ulysses the cat, finding her unexpectedly still, jumped on her lap. She stroked him for a bit until he started kneading her with his claws and the hairs which floated up from his lavish coat made her sneeze.

In the end she went out into the garden and cleared a bed she'd been thinking of redoing for some time although she hadn't decided what she wanted to do with it. Ulysses came with her, trying to imply that gardening had been his idea all the time.

She'd always liked gardening and hers looked wonderful in the spring. Little daffodils bloomed next to miniature irises and grape hyacinths, drifts of yellow and blue like water and sunshine. That had been her plan when she'd planted them but now, although she still found them pretty, their loveliness enhanced her sadness instead of cheering her up. She and Helena hardly ever fell out and it was heartbreaking.

However, she felt better when she came indoors and decided to do what was so often the best thing — nothing. She would carry on as normal and the right decision would occur to her. And as Leo was coming to dinner to plan their trip to Vienna that evening, she could distract herself with cooking.

She was doing slow-roasted pork belly because Leo had once mentioned liking it. And it was going to be perfect. In the kitchen, Gilly had control and right now this was a great comfort to her.

All the time she cooked she thought about Leo and all the time she wondered what difference, if any, Helena's information made to her feelings.

As she scored the pork fat with the Stanley knife she kept for the purpose, she realised she hadn't actually heard the details. It was perfectly possible that Leo had got caught up himself in some scam or other without being aware of it and he had just been brought down by others. But then, unexpectedly, the vision of the car on the wrong side of the road hurtling towards her carne into her head. It had given her nightmares for months. Could she love a man who drove so dangerously? But it had happened years ago! He didn't seem to drive dangerously now. A bit fast, perhaps, but Gilly thought that about pretty much everyone, including Helena.

And so what if he'd done time in prison?

135

People were allowed second chances. Of course they were. And abandoning someone you loved because they'd made a mistake in their youth was not only unkind, it was ridiculous.

As Gilly peeled potatoes she pushed away the thought that Leo hadn't been that young when he'd nearly killed her. She'd been the mother of a university student herself. While they hadn't ever talked about their ages she guessed he was a few years older than she was. But still! She was going to ignore everything that Helena had told her.

Gilly set a small table and chairs in the sitting room. Leo wasn't the sort of man who'd want to eat in the kitchen and the dining room was far too large for dinner a *deux*. But a little table in the window embrasure and the fire lit to add warmth and sparkle to the evening would be perfect. If she had only two guests who wanted dinner she put them there and everyone enjoyed it.

She polished the glasses and opened the wine. Leo had offered to bring wine but she had protested and bought some herself. She felt confident in her choice because she'd met William in Waitrose and he had helped her find one that had been praised in the *Sunday Times*.

She was very happy with her meal by the time it was ready. A small clafoutis of vegetables in individual ramekins to start — the belly of pork was a substantial dish. Then the pork with amazing crackling, mashed potato that had been through the ricer and was as smooth as silk, softened with an indecent amount of butter, and some green beans. Then for pudding she just had a simple orange salad with chips of caramel. It was all about the pork, the rest were just grace notes to the main event.

In spite of her determination to put everything Helena had told her out of her head there was a touch of anxiety in the excitement she felt at the prospect of seeing Leo.

One of the many things she liked about him was that he always arrived when he said he would, and he did tonight with a bottle of wine under his arm.

'Hello, you,' he said, kissing her on both cheeks.

'Hello, Leo,' she said. 'Come on in. It's so lovely to see you.' Being with him was very reassuring. He was a solid presence and it was easier to forget all she'd heard about him when he so obviously wasn't a jailbird. Whether or not he drove too fast was less clear.

'I brought you this — I know I said I wouldn't but I couldn't resist . . .'

Gilly looked at the bottle and laughed. 'It was on offer at Waitrose! I got a bottle too. Now that's a good omen.'

'Why would we need a good omen?' he asked.

'Oh, you know! It's just something you say.' Gilly took the bottle. 'Come and sit by the fire. It's a chilly evening. You know what they say: 'As the days get longer the days get colder,' or some such. What would you like to drink?'

'A glass of that sherry I brought you would be nice.' He paused. 'Have one too. It will help you relax. You seem a bit on edge this evening.'

'Do I? Just worrying about the meal, I suppose. I'll go and get the sherry.'

Gilly wasn't remotely worried about the meal — she knew it was going to be perfect — but she was agitated. In spite of telling Helena she didn't care about anything she'd told her — except perhaps the part about Leo being the man in the car on the wrong side of the road — it wasn't true. And she'd thought about little else.

Sherry consumed, some fairly normal conversation enjoyed, Gilly went to get the starter. She released the little ramekins on to warm plates and was pleased to see the batter was perfectly set. She'd eaten the dish in France once and had been pleased to find a recipe.

Leo had filled both their glasses with wine and for once ignored the jug of water that was also on the table. How was he getting home? Gilly wondered. She had no guests in that night and had deliberately kept this evening free, so she could easily put Leo up if he wanted to stay. But would he want his own bedroom or would he want to share hers? In spite of him being so ardent in many ways, he hadn't actually kissed her properly yet. She didn't know if he was biding his time (she really hoped that was it) or didn't fancy her. She herself had decided their trip to Vienna was the time to pursue their relationship further.

'This is very delicious,' said Leo after a couple of mouthfuls.

'I'm so glad you like it. We're having belly of pork next so I wanted to do something light.'

'My favourite!' He paused. 'Not the sort of

thing your daughter-in-law Cressida would ever cook.'

A slight concern that she kept forgetting about came into Gilly's head. 'I'm sure you've told me . . . ' She wasn't sure but she said it anyway. 'Did you meet Cressida and Martin at mine that time we all had Sunday lunch? Or did you know them before?'

He hesitated just a fraction too long for her peace of mind. 'I met them here, of course.'

It didn't ring true but Gilly was determined not to spoil her evening.

'So what news of Vienna?' she said later, when they were halfway through their pork and the best way to achieve the perfect crackling (which this definitely was) had been discussed at length.

'Oh! All booked!' said Leo. 'I'll give you the details after supper. I can guarantee you're going to absolutely love what I've planned. More wine?'

He topped up her glass and then his own.

For whatever reason, Gilly was not enjoying Leo's company as much as usual. Previously she had revelled in the sound of his voice — it was beautifully modulated — and he was extremely well read and full of information about (it seemed) everything from gardening to ancient Greek literature and everything else in between. She knew she didn't always listen to what he was saying and just let his voice wash over her. But now she was paying attention, waiting for a suitable gap for her to say something.

'Would you like some more?' she asked eventually, after a brief lecture on the life and

139

works of Gustav Klimt which they would see when they went to Vienna.

He patted his stomach, currently covered in very fine wool tailoring. He cared a lot about his clothes and while Gilly liked clothes too, she did wonder at his choice of tie sometimes. Now was one of those times; the pattern was a bit too busy for her. 'Just a soupçon more would be lovely. I should probably decline as I'm sure you've got a wonderfully rich chocolate pudding for afterwards but my greed has got the better of me.'

While Gilly was in the kitchen refilling his plate she wondered if it was greed that had got him into trouble before. She also worried that he'd be disappointed by the pudding even though she'd taken such care to remove the pith from the oranges and had been liberal with the Grand Marnier. The caramel was perfect too. So often people didn't cook the sugar for long enough, in Gilly's opinion, so you didn't get the proper caramel taste. Aware she was spending longer in the kitchen than was strictly necessary, she took Leo's plate back through to the sitting room, the heated-up jus in a separate jug.

'You are the most amazing cook,' said Leo, gazing fondly at her. 'And yet somehow you've managed to maintain your good figure. You're not super-slim, of course, but still perfectly presentable. Figurewise,' he added quickly, possibly feeling Gilly stiffen at this faint praise.

'Thank you,' she said, not sure if she was thanking him for his praise for her cooking or her 'perfectly presentable' figure.

She watched him eat, wondering if his rather

flamboyant eating style would begin to grate on her eventually. She'd once known a woman who'd ended a relationship because she couldn't bear the way her beloved ate boiled eggs. And as her mind strayed into irrelevant thoughts and memories she wondered if they were all because Helena had put doubt in her mind.

'So, dear Gilly . . . ' He put a well-manicured hand on hers. 'What cocoa — and cholesterol-filled delight have you in store for us?'

'Actually, pudding is very simple and not really very fattening. Maybe I had our figures in mind when I planned it.' She didn't see why the prosperous curve of his stomach should be over-looked while her own curves could be commented on.

'Oh! Well! Very sensible, I'm sure.'

'Not sensible,' Gilly said firmly, 'delicious! I'll go and get it.'

As she had taken the trouble to dig out her very pretty green glass dishes with stems to serve the oranges in, she wasn't going to have dessert disparaged.

'Well,' said Leo, when she'd put the oranges with caramel in front of him. 'Not quite what I had in mind but, actually, it will go nicely after the pork.'

'Thank you,' said Gilly, irritated. 'That's what I thought.'

'I don't suppose you have a pudding wine, do you? I'm partial to a nice muscat at a time like this.'

Gilly got up and went to the fridge. She knew about his predilection for pudding wines; he'd

141

mentioned it before.

She had poured them both a glass in her favourite vintage sherry glasses. She had stopped worrying about whether or not he was over the limit — she had empty bedrooms she could put him in. She didn't offer coffee. She was tired.

'This is what we're doing,' he said, having produced a file from his briefcase. 'First, a cab to the airport — saves all that airport parking annoyance, although I did consider valet parking. We have a civilised flight time. I've booked business class — a bit extravagant but you're worth it! And then, a really nice hotel. Here it is.' He produced his laptop and found the site.

'Oh my goodness, that hotel is amazing!' said Gilly. 'It must be fantastically expensive.'

'I hope you're not going to offer to pay your share, Gilly. I wouldn't allow it.'

Gilly swallowed, then took another sip of muscat. Her glass had been refilled. 'OK,' she said, encouraging him to go on.

'Then I thought we'd have a car for the first day, to take us around to the major sites. Of course we'll visit the opera, and the Spanish Riding School. Is there anything in the art line you'd particularly enjoy? Apart from Klimt, of course.'

'Actually, Leo, this is quite overwhelming — '

'I want you to be overwhelmed! Overwhelmed with luxury, art, culture — there are some amazing churches to visit. Sigmund Freud's house . . . '

'So how many days have you planned to stay?'

'Five days. That should give us time to eat our body weight in Sachertorte and schnitzel.'

Gilly's eye had been caught by the date on one of the many bits of paper. 'Leo! The booking is in June. I'm sure I said I couldn't go then! Let me get my diary.'

The time she spent getting it, although not long, was time for her to get her feelings in order. She produced the family calendar that ruled her life. 'Look. I have bookings. I know I told you about them!'

'You did, darling,' he said smoothly, the first time he'd used this endearment. 'But I decided if we stuck to your schedule we'd never go. You can easily cancel your visitors or get your friend to accommodate them.'

Gilly didn't respond. She didn't know how to. He'd arranged a truly amazing trip for them and now she didn't want to go. It was odd, Gilly thought. A couple of days ago, if Leo had done this she'd have thought he was being wonderfully masterful and she'd have found the whole thing very sexy. She'd have passed her bed and breakfast guests on to her friend and tried to make it up to them later. Now she was determined not to rush into cancelling her bookings.

Was it Helena's ridiculous revelations that had done it? she wondered as she let Leo continue to talk about the cultural joys of Vienna, not having really acknowledged her doubts. Or was the dizzy, wonderful feeling that she associated with Leo always destined to be fleeting?

'You don't seem to be paying attention, my love.'

143

Gilly turned to Leo. 'Sorry, do go on. Vienna sounds fascinating.' Even if she didn't intend to go there.

'I'd actually asked if you had any brandy — or, better, port.'

Gilly got up quickly, the hostess within her still willing to please. 'Oh yes, of course. I'll get it.'

When she'd come back to the table spread with maps and guidebooks she poured him the port.

'Thank you,' he said. 'Now after Vienna, I suggest we take the train . . . ' He paused. 'Now what?' He sounded impatient. He wanted his audience to pay proper attention.

'Sorry! I was just wondering how you were going to get home. You've had far too much alcohol to be safe to drive.'

'Isn't that my decision?' he said coldly.

'Would you like me to call you a taxi?'

He cleared his throat. 'I was rather hoping to stay with you tonight.' He looked at her in a way that last week would have had her half fainting with lust.

'Sorry, but I'm absolutely chocker. Not a spare bed in the house.'

'Really? I haven't heard a soul and you haven't jumped up from the table once.'

Except when I've been tending to your needs, thought Gilly. 'They're all coming in much later. By arrangement.'

He was silent for a few moments — rare for him, Gilly realised. 'Maybe you'd better call that cab,' he said at last.

Gilly went to get her phone. She had a

number of cab companies on 'Favourites'. As she looked through the list she wondered if she should tell him to cancel the trip to Vienna and decided 'no time like the present'.

She waited until the cab had arrived, however. 'By the way, Leo, I don't think I want to go to Vienna after all. At least, not in June. It's just too inconvenient.'

He sighed, obviously being patient with the whims of a woman. 'Why don't you sleep on it? I'll leave the information that I've printed off. It's got a link to the hotel on it.'

Gilly smiled and nodded, feeling cowardly but also that she'd been run over by a Savile Row-suited steamroller and so her cowardice was justified.

As he left Gilly noticed he had cat hair on the seat of his trousers. He would not appreciate that. But she'd had Ulysses a lot longer than she'd known Leo. If she had to choose between them, it would have to be Uly.

Gilly's emotions were mixed. Part of her felt she'd probably lost the silver fox that her friends envied her for having and so was regretful. The other part hoped she had: the thought made her feel liberated, in the same way she had when she'd finally navigated the tortuous divorce proceedings her ex-husband put her through. After all, Leo might be a silver fox but he was high maintenance. She enjoyed cooking for people and loved to be appreciated, but she wondered if she would ever get to the stage with Leo that they could just eat cheese on toast in front of the telly. He'd probably want her to go on a diet, too, in case she got just a bit too plump to be presentable.

After she had put on some music to tidy the kitchen by, she examined her feelings. Supposing she couldn't go to Vienna, how did she feel? Relieved, she realised. It wasn't that she didn't want to go, she did, but not in the high-powered, high-end way that Leo would arrange.

She switched on the overfilled dishwasher. Next question. How would she feel if she never saw Leo again? This wasn't quite so clear, she realised. Part of her was definitely relieved but part of her would wonder if she'd made the right decision. He was gorgeous, by anyone's standards, and the fact that he was courting her, a middle-aged woman, was very flattering.

Now she wished she'd gone for a rich and creamy chocolate dessert instead of the lighter, diet-friendly oranges in caramel. That would have been good — something really fattening and rich to indulge in so that the faint nausea she'd feel afterwards would match her mood. Fortunately she'd brought some cream just in case (in case of what, she never asked herself) and although it curdled slightly when poured over the oranges, it tasted nice. After she'd eaten it and poured herself some Grand Marnier she did the full number on the kitchen. Usually she'd just do the minimum and finish in the morning. She much preferred cleaning in daylight but she suspected she'd be feeling low when she came down the next morning and having a clean kitchen might help.

Before she settled down to sleep she texted

Helena, hoping her daughter hadn't taken her phone into the bedroom as she didn't want to disturb her. *I'm not going to Vienna with Leo,* she said, and added a grinning emoji.

Helena must have seen her mother's text early because she was in the kitchen by eight.

They hugged.

'Oh God, Mum, I'm so sorry! I would never have told you all that stuff about Leo if I hadn't been really worried!' Helena said, still clinging on to her mother.

'I know you absolutely did it for the best and I don't know if it was what you said, or him, but I'm going off him.'

Helena gasped in delight. 'Have you dumped him?'

'No. He may dump me first.'

'Oh, don't let that happen,' said Helena, possibly worried that Gilly might keep him. 'Far better for you to do it!'

Gilly didn't really want to talk about this now. She wanted to make up her own mind in her own time. But she knew Helena would put pressure on her if she showed doubt. She changed the subject. 'Would you like some belly of pork? You could heat it up for Jago next time you see him.'

Helena looked a bit guilty. 'I could and that may be quite soon.'

'Why?' If it hadn't been for the guilty look Gilly would never have asked. She felt that if she wanted her privacy respected she should respect Helena's but she was her mother. There were a few privileges.

'Because we're living together. No! Not like that! I'm renting a room in his house. For money. So we're sharing a house really, not living together. Although we do share meals — or we have so far.'

Gilly smiled again, hoping she didn't look too fond and clucky for her independent daughter. 'I'll give you all the pork belly then.'

★ ★ ★

Later Gilly found herself in Waitrose staring mindlessly at the chocolate display. Usually she was focused when she went shopping, had a list, knew what she wanted, but now her decision-making ability had deserted her. She still hadn't decided what to do about Leo.

She became aware of someone at her elbow. It was William. 'Oh, hello!'

'Hello.' He paused. 'I'd ask how you are but I think I know the answer.'

'Oh God, do I look awful?'

'Not awful, never that, but you don't look happy.'

Gilly started a smile and then decided it probably looked ghoulish and stopped.

'When I feel like that, I go gliding,' said William.

'Do you?'

'Can I take you gliding? Would you like that?'

At that moment she couldn't decide what chocolate bar to buy, how could she make a decision about going gliding?

'I don't know. I've never been. How can I possibly tell if I'd like it?'

'I expect the thought makes you feel a bit apprehensive,' said William. 'Can we find a day when I can take you to look at the glider and — if it's sunny and you feel like it — we can go up? But if you don't fancy it we'll just go out for lunch?'

'William, it's terribly kind of you but — '

'I'll email you,' said William, 'then you can think about it and reply accordingly. I shouldn't have put you on the spot while you're shopping.'

Now Gilly felt guilty. 'I'm sorry! It was such a kind thought but — '

'It came at just the wrong moment.' He smiled. 'I'll email you.' Then he walked off towards the wine department.

Gilly watched him go. It was so kind to try to offer comfort when she was obviously suffering. On the other hand she could have done with him not being quite so quick to notice when she'd put on a good layer of 'I'm absolutely fine' make-up. Still, if it hadn't worked, it hadn't worked. She picked up the first chocolate that came to hand and put several bars into her trolley. Then she headed to the baking ingredients department. She saw William passing through towards the checkouts. He gave her a wave and a smile and she smiled back. Gliding, she thought, not her sort of thing at all. Which was rather a shame.

★ ★ ★

Gilly was very surprised to open her front door and see Leo standing there just after she'd put her shopping away. He had a huge bunch of flowers in his hand and a very humble expression on his face.

'Forgive me for just turning up like this but I thought you may have blocked my number,' he said, 'and I really wanted to say how sorry I was about my behaviour last night.'

Gilly opened her front door, her feelings very mixed. 'Come in. And there's no need for all this.'

He came in and put the flowers into her hands. 'There was very much a need.'

'I'll just put these somewhere. I expect they could do with a drink before I arrange them.' Leaving Leo in the hall she went to her utility room and found a bucket. When the flowers were in water up to their necks she went back to her unexpected guest. Her short encounter with a cold tap had been enough for her to gather her composure.

'Can I offer you some coffee, Leo?' she asked. 'Having given your lovely flowers a drink I think I should show you the same courtesy.' She smiled.

'Can I suggest something different? Can I suggest I take you to my house for coffee? I'd like you to see it.'

The sensible part of Gilly would have said no but her curiosity squashed common sense in a second. 'That would be delightful,' she said. 'Go and make yourself comfortable in the sitting room while I get ready.'

Gilly wanted to suggest she took her own car but then decided it looked a bit rude. Helena would have chided her for her inability to be rude to people but good manners were in every fibre of her being and Leo was making a huge effort. Saying sorry was obviously hard for him and he was doing it with very good grace.

Unusually for Leo, he didn't talk much as he drove so when Helena rang the call broke the silence. Gilly felt awkward talking to her daughter because she knew Helena would not approve of what she was doing. At least Helena would understand her desire to see a possibly lovely house, but she wouldn't want the house to be Leo's.

Twenty minutes later, Leo drove through huge, wrought-iron gates that opened with the aid of a gadget in his car. He drove up the drive and drew to a halt in front of the house.

Gilly drew breath. Her own house was lovely, but this — lit perfectly by the spring afternoon sunshine — was spectacular.

It was a classical Georgian house, possibly an old rectory. The garden in front was beautifully tended and beyond the lawn there was a gate into the churchyard; beyond that was an old church. Gilly couldn't suppress a sigh.

Leo ran round the car so he could open the passenger door. He handed Gilly out.

'Come through to the kitchen. It doesn't have anything like the charm that yours has, but it is quite smart.'

The kitchen was reached via a generous entrance hall, stone-flagged, light and perfect for the tallest Christmas tree. Now it had an antique desk and chair and a chaise longue.

'Quite smart' as a description of the kitchen was an enormous understatement. Firstly, it was huge and secondly, unless Gilly was very much mistaken (and she did her fair share of looking on the internet), cost the same as a decent-sized house in some parts of the country.

Painted a darkish green (Farrow and Ball, Gilly recognised), it wasn't gloomy but stylish. A fouroven Aga the same colour took up quite a lot of one wall, fitted into what had once been an inglenook (another house-sized amount of money.) All around were cupboards and (she was willing to bet) pan drawers. There was one of those taps that provided boiling or icy cold water and a sneaky look at a tall cupboard that looked rather like an antique armoire (though not enough to make Gilly believe it was one) turned out to be a fitted larder.

Gilly had always wanted a fitted larder cupboard. She had a larder but it was damp, full of surplus kitchen gadgets (pasta maker, ice-cream maker, spiraliser, mincer) and wasn't full of decorative jars of spices. Basically, it didn't look as if it was owned by Nigella.

Leo drew out a stool from the breakfast bar and invited Gilly to sit. Gilly was not a fan of high stools but she clambered up and rested her hands on the marble island. It would be so perfect for making pastry, she thought.

He made them both coffee from a complicated machine and handed Gilly a mug. 'Take it with you while we do the tour. I have an appointment later or I'd invite you to lunch.'

'I've got things I need to do later, too,' said

Gilly, hoping she hadn't forgotten anything important.

Every room was more lovely than the last. There was a huge, elegant drawing room, a dining room, painted traditionally in deep red, and, as well as an office, a snug and a wine cellar, there was a magnificent orangery. Gilly had a conservatory and a wine cellar but her wine cellar was actually in the cellar and you had to go down steep steps to get to it. This was near the dining room and kitchen, incredibly handy.

'This is just so lovely,' said Gilly when the tour was over and they were back in the hall.

'It's home,' said Leo simply.

Gilly suppressed a sigh. She didn't want him to see quite how impressed she was. It would make his head swell and she didn't want him to have a problem going through doors.

'Well, now I must go back to my far more humble one.'

'I wanted you to see it, Gilly, not so much to impress you but so you'd know you wouldn't be giving up a lovely place to live if you threw your lot in with me.'

'I think we're getting ahead of ourselves,' said Gilly, channelling her inner playgroup leader. 'But thank you.' She gave Leo the sort of smile she usually kept for potentially difficult bed and breakfast guests. It never failed her.

'Let's get you home.'

As they drove back through the lanes of Gloucestershire, Gilly thought about Leo's wonderful house. And the more she thought about it the more she realised that no house, however wonderful, was better than her house. Fairacres was home, damp patches, deathwatch beetle and all.

'I'll be in touch,' said Leo, looking down into her eyes, his expression sincere.

'Lovely,' said Gilly, looking up into his eyes, mirroring his expression.

Neither of them meant those warm looks, she realised, but she wanted to get away politely. It was only later that she wondered whether Leo did too.

17

'Listen,' said Amy to Helena on the phone later in the morning after Helena had been to see Gilly and come away with a lot of pork. 'Are you sitting down?'

'I am now.' Helena was telling a lie. Amy sounded so urgent that standing up seemed a better choice. It was probably that Amy had forgotten to tell her they had a workshop in Cornwall tomorrow and they had to set off immediately.

'OK, well, you know the Springtime Show?'

'Yes,' said Helena, slightly sarcastically, 'the show where all the really high-end crafters display their work and it costs a grand to get in.'

'Right. Well, I've got you in!'

Helena exhaled and perched on the edge of a very broken-down armchair that had apparently once been leather. 'Calm down and breathe. How can I possibly be 'in'? It's booked up the year before it's on and — in case you missed it — costs a grand to enter. Am I sharing your stall?' Amy had indeed booked her stall at this show the previous year.

'No! The stalls are tiny. There was a cancellation. I was with some other people and one of them got the call. None of them wanted to take the place so I said yes. For you!'

'Amy! How can I go? I'm busy enough getting stuff together for Woolly World and I couldn't take that stuff to Springtime, it's too rustic. Quite apart from the money.'

'I've paid for your entrance. You've got just under three weeks to create some suitable stock and you'll get your money back — my money — no problem. Helena, this is the perfect opportunity for you to weave in silk.'

Helena wiped her arm with her forehead. Amy knew about her long-held ambition to work with silk, one she had batted away numerous times as being impractical. But at a show like Springtime, where people who would willingly spend well over a hundred pounds on a scarf visited with credit cards and a lust for luxury retail opportunities, silk would be perfect!

'I haven't got time — '

'You've got nearly three weeks. You won't have time to make that much but you could make samples and take orders. Hels, you've got all that silk at your mum's house and that handy little loom — '

'But I'm known for my blankets!'

'You can change. And you could take a few of your best blankets just to fill up the stall. But as I said, the stalls are tiny anyway.'

'It'll take me three weeks to thread the loom!'

'But, Helena' — Amy was talking soothingly now as if her friend were a traumatised horse — 'you've got all those beautiful cones of silk yarn that someone trusted you enough to donate to you. They might get eaten by clothes moths if you don't use them soon.'

'Do moths eat silk?'

'Definitely! Anyway, you have to do it or you'll

157

never be able to pay me back my grand.'

The conversation continued for a while. When Helena put the phone down she noticed there was a mug of tea on the table. 'You are such a star!'

Jago nodded, acknowledging his starriness. 'My reward is that you tell me what that was all about. It sounded really exciting from this end.'

Helena sipped her tea. 'OK, but it's a bit of a long story. Aren't you busy?'

'I'm having a break.'

'Well, when I was at art college, before I'd discovered weaving really, there was this amazing woman. She was in her fifties and I think I was missing Mum a bit and she took me under her wing. She gave me her loom. People often give weavers looms! Although I wasn't one then, I think this woman, Julia Coombs, saw that that was where I was headed. And, with the loom, she gave me a whole load of silk yarn. Beautiful colours. I longed to make something with it but someone told me I had to start with wool. Can't even remember why, now. So I put all the lovely coloured silk into bin liners and took it home and it went in the attic — although Mum put it in plastic boxes. The loom went up there too.' She gave a rueful laugh. 'My brother would say it's one of the reasons I don't want Mum to move except I don't think he'd remember about my stuff in the attic.'

'So what does Amy want you to do?'

Helena went on to explain about Springtime, how it had been a showcase for great artists and masters of their craft and how utterly impossible it would be for her to get enough work done in time even if woodworm hadn't got to the loom and moths to the cones of silk thread.

'I guess Amy could probably find someone else to take the spot, get her bag of sand back,' said Jago.

'Her what?' said Helena, distracted for a moment.

'Bag o' sand, grand.'

'Love it!'

'But you should go and check out your mum's attic and see what's survived.'

Helena sighed, feeling suddenly overwhelmed by the whole thing. Amy had such faith in her; her wonderful mentor, Julia Coombs, had had such faith in her; this was her chance to show them she was up to it.

★   ★   ★

Helena hadn't thought to ring her mother before she went up to visit the attic and tell her the news about the show, but her car was there so it was slightly surprising to find the back door locked. Helena used her key and let herself into the house.

'Mum?' she called but the kitchen had that empty feel that indicated no one was home. Ulysses the cat got up from the chair he was snoozing on and came over to say hello. 'So where is she, Uly?' Helena asked. 'I'd better ring her.'

She dialled. 'Mum? Where are you? I'm at the house and I want to go into the attic.'

'Oh, hello, darling!' said Gilly.

She sounded a bit awkward, Helena thought. 'Are you OK, Mum?'

'Of course, I'm perfectly all right. I'm with a friend.'

Helena got the impression she wasn't with a close friend and wasn't entirely happy about it either, so although she knew her mother hadn't been kidnapped she felt obliged to ask: 'You haven't been taken anywhere against your will, have you? Say Ulysses if you have.'

Her mother's laugh was rather brittle. 'Don't be silly and be careful going into the attic if you're on your own. The ladder isn't very secure. Promise?'

* * *

'Is that you, darling?' Gilly called.

'Yup,' said Jago, appearing in the hall with a large plastic box in his arms.

Gilly laughed. 'Is my daughter with you? Or are you burgling me?'

Helena appeared with a slightly smaller box in her arms.

'Is that the family silver in there?' asked Gilly.

'No. It's all that silk yarn you've been keeping for me in the attic and that small loom,' said Helena. 'Did I tell you? I'm going to start weaving in silk!'

'But I thought you were working flat out for World of Wool?'

'I'm doing something quite different now!' She looked at her watch. 'We must go — Jago has to

160

be somewhere — but I'll ring you and tell you all about it. It's all Amy's fault!' She followed Jago out of the back door. 'And thank you so much for keeping everything in those boxes,' she added. 'It's completely saved me!'

*   *   *

Although Helena was trying to remember the eccentricities of the loom that was travelling in pieces in the back of Jago's pickup along with the plastic boxes, one part of her mind was on her mother. Did she look guilty? Unsettled? Just a bit odd? 'I wish I'd remembered to ask my mother where she'd been when I called her.' She paused. 'Did she look shifty to you?'

Jago laughed heartily. 'No! And I think your mum is entitled to a private life, Helly.'

He hadn't called her that before and Helena took a moment to decide if she liked it or not. She concluded that she did. 'I know, it's just I'm in the habit of looking out for her. And she looks out for me.'

'Is that what they call a 'co-dependency'?' Jago enquired.

Helena thought about this before acknowledging there was possibly some truth in his comment. 'The trouble is, she was a bit of a wreck after the divorce. She was really strong all the way through it, but afterwards she sort of slumped for a bit.'

'She's lucky to have a daughter like you.'

'And I'm lucky to have a mum like her! Totally keeping the moths away from my silk thread was amazing!'

161

'So you'll stop worrying about Gilly and just focus on your new project?'

'I will.'

Jago stayed to help her assemble the small loom and then said, 'I must dash. I'm looking for my next project. Always have to think ahead in this game.'

Helena was aware this gave her a slight feeling of loss. 'Oh, OK! I'll see you later. Maybe I'll cook something?'

'Or maybe you'll get so involved in threading your new loom I'll cook something?'

Helena beamed. 'An even better idea.'

Threading the smaller loom did take forever, especially as the silk strands were so fine. She needed 125 threads per inch and she wondered if she was mad to start doing this when she had so little time. But the time flew by and when Jago put a monster sandwich by her she had no idea where she was in the day.

'Is that lunch or breakfast?' she asked, suddenly starving, her hunger triggered by the sight of food.

'Early supper. Shouldn't you stop now? Can you still see?'

Helena blinked. 'Actually you're right, I'm not functioning all that well at the moment.'

'Why don't you bring the sandwich into the kitchen and have a glass of wine with it while I cook us something else?'

'That sounds like a very good plan!' said Helena and picked up her plate.

As she followed him through the house she remembered he'd been on a mission too.

'Did you get the property you were interested in? Were you buying or just checking out?'

'Checking out. No point in buying something if it's never going to get planning permission. So how did setting up a different loom go?'

'Well! Although it took me a while to find my way around it, and I had forgotten quite how long it takes to thread a loom with thread so fine. I reckon I can get three good scarf lengths out of every time I thread the loom, but I am going to have to charge a lot to make it worth it.' She took a large bite of her sandwich and sighed happily.

'But there's the honour of being in the show?' He put down a full glass of red wine and she knew it was her favourite.

She took another bite before answering. He did have a way with a sandwich: the right bread, the right condiments, all perfectly balanced. 'There is, but you can't pay your bills with honour, can you? You have to have actual money as well. There's no point in creating beautiful pieces if people won't pay enough for them.'

'But didn't Amy feel fairly sure you'd make back your thousand pounds without difficulty?'

'Amy is dreadfully optimistic!'

'When I last looked, being optimistic wasn't considered a bad thing,' said Jago.

Helena looked at him, biting her lip to hide her smile. 'There's being optimistic and being foolhardy. And that was possibly the most delicious sandwich I've ever eaten.'

He nodded gravely. 'You were hungry. That helps.'

Over the following days, Helena hardly

163

stopped weaving. Jago brought her food during the day and dragged her to the table for the evening meal. She sent her mother a text to say she was fine but working very hard. She didn't tell her how late and long her hours were. Mothers didn't need to know everything.

18

Helena having to weave day and night was a relief to Gilly. It meant she wouldn't have time to wonder about what her mother was up to. Gilly did her bit to support her daughter, sending over casseroles which, she realised, mostly helped Jago, who seemed to have taken on the feeding role. But she was glad not to have her daughter's beady eye upon her. While she was very nearly 100 per cent sure she didn't want to go out with Leo any more, she was curious. He had more or less asked her to live with him and yet he hadn't tried to seduce her. So what was going on?

She took advantage of Helena being so occupied to invite Martin and his family for Sunday lunch. She had asked Helena via text but said, *Completely understand if you're too busy. I know how under the cosh you are at the moment.* While she would have been fine if Helena and Jago had accepted she was glad to be able to have lunch with her son without any twitches between him and his sister to deal with.

She had just settled them in the sitting room with a glass of wine and elderflower and something suitable for Ismene when her phone rang. She saw it was William.

'Do you mind if I answer this?' she asked, getting up so she could take the call in privacy. She knew that both Cressida and Martin would be looking at their own phones the moment she was out of the way so didn't feel too bad.

'William? How are you?'

'I'm well and I hope you are too? I was just calling to fix up a time to take you gliding. We've got a nice high coming up tomorrow I'd like to take advantage of. It will be perfect for a first flight.'

Gilly sighed. 'Oh, William! I'm so sorry! I do hope I didn't give you the wrong impression, but really, I don't think gliding is for me. I am an awful coward and I don't much like flying in small planes. I'm sure to be absolutely terrified.'

There was a long silence and Gilly was aware of having disappointed William. She didn't feel happy about it.

'I really do believe you might love it if you just let yourself give it a shot.'

'It's a terribly long shot, William.' She heard him sigh and felt desperate to offer him something. He'd been kind enough to want to share his hobby with her and she'd turned him down because she was a coward. He deserved better. 'I'd love to do something else — bird-watching, angling — something where you don't have to defy gravity.'

He laughed gently. 'OK, I'll let you off gliding, for now. I'll find somewhere good for birdwatching. Flicking metal hooks around at the end of a line might be a bit nerve-racking for me.'

She realised she was smiling. 'Thank you! Let me know.'

She walked back to Cressida and Martin; Ismene had found the magnetic atlas jigsaw that Gilly had bought for her. 'Right, can I get anyone

166

something to nibble? Lunch won't be long.'

'Who was that, Mum?' asked Martin. 'Not Leo?'

Gilly winced internally. Was she obliged to tell them about her relationship with Leo? She thought not. 'I was just talking to a friend about going gliding.'

'Gliding!' Cressida could not have been more horrified if Gilly had said she was going pole dancing. 'Gilly! You would never go gliding! It would be absolutely terrifying for you.'

'Yes, Mum, I hope you said no. It would be really unsuitable for someone of your age and state of health.'

'There's nothing wrong with my health!' said Gilly indignantly.

'Physically, you're fine, but you are nervy. Always have been,' said Martin. 'Gliding would be the death of you.'

Gilly took a couple of slow inward breaths. 'Excuse me. I must just check something in the oven.'

She walked quickly out of the room, her phone in her hand. When she was well out of earshot she got her phone and found 'Recents'. 'William? I've changed my mind. I do want to go gliding after all.'

'Gilly?' said William. 'Are you all right? You sound a bit as if someone has forced you into saying that.'

She couldn't help laughing. 'Really? No, don't worry, I just decided not to be such a wimp. It's turning me into an old lady before my time.'

'Never! I'll pick you up tomorrow just after eight. I am so pleased about this!'

167

Just as well she was an early riser, thought Gilly the following morning as she sat next to William in the car, trying to focus on the burgeoning hedgerows and the beauty of the emerging spring. She was breathing deeply, concentrating very hard on not thinking about taking to the air in an unpowered vehicle. Although to be fair, it wasn't the unpowered bit that terrified her, it was the tiny insubstantial scrap of metal she was going to be in at the time.

'We have the perfect day for it,' said William. 'I'm confident you're going to love it.'

Gilly's answering smile was rather strained. 'It's certainly a lovely day. How long are we likely to be in the air?'

'On a day like today, with a bit of luck and some good thermals we could go for miles but as it's your first time I think twenty minutes will be about right.'

Twenty minutes of her life. That wasn't a big sacrifice and when she came down she could say that she'd done it, she wasn't a coward and could carry on with her feet on the ground.

'I'm not likely to be sick, am I?'

William shook his head. 'Not on a day like today.'

'Am I wearing the right clothes?'

He glanced across at her. She was wearing a smartened-up version of what she'd garden in: flexible (so she could clamber in and out of the glider) and warm. Gilly was aware her fear of being cold identified her as being an older

168

person but it was too bad. She would never sacrifice comfort for fashion. A silk scarf added a certain aviator touch, she felt.

'They seem perfect to me. You can move about freely?'

'Yes. I did a bit of YouTubing to look at gliders and they seem . . . small? And will take a bit of getting into,' she said, pleased with herself for avoiding the words 'cramped' and 'claustrophobic'. 'I hope I'm athletic enough.'

'I'm sure you are.'

'And we wear parachutes?'

'Yup. Partly for safety and partly because if you didn't the seats would be really uncomfortable.'

'Oh, like when you lose the lining of your shoe and it's too big and unpleasant against your foot?'

He nodded. 'I expect so.'

She didn't speak for a while, aware they were getting nearer and nearer the airfield.

'Don't overthink it, Gilly,' said William eventually. 'If you really don't want to go, we won't go. It's not a big deal.'

Yet having been offered a way out Gilly realised she'd feel disappointed if she didn't give gliding a try. And Martin and Cressida would be so furious when she told them she'd been — any amount of fear would be worth that.

In spite of her bracing inner thoughts, Gilly found the age it took to drive the perimeter of the airfield agonizing. She was here, she wanted to do it and she didn't want it spun out with scenic drives around large open spaces.

After seemingly hours, but in reality only a few minutes, William parked the car near the clubhouse. He held her arm encouragingly as they walked past where a number of gliders were kept under cover towards the building where, according to the jaunty sign on the outside, the fun began.

William was obviously a popular member of the club; everyone greeted him with warm smiles, and there was the odd joke that indicated they appreciated his gentle charm. She received a fair amount of curious looks and shy nods herself and she couldn't help asking herself how many other women he'd taken gliding. She was surprised to feel a bit jealous; she wanted it to be only her. And then she wondered why.

'Come on,' said William. 'Let's get it over with!'

Gilly laughed. 'Do I look that terrified?'

'Yes,' said a couple of the other people.

'But no need,' one went on. 'You're going to love it.'

'It's traditional to have a big cooked breakfast after your first flight,' said another, 'no matter what time you go up.'

Gilly managed some sort of smile; now her ordeal was nearly on her, she was getting more and more frightened. She started breathing deeply. That was always a good idea.

'Is this your glider?' she said as they approached the machine, which seemed hardly bigger than a dragonfly.

'No, this belongs to the club. Mine is a singleseater. I thought it was a bit early to put you up in that.'

170

It took Gilly a couple of seconds to realise he'd made a joke. She whimpered in response.

'It's tiny!' she said, looking at the space she was expected to climb into. 'I swear this must be one of the few activities where you can be claustrophobic and agoraphobic at the same time!'

'Here, let me help you. You get in the front, but don't worry, you don't have to drive. Gilly cast him a terrified glance before getting herself up and into the tiny seat. Then the Perspex top came down and clicked into place.'

He handed her a headset. 'Here, put this on. It means we can talk to each other.'

There were a few minutes of bumping along the grass, the wings of the glider being supported by cheerful men, and then suddenly the glider took flight. Gilly gasped, breathed deeply and gradually felt her fear being replaced by amazement. She forgot about the flimsy machine and just felt joy at being in the air in almost complete silence. Only the sound of the wind rushing past disturbed it and Gilly found she tuned it out quickly.

'All right?' came William's steady voice from behind her.

'It's wonderful!' she said. 'It's like being a bird! Look! I can see the Severn! My goodness, this is amazing!'

'Can you see the mountains beyond the river?'

'Are they the Brecon Beacons or the Black Mountains? Oh, there's the Sugar Loaf, that's the Brecon Beacons, isn't it?'

'Do you want to have a little go on the controls yourself?'

'No thank you. I just want to swoop about, pretending to be an albatross, though I think they mostly fly over the sea, don't they? Oh, look! There's Dead Man's Acre.'

'What?'

'Doesn't matter.' If William didn't know the story she didn't want to waste time telling it to him now.

Gilly became totally absorbed in looking at the fields and villages, woods and hills spread out beneath her like toys. She could see the escarpment and where it dropped to the Severn plain.

There were sheep dotted about like blobs of cotton wool, cows in groups next to hedges splashed with blossom — blackthorn, she reckoned — and hawthorn. Smaller rivers, canals and ponds flashed silver. She saw a group of deer near a spinney and sighed with happiness.

The twenty minutes was over very quickly. The landing was very smooth.

'I've been on scheduled flights that bump more than that,' said Gilly, hoping her legs hadn't stopped working while she'd been airborne. 'I really hate the airline that plays that horrid cock-a-doodle-do thing if they arrive on time. I'd rather be late.'

Her legs had weakened a bit and she was glad of William's supportive presence as she extracted herself from the tiny space and got to the ground.

'So,' he asked, looking down at her in a fond and proud way, 'do I gather you liked that?'

'I loved it! I never thought I'd be able to get through it without having some sort of fit but it was magical!'

'Next time, we'll stay up longer, go a bit further.'

'So there'll be a next time?' Gilly asked, feeling like a child asking for a treat.

'There will be if I have anything to do with it!' William put his arm round her and together they walked back to the clubhouse.

'That went well, then?' asked one of the friendly men.

'I loved it!' said Gilly. 'I never thought I would. I'm such a coward about these things normally.'

'What things?' asked the man.

'You know — roller coasters, scary things generally.'

'So, are you up for a breakfast?' the man went on.

Gilly looked at William. 'I'm terribly sorry,' he said, 'although I hate to break with tradition, I have to get to work.'

'I have to work too,' said Gilly. Her work involved hanging sheets on the line. It seemed mundane but when you washed as many sheets as she did, good drying days became very important.

'I'm so glad you liked it,' said William as they neared her house.

'So am I!' said Gilly, unaware until very recently how very important it was that she did like gliding. She wanted to like it for William's sake. 'And I didn't just like it, I loved it!'

William didn't speak but smiled across at her when he'd parked the car. He looked very happy, Gilly realised.

'Have you time to come in for a coffee?' she asked him.

'No, I've got to rush back to the office,' he said, but got out of the car. He was at the passenger door in an instant and handed her out.

'Thank you so much for taking me,' said Gilly.

'It was my absolute pleasure,' he said, and kissed her cheek; then he cupped it with his hand, looking into her eyes without saying any more.

As she watched him disappear down the drive she felt that these two simple gestures were somehow more meaningful and touching than the most full-on kiss would have been.

19

Gilly wanted to see William again but didn't quite know how to go about it. She had written him a card after he had taken her gliding, taking care with it so he would realise how much she had loved the experience of seeing the landscape from the sky. He hadn't responded and that was over a week ago. On the other hand, she was delighted that she hadn't heard from Leo.

She looked at her calendar, the mocked paper 'family calendar' that caused mirth or disapproval depending, and saw something she thought could be useful: an opportunity to see him again without looking needy. No woman ever wanted to look needy, especially one of a certain age.

She composed an email, inviting him to Helena's upcoming show, implying he would be a guest of the family group. Later she would ask him for a lift — her car was going in for a service at the perfect time.

But while Gilly was writing her email, Martin rang.

'Hi, Mum! Just making plans for going to Hel's show.'

Gilly was surprised at his enthusiasm — surprised he planned to go even, let alone make plans. 'Oh? Are you and Cressida going?'

'We certainly are. We have to support the old skin and blister, don't we?'

175

This didn't sound like Martin. He wasn't usually bluff and friendly when he referred to anything his sister did. 'That's great! Really glad you can make it. She'll be thrilled.'

'So we'll pick you up on our way through.'

'Oh — I was going to go early, so I can give Helly a hand setting up —'

'But Mum! Your car is due for a service! I arranged it, don't forget.' It was the one helpful thing he did for Gilly and as she could have perfectly easily done it herself she was never that grateful.

'I was going to rearrange the date . . .' Another lie: they were falling from her like beads out of a beanbag.

'And now you don't have to. If you want to help Hel, you can stay later and get a lift back with her.'

When Gilly disconnected her phone a little while later she felt bulldozed. Martin did that to her sometimes. She was sure he meant well — fairly sure anyway — and wished she'd been able to tell him she could make her own arrangements. She went into the kitchen and put the kettle on. Perhaps William would get in touch, offering to pick her up, then she'd cancel Martin.

★ ★ ★

It was the day of the Springtime Show and it was five o'clock when Helena finally decided to get up. She'd woken every hour since 3 a.m. and thought she may as well avoid the agony of

176

trying to get back to sleep again. Her alarm was due to go off at six, anyway.

Amy was going to meet her at the venue and show her the ropes before she sorted out her own stall. That was OK: once the setting up was done, the hardest part was over.

She made a quick cup of tea, trying not to wake Jago whose bedroom was just next door, and then she surveyed her list. She'd been tempted to pack Jago's pickup (she was so grateful to him for swapping vehicles for the day) the night before, but then she worried about it raining or the truck being stolen or indeed anything she possibly could worry about. At least now she didn't need to worry about being late. She spent longer than usual getting herself ready. Moving boxes around was likely to disturb Jago and she preferred to do that at a less unearthly hour.

There were so many boxes. There were boxes of stock (quite a few of those, to her relief), there was her loom, the small one that she didn't have to assemble if the space really was as small as Amy insisted it would be; there were yarns, a selection of shuttles, beaters, combs and needles. She was aiming to make her stall look so interesting people would come over even if they had no interest whatsoever in buying a scarf. And although she had intended to only sell her silk scarves (Amy had got her in on this high-end product) she'd also brought all the rugs and throws she'd made for World of Wool which was later in the month. She wouldn't sell them in this posh venue, she was sure, but they added life and colour to her stall. Then there were the boxes of cheese straws, tiny savoury scones and little vol-au-vents her mother had insisted she brought with her.

'You never know when you may need a snack,' Gilly had said, 'and knowing you quite well, you need one quite often.'

'I have my sandwiches!'

'You may need to offer other people a nibble.' There had been a pause. 'To serve with the Prosecco someone may bring.'

Helena hugged her mother. 'Someone is so very kind! The best someone in the world!'

It was a really beautiful May morning. The early sunshine shone through the new green leaves sending dappled light on to the road. As the show was nearly an hour's drive away, Helena had time to enjoy the countryside that she didn't often see quite so early. Especially recently when she'd been working so hard.

But as she got nearer, Helena began to get nervous. Would her products look clunky, homespun and rustic next to all the other exhibitors? She was used to exhibiting at shows where the handmade chunky look was not only permitted, it was obligatory.

This was very different. Everything would be sleek, highly finished, shiny, totally professional. Like many creative people Helena suffered badly from 'fear of being caught out', as if she was someone who didn't know what they were doing and just loved doing it, like any old amateur creative.

Also, she wouldn't know everyone else

178

exhibiting. At one of her usual shows she would meet loads of old friends, fellow weavers, spinners, knitters and producers of wool and yarn. Apart from Amy, she wouldn't know anyone at Springtime. The other people could be snooty and not deign to talk to a humble worker in wool.

At least the event was really well signposted, she thought with relief as she arrived. She found the exhibitors' car park, near the back entrance to the building, and waiting for her was Amy.

'I knew you'd be early,' she said as Helena got out of the pickup. 'So I made sure I was earlier. Jago not with you?'

'No. He had to be somewhere else. He lent me his pickup though.'

'I can see that,' said Amy.

Helena felt a bit on the defensive. She thought she ought to defend Jago for being an unsupportive boyfriend when he wasn't actually her boyfriend and was actually very supportive. 'Let's get into the building,' she said instead.

Helena's stall was in a long gallery, with floorlength windows all down one side. The other side was panelled wood with a stuccoed ceiling. It was incredibly beautiful and originally designed (said a helpful notice) for women of the house to walk in for exercise when inclement weather made the garden unsuitable. Helena was very pleased with her spot. It was near enough the entrance so people wouldn't be tired by the time they'd got as far as her and yet not so near the door that people would just plunge on past, assuming the better items were further in.

'I'm afraid I have to push off to my stall when we're set up,' said Amy during one of the trips from the pickup to Helena's spot. 'But mine won't take as long. We've got time to make it all look nice.'

Helena smiled. She didn't say that she was perfectly capable of making it all look nice herself because Amy was very good at it and she was grateful for her help. And Amy had got this gig for her and although Helena was fairly terrified at the moment, she knew she'd settle once she was in. As far as she could tell (no one was fully installed yet) she had a goldsmith on one side and a leather worker on the other. Both of her neighbours had really lovely pieces on display.

'Would you like me to look after your credit card for you?' she said to Amy before she left to set up her own stall. 'How else will you avoid losing control of your spending?'

Amy looked longingly at a bright yellow handbag in butter-soft leather with gold buckles. It was open, revealing a contrasting silk interior. 'I may have to buy that right now.'

'Why don't you wait until the end of the show?' said Helena. 'If it's still there — and not everyone wants a yellow handbag — you could probably get a bargain.' She felt obliged to help her friend save money.

'Will you negotiate for me?' asked Amy.

Helena laughed. 'Of course!'

'You'll be best friends with the maker by then,' said Amy.

The public were due to arrive in half an hour and everyone was set up and waiting. Helena had tried a few tentative smiles at her fellow artisans but hadn't got a lot of response. Then she decided to bring out her secret weapon: her mother's well-filled Tupperware boxes.

'I know it's a bit early,' Helena said to the creator of the yellow handbag, 'but would you like a snack?'

The woman, who had deep red hair cut in a very elegant curly bob, looked in the box Helena was holding. 'Blessed be the day when we can have a cheese straw for breakfast. Thank you!'

Everyone Helena offered snacks to was equally grateful. 'We none of us had time for breakfast,' said one, 'so a sausage roll is bliss!'

'I'll do a coffee run when they're open,' said a third, having had two cheese straws and a vol-au-vent. 'So sensible to bring food!'

'It's my mother,' Helena explained. 'She hardly lets me leave the house without a food parcel — certainly not her house anyway. She's a feeder.'

'I love her already,' said the handbag maker, whose name was Venetia.

'She's coming so you'll be able to tell her,' said Helena, relaxed and happy now.

A slight rumble of conversation was heard. 'Oh! To your places, it's show time!' This was said by a wonderfully camp jeweller whose pieces made even Helena's abstemious heart beat faster. He was as kind as he was camp and had made Helena feel extremely welcome.

Helena greeted her first potential customer, hoping she didn't have flaky pastry down her front. She had dressed up for this occasion, put on make-up and tonged her hair into fat curls that fell over her shoulder: she didn't want the effect spoiled by a moment of carelessness.

She and Amy had made her stall look great. The loom, which was already threaded with the beginnings of a scarf on it, was now assembled. It was the centrepiece, and all around hung her creations. She put the big mohair blankets destined for World of Wool at the back. They were monochrome but the shades were vibrant, bright yet subtle, and made a very colourful background to her more subtle and vastly more expensive silk scarves.

'What a lovely stall!' said the woman. 'I love your scarves! I am a bit addicted,' she went on. 'My husband says I have the largest collection of them in private hands. How he would know, I have no idea.' She frowned. 'Unless he found my private stash of them under the spare bed.'

The woman didn't add to her collection by buying one but she took a card and promised to keep an eye on her website. Helena was grateful she'd remembered to bring her cards as she nearly always forgot. They were important, Amy was always telling her. Although she made most of her money through weaving workshops, she did sell things online.

But a member of the second group of people did buy a scarf and draped it round her neck. It looked stunning on the woman's rather formal black jacket, giving it the lift it needed.

'What's so good about these scarves,' the woman said while Helena was processing the purchase, 'is that they do for men and women.'

Helena smiled as she handed the woman her receipt. 'True.'

'And what's good about that is,' the woman went on, 'a woman can buy it for her husband — men are always so hard to buy for — and then wear it herself if he doesn't appreciate it.' She looked down at the scarf. 'In fact — can you wrap this up for me after all? Alexis has a birthday next week. That makes the scarf practically free!'

★ ★ ★

'Do you want a quick whizz round the other stalls?' asked one of Helena's neighbours an hour or so later. 'My friend has come and can mind my stall and it's a shame not to see what other people produce.'

'Oh, that is very kind! I was expecting my mother but she's coming with my brother and his wife and they're obviously delayed. I'd appreciate a trip to the loo as well. If you're sure.'

After a quick chat with Amy, whose stall was right up the other end, Helena took her tour of the show.

There were some exquisite things to see. Even if one wasn't intending to buy anything, just seeing the skill and beauty of the items made it very worthwhile for visitors. It could be a museum of the future, Helena thought.

There was a furniture maker who was an artist in marquetry. His jewellery boxes were like puzzles, full of secret drawers with hidden springs. She instantly thought about Ismene. She would love one of these boxes and she was so difficult to buy for. Helena considered for a few minutes and then, although the boxes were way above her normal budget for presents, chose a small oval box. There was a picture of a running horse and the secret compartment was very well concealed. While she would never be able to spend so much on her niece, Gilly, the ultimate indulgent grandmother, would have no trouble.

Having taken up time buying the box, Helena hurried past a violin maker, a glass blower (although not blowing currently) and a ceramicist.

Her purchase having been admired and approved by Jennifer, who'd been minding her stall, Helena said, 'The standard here is really high, isn't it? I was so lucky to get in.'

'But your work is lovely,' said Jennifer. 'I sold two of your blankets while you were away. Cash sales, thank goodness.' She handed Helena a wodge of notes.

'Oh, thank you! I'm only here because someone else dropped out.'

'Was that the woman who made garden ornaments?' asked Venetia from two stalls down. 'Rather a second-rate artisan if I may say so.'

Helena laughed. 'As long as you don't call me that the moment my back is turned.'

'Of course not!' said Venetia, horrified. 'Your work is of the highest standard! I'm talking casts

184

of gnomes with wheelbarrows and unfortunately placed fishing rods. From the back they looked horribly vulgar.' She bit her lip. 'They were quite funny though.'

Reassured, Helena smiled. 'Oh! Here's my mother.'

'Will she be bringing more snacks?' said Jennifer.

'Quite likely. As I said, she is a feeder.'

'Excellent. Anything she wants to buy from me she can have at a discount.'

But Helena's initial pleasure at seeing her mother, who was with her brother and sister-in-law, was dimmed when she spotted Leo marching across to join the party. He kissed her mother's cheek and stood beside her while they waited for a gap in the throng.

Honestly, thought Helena, how many times did she have to tell her mother he was a not a good person? But then she noted that her mother didn't look at all happy about his possessive attitude and guessed Leo's presence was something to do with her brother. She wondered whether, if she told Martin what a bad lot Leo was, he'd stop being his friend. But Martin was quite likely to say, 'I'll make my own judgements about people, thank you,' and carry on as before.

★ ★ ★

Usually Gilly was delighted when Martin showed any interest in Helena's work. However, today, she'd have very much preferred to go early, on

185

her own, help Helena for a bit, and then go home when she felt she was no longer useful. She hadn't heard back from William and now felt foolish for having invited him. Cressida even tried to make her leave behind the box of snacks she'd made.

'Does she need the empty calories?' she'd asked, eyeing Gilly's basket critically as they got in the car. 'Biscuits are just an evil combination of sugar and fat and Helena already has a sedentary occupation.'

'Yes, she does need them,' said Gilly, possibly more sharply than she'd intended. 'And she may want to share them with people.'

'Put the basket in the boot, then,' said Cressida.

'It's fine on my knee. Do you mind if I go in front? I have a slight tendency to car sickness if I'm not driving.' She kept the cool bag with three bottles of Prosecco near her too. Cressida was sure to disapprove of that.

Thus, she had managed to annoy her daughter-in-law before they were hardly out of the house. Usually she avoided it but just occasionally she couldn't resist asserting herself, just a little.

Cressida and Martin spent the journey to the exhibition discussing the benefits of private education, not Gilly's favourite topic. Her ex-husband's parents, who liked to be known as Gan-gan and Pops, cheery names that completely belied their very formal way with their grandchildren, had gone on about private education a lot. They seemed to think that Martin and Helena would have hugely benefited from being sent to 'a jolly good boarding school where they'll make friends who'll be useful to them all their lives'.

Martin, rashly in Gilly's opinion, referred to this now. 'Dad's parents were always sad we weren't privately educated, I know that.'

'Yes,' said Gilly, 'they were of the opinion we should sell the house — my house — and live in a hovel to fund your private education. But that's not the route you're going down, is it? Mind you, I think you're absolutely right! Education isn't only what goes on in school hours; at least half of it goes on in the home. In my opinion.'

Gilly spent the rest of the journey looked pointedly out of the window. No one said anything else until Cressida noticed an AA sign to the venue.

'It must be quite a big deal, this show,' she said. 'Good for Helena, getting in.'

Gilly softened towards her daughter-in-law by a millimetre.

★ ★ ★

Gilly was buying tickets when Leo came up to her, full of bonhomie and no sign of awkwardness. He kissed her cheek. 'This is such a lovely occasion, supporting Helena as a family.'

She was too polite to say, 'You're not my family,' so instead she murmured, 'Hello, Leo,' and smiled faintly. 'I didn't know you were coming.' Helena wouldn't be pleased to see him, even if he was trying to be supportive.

'Cressida suggested I came, said how pleased

187

you'd be if I did. Are you pleased, Gilly?'

'Of course,' she said, 'if you buy one of Helena's scarves.' She really hoped that he would buy one and not think she'd be pleased for any other reason. She wished she'd heard definitely if William was coming or not. But with Leo here, she'd rather he didn't. Her life suddenly seemed rather complicated.

At last they were at Helena's stall. When Cressida and Martin had said hello, Gilly kissed her daughter and handed over the box and the cool bag.

'Oh, thank you, Mum! My new friends are addicted to your baking. The savouries went down so well this morning.'

'Well, now it's a bit later in the day you can have a glass of Prosecco to go with the snacks,' said Gilly.

'Hello, Helena,' said Leo warmly. 'I thought I'd come and give you some support. Not that it looks like you need it.'

Helena's smile was a little tight. 'It has been really busy.'

'You don't seem to have a lot of stock,' went on Leo. 'I gather it was all rather short notice so maybe you didn't have time to make enough?'

'I did have loads of stock,' said Helena, 'but I've sold a lot of it. I've had to ask if some people can leave their purchases until the end of the day so other people can see examples of my work.'

'Goodness me! I was going to buy something for your mother but I may be too late.'

'It's OK,' said Helena, obviously making an

188

effort, 'I give her anything she takes a fancy to. Now will you excuse me? There's a gentleman . . . '

Gilly took a step back and watched Helena do her thing with a man who seemed very interested. She gave him a business card and he gave her one back. It would be good if that meant he'd commissioned a scarf. Leo wasn't going to order one, she realised.

Gilly stepped forward when Helena was free to talk again. 'Would you like me to take over for a bit? Give you a chance to look around?'

'I had a look around this morning, but a loo break would be good.'

Leo insisted on standing next to her while Gilly stood in for Helena and she wished she could ask him to go away. Eventually she saw William trying to push his way towards Helena's stall. He was quite a way away. If she was quick she should be able to get rid of Leo. 'Leo! Would you be very kind and get us some tea? Then we can have a piece of shortbread? I didn't have much lunch.'

'If that's what you want,' he said fondly, and kissed the top of her head.

She moved away from him, feeling horribly patronised. Then she looked up and felt even worse. William had stopped and was looking at her, confusion on his face. He had obviously seen Leo's possessive gesture and didn't know what to think.

She tried to smile reassuringly but it was difficult to say, 'I didn't invite this man, I didn't want him to kiss my head, it's you I'm interested

189

in,' in a gesture like a smile, however hard you tried.

William raised a hand in greeting and then turned back. Gilly felt bereft.

Cressida and Martin came up. 'Are you OK staying for a bit, Gilly?' said Cressida. 'There is some amazing stuff here! There's a handbag over there that has my name on it. I might persuade Martin I need an early birthday present.'

After they had gone and Helena had come back, Gilly told her where Martin and Cressida were headed.

Helena raised her eyebrows. 'There's nothing on that stall that is cheaper than a month's mortgage payments. I'm glad they're feeling so flush. The man who makes the leather belts is so nice and I'd love to buy something from him, but I just can't. Oh, I did buy something that you might like to give Issi for a present though. It's way above my budget but knowing how generous you are . . . '

Gilly looked at the little box that Helena put into her hand. 'It's amazing! I love it! And it's perfect for Issi. I must go and have a look at the other stalls. Would you be all right here for a moment?'

'Absolutely! Take the shortbread; it may get you a discount.'

'Oh, here's Leo with the tea,' said Gilly, suddenly very depressed.

'Ooh,' said Helena. 'I must just pop over to George with the shortbread. I forgot he brought me a cup of coffee earlier, I promised him something if you brought food.'

190

Gilly recognised a quick excuse to get out of the way when she saw one but was grateful. Leo and Helena together would have made her extremely uncomfortable.

'Sorry it took so long,' said Leo when he arrived. 'There was an enormous queue and then I met some people I know and couldn't get away.'

'That always happens to me,' said Gilly, taking the polystyrene cup. The tea in it was tepid, but she drank it anyway. She realised that Helena would be opening the Prosecco soon and she might well miss the opportunity to share it.

'And I hope you won't be disappointed,' said Leo, 'but I'm afraid I've got to go. I was intending to stay a bit longer, but something has come up.'

Relief made Gilly smile warmly. 'Oh no, don't worry about it. It was lovely of you to come at all.' 'You'll give my love to Helena, won't you? Tell her how much I like her scarves.'

'Absolutely,' said Gilly warmly, ignoring the thought that if he liked them so much he could have bought one.

Helena reappeared the moment Leo had gone. 'If you really like him, Mum, I will make an effort. It's just seeing him gives me flashbacks to that time we nearly died.'

Gilly was aware her daughter really meant 'the time Leo nearly killed us'. 'I don't like him but Cressida and Martin seem to adore him! It wasn't my idea to invite him to this.' She omitted to mention William; Helena had enough to think about. 'I should have asked him for a lift home

191

really, but I couldn't bring myself to. He'd have taken it as encouragement.'

'We could tell Martin to hurry up,' said Helena. 'I will if you'd rather not.'

Gilly was well aware that Helena thought that Martin and Cressida bullied her a bit and her daughter wasn't entirely wrong.

'Or Jago could do it!' said Helena. 'I'm sure he wouldn't mind. I know he's only coming to support me. I gave him one of my free tickets. This is such a brilliant event,' she went on. 'I've earned far more than my entrance fee although I have also sold practically everything I've made so God knows what I'll have to take to Woolly World at the end of the month.'

'I could always give you back all the rugs and throws you've made for me over the years. Not that I don't love them but — '

'Brilliant idea, Mum! I can remake them for you after the show! Oh, and here's Jago.'

As Jago drove Gilly home in Helena's car she thought what a nice man he was. Why did she think there was something a bit odd going on between him and Helena? They should be all over each other. Still, she decided, maybe she should sort her own love life out before starting on her daughter's.

20

The show was over and everyone was packing up when Jago reappeared.

'Hi! A mate was coming back this way so I thought I'd drop your car at home and get a lift back with him. I thought you might like a hand clearing up. Where's all your stock?'

'Sold! But, Jago, that's so kind! After you've taken Mum home and everything — to come all the way back to help me with this lot.' Helena gestured to the loom and other bits of equipment she had used to dress her stall.

''S OK. It's what mates are for,' said Jago. He started dismantling the loom which, as he'd helped her assemble it when she first decided to move into weaving with silk, he knew how to do.

'But you must let me take you out to dinner, in return,' said Helena firmly. 'I've done so well today, it's the least I can do for you.'

'I was going to have to knock up something out of leftovers for us, so I'm well up for eating out.'

She smiled. 'Anywhere you fancy?'

'There's a gastro pub I've read reviews of. It's a bit off our patch so it would be nice to go there while we're over this way.'

'Great! If you know where it is, I'm happy to go.'

'I'll drive, then you can drink.'

She paused, a large plastic box in her hands.

'You didn't come all the way over here so you could drive the pickup and not risk it with me for any longer than you had to?'

'No,' he said shortly. 'I have many faults but I am not possessive about my pickup. You drive it as well as I do.'

Helena's heart warmed to him another bit. At this rate she'd be in love with him before the summer.

They found the pub without too much difficulty and went into the bar. 'If we don't like what's on the menu, we don't have to stay,' said Jago.

'I think we will like what's on the menu,' said Helena, looking at it. 'It's got chips on it and I think after my long day I deserve some.'

'Then you shall have chips!' said Jago. 'And a large steak to go with them?' He inspected the menu carefully. 'You can have sweet potato chips instead if you like.'

'Nooo! Nothing wrong with sweet potatoes but if I'm having chips, I want proper ones.'

They had ordered and Helena was sipping a large glass of red wine when she looked across at a table and then leaned forward so she could speak to Jago privately.

'I recognise those two men over there,' she murmured, shifting her chair so she wasn't facing them. 'One ordered a scarf from me today — didn't catch his name but I've got his card and I know exactly what scarf he wants — and the other . . . ' She laughed. 'Although you would never guess, he has recently run a half-marathon with his colleagues.' She frowned.

194

'Or maybe he was just in the photograph with the runners. It was in the local paper.'

'So you don't know these people in real life, you just recognise them with your superpowers?'

'No, the first one I met.' She found her handbag and burrowed about in it until she came up with a card. 'Here you are! It's him.'

Jago took the card and then at Helena. 'Really?'

'Yes. Do you know him?'

'Of him. We're in the same business only he's a massive company and I'm a one-man band.'

'You mean you couldn't afford one of my scarves?' Instantly she began planning the design for one she'd make as a present for him. She took another sip of her wine. It was delicious, and she was glad Jago had led them here. 'How was Mum when you drove her home?'

'She was her usual charming self but she did seem a bit twitchy. When I asked if she'd enjoyed the show she said it would have been better if she could have driven herself there and was annoyed she didn't just change the date for her car being serviced.'

'Oh!' said Helena. 'Martin always arranges for her car to be serviced. Since the divorce. Cars are a blue job, you know. Women can't ring up a garage and make an appointment to have one serviced.'

'Really?'

'Mum indulges him because it's the only thing he does that's remotely helpful and she doesn't want to undermine him.'

'So, what's all this colour-coded job thing?'

'Cressida thinks it's simpler for men if jobs have colours. Blue and pink. Cars are blue, doing the online grocery order is pink. Don't get ideas of it going on between us. I prefer everything to be mauve.'

'Which means?'

'Whoever has time and thinks of it, does it.' She paused. 'It seems to work OK, doesn't it?'

She looked at him, wondering how he felt about her, whether he felt anything beyond friendship. They — well, he — had come up with the idea of pretending to be an item because it suited them but supposing one of them, i.e. her, wanted to change? To stop pretending? Because she did want them to be a real couple, who touched, who slept together.

Annoyingly they hadn't added a clause to their casual arrangement which told them how to deal with this situation. Supposing now, her inhibitions softened by wine and tiredness, she reached her hand across the table and put it on his large, roughened, very slightly hairy one? Would he get her unspoken message? And if he did would he look slightly horrified and embarrassed? Say, 'You're a lovely girl but I've never seen you like that?' Or something similar.

Helena decided she would die of embarrassment if this happened and took another sip of wine.

'I think you need another one of those,' said Jago. 'And here comes the food. Those chips look amazing! Can we have some mayo to go with those?' he asked the waitress. 'Thank you so much!'

The food was as good as it looked and Helena crunched her way through it, too tired to talk much. That was one of the many joys of Jago: he was perfectly happy to be silent. When she'd finished her steak she felt a lot better.

'Now, pudding,' she said. 'I'm paying and I'm insisting. I won't feel I've taken you out for dinner if you only have one course and no alcohol.'

'Oh, right! I'll hop up and get the menu.' Having done this he perused it. 'I think steam pudding with custard, cream and ice cream.'

'I'll join you!' said Helena, feeling bold and a bit anxious. 'I sort of wish Cressida was here.'

'Really?'

'She'd be so utterly horrified! And although I know it's childish of me, I do quite like horrifying her.'

He laughed. 'I know what you mean. I can't resist shocking my sister either.'

'Oh? How's Zuleika and her kitten?'

'The kitten is growing rapidly and is hardly ever out of trouble, apparently. My sister is going to keep her.'

Helena smiled. She had reason to be very grateful to that kitten. Without it her first meeting with Jago would have been very different.

'So,' Jago said, after several spoonfuls of pudding, which included fresh raspberries and was very much lighter than its title suggested it might be. 'What are you going to do with yourself now this show is over? You've worked so hard!'

Helena gave a laugh that was almost a sigh of

197

exhaustion. 'I'm going to work even harder! I've sold every blessed scarf, rug, throw and cushion cover, lots of it destined for the big World of Wool show at the end of the month. It's going to be pretty much impossible to restock in time.'

'Oh, Helly!' said Jago, putting his hand on her shoulder. 'I didn't realise.'

'Mum suggested that she give me back everything I'd ever given her which is something. I'll ask Cressida for her stuff too, but it's not going to be that much.'

'Can I make a suggestion? I'm not any kind of an artist or creative person but could you do something weird, huge, that wouldn't take you long? Weaving with rags, that sort of thing?'

'I'm not a massive fan of rag weaving but I could think along those lines, cutting up blankets and using them.' Her imagination was sparked. 'I've got some blankets that got terribly eaten by moths. I should have thrown them away but I put them in Mum's freezer instead. I could use those!'

Jago smiled, clearly pleased to have had the original idea.

'After all,' Helena went on, 'although obviously they'd have to be up to standard, I wouldn't have to love them. As long as I had, say, three . . . wall hangings perhaps?'

'With 'found objects' woven into them?'

'If I was desperate,' said Helena. 'I have always insisted on things being functional.'

'Wall hangings are functional if they're hiding an unsightly wall,' said Jago. He paused. 'Are you going to finish your pudding?'

'Not if I can avoid it. I feel a bit sick. Please . . . ' She pushed her bowl towards him. 'Go for it!'

She gave a massive yawn as he put down his spoon. 'Come on, let's get you home,' he said. 'You're dead on your feet.'

'Dead in my chair,' she corrected him but smiled. Even if they were just friends it was lovely to be with someone who looked out for her. 'I'll just go and pay the bill.'

She almost fell out of the pickup when they got home. 'Do you mind if I leave things here in the back, or do you need it first thing?'

'Don't you worry about it. I'll put it under cover in case it rains, but you get to bed.'

She set aside her concerns about keeping their relationship platonic and went to him with her arms open for a hug. He hugged her back, very hard, and it was lovely. 'You've done so well today, Helly,' he said. 'I'm so proud of you!'

She didn't quite know how to respond to this. 'And I'm so grateful to you, you've been brilliant, feeding me, looking after me, making it possible to work ridiculous hours.' A thought of how resentful her father had been of anything her mother did that didn't involve him floated through her mind. 'And now I've got to do it all again!'

'But you will. You'll do something amazing. Because you're amazing. Now go in. I'll bring you in a mug of hot chocolate and a hot-water bottle shortly.'

'I can't believe you've got a hot-water bottle,' she said, utterly amazed at the thought.

'I borrowed one from your mum when I dropped her off earlier. She was quite surprised when I asked but totally understood when I explained why. She gave me a hug.'

'That is so sweet! Now I'll have a quick shower and then bed.'

The hot-water bottle was in her bed and the mug of chocolate on the tea chest that was her bedside table by the time she was out of the shower. She realised that if she hadn't fancied Jago at all she'd still want to marry him and bear his children. And she did fancy him. A lot.

21

Helena was somewhat surprised to find a text from Cressida asking her over when she finally opened her eyes the following morning. She really needed to get on with her work but as she was still bone-tired and wanted to ask Cressida for the blankets and throws given to her over the years, she decided to go.

She did take the time to attack her hair with straighteners before she went, though, having gone to bed with it wet. She didn't want to arrive looking like one of those dogs who have dreadlocks.

She finished her breakfast and had a banana — there was no guarantee of biscuits, or indeed anything, at Cressida's house. She planned to visit her mother on the way home. Knowing how many blankets she could come up with before she started would give her courage to jump into another killing work schedule.

Cressida was unusually friendly when she opened the door to Helena. 'Helena! Come in! I'm so glad you had time to come round, but I just wanted to tell you how amazing the show was! I've never seen so many truly beautiful things in one place before. Come in! I've got the coffee on. Martin has taken Ismene to a museum — it's their Sunday treat if we're not doing anything else.'

Not only was there coffee, but there were

gluten-, dairy-, sugar — and taste-free biscuits on offer. Helena was suspicious. Surely all this wasn't because Cressida had liked the show? Although she knew she would like it — high-end, expensive and impeccable quality, it was perfect for Cressida's aesthetic taste.

'Well, this is very nice,' she said, hearing her mother's voice in hers.

Cressida gave a self-conscious little cough. 'You've probably guessed, Helena, that I haven't just asked you here to congratulate you on your show — which was fantastic.'

'Yes?'

'I'm a bit worried about Gilly.'

Guilt came over Helena like a fog. She had been so immersed in her work that she hadn't been paying any real attention to her mother, beyond accepting meals and biscuits. 'Why?'

Cressida pursed her lips and searched for words — unlike her, who usually knew exactly what she wanted to say and said it. 'I don't know if you're aware, but Gilly's been romantically involved with Leo.'

Helena nodded. She did know this — or rather — she had known it, but now she thought it was over.

'I think Gilly senses you're not entirely happy about it which is probably why she hasn't confided in you.' Cressida managed to imply that Gilly had confided in her, which Helena very much doubted.

'Go on,' said Helena, trying to appear dispassionate.

'The thing is, I know it's difficult when it's

your mother, but this could be her last chance of happiness. Leo is really lovely and has an amazing house. She's not getting any younger and having seen that having a new life with a gorgeous man is possible, you mustn't snatch the dream away from her.'

'I would never do that.' At least this was something that Helena could say with total sincerity.

'Please tell her she has your blessing! She's been behaving strangely lately. You've been so busy you may not have noticed.'

Guilt swamped her again. 'I have been working all hours getting ready for this show.'

'I know! And please don't think I'm judging you, but we're family and if you can't look out for your mum then I will. And I have!'

'I'm very grateful,' muttered Helena, feeling anything but gratitude.

'And I don't know if you know this, but she said something about going gliding.'

'Gliding!'

'I know!' said Cressida. 'I was horrified too. Imagine Gilly doing anything like that! Even hearing her talking about it was worrying. To be honest, she'd be better off with a man to take care of her.'

Helena may have wanted to keep things between her and Cressida civilised but she could not swallow this. 'That's not very feminist of you! Besides, she's looked after herself perfectly well up to now.'

'You have to remember', said Cressida, as if confiding a great secret, 'that women's bodies change. Hormones kick in and we can go crazy.'

Cressida said this in a way that made Helena absolutely confident that this would never happen to her sister-in-law. The way Cressida had said 'crazy' indicated a lack of control that was physiologically impossible for her. Her hormones were far too well disciplined.

Remembering she had a favour to ask meant Helena bit back any protest.

'I'll go and see her, but, Cressida, although I am so grateful you've been looking out for Mum for me, I do have another favour to ask you. It's a bit of a funny one.'

'Oh?'

To give herself confidence Helena imagined her sister-in-law doing a Tough Mudder — something that physically she'd be more than capable of, but would she be able to get covered in sludge to prove her fitness? Possibly not.

Helena cleared her throat. 'This is a really odd request. You know I sold absolutely everything I had in the show yesterday?'

'I didn't know but that's really good, isn't it?'

'Well, yes, but I've got another show coming up really soon and absolutely nothing to put in it. Mum suggested she gives me back all the blankets and throws and things I've ever given her, just so I've got something to display. I was wondering if you'd give me back the ones I've given you, too? I can put 'sold' stickers on them if you're really fond of them, but otherwise I'll replace them when I can.'

A strange look tweaked at Cressida's features, an expression strangely like embarrassment,

204

which was not an emotion that often touched her life. 'I'm afraid I had a big Marie Kondo session, Helena, and I found they didn't spark joy. They went to the charity shop.'

Helena caught her breath. 'Was this recently? Is there any chance I could buy them back?'

Cressida shook her head. 'It was when Marie's book first came out, so no.'

Somehow Helena got herself to the door and out of it, muttering conventional thanks as she went. But inside she felt kicked in the stomach. And when she'd stopped feeling quite so offended she felt angry about the waste. From now on she resolved to only give Cressida and Martin boxes of chocolates (Milk Tray for preference) as presents. Nothing she'd put any effort into.

She'd calmed down a bit by the time she'd got to Fairacres and was determined to find out what was going on with her mother. She was still feeling terribly guilty for ignoring her — or at least only eating her food but not actually paying attention. Was Gilly really in love with Leo? And what was all this about going gliding? Her mother would never do that! But first and foremost, she had to tell her mother about Cressida's despicable action.

★ ★ ★

Gilly heard Helena come in through the back door and came downstairs, a bundle of dirty linen in her arms. 'Hi, darling, how are you? You did so brilliantly yesterday! I was so impressed!'

205

They went into the kitchen, and Gilly put on the kettle for coffee.

'So what are you grumpy about?' asked Gilly when Helena had pulled out a chair and sat down.

'Cressida!'

Gilly felt slightly anxious. She hated it when her daughter was at odds with her daughter-in-law. She was also a bit worried about what Cressida might have said to Helena about Leo.

'What?'

'She Marie Kondoed all the woven things I've given her over the years! They didn't 'spark joy'.'

'Oh, Helly! Don't say she 'regifted' them?'

This made Helena smile. 'I know how much you hate that expression but what she did was worse!'

'Is that even possible?'

'Yes! She gave them all to charity and she did it ages ago so I can't even buy them back. Don't you think that's rude?'

'It is really horrible to have a present you've thought about, and in your case made, but I suppose if they didn't fit in with her decor . . .'

'I knew you'd stick up for her! And to be honest, if I didn't need them I probably wouldn't be so upset.'

'Well, you've given me loads of lovely things over the years and I've still got them all, and most of them have escaped the moths. Although one or two blankets are . . . ' She paused, choosing her words. 'Early work.'

'Oh, that's fine!' said Helena. 'Jago had a

206

brilliant idea. I should cut up the 'early' or moth-eaten work and weave wall hangings from them. They'd be quick to do. I told him I liked things to be functional but he said a wall hanging was functional if it was hiding something unsightly.'

'I do like Jago,' said Gilly. 'He was so sweet to me yesterday — and asking to borrow a hot-water bottle! Adorable!'

'He is really kind, and a great housemate. Although if my next show goes as well as this one did, I'll be able to afford my own place.'

'Aren't you living together as a couple then? That's lovely and old-fashioned of you.'

Helena looked discomforted. 'Well, I want to pay my way. I don't want to just latch on to Jago . . .'

There was definitely something odd going on. Gilly resolved to find out more.

'Here's your coffee,' she said. 'You must be so tired after the show.'

'I am. Too tired to be creative really, so I'm taking the day off.' Helena looked at her mother intently and Gilly realised she'd missed her moment. Helena was going to interrogate her and not the other way round. 'Cressida said she was worried about you.'

'Why? I promise there is absolutely nothing wrong with me. I've never felt fitter.' She paused. 'I think I may have lost a bit of weight — although of course I never weigh myself.'

'You look great, Mum. I don't think it was your physical health she was worried about.'

'That's even worse! Has she caught me talking

207

to myself? Surely everyone does that.'

Helena began to giggle. 'No, nothing like that! And yes, everyone does talk to themselves — or at least I do. No, she said — and honestly I don't believe this but although she has her faults I don't think Cressida lies — she said you'd talked about going gliding.'

Gilly joined in the giggling, hoping it would disguise her blush. 'What is Cressida like?'

'I knew she was talking rubbish,' Helena went on before Gilly had worked out what to say. 'She's more worried about you and Leo.' Helena took a breath. 'She's worried that because I don't like him you feel you can't go out with him. She says he's your last chance of happiness and I mustn't blight the relationship.'

'Cressida is talking out of the back of her neck,' said Gilly firmly. 'She's convinced there's something going on between me and Leo, but there isn't.'

'Oh. Well, that's a relief! I would have done my absolute best to live with it if you and he really were in love, but I'm very glad I don't have to.'

'You don't have to,' said Gilly firmly.

'But Cressida says Leo might be your last chance of happiness.'

Helena obviously needed more convincing. 'Darling, if I feel lonely, I'll just go on Kinder and find a new man. Or is Kinder what I read books on?' Gilly was slightly worried that she may have overdone the dotty-old-lady act.

But as this sent Helena into further fits of giggles she knew it was all right. 'Don't worry, Mum, I'd never let you go on Tinder, you'd

208

never know if you had to swipe left or right.'

But after Helena had gone Gilly found herself wondering how she'd feel if Helena didn't like William. Would it be as easy for her to think she'd have to give him up because of her daughter? No, she decided, it wouldn't be easy at all. And she might not even try.

22

Gilly had been making beds, baking shortbread, picking posies and organising laundry for what seemed like every hour of every day since Helena's show. And while she liked to be busy she was tired. Also, although she was physically occupied from dawn to well past dusk her brain was free to worry about William.

When she'd first met Leo she'd been a bit swept off her feet. He was so stylish and charming, had treated her like a queen, and taken her to lovely places. But when she started to get to know William better she'd realised how much nicer, kinder and, now she came to think about it, more attractive than Leo he was. William was the quiet horse that came up on the outside without being noticed until he was at the finish line. But was he still interested in winning this particular race? How would she ever find out?

If only he hadn't seen her with Leo she could just invite him round for a meal or something. In fact, she was fairly sure, if he hadn't seen her with Leo he would have been in touch himself. But she didn't have the courage to email him and tell him she and Leo were not together when he may not have actually been looking at them at the show; he could have been looking at something quite different.

She wished she was braver. Gilly was sure

Helena wouldn't worry about things like that; she'd just email William and explain.

Thinking about Helena didn't help her either. What was going on between her and Jago? He was such a lovely man, she would be so sad if there was something dreadfully wrong with him that made him ineligible in some way.

A thought occurred to her. Could he be gay? It wouldn't be a thing that was *wrong* with him of course but it did make him unsuitable for Helena! It didn't seem terribly likely, but Gilly didn't trust her gaydar; was his sensitive caring of Helena something you could expect from a man who was heterosexual? Possibly not! Hot-water bottles were just a little bit camp, after all, however much everyone loved them.

But even if he wasn't going to be the father of her grandchildren, Jago was still a lovely man and a very good friend to Helena. She found the thought of Helena having a gay best friend comforting.

She was still musing about Jago's sexuality while she made yet another batch of shortbread, wondering at the same time if she had in fact got bored with making the same biscuit time after time, when the phone rang. Slightly hoping it wasn't another booking — she could do with a few days off — she went to answer it.

'Darling? Daphne here! How are you?'

'I'm fine, Daphne. How lovely to hear from you, and how are you?' Gilly wiped her hands on her apron.

'In the pink, sweetie, absolutely in the pink. Now, I've got a plan.'

'Sounds a bit worrying.' Gilly really hoped that if the plan meant her B & B being taken over by a lot of unruly women, she would have time to prepare properly.

Daphne ignored Gilly's wary response. 'It's William's birthday soon.'

'Oh?'

'Yes, and you know something? He's never had a party! Not ever, in all his life. So I thought I'd organise one.'

'What took you so long? He must be in his fifties,' said Gilly.

'I just assumed his parents were in charge of that sort of thing but no. I have to do it now!'

'OK, well, anything I can do to help . . . ?' She briefly wondered if she should offer to have the party in her house but then decided it would look pushy. If William didn't fancy her it would be awful — for him and for her.

'Well, you can come, and — if it wouldn't be too much trouble — make a cake? I'm sure I could get someone else to make one but I thought you'd make a much nicer one.'

'Of course! I'd be happy to. What sort of cake do you think he'd like? Sponge? Fruit? Chocolate?'

'Actually what he'd really love is one in the shape of a glider. It's his hobby, you know.'

This was a bit of a shock. 'I'd been thinking of a nice chocolate sponge with his name on it in white buttercream? Perhaps some candles?'

'Yes, a glider made out of chocolate sponge would be brilliant! Thank you so much, Gilly. I knew I could rely on you.'

Gilly's murmured appreciation of Daphne's faith was a bit half-hearted.

'It's going to be a surprise party, you know,' Daphne went on.

'Oh!' Gilly's protective instincts broke through her desire to seem helpful and supportive at all times. 'Are you sure he'd like that? I mean, not everyone has the temperament for a surprise party.' She'd been to a couple when the person was obviously not at all happy to have their friends jump out from behind bushes when they were unprepared and not wearing their make-up. 'William is quite . . . sensitive?' That wasn't the right word; it made him sound like a poet. 'I mean, he's got a quiet personality. There's nothing of the showman about him.'

'It'll be fine! Don't you worry. He'll be delighted. You just get that cake made.'

'You haven't given me a date?'

'Oh, sorry! Tuesday next week OK for you?'

'Yes,' said Gilly faintly.

'And I'm arranging a minibus to pick everyone up so no one has to worry about drinking and driving.'

Although she hadn't said as much, Gilly sensed that Daphne felt it was a bit silly to worry about drinking and driving.

'Great!' Maybe she could get the cake to the venue beforehand. Otherwise she'd be stuck in the back of a minibus with the cake on her knees. If it hadn't had to be a glider she could have put the cake in the special container she'd bought from a party years ago and had used at least twice. As it was, it would be more complicated.

213

'So I'll be back with all the details soon,' said Daphne. 'Lovely to chat to you! Byeee!'

* * *

Although her response to Daphne's glider cake suggestion hadn't been one of overwhelming joy, Gilly was a little excited at the prospect. She immediately put 'glider cakes' into her search engine and had a look. When her children were small she used to make amazing cakes in the shapes of pirate ships, ski slopes and mice and they'd always loved them. She really liked William so did he deserve anything less than a cake in the shape of a glider?

She considered ringing Daphne to find out roughly how many the cake was going to have to feed but decided Daphne would probably say something vague and unhelpful. No, she was going to go this alone and make William the best cake he'd ever had. Although going on what Daphne had said about him never having had a party, maybe he'd never had a cake, either? In which case it was bound to be the best one!

After ordering a couple of enormous cake tins from the internet, she made a list for the cash and carry. She added food colouring to the list of normal cake ingredients. And then she sat down and thought about her gliding experience. What had been so magical had been seeing the landscape from above, in the silence, as if one was a bird. Maybe it would be better to recreate the landscape in cake, from a bird's-eye view, and add the glider later?

She looked online again and saw that other cake makers had had this idea. But instead of sitting the glider on the cake, she would suspend it over the cake, from the corner. Yes! She was happy. She'd work out the engineering later.

She rang Helena. 'Hi, darling, I know you're busy but I'm going shopping. Is there anything particular you'd like or shall I just get what I think you need?'

'Oh, Mum! You read my mind! Jago has done all the housekeeping lately and it would be wonderful if I contributed something. I'll pay you back.'

'We'll discuss payment later. Shall I drop it round to you? Or will you pick it up?'

'I'll wait until Jago goes out and then pop over. It'll be nice to have a break and some company.'

★　★　★

But it wasn't until a few days after Gilly had rung that Helena finally got over to see her. She knew her mother would have put everything in the fridge and possibly made a lasagne or something as well. With garlic bread. She was also looking forward to a long hot bath in her mother's bathroom, with her mother's bath products. Washing arrangements in Jago's house were still a bit primitive.

Although she had kept up her rate of work since the Springtime Show, she was beginning to lose hope that she'd have enough work to fill a stall respectably at the World of Wool. She had a

215

good reputation as a weaver which meant all sorts of people would go to that event just to see what she was doing these days. There'd be fellow weavers, teachers, potential customers and just friends — she had to have enough good work or she might as well phone in sick. This was not something that self-employed artists could ever do! Jago had suggested wall hangings but she found herself completely lacking in inspiration. She wanted to display work she believed in, even if it was different from what she usually did.

She came into her old home through the back door to see her mother frowning at something on the kitchen table. Ulysses, the cat, was shut in his cat basket. As he quite often slept in there through choice this wasn't actually cruel but this time the door was closed. This was unusual. She went over to the kitchen table on which was an enormous cake.

'Mum? What is this? And what is it supposed to be?'

'Can't you tell? I've had to shut Uly up in case his hairs got in it.' Her mother sounded tired and disappointed.

Helena looked at the cake a bit more carefully. 'Oh! I get it now! It's a landscape, from above. And you've put in all the fields and hedges and the river. And the mountains. It's amazing! It's just like when we were little and you made us such brilliant cakes. I love your hedgerows made out of chocolate flakes. I don't like those shop-made cakes that are all smooth and professional but you know they won't taste nice.'

'I'm not a big fondant-icing fan either,' said

Gilly, looking more relaxed now.

'Look!' said Helena. 'There's a little caravan. Do you remember the caravan cake you made me for my Sylvanian Families? And a duck pond! With little ducklings!'

'I did get a bit carried away, I must admit. Once I'd started I couldn't stop adding detail.'

'You are so talented! You should enter *Bake Off*.'

'It's only a cake! Now, find yourself a towel in the airing cupboard and have your bath. I'll make you an omelette when you come down.'

'A Mummy-omelette! Yes please. Jago's out or I'd have brought him round for one, too.'

'Has he gone anywhere nice?' asked Gilly.

'Just a meeting, I think. He didn't seem overjoyed to be going.'

'Oh,' said Gilly. 'You go and have your bath then. I'll see how you're doing before I start cooking.'

Helena gave her mother a hug before going upstairs.

She turned on the taps and went to hunt for a towel in the walk-in airing cupboard. She wanted to find a non-B & B towel so her mother wouldn't have to wash it immediately when something right at the back on the bottom shelf drew her attention. It was a Harrods carrier bag and seeing it brought back a flood of memories. She pulled it out and saw that yes, it did still contain what she thought it did. Several old fleeces, dyed in eye-popping colours, rolled together in a felted mass. She'd forgotten about them but now she remembered the day she'd

217

dyed them, thinking she was going to spin and then weave them. And here they were, in her mother's airing cupboard, as vibrant as they were when they went in.

She got in the bath and lay there, as always her thoughts becoming more creative as the hot water did its work. She thought of her mother's cake — in theory it was a crazy idea but actually, it was lovely. Why didn't she make a wall hanging of a landscape from above? She could use the fleece. She could do another as a cross section of a piece of land, like a piece of cake. (She realised it had been ages since she'd had a good bit of cake!) And the cross section, starting from the bottom up, could show all the strata and layers of the earth ending with a hedge and possibly sky and clouds as the top layer. Once she'd worked out a pattern it should be quick to do. Fleece was lovely and fat! It would take up lots of space.

When she went downstairs later wearing her mother's dressing gown and smelling of her bath products she was excited.

The kitchen was no longer taken up by cake and a sulky Ulysses now sat in front of the range cooker, the end of his tail flicking with resentment.

'Mum — I've had a brilliant idea! I want to borrow your idea of a landscape from above. Wouldn't it be a wonderful wall hanging? And then I thought I'd do a cross section of the earth too. Just a slice, obviously. Once I've worked out what I need to do it'll be quite quick to make, I think.'

218

'Oh?' Gilly held the bread knife over the loaf, waiting for Helena to explain further.

'I found that bag of fleeces I dyed when I was in college. They were in the airing cupboard. Not only are they amazingly bright colours, fleece is really fat — '

' — and so will take up lots of lovely space? Darling, it sounds brilliant. Now, omelette coming up. Why don't you stay the night and then you can have wine with it.'

'And we can watch property porn on telly? I've been working so hard I've hardly had any time off. That would be lovely! I'll just text Jago to tell him not to expect me home.'

It was only after Helena had left following a proper B & B breakfast that she remembered she hadn't asked her mother whom she was making the cake for. 'I'm going to be a better daughter when this show is over,' she said out loud.

23

It was the day of William's surprise party and Gilly was pleased. Everything had gone to plan. The cake looked perfect and she had arranged to deliver it early. All the clothes she planned to wear were clean and none of them needed mending. Even her hair had gone right when she'd washed it the previous day — never a given. Nothing could possibly go wrong.

As Gilly felt that complacency was never a good thing she used her day wisely. She made a shepherd's pie for Helena and Jago (she thought of them as a couple although she was now convinced he was gay) and dusted all the bedrooms. She didn't make up the beds with fresh linen as she was expecting her help, a young woman saving to go travelling, in the morning and it was so much quicker with two. Also, she had to keep reminding herself, the minibus was due to arrive at six thirty, which was quite early. You really couldn't be late for a surprise party, she knew; you had to be there before the surprisee arrived.

It was just before six, when Gilly had had a change of mind about what jewellery she should wear and was in her bedroom inspecting her collection, when the doorbell rang.

Thinking it was a bit bloody early and that she would ask the bus to wait and that her current jewellery would have to do, she opened the door.

Instead of a minibus driver there was an anxious-looking couple in their late seventies. Her heart sank.

'Can I help?' she asked, just in case by some wonderful chance they were simply lost, or their car had broken down.

'We've got here!' said the woman, who seemed near tears. 'There was a time when I thought we never would. We are booked in here for tonight, aren't we?'

Gilly sighed. 'Well, I don't think you are, but never mind. I've got room.'

It took ages to get them settled and then, because they were too tired to go anywhere else, she made them omelettes and settled them in the guest sitting room with the heater and the television on. Ulysses, recognising a couple of cat lovers, had settled on the woman's lap. The minibus had been and gone and now she had to drive to the party as fast as she could and hope she got there before William did.

As no one was hiding when she arrived and the function room was full of people, she realised she was too late. She went straight to the kitchen to find someone in charge.

The cake had been put on the trolley used for wedding cakes; it was being treated with the respect Gilly felt it deserved. It really was a very good cake. And once she had suspended a model glider over the landscape she was entirely satisfied.

'That is an epic cake,' said the venue manager. 'The detail on it is amazing. We've been admiring it all day. If you fancied becoming a professional we would be happy to recommend you to clients.'

'I think I'm happier with an amateur status, thank you,' said Gilly. But she was really thrilled at his reaction.

'There you are!' said Daphne, bustling up in a vision of crushed silk in a bright olive colour that exactly matched the huge glass beads round her neck. 'What happened?'

'I am so sorry, Daphne. Some people turned up on the wrong day and I couldn't turn them away.' She was about to add that they were quite elderly but then realised they were probably the same age as Daphne.

'Oh dear. Poor you. How awkward. And of course you can never turn anyone away. But you have made the most magnificent cake I have ever seen! I can't decide what my favourite bit is. I think it's the tiny swans swimming on the river.' Daphne looked at the cake again. 'And you've added a glider! Much more sophisticated than making one out of cake. I don't know what I was thinking of when I suggested that.'

'I did lots of those sorts of cake for my children when they were little but felt you couldn't recreate the lightness of gliding, the flying sensation, if the wings were made with Victoria sponge.'

Daphne cackled with laughter. 'Excellent! You sound like an artist! Oh, you're wearing odd earrings. Is that a thing or is it a mistake?'

'Definitely a thing,' said Gilly, her hands flying to her ears to check what she was wearing in them. 'It's my artistic rebel streak.'

She wondered if the earrings were different enough from each other to look as if she'd done it on purpose. While she wasn't opposed to people wearing odd earrings, it had to look on purpose and not just an accident. Hers were definitely an accident. Still, most people wouldn't notice, she was sure.

'Right,' said Daphne, 'we'll do the cake. Some of the people here need to rush off.'

As they followed the cake, being pushed on its trolley by the hotel manager, Gilly asked, 'So how did you find out who to invite?'

'I got William's mother to find his address book, which she did and posted to me. I must say it did seem a little bit old but it was all I had to go on so I just invited everyone in it.'

'So his bank manager might be here?' asked Gilly, laughing in spite of trying not to.

'If his bank manager loves William enough to come then he's welcome,' said Daphne. 'Now, here we are!'

Feeling chastened, Gilly moved backwards so she was at the rear of the crowd which was now gathering round the cake. Daphne found William, took hold of his wrist and brought him forward.

Gilly studied him for signs of stress, of being utterly miserable, but he seemed to have risen to the occasion quite well. He always dressed fairly formally so although he might have had to remove his tie to look party-ready, he did look very nice. Very nice indeed, Gilly thought, and realised she was probably biased. She couldn't help wondering what ruse Daphne had come up with to make him come to the hotel.

'Ladies and gentlemen,' said Daphne, 'we are all gathered together to wish this young man a very happy birthday. But before we all make a hideous noise singing one of the dullest tunes in history, I think William would like to make a short speech.'

William looked around him easily, not rushing to speak but acknowledging his guests with a smile. 'I think when my aunt said I would like to make a speech, she really means she thinks I ought to make one. While I'm not one for speeches normally I am very glad of the opportunity to thank you all so much for coming. It is really great to have this chance to catch up with old friends — people I haven't seen for far too long.'

There were cheers and comments that indicated how fond his guests were of William and then there was the obligatory song.

Then Daphne bustled forward again. While she clearly adored William she didn't really like being out of the limelight. 'Now we've got that out of the way, I'd like to draw your attention to this wonderful cake! I think you should all have a good look at it before it's cut.'

It seemed to Gilly, who was suddenly overcome with nerves, that everyone with a phone took a picture of the cake. All she wanted was for William to like it, and maybe to say so. Then she could have a quick drink and slip away.

She reckoned without Daphne.

'Now,' Daphne said, brandishing a large knife she had got from somewhere, 'while this isn't a wedding' — pause for laughter — 'it is an occasion and this magnificent cake, which I think is a work of art, recognises that. And I'd like to introduce you to the wonderful woman who made it. Gilly!'

Gilly's hand was taken and she was dragged to stand in front of the cake next to William. She gave him an apologetic look and received a very amused one in return.

'Right!' said Daphne. 'Cut the cake!'

The cry was taken up. 'Cut the cake, cut the cake!'

Someone a bit more officious than the other guests came up with a proper camera and insisted on posing Gilly and William, both pairs of hands on the knife, looking at the camera before the first slice was cut.

'I am so sorry about this,' said William out of the corner of his mouth. 'This is desperately embarrassing for you.'

'I didn't realise Daphne had organised a photographer.' Gilly was talking out of the side of her mouth too.

'Put your arm round her, William!' called the photographer.

'That isn't an official photographer,' he muttered. 'I rather think he was in the gliding club at university. Haven't seen him for about twenty years.'

'But he came,' said Gilly, remembering what Daphne had said.

'Now could we get you to kiss?' called the old friend from the university gliding club.

Gilly was expecting William to baulk at this but as the crowed joined in with the instruction,

225

'Kiss, kiss,' he put down the cake knife, took hold of her chin and kissed her.

She hardly heard the cheers that welcomed this as she accepted the kiss, which was short but full of intent.

'I hope you don't mind,' said William afterwards. 'Our public demanded it.'

'I don't mind at all,' she said. 'One should never disappoint one's public.'

Daphne was in heaven. 'I am so glad you two have got together! Some people may call me interfering but I call it helping love along!' Then she moved away quickly, possibly sensing she'd gone too far.

'I am so sorry!' said William again. 'I'll go and explain. It's one thing her interfering in my life but she mustn't do it to you. I'll tell her you're with someone else.'

He started to go after Daphne.

It was now or never. Gilly caught hold of his jacket. 'No! Don't! I'm not with anyone.'

William stopped and then turned round slowly. Gilly was in agony, wondering if he would be embarrassed and awkward because he wanted her to be with someone. But when she saw he was smiling her panic subsided. His expression was amused and fond and, she realised, very pleased.

'I'm so glad,' he said. 'Let's go and find a drink. I don't know about you, but I think it's time!'

'Excellent plan!' said Gilly. She could pick up her car tomorrow and go back on the minibus tonight.

When they both had drinks, William went on a

tour of the guests with Gilly at his side. Because they were all friends from a long time ago along with William's fleet of aunts, no one was surprised to see Gilly. It obviously seemed normal that William should have a woman on his arm. A few enquired about the wedding, asking why they hadn't been invited, but William explained that he and Gilly hadn't been together that long. He patted her arm fondly, a bit possessively, and made her feel she was important to him. She realised how much she enjoyed feeling part of a couple after being on her own so long. Yet being with Leo hadn't given her this warm sense of belonging.

'Well, I think we've talked to everyone,' said William after a little while. 'It's time for cake!'

Alert for this moment, a waiter came up with two plates and they found a sofa to sit on while they ate it.

'It really is the most marvellous cake ever,' he said. 'I can't believe I actually know someone who is so clever that they could make something so beautiful and so delicious.'

'Thank you,' said Gilly, pleased. 'I've always felt it shouldn't be a compromise between beauty — well, not exactly beauty, just detail really — and taste.'

'I can't believe anyone would take so much time and trouble to make one for me,' William went on. 'Daphne explained that she'd offered to get it made professionally but that you'd insisted on making it yourself.'

It wasn't quite how Gilly remembered it. Daphne had definitely asked her to make it, but she realised it was all part of Daphne's cunning plan to bring them together. 'I do like making cakes. I haven't done one like this though since my children grew up. Now I just make cakes to serve to my B & B guests, or fundraising events.' She paused. 'Although come to think of it, I do make them for Helena.'

'Not your son?'

Gilly now felt a bit mean. 'His wife isn't a fan of cake.'

'Oh,' said William. 'It must be hard to connect with someone who doesn't like cake. For you, I mean. A fellow non-cake lover would find it easy, I suppose.'

'Shall we have another drink before the minibus arrives to take us all home?' suggested Gilly.

'Yes to the drink, no to the minibus. We'll get a taxi.'

24

William tapped his phone a couple of times and then ordered the taxi. 'Right,' he said. 'Brandy while we wait?'

'Why not?' said Gilly, thinking briefly about the risk of a hangover, before deciding she was enjoying herself so much any repercussions were worth it.

The taxi came and they both fell into the back. William's fingers entwined with hers as they sped through the countryside.

The taxi was obviously part of a fleet used by William as no money changed hands before it drove away. He was by Gilly's side at the front door in seconds.

'Would you like to come in?' asked Gilly, giggling as of course he had no choice.

'Yes please,' said William.

'We'll have to be quiet as I've got B & B guests.'

They entered the hall. 'Would you like another drink or anything? We can talk in the kitchen.' It was only now that the reality of the situation dawned on her. William was here, in her house, without a car between them. Although he could always order another taxi.

'What about your bedroom? Could we talk there?'

'Oh yes.'

'Then we should definitely go upstairs although I don't want to talk.' He paused, giving her time to back out.

She didn't have to think about this; she knew what her answer would be. There was no way she was ready to sleep with William: she didn't know him nearly well enough. Also, the preparation sleeping with him would take! The waxing, the exfoliation, the toenail varnishing — it all had to be done. She hadn't had sex since the last time with her ex-husband, which seemed a very long time ago now. It wasn't something that was possible in a worn PrimaDonna bra and a pair of old Sloggis.

Although she was certain in her mind her body had different ideas. She heard herself say, 'Come on,' and she took his hand.

When they reached her bedroom he shut the door behind them and took her into his arms. They kissed for a very long time.

'I'm so glad I had the brandy,' Gilly whispered as William undid her top. 'Or I'd never have the nerve to do this.'

'It'll be fine,' said William. 'Trust me. I'm your accountant.'

As the night drew on Gilly had time to wonder if the characteristics that made William such a good accountant also made him a good lover. Meticulous attention to detail, finding sweet spots in unexpected places, not giving up until every area was attended to.

It was a wrench when, before it was even light, William got up and said he had to go.

'The trouble with surprise parties midweek is that they don't always happen at a time suitable for the person the party is given for,' he said. 'I have a meeting at the other end of the county and I have to go home and get ready.'

'I wasn't sure you'd like a surprise party,' said Gilly, watching him put on his clothes. 'I think they're a bit Marmite — they work for some but others hate them.'

William came back to the bed and kissed her. 'I absolutely loved it!' he said.

★   ★   ★

Gilly was down early, ready to make breakfast for her B & B guests whenever they appeared. Usually she would try to get some sort of idea of when they might want to get up the night before but with trying to get off to William's party, she'd forgotten.

Some elderly people got up really early and were ready for breakfast by seven. Others, who didn't sleep well, sometimes got up much later because they wanted to catch up on the sleep they'd missed in the night. This couple, it transpired, belonged to the latter group.

She was grateful for the time to sort out her thoughts. She felt so giddy, so girlish, so — as Helena would put it — 'oved-up', she could hardly concentrate. She was grateful these guests hadn't stayed with her before so they would think it normal for their hostess to keep forgetting things and to put tomatoes on the wrong guest's plate.

They were still eating toast and marmalade when there was a knock on the door just after ten.

Gilly rushed to answer it, a smile on her face, convinced it was William, having changed his mind about the meeting. It was Leo.

231

You can't take back a smile, Gilly realised as she looked at him. Nor can you say, 'That wasn't meant for you!' You just have to back-pedal as best you can.

'Can I come in?' he asked, and as there was just enough gap between Gilly and the door frame for him to do so, he entered the house.

Gilly hoped she didn't have to ask her guests to rescue her from him and ushered him into the kitchen. Ulysses would spring to her rescue and shower him with cat hairs if necessary, she was sure.

'Gilly,' Leo said, holding her hands. 'Every time I try to talk to you it all comes out wrong. Will you give me ten minutes of your time?'

'Of course,' said Gilly, suspicious and a bit anxious. 'Coffee?'

Leo sat at the kitchen table in his beautiful suit, eyeing Ulysses the cat, who did seem to have a rescue plan, involving the suit and its beauty, and his ginger fur.

'So, Leo? What can I do for you?' said Gilly when she'd put coffee, hot milk and a plate of biscuits down in front of him.

He fiddled around with his coffee for a few minutes and then nodded his head towards the dining room where the sound of knives against plates could still be heard. 'Can they hear us?'

'I doubt it. They both have hearing aids.'

'Good. It must be such a nuisance not being able to say what you want in your own house.'

'I don't find it a problem,' said Gilly.

'Gilly,' said Leo, taking hold of her hand.

She extracted his hand and said, 'Please tell

me what you came to say. I'm going to be called away at any moment.'

'It's all wrong you having to do this bed and breakfast thing! But anyway . . . ' He reached for her hand again but she kept it in her lap. 'I don't think, before, I took into consideration quite how much you love this house.'

'Maybe not.'

'So if we were together we could live here and not in my house. You'd like that better, wouldn't you?'

'What? Better than living in your house?' It was his assumption that they should live together that really confused her.

'Yes! We could live here, in the house you love. How about that?'

'Well, I do like living here, that's for sure,' she said cautiously. While she could — and probably should — have sent him out of her house and her life forever, she was eager to know what his agenda was.

'Exactly!' He smiled as if her living in her house had been his idea all along. 'Which is why here is where we'd live.'

'But what about your lovely house? All your lovely things — '

'Not important. What's important is your happiness.'

'Thank you,' Gilly muttered, not sure how to respond to this.

'Right. Well, the thing is, I don't think I've made it quite clear what I want from our relationship.'

Gilly wasn't aware they had one but didn't comment.

'I want to marry you, Gilly. I think we could make each other very happy.' His statement sounded very rehearsed and strangely lacking in passion.

'Really?' said Gilly. She could imagine Helena's reaction to this suggestion. She wasn't sure Martin and Cressida would be all that delighted either.

'I know! And for someone who's always been a bit of a commitment-phobe, that's quite a thing!' He smiled as if he'd given Gilly a huge compliment. 'But I realise that while it's what I want, the prospect may be a bit daunting for you.' He smiled again, fond and patronising.

'Well . . . '

'The thing is, I know that women of your age aren't awfully keen on the physical side of marriage.'

This was news to Gilly who had very recent experience of the exact opposite. 'Oh.'

'They like affection and intimacy but not actual — you know . . . '

'Do you mean sex, Leo?'

He seemed a bit embarrassed by her bluntness. 'I didn't want to be quite so obvious, but yes.'

'Oh.' Her gaze flicked towards the dining room, willing her guests to want more toast, more tea or more anything. They did not respond.

'We could live here together, a happy, respectable couple, and keep each other company, do things — travel. I could take you to Vienna — '

'Haven't you cancelled that yet, Leo? I really think you should.'

He ignored this wifely suggestion. 'I can take

234

you to Venice! The world is your oyster.'

'I'm not sure I like oysters, Leo.'

'It's a figure of speech, Gilly!'

He sounded quite snappy, thought Gilly, and they weren't even married yet. 'I'm incredibly flattered, Leo,' she said, 'but I don't think we want the same things out of life. So, no thank you, I don't want to marry you.'

He seemed stunned. 'Gilly! I haven't asked a woman to marry me since my first wife! I don't think you've had time to think this through.' He got up. 'I'm not going to take no for an answer. I'm going to let you think about it.'

'Really, I won't change my mind — '

'Just think about it! Think about what you're turning down!'

Then he got up, pushed his chair back so it made an unpleasant grating sound on the floor and marched out to the front door, nearly tripping over Ulysses as he went. When the door had shut behind him — nearly but not quite a slam — Gilly heard something from the dining room. She went in.

Her bed and breakfast guests were looking at her. 'If I'm not mistaken,' said the woman, 'he's the man who tried to swindle us out of quite a lot of money with some 'sure-fire' scheme or other.'

'The man's a shower,' said her husband. 'An absolute shower. You did absolutely the right thing getting shot of him.'

'Well now,' said the woman, much more gently. 'We've had a really lovely stay but we must get on. We have an appointment in town shortly.'

235

Gilly was confused. She was convinced by now that Leo was on some sort of commission — that if he persuaded her to sell Fairacres, Martin and Cressida would reward him. But now he appeared to want to live in the house?

It was possible he'd realised she wasn't selling and so felt marrying her, living in her nice house, would give him some status he felt he lacked. She chided herself for being so wet that she hadn't made it absolutely clear how she felt about it all earlier. But her ex-husband had made her fearful of confrontation. Thank goodness she'd done it now.

After the couple left, Gilly suddenly felt tired and was clearing up at half her usual pace when William called.

'How are you, darling?' he said when she answered the phone.

She laughed and discovered she was smiling. 'I'm well. How are you?'

'Missing you.'

'That's nice. I'm missing you, too.' She thought of her bedroom, her bed still unmade, and how lovely it would have been to go back there with William.

'Um — you'll probably be a bit annoyed but I couldn't help investigating that Leo Simmons. I did it the other day, after I saw him with you at Helena's show.'

'Oh?' Gilly was apprehensive. She didn't want William to think that Leo was a close friend, especially not after what her guest had said about him being a 'shower'.

'Apparently he hasn't paid the rent on that

236

fancy house he lives in for a couple of months. I found out from a client of mine.'

'Goodness! Well, that does rather explain one or two things.'

'Care to enlighten me?'

'Yes, but not over the phone.' She paused, not wanting to seem pushy. 'Would you like to come here for supper tonight?'

'I'd love to. But do I have to wait until suppertime? Could I come after work? I'd bring some work with me and stay out of your way until it's time to eat.'

'That would be lovely! What's your favourite pudding? I'm only asking about pudding because I don't want to spoil you too much.'

'Crumble for me, always crumble.'

'Excellent!' She paused and then rushed on. 'I can't wait to see you again, William!'

'Nor me!'

It took them a long time to end the call but afterwards Gilly found she'd stopped worrying about seeming too forward. She realised she felt completely confident that William loved her and wouldn't let her down.

25

Helena came through the back door as usual, eager to see her mother. She was looking forward to a bath and some telly and an early night in her own bedroom while Jago was out. But her mother wasn't alone. In fact, as Helena looked around her she instantly spotted things were not as she expected. The little table by the window in the kitchen was covered by a cloth and there were candles. Sitting at it, now half rising from his seat was — her accountant? Really? Did they make house calls? Was her mother's financial state so bad that he needed to come round after office hours?

Her mother was greeting her, making welcoming noises, although Helena began to realise she was far from welcome and that she really shouldn't have turned up without warning.

'Oh, Mum, I'm so sorry! I'll go away again. I didn't mean to interrupt. Jago's watching something over at his friend's house so I thought I'd come and have a bath. I really should have asked.'

She felt overcome with embarrassment although at least this time there were no flashbacks to when she and her mother nearly got killed on the road.

'Darling, don't be silly,' said Gilly. 'You know you're always welcome. Have you eaten?'

'If not, I recommend the crumble, it really is delicious,' said William.

'Mum is really good at crumbles,' said Helena, trying not to look hostile. She didn't feel hostile at all, but after her reaction to Leo she worried that her mother would assume she hated anyone Gilly went out with. Or had an intimate little supper in the kitchen with, even.

'And cakes!' said William. 'She made me the most amazing birthday cake, a bird's-eye view of the landscape with a glider hovering over it.'

'Oh, I saw the cake!' said Helena, privately cross with herself for not asking at the time who it was for. 'It was brilliant! It actually inspired a wall hanging I'm doing for a big show.'

'Why don't you sit down and have some crumble and a glass of wine and tell us about it?' said Gilly.

Helena realised her mother was constitutionally incapable of turning away a potentially hungry person. Cooking and feeding people was so important to Gilly that Helena wondered if it was a way of compensating for her unhappy marriage and subsequent divorce.

'I'll just have a quick bath if that's OK?'

'I made a spare crumble for you anyway,' said Gilly.

'Oh, Mum! You're so kind!'

'I know Jago likes my cooking,' said Gilly as if achieving this situation was somehow challenging.

'Who wouldn't?' said William.

'You'd be surprised,' said Helena. 'Not everyone appreciates Mum's skill with butter and sugar. Now don't let me disturb you any more. I won't be long.'

239

As she went up the stairs Helena realised that in spite of her cheery words she was in a state of mild shock. Coming home to find her mother entertaining a man was the last thing she ever expected. And while she didn't disapprove of her mother having another man-friend, really quite soon after she'd got rid of Leo, now she'd had a few minutes to get used to the idea, William was her accountant. Wasn't that a bit odd? Was it even legal? And making him that cake? She knew her mother loved baking but would she go to all that trouble for someone she didn't care about? No, not even Gilly would do that. And she deserved all the happiness that came her way. No, it was fine for her to go out with whoever she liked, as long as they'd never nearly killed them in a car.

Up in the bathroom, she was pleased to see her mother had stocked up on her favourite bath oil and there were a few candles around the edge of the bath. Helena was about to light them and luxuriate when she suddenly wondered if her mother had planned to light them at another time, when she was not alone!

Helena had a quick bath, without candles, and then got out and dried herself briefly before pulling on her clothes again. She had to get out of the house as quickly as possible.

To her relief, her mother was alone in the kitchen when she got back down. She was wrapping foil round a Pyrex dish.

'Oh God, Mum, I'm so sorry! Interrupting your evening like that,' said Helena. 'I really should have called — ' A horrible thought struck her. 'He hasn't gone home, has he? William? I didn't drive him away?'

'No, darling. He's just getting a fire going in the sitting room. I know it's spring and all that but it's really quite chilly.'

'Oh, that's all right, I would have hated to ruin your evening completely.'

'No, darling, it's fine! And you don't have to rush off.'

Gilly's words said one thing, her body language quite another; Helena was fairly fluent in 'Mum' by now. 'Yes I do. But I will certainly take the crumble. You know how much Jago loves your cooking.' Then she realised her mother had said this earlier.

'While we're talking about Jago,' said Gilly, pausing in her foil manipulations, 'I just want to say while it's sad he won't be the father of my grandchildren, he's still a really lovely friend. I don't think you should have to worry about people knowing he's gay. There's no shame in it or even embarrassment.'

Helena took a breath. Her mum thought Jago was gay. And while she had never thought it before, she suddenly wondered if Gilly was right. 'Of course not — '

'I think he's far too nice to be heterosexual,' Gilly was saying. 'Although William is very nice too and he's certainly — '

'It's OK, Mum,' said Helena quickly. 'I think William is lovely but I don't think — '

'You don't think Jago is gay?' Gilly had that sad but loving expression that parents take on when they tell you your goldfish has died.

241

'Darling, he borrowed a hot-water bottle for you. I can't think of any straight men who would be so thoughtful. Can you?'

'Mum — '

'I knew there was something not quite normal between you. I didn't know what until it suddenly hit me. And while in some ways it is sad, as I said — he is so very handsome and the babies would be gorgeous — as long as he's happy and . . . ' She paused. 'I assumed you knew. You must be disappointed.'

Helena didn't know what to say. She only knew that she needed to find out if her mother was right as soon as possible. 'Can you give me the crumble? I'll sort this out with Jago in the morning.'

'You don't want to stay the night?'

'Certainly not! You're with your accountant — you probably want to talk business.'

Gilly laughed. 'Well, off you go now. And get in touch in the morning, or when you've had a chance to talk to Jago. But the friendship is the important thing.'

★ ★ ★

The thought that Jago might be gay had never crossed her mind before but now it began to make sense. She drove home thinking back on their friendship. Who else would offer so much with no strings? It was his idea to pretend they were a couple to get everyone off their backs. Why would he do that if there was no reason? Maybe he hadn't come out yet? Well, she'd ask him the moment she saw him in the morning.

She was surprised to see his pickup in the yard. She'd thought he'd intended to stay over with his friend (another possible indication of his sexual preferences, she realised now). But the sight of it strengthened her resolve to speak. No time like the present. And she was armed with a crumble and carton of clotted cream. The timing was perfect!

Jago was in the kitchen making a hot drink when she arrived.

'Hey!' he said, obviously pleased to see her. 'I thought you were going to sleep over with your mum.'

'I thought you were going to sleep over with your mate!' Now the thought that Jago was gay was in her mind, Helena couldn't get rid of it, and, yes, she was horribly disappointed at the thought.

'To be honest, he's so heartbroken about his girlfriend leaving he just wanted to get drunk and I wasn't prepared to have a hangover along with him. I'm really sorry for him and all that, but friendship only goes so far. I found I just wanted to get back.' He paused. 'What's your excuse?'

Helena went to the cupboard to find some bowls. 'Make me a cuppa and I'll tell you. Mum sent crumble and clotted cream for us.'

'God, I love your Mum!' said Jago and flicked on the kettle.

'She's very fond of you, too,' said Helena. Then, deciding it was best to get it over with, she went on: 'In fact, she thinks you're gay.'

243

At first Jago seemed confused and then amused. 'Why on earth would she think that?'

'Because you're so nice!' said Helena, having filled the bowls.

'Well, I can't deny I'm nice but I am not gay. If I was gay, why would I keep it a secret? Here's your tea.'

'So you're definitely not?' She put down the crumble and handed Jago a spoon.

'Definitely not.'

'Oh, OK.' Helena felt stupid now.

Jago picked up his spoon and then put it down. 'Will your mother stop making me crumbles if I'm not gay?'

Helena began to see the funny side. 'I don't think so. She said you would have fathered gorgeous babies so she'll take the news well.' In fact, Gilly had referred to him fathering her grandchildren but Jago didn't need to know that.

'That's a relief. I'd have been very sad if my hormones cut me off from your mum's amazing cooking.'

'Talking of hormones,' said Helena, keen to change the subject — she was feeling such a fool — 'let me tell me you why I didn't stay the night. Mum had a man there!'

'Not the creepy bloke, Leo?'

'No! It was her accountant. They've known each other forever but I didn't know there was anything going on between them.'

'And it wasn't just a friendly business dinner?'

'I did wonder that for about five seconds but even if they were friendly, she wouldn't give him dinner unless there was something else. And

244

actually, the look he gave her, he's very smitten.'

'Cool! She's an attractive woman, your mother. It's nice she's got a bloke who's into her.'

'Jago! This is my mother we're talking about!'

'Everyone is entitled to a private life, even gay builders.'

'But you said you weren't gay!'

'Would you like me to convince you just how ungay I am?'

Helena realised that yes, she would. She stood up. He stood up. 'How would you go about that, then?'

He came round to where she was standing and put his fingers round her face. He tilted her face upwards. 'Like this,' he said firmly. And kissed her.

After a while he said, 'If you're not convinced by now there are other things I could do to show you.

Helena pretended to think about this. 'Actually, I don't think I am quite convinced.'

'I would really hate for you to be in any doubt. Whose room? Yours or mine?'

'Yours,' said Helena. 'Bigger bed.'

Later, Jago came down to fetch the crumble. They ate it in bed before Jago did a bit more convincing.

★   ★   ★

William and Gilly sat on the sofa in front of a fire that was more for effect than heat. It was very pleasant but Gilly was starting to get a bit impatient. She yawned.

William, who had his arm round her shoulder, took it off. 'I should be going. It's late.'

'Must you?' Gilly was disappointed. 'For once I haven't got any guests . . . '

'Well, not if you don't want me to,' said William at once. 'I didn't want to presume you'd want me to stay.'

'It wouldn't be presuming, William,' she said. 'It would be lovely.'

'You know I never dreamed I'd find such happiness again after my wife died,' said William. 'I have had girlfriends, of course, but they've never come to anything. They most of them tried to persuade me to give up gliding. This time feels very different.'

'It does to me too,' said Gilly. 'And I love gliding.'

'I know you've had other offers — '

'Please don't remind me.'

'Then I won't. But let's not tell Aunt Daphne that we've got together just yet. I think it would be very bad for her to think her matchmaking worked so quickly.'

'She will be pleased though,' said Gilly.

'Delighted. But she'll become power mad and think she can reorder the universe.'

'If anyone can, it's Daphne.' She took a breath. 'Now, let's go upstairs . . . '

★ ★ ★

In the very early morning, when William got up to go (bringing a change of clothes would have definitely been presuming, he insisted), Gilly

246

looked at her phone. There was a text from Helena. *Jago definitely not gay. Love, H.*

Gilly settle back into the pillows, deeply satisfied. If there ever were any, the babies would be adorable.

26

Helena didn't rush to push her new-found happiness in her friend Amy's face. Of course she would tell her, but Amy had been away and the time to share this news wasn't now. Especially as the man Amy had had her eye on last month had not been interested in her. The perfect time would be when they were holed up in their favourite, regular Airbnb after the first day of World of Wool. She'd wait until they'd sunk half a bottle of wine and then tell all.

On Friday evening they drove down together in Helena's old Volvo that could pack everything in, as always exclaiming over the beauty of the countryside, debating and arguing the best way to get to a little corner of Wales that had no obvious route and getting excited when they finally arrived at the Airbnb.

Setting up the next morning was always fun as, unlike at Springtime, they shared a stall. When they first arrived at their allocated spot, they always felt they'd never make their stall look attractive, and yet somehow they always managed it. It was Helena's job to go on the first coffee and bacon butty run, finding the stall by following her nose. And she always came back with bits of news about who was there already, and who was expected, along with their breakfast. This time was no different and the show promised to be busier than ever.

★　★　★

'Well, that was an amazing day, wasn't it?' said Amy as at last they unlocked the door to their little home for the night. 'Best ever, I reckon.'

'I think it was!' Helena walked straight into the kitchen and found glasses. 'Do we need a corkscrew?' she asked. 'There's one just here.'

'You know I always buy wine with proper corks, or we'll lose the cork oaks,' said Amy, but without emphasis. They were dog-tired but happy.

When they both had wine and the ready meal was heating up in the microwave, Helena set to lighting the fire. It was one of their rituals and today they needed it more than in some years. Although it was late spring according to the calendar, the nip in the air said different.

'I never know if we do this show to display our work or catch up with our mates, or both,' said Helena, snapping twigs and piling them up carefully.

'Definitely both,' said Amy. 'It's so great being in our own tribe, surrounded by like-minded people who get us.'

'Yes,' agreed Helena. 'It's relaxing not having to pretend we're something that we're not. I loved doing posh Springtime, and we both made lots of money, but I felt a bit out of my depth. I'm an artisan, not an artist. The guys there today were all the same.'

'Even if some of them look a bit as if they spun and knitted themselves?' Amy was being provocative on purpose. 'You've always been a

249

bit more tolerant of the complete yoghurt knitters than I have.'

In spite of Amy's occasional snippy remarks, she had a heart of gold. Helena often thought the snippiness was partly to disguise her kindness.

When she was confident her fire wouldn't go out, Helena flopped back on to the sofa and picked up her wine glass. 'So,' she said, 'what was the best thing you saw today?'

'I'll tell you what the worst thing was — that blanket that looked if it was literally made out of what was picked up from the cow-shed floor,' said Amy. 'But I did love that alpaca stuff. Such fine wool. I must get hold of some and give it a go. And did you see Elaine? Isn't she looking great these days? She's definitely better fatter.'

They chatted on about the various people and projects they had seen, what was new and what was boringly the same.

'I must say I was relieved that my wall hangings went down so well,' said Helena, having stirred the beef and dumplings and put it on for a few more minutes. 'I was quite nervous about them, I must say. My work is usually far more ordered than that.'

'They worked very well artistically, and I loved the great chunky bits of fleece in them.' Amy frowned. 'Where did you get the idea from?'

'Can't I ever have invented anything? Do I always have to have got the idea from somewhere else?'

'I'm sure your brain is a simmering mass of inspiration but I'm sure you said something about cake that I didn't understand.'

Amy got up to find bowls into which she put the stew. She carved two huge slices from a loaf they'd bought at the show and put thick slabs of Welsh butter on them. She brought it all over and set it down on the coffee table. Helena opened another bottle of wine. It was going to be that sort of night.

'Yes, it was a cake my mother made for her boyfriend. I admit it.'

'What? Gilly's got a boyfriend! Oh — the silver fox my mum saw her with at the opera? That's great!'

'No, not him! He wasn't such a great catch, it turned out.' Helena went on to explain what was wrong with him until Amy was convinced.

'So, tell me about this other boyfriend?'

'Well, he's her accountant so they've known each other for years but have only got to know each other properly just recently. The cake was for a surprise party his aunt gave him. It was a bird's-eye view of what you see when gliding, apparently. Mum suspended a glider over it. I saw the pictures as well as the cake. And then I got the idea of doing a cross section of the earth.'

'Well, they looked amazing. And you produced quite a lot of other work considering you'd cleaned yourself out for Springtime.'

'That was because Jago was so amazing at looking after me so all I had to do was work.' She paused. 'I couldn't have managed without him.'

'I know you've been pretending you're a couple — don't think you can pull the wool over my eyes — excuse the pun — but are you really a couple now?' Amy sounded wistful.

'Yes.'

Amy nodded slowly. 'And you're sure about this? Obviously you've had boyfriends but you always said they were just a bit of fun, and it was only very recently you said you didn't have time for men.'

'It's amazing what you find time for when you fall in love.'

There was a long silence. 'So Jago is the real deal? The one, etc., etc.?'

'Yup.' To lighten the mood a little she added, 'And in case, like Mum, you were wondering, he is definitely not gay.'

'Gilly thought he was gay? Oh, that's adorable! Why?'

'Because he borrowed a hot-water bottle for me. She told me she thought hot-water bottles were camp.'

'That's so sweet! And so like Gilly.'

'I know.' They sat in silence for a little while, sipping their wine. 'So, Ames, how was your holiday?'

Amy had been on a yoga retreat, her unspoken agenda to find a man with a perfect and very supple body. 'Lovely, inspiring, a real break but man-wise a total failure. There was this lovely guy on the course but there were more lovely women and he picked one of them.'

'Oh, Amy, I am sorry.'

'So, your perfect, hot-water-bottle borrowing hot-sex machine — '

'I never said that!'

' — hasn't got a non-gay best friend, has he?'

Helena laughed, relieved to hear her friend wasn't too cast down by her failure to snag a yoga expert.

'Well, now you come to mention it, his best mate from forever, who I still haven't met, is newly single. You might be just the person to make him happy again.'

'I might be! Now tell me all about him.'

Helena realised she'd made an error. She knew very little about James apart from his name and that he and Jago went way back. She also knew he liked football and lager, neither of which was going to make him sound attractive to Amy.

'To be honest, I don't know anything — hardly anything — except he's a mate of Jago's.'

'Men do sometimes have very peculiar friends and if they're not peculiar they can be quite ugly.'

'They can.'

'So we look him up on Facebook,' said Amy. 'Where's my laptop?'

There were an awful lot of people with the same name as Jago's friend so Amy suggested they looked up Jago — in fact she had done it almost before Helena had realised her intention.

Helena wasn't really happy with what Amy was doing — it felt like prying. She and Jago had no secrets between them and somehow looking him up on Facebook without asking felt wrong. But she knew an open objection, or a protest that she didn't want to, would just encourage Amy in her investigations so she yawned instead.

253

'I don't know about you, Amy, but I'm done in. Can we do all this detective work tomorrow? Or maybe when we're back home? We've got another very long day tomorrow and then we have to drive home.'

'Oh,' said Amy, looking disappointed. 'I expect you're right.'

'And tomorrow is another day — you might meet the man of your dreams IRL — In Real Life,' Helena added with emphasis, just in case Amy was too tired to understand the initials.

'Yeah, right. I could meet a sheep farmer who knits his own hot-water-bottle covers out of old birds' nests — how sexy is that?'

'I think that could be perfectly sexy. But right now I need a shower and bed.'

She also wanted time alone so she could think about Jago uninterrupted.

★   ★   ★

The following day was similar to the first. There was lots of meeting up with old friends as well as new people coming along, asking tentative questions. Amy and Helena decided to arrange a few more workshops as so many people seemed keen to learn from them. They also wanted to know how to create the wall hangings Helena had made principally because they were relatively quick to make compared to the gossamer-fine silk scarves she had produced for Springtime, which looked so beautiful and took so long.

As they'd sold everything except the wall

hangings that had attracted so much attention, they decided to pack up early. Helena was longing to get back to Jago although she didn't confess this to Amy. It didn't seem fair when Amy had no one.

Helena had always felt perfectly contented without a man in her life. She hadn't felt incomplete, or in need of validation, or lonely, but now she had found love (she'd stopped pretending it was anything other than love) she felt this incredible happiness. And while she appeared to be the same, a normal, hardworking woman, in her head she thought of nothing but Jago. She hadn't believed such love was possible — at least for her.

And because she was so happy she wanted Amy to be as happy, and so she resolved to introduce her to Jago's friend James as soon as she could. It was unlikely they would be as perfect for each other as she and Jago, but they might go on a few enjoyable dates. It could be fun for all for them.

⋆   ⋆   ⋆

Jago must have come out of the house the moment he heard Helena's car arrive in the yard. It was nine o'clock at night — Helena had taken Amy home on the way back from the show — and she was exhausted. But her heart lifted the moment she saw Jago's frame coming towards the car. She opened her window and he leaned into it as if he wanted to pull out through it into his arms.

His kiss, his smell, the feeling of his cheek rough against hers made her weak with longing.

'Let me get out!' she protested, frustrated by the limitations of their situation.

She almost fell into his arms and he held her so tight she couldn't breathe — she didn't want to breathe — she just wanted to stay in his arms forever and ever.

But eventually she pulled free. 'Maybe we should get into the house?'

'Of course,' he said apologetically, 'it's just I've missed you so much. Are you hungry?'

The kitchen was warm and full of savoury smells and Helena realised how happy it made her just to be in it. 'I know this isn't the most top-end finished kitchen in the world,' she said, 'but it's welcoming and spacious and I wouldn't want to be anywhere else.'

'Oh, that's a shame,' said Jago, taking something out of the oven. 'I was hoping there were other rooms in this house that you like.'

She smiled at him, hoping she didn't look quite as soppy as she felt. 'I like lots of rooms.'

'Just as well. Now you sit there. I'm about to feed you and give you wine.'

'Amy and I drank a bit too much last night,' said Helena, taking the large glass he offered her. She took a sip. 'But it wasn't anything like as nice as this.'

'This is a special bottle — to celebrate your return.'

'Jago! I was only away two nights.'

'I know. But I missed you. Now, how hungry are you?'

'Very.'

As they ate they discussed the show. 'So it was a success? Worth all the work?' said Jago, dipping bread into the gravy of the chicken tagine.

'Absolutely. Loads of old friends came to see us and enough new ones to make doing a few more workshops definitely worthwhile.'

'How did the wall hangings go down?'

'Brilliantly! Everyone loved them! And lots of people want workshops to learn how to make them. Which will work well as they are comparatively quick.' She put down her fork. 'They didn't actually sell, of course, but hey!'

Jago laughed. 'Tell me when you've nearly finished — I have a surprise for you.'

'A nice one?'

'I think so.'

'Well, I don't think I can eat much more. I'm too tired.'

'Pudding? Sticky toffee? Bought the best brand.'

'Not now and I was brought up to believe that sugar at bedtime made me hyperactive.'

Jago laughed again. 'Maybe I should force-feed you some . . . '

'I'm sure that's not required,' said Helena primly, looking up at him, no longer caring if he could tell exactly how much in love with him she was.

He went over to the kitchen timer. 'I've set it for ten minutes. When it rings you're to come upstairs. Tell me when you're on the landing.'

'Supposing I fall asleep while I'm waiting?'

'The timer will wake you and if it doesn't I'll

257

come down and pour cold water on you! There's a crossword there I haven't been able to finish. Do that to keep yourself awake.'

Helena felt she might have nodded off for a few moments but as Jago had predicted, the timer woke her. She got up to turn it off and then, as instructed, went up the stairs.

'I'm here!'

Jago appeared. 'Now shut your eyes, I'm going to guide you.'

He put his hands on her shoulders. 'Now, about three paces forward — now to the left . . . '

She went where she was directed and was suddenly hit by warm, moist air smelling of lavender.

'You can open your eyes now!'

She was in the bathroom, but where before there'd just been a shower in the corner and not much else, now there was a bath full of hot, scented water and around the bath and on every surface were candles. There was no other light.

'Oh my God! This is so beautiful!' she said.

'It took me all weekend to put the bath in but I was determined to do it for you.'

'But I thought you had a big job you had to finish.'

'I have and I will finish it soon, but this took priority. Do you like it?'

'I absolutely love it, but I feel guilty that you took time away from your work to do this for me.'

'As they say in the adverts, you're worth it.'

She put her arms round his neck and pulled

258

down his head so she could kiss him. 'Thank you so, so much. You are so kind!'

'Let me add to my kindness and help you get your clothes off so you can get in,' said Jago.

'Only if I can help you with yours.'

* * *

Eventually they had to get out of the bath as the water was cold but Jago had found somewhere to heat a huge bath sheet that he wrapped round her. Then he picked her up and carried her to his bedroom. He lowered her to the bed and she had time to notice that there were clean sheets, dried in the open air, before he joined her. She felt she had never been so happy before in her life and certainly never had she been so in love.

It wasn't until they were having breakfast the next morning — early as Jago had to go to work — that Helena remembered to ask him about James. 'Amy is desperate to meet your newly single friend. Do you think he'd be up for that?' She didn't add that being so happy herself made her want to spread the joy.

He finished his mouthful, looking at her thoughtfully. 'Actually, my single friend is longing to meet you, too. He wants to check you out, make sure you're good enough for me. And Amy's a nice, jolly girl; I'm sure they'd get on well.'

'A jolly girl? You think Amy is a jolly girl?'

'Anything wrong with that?'

'Not really, it's just not very — I don't know — it's not how women like to be thought of.'

259

Jago shrugged. 'Nothing wrong with jolly,' he said. 'Currently I'm too besotted by another woman to be able to see her best friend as sexy or beautiful or any of those things. She is pretty though, I'll give her that.'

'Big of you! Do you want the marmalade?'

'Please.'

'So, what shall we do? Have them both to dinner?' She chewed her lip at the thought. It would be rather high pressure.

He shook his head. 'Let's keep it low-key. James will want to get a good look at you — he's quite protective of his old mucker — and I think it would be better if we went to a nice wine bar that does food so we can stay on and eat if we want to, but all go home early if it's a disaster.'

'That sounds great. No cooking or tidying involved.'

He gave her a heart-stopping grin. 'I think in American films in the fifties they called it 'double-dating'.'

Helena giggled. 'And me and Amy can go to the powder room to compare notes halfway through and say, 'I don't fancy yours much.''

'Perfect! I'll ask James. But if he says yes, can I leave it to you to set up, find somewhere nice? I've got so much on.'

'Of course! I'd like to do that.'

'You are a wonderful woman. Do you know that?' Then he gave her a toast-and-marmalade kiss and went to work.

★   ★   ★

A little later, Helena decided to go and see her mother. Gilly would want to hear about World of Wool anyway, and because she was Helena's mother, she'd have to put up with hearing how wonderful Jago was. But she was going to call first and make sure it was convenient.

'Mum? Only me. Can I come over?'

'Of course you can, darling. But why are you asking first?'

'You know why, Mum. I didn't want to disturb you if you had a friend with you.'

'I'm quite alone at the moment.'

It occurred to Helena that her mother sounded particularly upbeat and cheerful. Was it possible that she was in love too? Were she and her mother about to compare notes on their beloveds? The thought gave her mixed feelings. She was delighted, of course, but really, you didn't want to think about your mother — any parent really — having a sex life. It was weird.

Helena had never thought she'd feel about anyone as she felt about Jago. She didn't believe in that kind of love. But here she was, on cloud nine, mentally skipping about in the sky. For her mother to be in the same condition was just a bit mind-blowing.

27

Gilly put the kettle on when she'd disconnected from Helena. She felt the situation called for real coffee and freshly ground beans. Although it was still early days in her and William's relationship she felt a bit guilty that they still hadn't told Daphne or any of their friends about it. Helena knew, of course. And she should probably tell Martin although she felt certain that her son and Cressida would not be pleased.

She would talk to William the next time he called. Although mostly she let him do all the getting in touch (she was horribly old-fashioned), now she sent him a text to say that Helena was coming for coffee but that she probably wouldn't stay past ten or eleven. Helena, she realised, now kept builders' hours which meant she started early.

When Helena breezed through the back door a little later, Gilly's mother's heart soared with joy to see her daughter so happy. But a part of her was doubtful. She had had that madly-in-love glow herself when she had first been with her now ex-husband.

'Oh, Mum!' said Helena. 'You've made real coffee. Are there B & B guests here?'

Gilly laughed. 'Do I only make coffee when I've got paying guests?'

'Well, you know. But I'm not complaining. And shortbread! I've just had breakfast but I'm still starving for some reason.'

'I can't imagine what that would be,' muttered Gilly, smiling to herself. 'So how did World of Wool go? As successful as ever?'

'Pretty much,' said Helena, blowing crumbs. 'Everyone loved my wall hangings. Not enough to actually buy them of course — after all, at do's like that people make their own wall art — but I'm going to run workshops showing how to make them so they will have been worthwhile.'

'It was worth doing them then. After all, courses are the gift that goes on giving. You can only sell a wall hanging once.' Gilly didn't join her daughter in eating the shortbread, she was a bit sick of it.

'Deffo. But, Mum, the best bit was when I came home!'

'Really?' Gilly was fairly confident that Helena wasn't going to give her a kiss-by-kiss account of her nocturnal exploits but she was just slightly anxious.

'You know I have to keep coming round here to have a proper bath?'

'Yes.'

'Well, Jago spent the whole weekend putting a proper tub into the bathroom that just had a shower in it. It was amazing! He'd cooked the most brilliant chicken tagine and then he made me wait downstairs until the pinger went. Then I had to go upstairs and he led me into the bath-room. He'd put candles everywhere and some gorgeous lavender bath oil and it was lovely.'

'Oh, darling, how thoughtful! You're absolutely sure he's not gay?'

'Yes! But it meant he's now behind with his

work and he was so brilliant when I was working so hard, doing all the cooking and stuff, I'm determined to do the same for him.' She paused and made a face. 'But the trouble is, he's a brilliant cook and I'm not. I'm hoping you can give me some foolproof recipes.'

'Of course I can. And you can cook perfectly well; you just lack confidence.'

'I'll need a recipe for crumble, your cheese scones, soup — all the lovely comforting things that you make.'

'Those are the things that I don't really have recipes for, but I'll do my best. I've never seen you like this, Helly.'

'I know. I've never been like this before. Being in love is just so blissful, isn't it?'

Gilly sighed. 'Yes, it is. The trouble is, you can't just decide to feel like that. Some people seem able to fall in love all the time. I'm not like that.' She realised she had never loved Leo, she had just been flattered by his attention and had enjoyed all her friends envying her.

'I don't think I am either,' said Helena, 'or it would have happened before now.'

Gilly nodded.

'And are you in love now, Mum?' asked Helena.

Gilly nodded again. 'Yes, I think I am.'

Helena came round the table and hugged her mother. 'Long may it last,' she said.

'Indeed!' said Gilly, wondering if she would ever stop worrying about her children. She couldn't bear to see Helena's heart broken now.

★ ★ ★

264

'Thank goodness you're back!' said Helena when Jago came into the house later that evening, ridiculously pleased to see him again.

'Why? What's wrong?' He looked worried.

She laughed. 'Nothing really. Supper's ready when you are.'

She had come home from her mother's laden with supplies including a stew from Gilly's freezer (currently bubbling away), a box of broken shortbread, some frozen rhubarb (not turned into a crumble), recipes and a big bundle of herbs from the garden.

When she'd done most of her paperwork required to follow up after World of Wool, emailed several people about workshops, tidied the house and put some tools in a more sensible place, she set about finding somewhere nice for the 'double date' that was in prospect.

She had found a lovely wine bar, not too far away, with good reviews and parking, then ran it past Amy. This instigated a phone call that went on for some time but at least they had agreed a couple of possible dates and when they finally disconnected Helena felt she could text James with the dates and venue details. And all the time she worked she thought about Jago.

Now, he kissed her fondly and lingeringly. 'I'll just grab a quick shower first, then I'll be down.'

★ ★ ★

The following Sunday evening they were in Helena's car. Jago was driving. They'd tossed for it.

265

'I'm quite nervous!' said Helena as she fiddled with Google Maps on her phone although they knew the way.

Jago glanced at her. 'Why?'

'Because James may not like me!'

'I like you. Isn't that enough?'

Suddenly it wasn't. She needed him to tell her he loved her. He'd certainly shown her this was the case but now she needed the words. She wouldn't ask though. 'You know how it is. Your best friend! I'd have been miserable if Amy didn't like you and I was desperately upset when I thought my mother was getting together with Leo.'

'A mother is different, though.'

'Of course. I did wonder if I'd never want her to have a man in her life but I'm fine about William. I mean, it took a bit of getting used to and a lot of blanking out about what they do that isn't just having dinner or whatever, but basically I just want her to be happy.'

'I'm sure James just wants me to be happy. And I am,' he said. As they'd reached a set of traffic lights just then he took the opportunity to kiss her.

Helena was glad Jago was driving — a glass or two of Prosecco would make the whole date a lot easier, at least in the beginning. If James didn't like her, Jago would be torn between his girlfriend and his old friend forever. As for her liking James, she'd made up her mind to. A lot of things were a matter of choice, she realised, even those that didn't appear to be.

As arranged, Helena and Jago arrived first.

James appeared minutes later. Amy was due half an hour after that.

'Hey mate!' said Jago as he and James hugged each other.

'So this is Helena?' said James. He hugged her too and she took it as a good sign.

While Jago went to the bar, Helena and James inspected each other. She was a bit more intense with her inspection than he was. For her part she liked his curly fair hair, very blue eyes and intelligent expression, and thought Amy would too. He wasn't as tall as Jago and, in Helena's opinion, not as attractive, but he was quite good-looking enough, she felt.

When they'd finished studying each other she smiled and he smiled back. 'So, you're a weaver?' he said.

'Yes. But Amy and I do a lot of workshops together which are more lucrative than selling the things really. I hope you're not anti-weaver generally.'

He laughed, as he was supposed to. 'Certainly not. So far, I've never met a weaver I haven't liked.' He paused. 'Of course you are the first weaver I've met.'

She smiled. 'Amy is also a weaver.'

'Well, let's hope she fits the pattern.'

'I don't know if there's a pattern but she's bright, and fun.' She paused. 'Jago says she's jolly.'

'You don't agree with him?'

'Oh, I do! She and I have a lot of fun but I'm not sure it's a flattering description.'

'I'll let you know if I think she's jolly.' He winked.

Helena decided she liked James — he was definitely jolly.

* * *

As the evening was going so well, they decided to stay and eat. Amy and James seemed to hit it off and, Amy had confided, she fancied James really quite a lot.

But while they were sharing a selection of puddings, Jago frowned and got out his phone. 'Sorry,' he said, having looked down at it. 'I'll have to take this.'

Something in the way that he left the table made everyone else a bit less cheerful. 'I hope it's not something dreadfully wrong with one of his properties,' said Helena. 'We may need to leave at once to put buckets under burst pipes.'

'Well, if you have to go, maybe me and Amy can stay on for a bit? Would you be up for that, Amy?' James asked.

'I should think that would be all right,' said Amy. She sounded fairly relaxed about it but Helena guessed she was delighted by his suggestion.

Jago came back. 'We're going to have to go, I'm afraid,' he said.

'Burst pipes?' said Amy.

'No. Why should it be burst pipes?' Jago seemed confused.

Helena got down from her stool. 'We were just speculating about what your phone call was. I guessed a plumbing crisis at one of your rental properties.'

'If only!' he said. He pulled some notes out of his wallet and put them on the table. 'Let me know if that's not enough and don't go crazy, kids!' He gave a cheery smile but Helena could tell it wasn't sincere. He was obviously very worried.

He didn't volunteer any information after they set off for home and eventually she had to ask. 'I don't want to be nosy, but can you tell me what the phone call was about or is it confidential?'

He sighed. 'I do have a business problem, I'm afraid. Which means I'll have to be away for a while and I'm not sure how long.'

'Oh.' This was a shock but she didn't want to appear clingy by letting him see how much of a shock. 'But we'll be able to keep in touch with each other?'

He shook his head and looked straight ahead through the windscreen. 'I'm afraid not. There's no phone signal where I'm going. Or any Wi-Fi.'

'But what about your properties here? Will you need me to do anything for you?'

'Sweet of you to offer.' He gave her a warm smile and patted her knee. 'I'll sort things out before I go.' He was silent for a few moments. 'Will you be OK on your own in the house? It could feel a bit spooky with it being unfinished and everything.'

Helena didn't know if she'd be all right or not. She hadn't minded living on her own in her little studio, but he was right, the house was a bit spooky, being big and half a building site. 'I might ask Amy to come and stay if you wouldn't mind?'

'Of course not. She could have your old room.

She's fun, isn't she? I think she and James will enjoy each other's company even if they don't get together forever.'

Helena sensed he'd rather talk about Amy and James than his own situation. 'Could you tell if he liked Amy? And you know what I mean when I say 'liked'!'

He chuckled. 'I think he did. She's sparky and fun and she'll take his mind off his lost love.'

'As long as his lost love doesn't come between them.'

Jago was thoughtful. 'I don't think she will. She wasn't all that great, to be honest. Although she thought she was and James did too. Amy is a far better bet, relationship-wise.'

Helena laughed. 'Glad she's been promoted from being 'a jolly girl'.'

'You took that all wrong!'

They argued about it cheerfully for the rest of the journey home.

★ ★ ★

In the morning he left, early, before Helena was properly awake.

She tried to go back to sleep but couldn't and found tears slipping out of the corners of her eyes as she listened to the birds and saw the room get lighter.

In theory she had no reason to cry. Jago had been called away on business and had gone. It was no big deal. But somehow it felt like a big deal, as if something had changed — not necessarily between them but with him.

270

28

There was always plenty to do in the house and Helena's building skills had come on a lot since living with Jago. She was best at pointing but she also tidied up a few half-finished sections of bricklaying. But when she could do no more and it was no longer silly o'clock, she went round to see her mother.

'Hello, darling,' said Gilly, without looking up from writing something. It looked like a list. 'What's wrong?'

'Mum! How do you know anything's wrong? I've just arrived.'

'I'm your mother. Don't query the process.' Now Gilly did look up. 'So?'

'There's nothing wrong! Well, not really.' Helena pulled out a chair and sat at the kitchen table, putting her arms on it. 'Jago's gone away, that's all. I'm going to miss him.'

'Oh, sweetheart, I'm sorry. That's horrible. How long is he away for?'

'I don't know.'

'But you can keep in touch with him? FaceTime? See how he is?'

'No. He said he'd be out of contact.'

'That is a bit harder to cope with, love. But you didn't leave on bad terms or anything?'

'Oh no.' Although this was the first time he'd got up without making love to her, but she didn't need to share that with her mother. 'No, we're fine but I'm a bit worried about him. He got this phone call while we were out with James and Amy last night and we had to leave the wine bar right away so he could make arrangements. Then he went really early this morning.'

'If you want to come home for a bit, do,' said Gilly firmly. 'Whatever your old mother is getting up to doesn't stop this being your home, first and foremost.'

Her mother's invitation instantly made Helena feel better. She didn't want to move back home but knowing she could made the prospect of being alone in Jago's house seem less daunting. 'That's really kind of you, Mum, but I think I'll be fine. I'm a big girl now, after all.'

'You'll always be my baby, darling,' said Gilly, smiling fondly. 'Now, I planned to make some soup. Do you want to stay and help me chop up vegetables?'

'Oh yes, that would be fun.'

They made soup and chocolate cake and by the time Helena left with the cake in a tin she felt a lot better.

She was further encouraged by Amy's eagerness to come and stay. In theory it was to plan weaving workshops but Helena knew the signs: Amy wanted to talk about James.

To be fair to them, they did plan a couple and Amy was also keen to help Helena with her workshops to create wall hangings. They discussed sourcing fleece, dying it themselves or buying it already dyed and various other work-related subjects before Helena said, 'Shall we order pizza and open a bottle of wine?'

'Thought you'd never ask!' said Amy. 'But let's make pizzas in the frying pan. Cheaper.'

'I've got wine already and cake for pudding. So, how did it go with James after we left?'

'He is so lovely!' said Amy. 'Obviously it's far too early to say for sure but he sent me a text this morning saying how much he'd enjoyed meeting me.'

'Really? That soon? That's amazing!'

'I know! So unlike a man. He's very keen that we should meet up again though. No date made yet, but hey! And he is so nice.'

Amy went on to tell Helena every little thing she knew about James. Not, Helena realised, because Amy thought she needed to know all that, but because she just wanted to talk about him. She was attracted to him and had 'mentionitis'. Still, it was all good stuff and useful to know. He was Jago's best friend.

Suddenly Amy said, 'I know! Let's check him out on Facebook!'

'You don't expect me to believe you haven't already done that, do you?' Helena had found a mixing bowl and a packet of flour. Amy would make the pizzas.

'Well, no, but he may have put something about me up there.'

Helena couldn't help laughing. 'Really? What would he say?'

'I've met a gorgeous new woman, really hope she's as into me as I'm into her. Obvs.'

'Honey! There's pinging off a text to someone you've just met and there's turning that someone into a girlfriend . . . '

'I know there is a bit of time in between but I haven't felt like this for so long. Let me enjoy it!'

'I'm really not raining on your parade,' said Helena gently. 'I'm just managing your expectations.'

Amy was rueful. 'OK, OK, I know. But let's get these pizzas on and then we'll have a peek. I want to check out how he looks in swimming trunks.'

There was a good array of photos and, to Amy's delight, a couple of James on a beach. There was one of him in skiing gear, holding some kind of trophy, standing in front of a row of laughing friends.

Helena, crunching pizza, looked over Amy's shoulder. 'Hang on!' she said. 'That's Jago.'

'Where?'

'In the background. Look.'

Amy peered at the group of young men standing behind James. 'Which one?'

'There. Look.' Helena touched the screen with her finger.

'Helly! He's wearing a big hairband, ski goggles and is looking away from the camera. How on earth can you tell?'

'Well, I just know. It's him. I know it is.'

'You and your spooky 'super-recogniser' stuff!' Amy was dismissive but indulgent.

Now it was her man in the photos Helena was a bit more interested. 'But that's weird. He's tagged wrongly. You'd think James would get his best mate's name right.'

'It might not be him. And anyway, he may not have put the photo up there.'

'But it is him. And apparently he's called Jonathan Relto.' Something stirred in Helena's memory. 'Wasn't Relto the name of that company that was responsible for all those people nearly dying in a fire? There was a dramatic rescue and several fireman got medals for gallantry.'

'No idea,' said Amy. 'Let's google him.'

Helena's legs turned to rubber. She felt as if all her life force was escaping out of her body as she read. There were many more pictures of Jago available, ones that even Amy had no problem in recognising. Only he wasn't Jago, the man she loved. He was Jonathan Relto, nephew of one of the worst landlords in history. His uncle had only missed going to prison because of a very clever lawyer. Worst of all, Jago had worked for him. She developed a cold sweat and her mouth went so dry she couldn't speak.

'Oh, Helly,' said Amy, looking at her friend with concern. 'Would you like some water?'

Helena nodded. While Amy went to fetch her some, she tried to get her brain to work. Amy came back with water, she sipped some and managed to speak. 'I don't know what to do.'

'Is there any brandy in the house?' asked Amy.

'You're not supposed to give brandy for shock. It gives you hypothermia or something.'

'Don't be ridiculous!' Amy was dismissive of this namby-pamby response. 'I'll find the brandy. It'll make you feel a bit more in control.'

Helena remembered the first time Jago had offered her brandy, after she had rescued the kitten. That time she had asked for tea instead, but this required something stronger.

Amy had obviously managed to find it and held out a glass to her. Helena took it and sipped, and as she felt the strong liquor reach her bloodstream she realised that Amy was right, her limbs did feel more connected to her body. 'I feel as if I've been run over by a train,' she said.

'It must be awful. I'm so sorry!' said Amy.

'Jago — the man I thought I loved — is not who he said he was. He's this other, horrible person, very nearly responsible for people dying!'

'They didn't die though. And you don't know how much he had to do with it. He may have worked for the company but he could have been a caretaker or something.' Amy sounded as if she was desperate to say something comforting but couldn't think of anything sensible. 'If he was responsible, he'd have gone to jail and his uncle avoided that,' she added.

'Oh, come on! As if! Besides, he's lied to me. I can't forgive him. I'm leaving here.' She paused and looked at her glass. 'Tomorrow. I'm over the limit now.'

'You were over the limit a few glasses of Prosecco ago,' said Amy. 'And don't overreact. Jago didn't lie to you; he just didn't tell you everything.'

'That's as good as lying, isn't it?'

'Not really. I know you're living together but you haven't known him that long. It wouldn't be an easy thing to bring up. 'By the way, my uncle's company was responsible for that awful fire, when people nearly died, years ago.''

'But when would he have told me? Soon? Never?' Helena still felt horribly deceived.

276

'I don't know, Hells, but you can't think badly of him because he didn't blurt it out when you first met. Have you told him everything about you?'

'I may have kept quiet about some unfortunate music preferences when I was twelve, but mostly, yes. He knows all about my parents' divorce and how it affected me. He knows everything remotely important.'

Amy put her hand on Helena's arm. 'It needn't be a deal-breaker, Hel.'

Helena shook her head, still in despair. 'We haven't actually made any sort of deal. I just moved in as a lodger and then changed bedrooms. I feel such a fool! I feel I've shacked up with a complete stranger. I just fell in love and followed my heart and my lust.'

'I think you are overreacting.'

'Amy, you saw what was on Google!'

'I'm not saying the fire wasn't awful — not for a second — but just because it was Jago's — or Jonathan's — uncle's firm, it doesn't mean he had anything to do with it.'

'Then why change his identity? Is that what normal, innocent people do?'

'Well, maybe! Maybe having that name meant he couldn't get work, or start a business or anything.'

'I don't know, Ames. I just don't know. I just feel terribly let down.'

'But he's been lovely to you — '

'But who has been lovely to me? And why? Is it Jago or Jonathan?'

'He won't have a hidden agenda. What has he

got to gain from being nice to you?'

'He has a hidden past, why not a hidden agenda? I just feel I'm in the middle of a bog and everywhere I put my foot it just sinks in. I have to get away.'

'You're not being logical!' said Amy.

'Well, sorry!' said Helena. 'The man I've been living with — the man I thought I loved — has turned out to be someone completely different. Sorry I can't react in a calm and reasoned way.'

Amy was getting fed up. 'OK, I'm going to make tea and toast. We're going to eat it and then go to bed. I promise you, this will look better in the morning.'

'You sound just like my mum.'

'I'll take that as a compliment. Your mum talks a lot of good sense.'

'I'll sort out some sheets for your bed,' said Helena. 'If I think of this as a sleepover, maybe I won't feel so utterly miserable.'

★ ★ ★

After a drawn-out breakfast, Amy had persuaded Helena not to do anything rash until she had talked to Jago.

'He's entitled to give his side of the story,' she said. 'You've just seen a lot of stuff on the internet. We all know you can't trust everything you see on there.'

'I do get that,' said Helena, although she was still reluctant to accept it. 'But how do I speak to him when I don't know where he is, and can't contact him? I don't know how long he's going

278

to be away for and, frankly, I can't cope with waiting for him to get home. 'Hi Jago, or should I say Jonathan?''

'No, I get that, too. I think you have to find him.'

'But I don't know where he is!'

'I bet James does,' said Amy. 'They go back years and they're best friends. Ask him.'

'I hardly know him!'

'Do you want to find out where Jago is, or not?'

Helena made a face. 'I do but I'm also really nervous. Supposing I find out he's an insurance-swindling arsonist or whatever? Maybe I'm better off not knowing.'

'No, you're not. You can't spend the rest of your life wondering if you let the best man you're likely to meet go because of stuff you saw on Google, without ever giving him a chance to put his point of view.'

Helena knew Amy was right. She didn't want her to be right, but she was. 'I've just thought of something.'

'What?'

'James might not believe me about the picture on Facebook. You know? Me being a super-recogniser? I'll need proof I've seen him.'

'You don't need to tell him how you came to find out Jago's changed identity. Just ask him where he is! Right.' Amy looked at her phone to check the time. 'I've got to see someone about a workshop. I can leave you my computer with my Facebook page open. I'll be back at three to fetch it and find out how you've got on. Is that OK?'

'Yes, that will be brilliant. OK, I'll get in touch with James.' Helena didn't move.

'Do you want me to do it for you?'

Helena shook her head. 'It's a kind offer but I think I need to do this when I'm on my own.'

'But you will do it? Promise?'

'Absolutely promise.'

'Fair enough, but tell me everything as soon as you can. Call me.'

'I will.'

'Are you going to tell your mum about this?'

Helena shook her head. 'Not until it's resolved. There's no point in worrying her.'

Amy nodded. 'Get on the phone then.'

'I'm going to text. After you've gone, like I said.'

'I'll just clear breakfast.' Amy seemed reluctant to leave.

'No need. I'll do it. Now please go before I lose my nerve.'

'If you're sure . . . '

'Absolutely. But thank you so much for keeping me from overreacting. I might overreact again later, but just for now, thank you!'

They hugged and then Amy left and Helena went to find her phone.

She sent a text, grateful that because of Amy wanting to meet James she had his mobile number in her phone.

I've seen Jago's details on Facebook. Can we meet up soon?

After she'd sent the text she worried that James would think she was trying to pick him up the moment Jago's back was turned but she realised this was paranoia. But she felt paranoid.

It was like a waking dream — she didn't know what was real and what wasn't.

As she cleared the breakfast in Jago's patchwork kitchen she had to stop herself crying. She had to stop assuming that she was destined to pack up her things, including two looms, and leave. Where would she go? She personally could go to her mother, but her looms? Where would there be space for them?

Luckily for her sanity, James got back to her soon. *This would be better face-to-face. Could I come to yours at lunchtime?*

Sure, she texted back. *I'll make you a sandwich.*

Then she wished she hadn't said that. Jago was the sandwich expert, not her. Making one would just make her think about him. But then she realised that he had been the default setting for her brain for some time, and even thinking that she had been cheated on in the most complicated way didn't stop her loving him. Her heart would have to catch up with her head and it might take a while.

★　★　★

Helena was waiting at the door for James when he arrived.

'Hi, Helena,' he said as he got out of the car. He kissed her cheek. 'Did you really make a sandwich?'

'Yes, but of course it won't be as good as Jago's.' Then she found herself near tears again and wished she hadn't mentioned him. Although

281

considering the reason she and James were meeting it wouldn't be possible not to.

Soon they were sitting at the table in the kitchen.

'So,' said James, 'how did you find out about Jago?'

'We — me and Amy — were looking at Facebook. At you, actually, and his picture came up.'

'But there are no pictures of Jago on Facebook, not on my page, anyway.' He seemed so certain about this Helena was very glad she'd anticipated the problem.

She opened Amy's laptop and found the picture. James stared at it. 'OK, I remember the photo being taken but where is Jago?'

'There,' said Helena, pointing.

James frowned. 'I know it's him but how the hell do you know?'

'I have a gift — a curse a lot of the time — which means I can recognise people in a way other people can't. It's weird; I can't explain it.'

'But he's wearing skiing gear! He's not even looking at the camera.'

'Are you saying it's not him?'

James's indignation subsided. 'No. It's him. But how anyone could recognise him . . . '

'Well, I have. And he's tagged with a completely different name. Maybe you could explain that?'

James chewed his sandwich with agonizing slowness.

'It's not my story to tell.'

'But I can't live with all this stuff I've read

282

about him on the internet and not find out more.'

'He should tell you about it, not me.'

'Of course he should!' Amy had gone on about this long enough for Helena to be convinced. 'But I don't know where he is. I can't get in touch with him!' She took a breath. 'Do *you* know where he is?'

James nodded. 'I do. And I'll tell you.'

29

Helena and James were looking at Maps to find out exactly where the address Jago had given James actually was.

'The trouble is,' said James, 'postcodes in these remote areas are enormous so they don't help much.'

'I don't know the Wye Valley at all,' said Helena.

'It's very beautiful, I know that.'

'But if he didn't do anything wrong — I'm assuming he didn't do anything wrong — ?' Helena broke off, hoping James didn't feel trapped into saying what she wanted to hear.

'Look, I've said, it's not my tale to tell. I'm the only person he's stayed friends with from those days. We knew each other at school. Let's just say I'm not surprised he wanted to cut himself off from everyone else.'

'And you didn't want to cut yourself off from him?'

'Nope. He's a good guy.'

A modicum of relief relaxed Helena's shoulders a little. 'Well, that's something, at least.' 'He'd probably kill me if he knew I'd said that,' said James, frowning as he studied Maps on Amy's computer.

'Why? Why would he mind you saying he was a good guy?'

'Because he doesn't feel like a good guy.'

James took his fingers off the keys. 'Helena? I need a proper map. Satnav and all that are OK as far as they go, but they don't give you a chance to plan or see where you're headed.'

'My mother would have one.'

'Could you borrow it?'

'I'm sure I can.'

'Would she ask why you wanted it? Where you're going?'

Helena nodded. 'I hadn't planned to tell her until it was all over. She's a bit of a worrier. But I will have to tell her if I need a mapbook.'

'You might be away for a few days, too.'

'I hadn't thought of that,' said Helena. 'But I suppose that's true.'

'If you started really early tomorrow morning, didn't get lost and you and Jago had your conversation really quickly, you could get back in a day, but honestly? I think you guys need time to talk this through properly.'

Helena nodded. 'I'll have to tell Mum, then.' She looked at James. 'Do you know why he rushed off so suddenly? Was it his past coming back to haunt him, as they say?'

'I really can't say. I promised I wouldn't.'

Helena sighed. 'OK. I'll see if my mother is around.' Helena called her mother and discovered she was out but able to answer her mobile.

'Darling!' said Gilly, sounding happy. 'Why don't I come and see you? I'd love to see where you and Jago live!'

'Oh, Mum, I need to borrow something. And tell you something. When will you be home?'

Helena wanted to cry all over again and hoped

285

she'd get through the process of putting her mother in the picture without actually sobbing.

'Oh. OK. Well, I'll be back in an hour. Everything all right?'

'Not really, but I'll explain when I see you. Now I must call Amy; she left her laptop here this morning and she'll probably need it.'

Having brushed off her mother with a kind of lie that happened to be true, Helena did call Amy.

'So I'm going round to Mum's in a minute to borrow her mapbook and then tomorrow, bright and early, I'm going on a road trip.'

'It sounds fun in a way. I mean, finding your way to a hidden location and reuniting yourself with your lover.'

'If that's what it was I'd agree with you. It's a mission, anyway.'

'Although it's Wales, the Wye Valley, so not miles and miles away.'

'Actually, that's what I thought but James put it into my head that it might not be easy to find. Hence the physical map, so I can see all the little tiny roads. I'm not going until tomorrow, anyway.'

'And you'll be OK on your own?'

'Of course!' Helena sounded brighter than she felt.

★ ★ ★

Gilly put a meringue on Helena's plate. 'You can tell I bought these. I just felt I wanted you to eat something.'

'Did you buy them before or after I called you, Mum?' asked Helena, recognising her mother's compulsion to feed her family if she was worried about them.

'Not the point. Just have a bit of sugar — I know! It's poison! — a sip of tea, and then tell me everything you think I need to know.'

'You'll have guessed it's about Jago.' She sighed.

Her mother nodded and broke off a bit of her own meringue with her fork.

'And my wretched super-recogniser thing comes into it.'

Gilly looked up, anxiety making her frown. 'Did you see him on a rerun of *Crimewatch*?'

Helena found herself laughing, not sure if her mother had been deliberately funny or was just being naïve. 'I wish! No, I found him on Facebook.'

'And that's bad?'

'Yes — when he's got a completely different name! He's not who he says he is, Mum. He's a different person with a different name.'

'People are allowed to change their names if they want to,' said Gilly.

'Yes, and he had good reason, but I feel like he's lied to me!' She had been going to give Gilly a carefully edited version of what she'd discovered but found herself wanting to tell her mother everything. 'His real name is Jonathan Relto and his uncle owned the company that was responsible for all those people nearly dying in that fire. Do you remember? All those firefighters got awards for bravery, rescuing them. Let me show you.'

Soon they were both peering at the screen of

287

Gilly's computer. 'It does look bad, I know,' said Gilly, 'but my instinct tells me he's a good man.'

'You thought he was gay!'

'I rest my case,' said Gilly primly and then laughed. 'I know it must be a horrible shock for you and you're quite right to try to find out the facts as soon as you can, but I'm putting my money on Jago being one of the good guys.'

'Oh God, I hope you're right, Mum!'

★ ★ ★

Helena didn't go back to Jago's house that night. She stayed with her mother and allowed herself to be mothered. Comfort food, wine, a bath, girly telly. It didn't cure her from doubt and a sense of being enormously let down, but it did cushion her from it a little.

And in the morning, although she should have gone to her own home to pack a case, she preferred to manage with some clothes she'd left at Fairacres for years and things she could borrow from her mother. This included a slightly moth-eaten cashmere cardigan, a long cotton nightie (which she'd borrowed the night before) and a few pairs of her mother's knickers (which was a bit weird). Gilly had provided a new toothbrush and a small pot of moisturiser along with a new mascara and a stub of a kohl pencil. It was pouring with rain.

'Well, the saying is, rain before seven, fine before eleven,' said Gilly as she and Helena looked at the rain-drenched sky.

'It's half past seven, Mum, and I do hope to

get there before eleven.'

'I meant it will be nice when you get there.'

Gilly sounded feeble, and Helena knew she was struggling to be optimistic.

'It'll be fine,' said Helena and made a dash for the car.

Her raincoat held over her head, Gilly followed her, apparently trying to disguise her reluctance to let her daughter drive off into the storm to an unknown destination. Helena knew exactly how she felt.

'I'll be OK, Mum,' she said, when she was sitting in her car, Google Maps on her phone, the map open on the seat beside her and a list of places to aim for on the dashboard. She also had a packet of sandwiches and a tin of shortbread.

'I know you will,' said Gilly, sounding very confident but not fooling her daughter. 'And I know it might be difficult to keep in touch, but if you can, do. You've got your phone charger?'

'Yes. It's plugged in right now. Google Maps eats battery.'

'Off you go then!' Gilly stepped back from the car and started to wave.

The weather was completely in tune with Helena's mood. It was dreary, persistently grey and visibility was affected. She didn't really know what she was going to find when she reached Jago — if indeed she did reach him. Would he be pleased to see her? Probably not or he'd have asked her to go with him. Still, she had to find out his side of the story. If he was as bad as the internet made him out to be she had a fallback position — she would go to the little cottage she and Amy always rented for World of Wool and hope it was available. It was midweek and in a less touristy part of Wales, so she was in with a chance. Then she'd have to start putting her life back together.

She switched on the radio for any traffic news and for cheering music and discovered that the Severn Bridge was closed. This didn't make it impossible to get where she was aiming, but it did make it more complicated. She pulled in and had a good look at the mapbook and Google Maps. The bridge being closed would make her journey a bit longer. Then she sat off again.

The weather got worse as Helena drove, and while she was on the motorway the sound of the rain on the roof was deafening, relieved only by the brief spells spent driving under bridges. She slowed right down, wishing her fellow drivers would do the same.

Following the directions on her phone she turned off the motorway and started climbing into the Welsh hills. The rain seemed to come down harder and in places the road turned into shallow streams. Still her road led her upwards — which surely was a good thing?

Her phone lost signal at the same time as Helena came across a 'Road Closed' sign. As water was pouring down the road in question this didn't seem unreasonable. She pulled into the side and got out the map again. She set off when she had found herself an alternative route, hoping her phone would pick up another signal.

When she had a second to glance at the scenery, she saw that it was very beautiful but the road was getting narrow, steep and winding. Cow parsley lined both sides and the verges seemed full of wild flowers. At another time she would have either stopped and walked a little to identify the flowers or driven slowly and just admired the beauty but today she was on a mission. Her optimism with regard to the success of that mission was waning, being washed away by the rain.

She thought she was nearly at her destination when she came across another sign. This one said 'Road Ahead Closed'. It did not specify how far ahead and this was important because nearly at the end of the road there was a little turn-off which was the one she wanted. There was no water running down this road — or at least not an unreasonable amount. Should she risk having to turn back? Or search for another way now?

The map was not encouraging. She'd have to turn round and start again, more or less, and who knew how many more roads would be closed now? She decided to risk it and take the road that might close before she reached her turn-off.

The rain started to ease and eventually Helena realised it had stopped and that the sun was appearing through the clouds. Mist gathered about her, touched with gold.

Her hope that the road wouldn't close before her turning increased as a car came towards her. But then it got narrower, becoming single track with passing places. She reckoned she had about half a mile to go before her turn-off when she went around a corner and found that the road was blocked.

She pulled her car off the road and got out.

She stretched. Undid her plait, shook out her hair and considered her surroundings. It was blissfully quiet. The only things she could hear were birds singing and somewhere out of sight the sound of running water.

Just for a bit she allowed herself to rest and then she considered. She could turn round and go back — there was room — or she could abandon the car and walk.

She looked at her phone. No signal. So she got out the map and tried to work out roughly where she was in relation to her destination.

There was no quick solution, she just had to walk the next bit and hope it didn't become impassable. What was really worrying her was getting away quickly if Jago didn't want to see her. She didn't fancy running; it would look desperate.

She put her water and sandwiches into her rucksack but left the rest of the food that Gilly had pressed on her. Then she put the map on top, just in case. She locked the car and set off up the road, past the barriers.

If she hadn't been fretting about what her reception might be, or worried that she might get lost, she'd have enjoyed the walk. The world had a newly washed feel to it after all the rain and although it was muddy she was wearing sturdy trainers which were coping OK.

The scenery seemed to get lovelier with every step but the road got steeper and it seemed to take a long time before she reached the turn-off she was aiming for. She had bundled her hair on top of her head to keep it off her neck but there was still sweat running down her spine and the minimal amount of make-up she had put on that morning had long gone.

She had a drink and then set off again, acutely conscious of how far she'd have to walk back if she'd made a mistake — a mistake in her direction or a mistake in coming at all.

The road trailed through fields and small woods and the occasional cluster of farm buildings. It was lovely but it was long and Helena's confidence wavered. Should she turn back now? She'd been going for nearly an hour. Say half an hour back to the car (it would be quicker going downhill), but it would still be at least two hours to get back to her mother's house, probably three or four.

Then she heard a lark singing in one of the nearby fields. The sound of it soaring up and up and up filled her with hope. She would go on until she reached the address James had given her. She would face this dilemma head on.

★ ★ ★

She was seriously sweating, out of breath and tired when she finally looked up and saw a small cottage further up the lane. She knew it was the right one because it had Jago's pickup parked outside it.

She was here; she had arrived. Now all she had to do was walk up to the front door and knock. But at that moment she would have preferred to walk over broken glass.

She decided to have a drink of water and then

293

use a bit of it to wash her face. She went behind a tree, out of sight of the house, so she could prepare herself in private. When she was as clean as she could be given the small amount of water she had, she ate a sandwich. She chewed slowly to avoid indigestion, reluctant to admit to herself she was killing time, too scared to actually confront Jago now she was here.

She slid down so she was squatting, wishing the ground wasn't so wet and she could sit, and rested under the tree for a while. Then her legs began to cramp and she straightened up again. She spent a few minutes shaking out her hair (very damp round her neckline) and retying the scarf holding it back.

She was just wondering what more she could do to use up time to put off the inevitable when she heard a voice.

'Are you going to stay there all day or are you going to come in? I suggest you come in. It's going to rain again.'

It was Jago.

30

'You managed to find me, then?' Jago said.

'Were you hiding?'

'No. You'd better come in and meet Fred. I'll make a cup of tea.'

His words were hospitable but his manner wasn't. But as she didn't have a choice, Helena walked up the path to the house and followed him to the threshold of the back door. There she stopped and started unlacing her trainers, which were caked with mud.

'Don't worry about that — ' Jago began and then saw just how dirty her shoes were. 'OK, take them off. I'll find you a pair of clean socks to wear on top of yours.'

'My socks are soaking,' she said, peeling one off.

'Thick socks then.'

Helena removed the rest of her footwear and leaned against the doorjamb, taking in the view. A series of valleys, small woods and fields lay like a bumpy quilt before her, leading down to a thread of silver that was the river. The sun coming out after the rain caused mist to drift across the landscape like skeins of carded wool. She couldn't help planning a wall hanging inspired by the spectacular scene — or maybe an actual quilt that could go on a bed or sofa.

She was summoned back to the present by Jago's 'Here!' He was holding two pairs of socks,

295

one pair of them extra thick, designed to go inside climbing boots or wellies. It took a few moments to get the thinner pair on over her damp feet but when she had the second pair on she had hope that her feet would one day be warm again.

'Come in. I'll get the fire going. It's not that cold but Fred needs to be kept warm,' said Jago.

The thought of a fire encouraged Helena to go into the house.

Jago was in the kitchen, a lean-to attached to the back of the property: a cottage, one room deep, that smelt of damp and slightly rotting vegetables. There was a small piece of land outside the kitchen window and then there was the hill. 'Go through into the front room. Fred is there.'

'Is there a bathroom of any kind I could use? I need to get the mud off my hands.' She was expecting to be shown to an outdoor privy. It was that sort of house.

'Oh! Of course, sorry.' He indicated a door just off the kitchen. 'It's in there. Not very salubrious, I'm afraid, but it has running water.'

There was an ancient lavatory with an overhead cistern and a cracked handbasin, both of which were fairly stained but, because of the broken window, the little room didn't smell. She felt a lot better when she came out.

'Right,' said Jago, who had obviously been waiting for her. 'I'll introduce you to Fred.'

Although he was making all the right gestures, Jago's manner was making Helena feel unwelcome and if she had had her car outside she would have got into it and driven away. But she didn't have that choice.

Jago ushered her into the front room, which was small but had the most amazing view. An old man was sitting in an armchair there; next to him was a small table covered with invalid paraphernalia. Going on what she could see, Fred was in need of quite a lot of support. 'Fred? This is Helena. Helena? This is Fred. Right, I'll make tea.'

'Don't rush off, lad,' said Fred, who looked frail but seemed to be in command of all his senses. 'Is Helena your girlfriend?'

Jago looked at Helena and gave a tiny shrug, as if he didn't know. Then he went to make the tea.

'Yes,' said Helena firmly. 'Yes, I am his girlfriend.' She went further into the room and sat on the chair next to Fred's. 'This view is wonderful! I could look at it all day.' It was similar to the view that had inspired Helena so much from the kitchen doorway but at a different angle and there was no river at the bottom.

'That is pretty much all I do these days: look at the view. And yes, I'll miss it,' said Fred.

'You're leaving here?'

'Didn't Jon tell you? I can't manage here on my own and my daughter is going to have me with her. But she's having the house made suitable and there are complications. Aren't there always when there are builders involved?' He said this with a twinkle but Helena realised he was a bit fed up.

'I suppose when you start building work,

297

problems you never knew were there are revealed,' said Helena.

'Yes, well,' went on Fred, 'they wanted me to stay in hospital until the work was done, said I couldn't come out and live here as it wasn't fit for an elderly and infirm person who'd just had a serious op. Well! I wasn't staying in that place with all those ill people. They'd call me a bed-blagger — blocker — one of those things. I put in a call to Jon and he came straight up here.'

'He's very kind,' said Helena. This was demonstrably true and she'd experienced it herself. But there were still an awful lot about him she couldn't be anything like as sure of.

'He's a good lad. It wasn't fair, what happened to him.'

'What did happen to him?' Although it felt a bit wrong to grill a sick old man for information this did seem too good an opportunity to miss.

Annoyingly, before Fred could tell her anything, Jago — Jonathan — came back into the room with a tray. He found another little table and put the tray on it. On the tray were three chipped mugs of tea and a packet of Rich Tea biscuits.

'The biscuits are a little stale, I'm afraid,' said Jago. 'I haven't been able to go shopping.'

'I've got shortbread in my car,' said Helena. 'Sadly it's down the hill and quite a way away. The road was closed, which was why I walked up.'

'You walked up the hill to see me?' said Fred, astonished.

'Sorry to break it to you,' said Jago, 'but I

think she may have walked up here to see me.' He gave her a sideways glance and a little smile that reminded her of how he had been when they'd been together. Why was he so different now?

'It's quite far,' said Helena, 'or I'd run back down and fetch them. The running down part is fine but walking back up is a bit exhausting.'

'Why don't you go down in your pickup, Jon?' suggested Fred. 'Leave me and your young lady to talk.'

'That's a good idea!' said Helena.

'No it's not, not even for shortbread, even though Helena's mother does make amazing shortbread.' Jago was firm. 'Now, Fred, do you want tea? Or are you full of healthier fluids?'

'Tea doesn't taste the same any more,' said Fred sadly. 'But shortbread would.' He looked pleadingly at Jago, who shook his head.

'Maybe later Helena could sit with you while I go shopping and collect what she needs from her car. But she's only just arrived and she can't be in charge of you without the proper training.'

'Really?' asked Helena. 'Did you have training, Ja — Jonathan?'

'No, he didn't,' said Fred. 'And he lied to the woman from social services and said he was my son. Poor woman was so overworked and desperate for my bed that when Jon said he'd take full responsibility she let him.'

'And also Helena probably needs to get back. When were you thinking of leaving?'

Jago obviously wanted her gone. Helena's heart sank. 'As you know, I've only just arrived

299

and, having come all this way, including walking up a very steep hill, I'd like an opportunity to get to know Fred a bit.'

'Considering you didn't know Fred existed until a few minutes ago I'm surprised at your enthusiasm for his company,' said Jago.

'But now she's met me, she's in no hurry to leave. Isn't that right, Helena?'

Fred was obviously enjoying the argument and Helena hoped that there would be plenty going on for him to enjoy when he moved to his daughter's. While the scenery was spectacular here it was very isolated.

'That's right! But why don't we have our tea, and then Ja — Jonathan can start the training programme so he can go shopping.' She sipped her tea. It was starting to go cold.

'Bring your tea,' said Jago, 'and I'll give you a tour of the house.'

'Won't take long!' said Fred cheerfully.

Apart from the kitchen there was one room that was obviously Fred's bedroom and another smaller room with a single bed in it.

'Oh,' said Helena, taking in that there was nowhere for her to stay. 'Sleeping in shifts then!'

'Actually, if you are here, that would be good. I don't like to leave Fred unattended, even at night.'

'So you stayed up all last night?'

'I dozed in the chair for a bit.'

'But you don't want me here,' she said, a statement not a question.

He didn't answer for a long time and when he did his expression was bleak. 'I want you here

300

but I don't want you to be here for the reason that you are.'

'Which is? That was quite a complicated sentence.'

'I don't want you to have found out about my past. James must have told you, right?'

'No, I saw your picture on his Facebook page. And to be fair, only I would have recognised it. You're just really unlucky having a girlfriend like me.'

He didn't answer for so long Helena thought he was never going to. 'Not unlucky. Terribly, terribly lucky.'

'I came to hear your side of the story.'

'I will tell you, I promise. But not now. I must take advantage of you being here to get some urgent supplies.'

'But Fred knows?'

'Fred doesn't know I reinvented myself. He's part of the story.'

They heard a noise from the living room and Jago moved quickly to get there.

Fred was fine. 'Sorry! I just knocked my glass of water off the table. Sorry to frighten you, love,' he added, smiling at Helena.

'If you can stop him causing chaos while I'm away for a couple of hours, I'll go shopping,' said Jago, when everything was cleared up.

'How are you going to do that with the road closed?'

Jago grinned. 'I'll do what I did on my way up here: move the barriers, drive round the hole and then put the barriers back again. Simples!'

Seeing him smiling again was like the sun

coming out. And then he was gone, with a shopping list and a promise to text Gilly to tell her Helena was safe.

'So it's just you and me then, Fred,' said Helena, hoping Jago wouldn't be too long but knowing the nearest town was miles away and he wouldn't be back for a couple of hours.

'That's right. How are we going to pass the time?'

'Well,' said Helena, 'I was hoping — '

'Tell you what,' said Fred, who didn't seem to have heard her, 'what I'd really like is for you to read to me.'

'Oh, what? The newspaper?' Helena hid her disappointment that she couldn't spend the time grilling him.

'Dick Francis!' said Fred gleefully. 'They're all there on the shelf. Haven't been able to read them for years! You've got a nice voice.' He smiled. 'See if you can find the first one. *Dead Cert*, I think it was.'

Helena consoled herself with the fact that she quite liked Dick Francis too.

'I'll get myself a glass of water before I begin.'

31

In the end it was three hours before Jago got back. By this time Helena and Fred were close friends. She'd read quite a lot of *Dead Cert,* made him a sandwich and a cup of tea, watched while he had a nap and, frighteningly, helped him to the loo. Fortunately once he was in there he could manage. But the unevenness of the floors and how hard he found it to manage them demonstrated that he urgently needed to live somewhere else.

Fred was asleep again by the time Helena heard Jago's pickup arrive. She ran out to meet him.

'Hi! Did you manage to get everything? Did you text Mum?'

'I did and she rang me immediately so I was able to convince her you were fine but wouldn't be back for a while.' He studied her carefully. 'I didn't specify any time so you don't need to worry about her worrying about you — but of course you can go now if you want to.'

She studied him back, trying to interpret his wishes from his calm, serious expression. She failed. 'What would you like me to do?'

'Honestly? I'd like you to stay — it's too late for you to set off back home today in any case.'

Helena took a breath to ask if it was only concern for her that made him not want her to leave or if there were any other reasons but her nerve failed her. She didn't feel she knew this

Jonathan/Jago very well and couldn't predict his response.

'OK, well, let's see what you've got and then think about supper. Fred had a cheese sandwich for lunch.'

'Really? He managed that?'

'I took the crusts off and cut it into very small pieces but he did find it a struggle. He enjoyed it though. I read him an awful lot of Dick Francis, too.'

'So you didn't talk much?'

Helena suppressed a sigh. 'No, we didn't talk much.' Every time she'd tried to talk about Jago, Fred had changed the subject. 'He didn't tell me any of your secrets but I need you to tell me them. I can't cope with not knowing who you are for much longer.'

Jago didn't bother to suppress his sigh; it was loud and heartfelt. 'I know. But it'll take a while and I'm so tired and busy. Oh, by the way, I broke into your car and retrieved the shortbread and your overnight bag.'

'Useful and worrying at the same time, but mostly useful so thank you.' Then, remembering he hadn't slept properly because he'd been sitting up with Fred, she went on, 'Why don't you have a nap? I'll do supper and maybe put the telly on for Fred to keep him amused?'

'That would be great, if you don't mind? Fred is my responsibility, not yours.'

'He's my friend, which is also important, and when you wake up, when we've a suitable moment, you're going to tell me just why he's your responsibility.'

'OK.' Jago seemed very tired, more tired even than a night dozing in an armchair should make you. He took a couple of steps out of the kitchen and then turned back. 'Good luck with the telly. Only three channels and one of them is Welsh. Luckily I bought a paper . . . '

★ ★ ★

By six o'clock Helena had made a cottage pie out of the mince Jago had bought, and given Fred some. He was very enthusiastic about it but didn't actually eat very much. Helena didn't eat very much either. She and Fred were drinking tea and looking at the view (Jago had been right about the telly not being up to much) when Jago came in.

They were both pleased to see him. Although happy with each other — Helena was learning how best to help Fred all the time — they were both aware of Jago's absence, although Fred called him Jon.

'Go and get yourself some pie and then come and entertain this young lady,' said Fred. 'She's bored with me.'

'I am absolutely not bored with you!' said Helena indignantly. 'But do help yourself to pie, Jago, and then join us. I want to know how you two met.'

It was a simple question and Helena said it in the bright way people do when they're making small talk. But no one was fooled.

'This may need a drink,' said Jago. 'I bought a bottle of rum. I know you like it, Fred.'

'Not really allowed it now, but you could put a drop in my tea and no one would notice,' he said.

'Just more tea for me, please,' said Helena when Jago looked at her enquiringly. 'Oh, and ginger biscuits please. For dunking.'

'Good idea,' said Fred.

While Jago was away Helena smiled at Fred. 'So you and him go back a long way?'

Fred smiled too, but shook his head. 'I'll let him tell you.'

There was a lot of moving small tables and shifting chairs slightly and seeing Fred was all right before Jago finally said, 'OK. Well, it was about ten years ago, wasn't it, Fred?'

Fred nodded. 'Ten years. I was a relatively fit man then.'

'And you met where?' said Helena, who was by this time beside herself with impatience. She was crunching into ginger nuts as if they were the enemy.

'You'd better start at the beginning, lad,' said Fred.

'I don't know how much Helena knows. There's stuff on the internet and she'll have read that,' said Jago.

'You tell her,' said Fred firmly. 'There were a lot of lies told at the time. She'll only hear the whole truth from you.'

'What have you read?' Jago asked Helena, obviously terribly unwilling to say a word more than necessary.

'I read about the fire in the block of flats where five people were nearly killed. The fire

306

brigade got awards for saving them. It was thought to be shoddy building work that made the fire spread once it had started. The building company — Relto — was condemned for its bad practice. The head of the company was sued for manslaughter but got off. Clever lawyers, everyone thought. The world was outraged. I actually remember it although I was quite young and didn't pay much attention to current events.'

'So was I,' said Jago, 'though I was of working age.'

'You were just a lad, Jonathan, and they tried to blame you for everything,' said Fred. 'His uncle' — Fred addressed Helena — 'he owned the business; he was responsible. What he said, went. Young Jonathan was in quite a different part of the business. He was selling the properties that his uncle threw up.'

'Did you work there too then, Fred?' asked Helena.

He nodded. 'I was on the construction side.'

'So you met through work?' Helena went on, hoping she'd get the whole story.

'Not at the time,' said Jago. 'I met Fred after it had all gone horribly wrong.'

'Oh?' Helena felt she had to keep prompting because both Fred and Jago were so reluctant to tell her what had happened.

'For some reason,' said Jago, 'I got all the flack, the doorstepping, pilloried in the press, all that stuff.' He paused. 'Long sessions with the police which actually worked in my favour in the end because I got to know one of the younger ones. He was my contact when I wanted to find

307

out about that Leo your mother was going out with.'

Fred wasn't interested in any upsides, he was too indignant. 'You got that because your uncle kindly redirected all the stuff that he should have dealt with to his nephew.' Outrage gave Fred energy and he seemed to have stopped being old and frail for the time being. 'He blamed everything on the apprentice who was working his way up from the bottom, to keep himself out of prison.'

'Is that true?' Helena was outraged.

Jago nodded. 'I was in a bad place in every way when I met Fred.'

'We met at the site of the fire, by coincidence,' said Fred. 'I recognised him, we got chatting and I offered to teach him bricklaying.'

Jago grinned. 'You told me it was time I got calluses on my hands and actually learned how to build. He took me on, and I learned my trade.' He paused. 'I decided to change my name by deed poll before I did that. Grew my hair and a bit of a beard. No one recognised me.'

'I never agreed with you having to change your identity,' said Fred. 'It looked as if you'd done something wrong.'

'Maybe it was cowardly, but I was so ashamed of my name, I didn't want to be known by it any more.'

'How did you choose your new name?' asked Helena.

'Jago was a nickname from school, and Pengelly was my grandmother's name. There is a Cornish connection so I'm not a complete fraud.

308

Anyone else for more tea?'

While he was out of the room Fred said, 'We've kept in touch and he's always helped me out if I'm in bother. He's supported my family, too. Not with money but with jobs and accommodation once or twice. He's built a new life for himself. I'm proud of him.'

Helena's throat suddenly closed with emotion as she realised she felt proud of him too.

After Jago had brought the tea, he went out again and came back with a bowl of jelly and ice cream for Fred. 'My favourite,' he said happily as Jago put it in front of him.

'I suppose it's nice and easy to eat,' said Helena.

Fred gave her a funny look. 'It's bloody delicious. It's always been my favourite.'

Seeing Fred's, Helena wanted jelly and ice cream too. When they had all had it, Fred yawned.

'Tell you what, it's turned into a lovely evening out there,' he said to Jago. 'Why don't you take Helena outside and tell her the rest of the story? There's a nice bench a little way along. Perfect for looking at the view and talking.'

Helena looked at Jago, who then looked at Fred. 'You'll be OK?'

'I've got my bell. I'll ring if I need you.'

Jago got up and held out his hand for Helena's so he could pull her up too. 'This calls for rum.'

'And more ginger biscuits. For dunking,' she said.

'Really?' Jago and Fred both looked horrified.

'Don't knock it till you've tried it.'

Jago had to go back inside for an old mac and cushions as the seat, although perfectly positioned, was soaking wet.

'It is an idyllic spot,' said Helena. 'You get a bit of both views, the one at the front and the one at the back.'

Jago nodded. 'My plan is to make the cottage habitable — extend it a bit — and then Fred could maybe come up for holidays with his daughter and her family.' He looked down at her. 'Maybe we could come up here too?' He had become tentative as if not quite sure how he stood with her.

She picked up on his doubt and became shy. 'I would like that.'

He handed her a glass of rum and the packet of biscuits. She took one and dipped it in. 'So?' she asked. 'What's the rest of the story?'

'It's more background really. Before the fire I was engaged to be married. We were young but we were in love and she had a big wedding planned. All the bells and whistles, country house hotel, a band for the day and another for the night. Her dress cost several thousand pounds.'

'Oh my goodness.' Helena crunched into a rumsoaked biscuit for support.

'But after it all blew up she broke off the engagement. Said she didn't want everyone to be putting up pictures and mocking her for marrying a man who could have been responsible for people dying.'

310

'Although they didn't die.'

'And I wasn't responsible. She knew that, but the rest of the world thought I was. She had a point.'

Helena sipped the rum without the biscuit and found she liked it.

'I suggested we elope, so we'd be married but we just wouldn't have the big party. It turned out it was the big party she wanted really, so our relationship probably would have ended in tears anyway.' He smiled ruefully. 'She liked being engaged to the nephew of a major property developer; she didn't want to be shacked up with a simple builder who was going to have to start again with nothing.'

'There's that song,' said Helena. '"If I were a carpenter, and you were a lady . . ."'

'Believe me, that song was often in my head in those early months.'

'So, you not only lost your job and your reputation, you lost the love of your life as well.'

Jago nodded. 'Except she wasn't the love of my life as it turned out; she was quite selfish and a bit irritating.' He paused. 'She would have never put aside her claustrophobia and got covered in mud because a stranger asked her to rescue a kitten.'

'Oh.' Helena's mood had been pensive but it took a little uplift now.

'Although I suppose I can't blame her for wanting the huge extravaganza. It's what every little girl wants, isn't it, from when they're nine years old? That's what she told me.'

Helena shrugged. 'Is it? I don't know.'

'Really?' He seemed surprised, almost disbelieving.

'I may be on my own here, but I haven't given my wedding any thought at all.' Now she did think about it she realised she wanted something quite low-key, at her mother's house. Tent in the garden, lots of cake.

'But don't you want to get married?'

She couldn't read his expression. He was confused, she decided, possibly a bit disappointed, and disbelieving. 'Well, I haven't ruled it out. But my life has been focused on different things: my weaving, my career, earning a living.' She paused. 'I would like children, eventually — I can't deprive my mum of grandchildren she's allowed to feed — but I haven't really thought about it.'

She sipped her rum but didn't quite have the heart to dip another biscuit in it. She did want to get married, but there was only one man she wanted to get married to, and right now she had no idea what he wanted. And although he'd told her about his name change and the reasons for it, could she trust him? Also, while he was talking about marriage and asking her about weddings, he wasn't asking her to marry him. And he might have told her about his past now, but he hadn't said anything before. Had he been hoping to avoid telling her, ever?

She suddenly felt desperately tired and wanted her own bed and a novel where nothing bad happened. She yawned and then got up. 'What time does Fred go to bed?'

'Why do you ask?'

'Because I want to go to bed now. I think it's the rum.' It was better to blame it on the rum than to explain the turmoil he had caused her.

'I could start getting him into bed any time now but why don't you go now and get some sleep? I'll be fine until about four o'clock in the morning.'

She felt a wave of fondness for him. He was being very kind. 'You don't have to stay up that long! Let me have a couple of hours and then wake me.'

'All right.'

Something about the way he said this made her realise he wouldn't wake her unless or until he was passing out with tiredness. 'I'll set my alarm, just in case,' she said.

He made an indignant face. 'In case of what?'

'In case you forget to wake me.'

He laughed. 'OK, I'll wake you after two hours or so then.'

When she was finally convinced he wouldn't take the entire night shift on his own she went to bed.

It was odd going to bed in the little narrow bed he'd been in so recently. The mattress was old and had a dip in the middle, which meant it had a coffin-like feel, but Helena decided it was cosy. The room was full of things cleared out of the living room, probably to make space for Fred's medical paraphernalia. But underneath the piled-up furniture and boxes she found a cache of Mills and Boon novels.

'Oh, lovely!' said Helena out loud and found a couple she liked the look of. But she was asleep

313

before she'd even properly opened the first one.

She was awake as soon as she heard Jago's tap on the door. She called to him that she was up and pulled on some clothes. She left her hair in a tangle, thinking she could brush it when she was watching Fred.

'That was quick,' said Jago, looking at her a bit strangely.

'I did my best. Now you go and get your head down. The bed is all warmed up for you.'

He didn't go immediately. 'I like your hair like that,' he said.

'Really?' Helena didn't believe him.

'You know what to do? Help Fred to the loo, get him anything he needs and if he's too heavy, or anything happens, call me immediately. OK?'

She nodded. 'On your way, bonny lad,' she said with a smile and a bad Scottish accent.

The moment he had gone she looked in the mirror. Her hair was a tousled mess but, she realised, it was also a bit sexy. At least Jago couldn't possibly think she'd done it specially.

It was quite peaceful sitting in a dark room with a table lamp and a good book. She took Fred to the bathroom once, which took a long time, and before she knew it, it was nearly time to wake Jago. She decided she needed a cup of tea and made one for Jago, too.

Jago was facing the wall and stirred when she put the mug down on the bedside table. 'Jago? Are you awake? It's time for a shift change. I've brought you tea.'

Jago turned over and before she knew what he was about to do he had reached up and pulled

314

her down for a kiss. She found herself in his arms, half lying on the single bed. For a second or two she allowed herself to stay there, wrapped in his arms, in the dark, just the two of them. And then thoughts of Fred, possibly needing the bathroom again, made her pull away.

'We haven't time for this,' she said. 'Drink your tea and then get up.'

She heard the shower going — an attachment on the taps in the narrow bath — and shortly afterwards he appeared in the living room.

'OK, I'll take over now,' he said. 'Thanks for the tea.'

She thought she'd never sleep but the bed was warm and cocoon-like and the room very dark. While she did spend quite a bit of time thinking about Jago and how she felt about him now, she did drift off and soon Jago was shaking her arm.

'Hey! Wake up! You must have been very deeply asleep. I've been knocking and calling for ages.'

She sat up in bed. 'Oh, gosh, sorry! What time is it?'

'Just after four. Dawn is breaking and the birds are singing loud enough to deafen you.'

'Have you made me tea?'

'I have. It's getting cold so hurry up!'

The dawn was so lovely it made Helena (who was a bit sleep-deprived) feel almost weepy. The sun was coming up, sending shafts of sunlight through woodlands, across fields and into the valleys. In the background the birds were so loud they could have been a music track.

She sat in the chair that Jago had moved so

she could see the view and sipped her tea. As she watched the mist, which again reminded her so much of carded wool, drift across the landscape she saw a little group of deer emerge from the trees and start grazing in a field.

'Look,' she whispered. 'The deer!'

'You don't have to whisper,' said Jago, who'd reappeared behind her. 'They won't hear you from here.'

She dug him in the arm with her elbow. 'Not them — Fred! How is he? Anything you need to tell me?'

'Not really. He gets up early though so there's no point in my going back to bed really.'

'Go for a couple of hours. You can get him up when he's ready. I'll wake you.'

She had been planning to read but instead Helena sat and watched the day slowly wake with the promise of sunshine and light. But distracting her from the beauty, even more than the progress of the deer, who ate the grass for a bit and then meandered across to the next wood, were her thoughts of Jago. She had to get them into order, she decided.

Did she still love him? she asked herself. She decided she did because the thought of anything bad happening to him made her really sad. She tested the theory by imagining something awful happening to Cressida or Martin. She was upset and really didn't want it to come about but she didn't mind as much as when she thought of Jago suffering.

Could she forgive him for not telling her about his past? Well, she decided, he probably would have told her eventually, and so yes. Except she didn't know this for sure. Doubt waved in and out of her mind. He'd worked hard to create a new identity, why would he risk telling anyone about his old one?

Abandoning the back-and-forth this created she asked herself other questions. Was Jago a kind man? Easy — yes, he was. She'd experienced it herself and seen it with Fred. He was extremely kind.

Did she fancy him? Another easy one: yes she did, a lot.

Hard question. Did she love him enough to overlook her doubts? Probably yes.

Hardest question. Was he so disillusioned by women that he wouldn't be able to commit to a relationship again? Answer was definitely 'don't know' followed by 'hope not'.

Final question. How did he feel about her? He certainly fancied her and liked her as a person, but love? She couldn't know. He hadn't said as much although he had come near it.

She was grateful when Fred stirred, wanting the bathroom. She was driving herself mad with her questions.

32

The day progressed slowly, filled with small tasks until after lunch Jago said, 'I think I'll go somewhere and pick up emails and things. Do you want me to take your phone? Your emails would download and then you could read them.'

'That would be nice,' said Helena.

'Get me a newspaper with a decent crossword in it,' said Fred. 'And if you can get in touch with my daughter, tell her I'm being very well looked after but I need to get somewhere I can move about more easily.'

'I think she knows that, Fred,' said Jago. 'But I will pass on the message.'

Helena walked out with him to the car. 'The trouble is,' he said, 'Fred's daughter is struggling to afford the alterations. You do get some help from the government but not everything she needs.'

'Oh dear, that's worrying.'

'It wouldn't be worrying if she'd accept help from me! But she says her family has had enough from me and won't take any more.'

Helena let her gaze take in what she now thought of as the Back-door View. 'Isn't there some way they could raise money from this place? It's in such a heavenly spot. It would make the ideal holiday home — or rental. Anything really.'

He frowned. 'Well,' he said after a bit, 'I

suppose I could buy it from them, if they wanted to sell. I would be taking on a far greater mortgage load than I'm happy with, but if it did the trick for them I'd do it.'

'Or maybe you pay for the renovations, etc., and pay yourself back from the lettings. Once you're reimbursed the rental income would come to them. And they could come and stay too, when it's done up. The cottage and the view would stay in the family.'

'Why didn't I think of that? It's the perfect solution! Clever you! I'll still have to borrow a fairly hefty amount but nothing like as massive.'

Excited, he put his arms round her and lifted her off the ground before giving her a big kiss on the cheek. 'I'll put it to Maureen; see what she says.'

When he came back from his trip a few hours later, he said, 'First, the road's back open; second, Gilly wants to hear from you ASAP; and finally, Maureen was delighted with your suggestion. I had to explain that the money for the repairs would be a loan and not a gift and she was quite happy. They'd thought they'd have to sell Fred's house and although they knew it was for the best, they were very sad at the prospect. This way they can have their cake and eat it, so to speak.' He grinned. 'And as she's accepted a quick injection of cash from me, her house will be Fred-friendly very soon.' Now he looked more serious. 'Then we can go home.'

★   ★   ★

319

Two mornings later Maureen and her husband came for Fred, which was a relief, for although Helena and Jago had developed techniques for looking after him, it had become increasingly clear he needed a properly modified home. When Helena heard a car drive up while Jago and Fred were in the bathroom, giving him a shower before his journey home, she went out to meet it.

'So,' said Maureen, a pleasant-looking woman in her fifties with a warm smile. 'Are you the wonderful woman Jon has been talking about?'

Helena was thrown — partly by Maureen's use of Jago's old name but more by his apparent description of her. 'I'm Helena,' she said. 'I can't answer for anything else.'

'You are wonderful because you've been helping Jon look after my dad so just accept the compliment.' She gave Helena a quick hug. 'It's been a bit of a nightmare, getting the house ready for Dad.'

'I bet,' said Helena.

'But Jon has saved the day, again!'

'Well, he told me that Fred saved him when he was in a very dark place. So he's delighted to be able to give something back.'

'He's given back with interest!' said Maureen.

'Come in,' said Helena. 'Though it's your house really. I put the kettle on ages ago. It's probably boiled dry by now. Jago — Jon is giving Fred a shower for the journey home.'

'Not easy with that dreadful thing you put on the taps. I never have been able to work it without soaking the bathroom and myself.'

320

'Oh no, nor me!' said Helena. 'Now, tea — or would you prefer coffee?'

They had a quick chat before Maureen said, 'Well, Dad, it's time we were getting off.'

Fred looked as if he would argue and then said, 'I suppose you're right. Not that Newport is that far . . . '

'It will take us a while to settle you in the other end,' said Maureen. 'And the family are all eager to see you.'

Fred smiled. 'They're a good lot. I'm very lucky.'

★ ★ ★

When the car had driven away, leaving them waving on the hilltop, Helena realised she would miss Fred. She'd become very fond of him and remembered her mother saying that when you look after something or someone you begin to care about them.

'He is a lovely person,' she said. 'I really like him.'

'And he likes you, too.'

'Really? How do you know?'

'He told me. He said, 'Don't let that one slip through your fingers, young Jonathan. You'll regret it forever.''

'Oh,' said Helena, feeling herself blush.

'Yes. He's very wise, is Fred.' He moved around so his arms encircled her. 'What do you say to us making us a permanent thing?'

'What do you mean?' She looked up at him, fairly certain she knew but not quite sure enough

321

to reply without clarification.

'I'm asking you to marry me.' He gazed down at her, a sense of wonder in his expression. 'I'd decided I wasn't going to try the whole marriage thing again. It was such a disaster before. But you're different.'

A thousand thoughts and questions floated through Helena's mind like motes of dust. Could she trust him? And did he love her as much as she loved him?

Her silence made him talk more. 'I've never met a girl like you, Helena, so sweet and kind and yet so maddeningly attractive! I didn't realise girls came in that model. I thought they were all selfish and narcissistic. But, to be honest, I think I'd have fallen in love with you even if you hadn't rescued the kitten or done anything kind. I know it hasn't been long but it feels right. I feel I've met my other half.'

'But how do you know it's real? You thought you were in love before.'

'Because it's happened without me realising it. I love you, Helena, for better, for worse. And if you leave me, you should know I'll go on loving you for the rest of my life. I realise it's not easy for you because you don't know who is declaring their love to you. Is it Jonathan? Or is it Jago? Well, I'll tell you, it's Jago. Jonathan was the boy who was made a man by bad things happening to him. But can you believe me? Can you trust me?'

Helena's uncertainty left her as surely as if had never been there. Of course she could trust him — and he had told her he loved her pretty clearly. 'Oh, Jago! Of course. And yes, I'd love to marry you.'

He gave a deep sigh of relief before his hold on her tightened and he kissed her.

33

Gilly had put on a brave mother's smile while she waved off her daughter into the rainstorm but she was very worried. Watching your child get over heartbreak was, she knew, one of the hardest parts of being a parent, and she really hoped she didn't have to do it for Helena and Jago. They were such a good couple, so well suited, and whatever his past, she was certain Jago was a good man.

She was delighted when William called. 'Gilly? Are you very busy? Could you tunnel out for a visit somewhere?'

It was lovely to hear his voice and she particularly loved hearing him say her name. 'I'm not that busy, as it happens, being midweek. What did you have in mind?'

'I want you to come and see my house.'

Just for a moment Gilly had a nasty flashback of when Leo took her to see his house — the beautiful house he didn't own. 'Oh,' she said.

William seemed to know she was having a wobble. 'I just thought you ought to know where I lived. After all, we are a couple now, aren't we?'

'We definitely are.' Gilly gave a little sigh of happiness. 'When will we go?'

'Tomorrow. I'd like to take you out to lunch first, nearby, and then show it to you. I'm planning to take the afternoon off.'

'I do love an outing when a bit of bunking-off

324

is involved,' said Gilly. 'Will you pick me up? Or shall I meet you somewhere. I've got to do some shopping so it would be no trouble.'

'I'd prefer to pick you up, if you don't mind, then it's more like a date and less like an estate agent's appointment.'

Gilly laughed and shortly afterwards they disconnected.

★ ★ ★

William lived in a nearby town that was famous for its antique shops. Fortunately it also had a fair number of very nice places to eat. He took her to a Italian wine bar that was also a delicatessen where he was greeted like an old friend.

'William! Your table is free. I'll bring the board over when you're settled.' The proprietor gave Gilly a bow that was respectful and curious at the same time.

'Hello, Franco. This is my good friend Gilly.'

Gilly dipped her head nervously and smiled back; then she followed them to the table.

'I'm not going to bother to ask if you come here often,' she said when they were both seated.

He laughed. 'It is my regular. I live very nearby.'

'A town house?'

'Yes.'

'I can't wait to see it.'

'Could you imagine yourself living in a town, Gilly?'

Gilly thought about it. 'This is a very nice

325

town. Lovely shops, lovely places to eat — ' She guessed he was showing her his home before asking if she'd like to move in with him. It was terribly early days. While she was completely sure of William, she wasn't sure she was ready to throw up her life to be with him. It made her very twitchy.

He laughed, aware she wasn't answering his question.

'What are you going to have to eat?' she asked.

'I usually have whatever Franco tells me is best. It saves me having to decide.'

'I'm not good at decision-making either,' said Gilly, 'if it doesn't particularly matter.'

'But if it does matter?'

'I'm usually OK on those.'

Franco came up. 'So, what can I get you?'

'What's the special?' asked William.

'Asparagus with a little pasta,' said Franco.

'That sounds delicious,' said Gilly.

'We'll have two of those then.' He looked at Gilly. 'A glass of wine?'

'Yes, please,' said Gilly. Wine would help.

'A glass of wine for my friend, sparkling water for me,' said William.

'It's the first asparagus I've had this year,' said Gilly when they had been served. 'And I've never thought of having it with pasta.'

'I suppose it comes naturally to an Italian, to put pasta with things.'

It was completely delicious.

'You are so lucky living near here!' said Gilly enthusiastically. It was always a safe thing to say.

'I am,' said William, 'but it has its downsides.'

'Really?'

'Not that near the gliding club, for example.'

'Oh,' said Gilly. 'Have you been gliding lately?' She tried to think if he'd had the opportunity to go gliding but, in spite of the wine and the lovely food, she was still a little on edge and couldn't remember his schedule. 'And could I go again?'

'Of course! Any time! We must make a date for it.' He smiled warmly at her. 'I have to say, you are the first girlfriend I've had who has wanted to go gliding.'

'Have you had a lot of girlfriends?' Gilly felt this was an opportunity to find out about William's past without appearing nosy.

'A few since my wife died. None of them remotely serious.' He put his hand on hers and looked into her eyes.

Before she could respond Franco carne over. 'Can I get you dessert? Coffee? Peppermint tea?'

William looked at his watch. 'I think maybe we'd better have coffee at my house, if you don't mind, Gilly?'

'Not at all,' said Gilly; she was keen to see it, and to find out if William had invited her here for more than just a look at the place where he lived. She turned to Franco. 'But another time I'd love to try your desserts. That pasta was amazing.'

'A woman who eats desserts,' said Franco with a satisfied nod. 'Excellent.'

William's flat was just across the road. 'I own the whole property but as you see, the bottom part is currently an antique shop.' He opened the door and ushered Gilly in.

'Ooh, what a lovely shop!' said Gilly, although she realised the antiques were all very high-end and beyond what she would have permitted herself to spend.

'Don't get distracted,' said William firmly. 'Hello, Peter. We're just going upstairs,' he said to the proprietor.

As Gilly went up the steps ahead of William she wondered if the look Peter had given her had been as speculative as Franco's. She was getting the impression that William bringing a woman home was unusual.

He unlocked the door. 'There,' he said. 'Go in.' Gilly was in a beautiful first-floor sitting room and found herself moving to the triple window that overlooked the street. The room was large and had a beautiful stone fireplace. It appeared to have been furnished from the shop down below.

'Of course, it would be perfectly possible to take back the shop and incorporate it into the house,' said William. 'The kitchen is through here and rather small.'

It was small but very well fitted and perfectly big enough for one — or even two.

William opened another door. 'Bedroom, en suite, dressing room, etc. There are two more rooms upstairs. There's a bathroom there too. You can't have guests coming down the stairs in the night, especially if they're Aunt Daphne.'

Gilly laughed, pleased to think of Daphne being here. Personally she felt a bit over-whelmed.

'Imagine a big kitchen downstairs, opening

out on to the courtyard garden.'

'I'm doing that. It's huge!'

'Yes, too huge for one person, which is why I've never done it.'

'Have you had this house long?'

He nodded. 'Yes. I bought it about twenty years ago — it was derelict. I had a small legacy that helped with the deposit. The rent for the shop covered the mortgage.'

'You're telling me very clearly that you own this house,' she said. 'Because . . . '

'Because of what that scoundrel Leo did, implying he owned a house he rented.'

'I love the word 'scoundrel' — it's so charmingly old-fashioned.'

'I am charmingly old-fashioned,' said William.

Gilly laughed. She was beginning to relax a bit. She wandered around this amazing flat and tried to picture herself in it.

She would like being near the shops. She'd love to be within walking distance of nice restaurants. But how would she cope without her B & B guests? She needed work — not just for money but because she believed work was good for people. She went into the kitchen which was at the back and looked down at the courtyard garden. She could see Ulysses there, possibly curled up on top of one of the stone sinks, crushing the succulents or auriculas or whatever was growing there.

'So,' said William, who had let her roam about and explore. 'Could you live here?'

She sighed and bit her lip.

'If I was to offer you my heart and my home,

329

so to speak. I mean, if you took my home and didn't want my heart I would have to find somewhere else to live.'

She managed a laugh.

'And I'm thinking that we will have to decide if we want to live together or carry on as we are.' He looked at her with a mixture of seriousness and gentle humour. 'How do you feel about it? I know it's awfully soon to think about these things but I feel I've wasted enough of my life hoping you'd have a problem with your VAT so you'd come and see me. I want you there every day. Greedy though it sounds.'

She considered her answer. It was a big step and very early days and yet somehow she felt ready to face it. 'I do always feel sad when you go home in the morning.'

'So do I.'

'But although this is a really lovely house — flat — whatever — I'm not sure it's quite for me. The thing is, could you live in my house? I mean, I feel I'm asking you to choose between an amazing, prizewinning racehorse and a big, clumsy old Clydesdale with feet the size of dinner plates, hairy fetlocks, a head the size of a small child, which, however well groomed and polished, will always be a bit of a lump.'

He laughed. 'I love that analogy! And I do have to tell you that I've always been very fond of heavy horses — and old houses in the country.'

'And of course you could bring any favourite pieces of furniture. I could get rid of some of my stuff. Pass it on to Helena, possibly.'

'Not your son?'

'No. Martin wouldn't want it. He and his wife have quite a different style to mine.'

'I'll think about what my favourite bits of furniture are.' He frowned slightly. 'I can't think of anything except the desk that was my father's.'

'You wouldn't want to bring that beautiful fireplace? I'm sure I could find room for it!'

'I think you'll find it's fairly firmly attached to this building.'

'Oh, shame. I was hoping for an upgrade,' said Gilly. Then she became serious. 'But what about the B & B? How will you feel about having to share your home with strangers? It's not for everyone. Sebastian, my ex-husband, was horrified at the thought and he didn't have to do it. Martin thinks it's awful.'

'I don't think it will worry me. We could have our own space, after all.'

'And you don't have to sell this house. You could rent it. Keep it in case . . . ' She paused, worrying if she was saying too much. 'If things didn't work out.'

'You know what? I think things will work out.' He paused in his turn. 'Shall I tell you when I decided to stop looking for women who might become life partners and only had very casual girlfriends?'

'If you like . . . '

'It was when you became a client.'

'Oh!'

'You were in a dreadful state and I knew that I had to bide my time — and it might be a long time — before I could do anything about it, but

331

I fell in love with you the first moment you came into my office.'

Gilly took advantage of the sofa that was just behind her and sat down rather quickly. 'Really?'

'Yes. I hope that doesn't seem stalkerish to you?'

'It is a bit — surprising.' She imagined herself as she had been that day, red-nosed, swollen-eyed, unable to think clearly.

'It surprised me too, I must say,' said William cheerfully.

'Well,' Gilly said after a long pause. 'I'm glad you decided to do something about it eventually.'

'Me too. And we mustn't forget Daphne's input. Although I did rather resent her interference at the time.'

'I think we should tell her we're together,' said Gilly. 'Have her to dinner or something.'

'Mm. I've had something a bit more ambitious in mind.'

Gilly felt she should stop being surprised by William, given that at one time she had thought he was just a really nice accountant, but it was difficult.

'Which is?'

William came and sat beside her. 'Remember my surprise party?'

'It wasn't long ago. Even I can remember that far back.'

He laughed. 'Well, it wasn't quite the party I'd have liked because Daphne had got an old address book and so missed out on people I would have loved to have there. So I thought if I gave another party — same venue probably; it was OK — you could invite your friends and family too and we could announce ourselves as a couple.'

'Unusual,' said Gilly.

'Well, I'd prefer to be able to announce something a bit more conventional but I feel it's too soon.'

Gilly felt she knew what he meant but wasn't quite sure enough of herself to follow this up. 'Well, to be honest, I'd much rather have it at my house. We could have a marquee in the garden. It would be lovely. And it would make sense of the whole thing if you're going to move in with me.'

'It would be an awful lot of work for you. Although of course we'd get a caterer.'

'I'd like to do the puddings myself — the fun part of a party.'

He took her into his arms. 'That would be amazing! How soon do we think we could do it?'

'I don't know . . . '

'I'd like to do it as quickly as possible. Would a fortnight be too soon?'

'Shall we see about the marquee and then decide?' said Gilly. 'I have a favourite firm I use.'

'Excellent. Franco would do the catering if we asked him.' He paused. 'He's been wondering out loud why I'm single for long enough.'

'Maybe we should go back and tell him we're 'coupled up'.'

William kissed her again. 'One of the reasons I love you — you're so 'down wid da kids'.'

Gilly found this thought so hilarious she had to have a drink of water to calm herself down.

Gilly was very happy when William dropped her off, particularly as he had promised to be back for supper. She walked around the house thinking about what furniture she could get rid of so William could have enough things to make the house seem partly his. He'd need space for his desk. Would under the window in the sitting room do or would he actually like a proper study? In which case the room Gilly currently used for flower arranging and as a general dumping ground could be cleared out and made very nice.

But in the meantime, if she moved Martin's old desk, which wasn't very special really, William's desk would fit. She'd ask Martin if he wanted it although it wouldn't really fit into his and Cressida's minimal, modern decorative scheme.

Thinking about Martin made her realise she'd better let him and Cressida know about William and that she should do it face-to-face. She'd email him to invite them over. But the more she thought about telling him, the more nervous she became. She ought to phone but didn't want to.

She didn't escape talking to him. He rang right back as soon as he got her email. 'What is this thing you want to tell us, Ma? Nothing silly, I hope.'

'What do you mean? What could I be telling you that's silly?' She knew exactly what he meant though, and in his eyes, yes, it was silly.

'I don't know,' he said. 'But I think it would be

334

better if you came here to tell us whatever it is.'

'I was going to make the stew you like with the cheese scones.'

'So, you wanted to butter me up with my favourite food.'

She didn't bother to deny it. 'I just thought you'd like it.'

'Come to us. Tomorrow night? About seven. Cressida would never eat stew and scones.'

34

She brought flowers from her garden, already in her jam jar so Cressida wouldn't have to worry about finding a vase (she might not even have a vase), some cheese straws (Martin loved anything cheesy) and a book for Ismene. She also got out a bottle of wine from the cellar which she thought looked OK although she couldn't remember much about it. She'd bought it after a long and persuasive phone call from a famous wine merchant some time ago. Now she really hoped it was nice. On Martin and Cressida's doorstep, waiting for the bell to be answered, she wished she'd brought two bottles.

'Mum! Hi!' said Martin. He hugged her briefly. He made Gilly feel wary.

'Hello, darling. How lovely to see you! Is everyone well? It seems ages.'

'Well, come in. Oh, thank you for this,' he said, taking the bottle and leaving Gilly with her arms still fairly full.

Cressida, looking very well groomed and thin, was perched on the edge of the sofa, her knees clamped together. She had very tense legs, Gilly felt, and now, when she got up, every sinew of them was visible. 'Gilly! You brought flowers, how lovely!'

'Yes,' said Gilly, handing them over. 'They just need some water. You don't need to rush around trying to find a vase for them.'

'Very thoughtful,' said her daughter-in-law, although Gilly suspected she was the sort of person who thought flowers in jam jars was a bit 'shabby chic' and not her style.

'And where's my lovely granddaughter?' she asked. 'I've got a book for her that she might like.'

'She's staying with a friend. We felt we could relax more if she wasn't here.'

'Oh. Well, let me know if she likes the book. I could get more by that author.'

'Very kind. She loves reading, as you know.'

'She's a credit to you,' said Gilly, wishing her granddaughter were there in person. A little light relief would have been very welcome. And she loved Issi.

Martin handed her a glass. 'Sherry, Mum?' he asked.

She took the glass. She did like sherry but the Tio Pepe Martin served was very dry and she yearned to tell him she liked something a bit sweeter. A nice amontillado was much more her thing.

'So,' she said, having taken a sip. 'Shall we get what I have to tell you over? Tell you now?'

'No!' said Martin urgently. 'Not yet!'

'It's no big deal really,' said Gilly. 'It's only that — '

'Stop!' said Martin, holding up a commanding hand. 'Dad's coming.'

'What!' Gilly stopped trying to be well-mannered and restrained. 'Why? What did you invite him for?'

'I thought if you were going to be telling us

337

something potentially serious he should be here,' said Martin.

Gilly took a breath, forcing herself to remember that Martin was away for most of the acrimonious divorce proceedings and she'd made a point of not telling her children quite how awful their father was. Helena knew a lot more, of course. It had been harder to hide it from her.

'What I have to tell you, Martin, is absolutely nothing to do with your father!'

'Well, it must be something important or you wouldn't be making such a big deal of it,' said Martin.

Gilly drained her sherry glass. This was going very badly. Martin was so hostile. Maybe she should just say that she wanted to get rid of his desk but not say why? But then it would look dreadful if the next time Martin and his family came over William literally had his feet under the table. And there was the party. She'd have to invite Martin and Cressida to that.

She took a breath. 'Well, there are two things. The first is, I don't want to sell my house but I do want to get rid of some bits of furniture. I wanted to see if you wanted them.'

There was a short, tense silence. Martin pursed his lips. Then he said haughtily, 'Well, it's a shame you don't want to help out your family, but I accept your decision. And the second thing? It can't only be that or you wouldn't be here.'

If Martin hadn't been such a serious person she'd have said, 'You've got me bang to rights.' As it was she made a non-committal little sound.

The doorbell jangled and Gilly had time to wonder if it was the most irritating one she had ever heard. Then she heard her ex-husband's deep, loud voice. 'She's still got that sardine can of a car, I see,' he said. As he was still in the hall it was possible he didn't intend Gilly to hear him, but it was unlikely.

'Hello, Sebastian,' said Gilly.

'Hello, Gilly,' he said and bent to kiss her cheek.

The smell of his aftershave made her shudder. 'It's been a while,' she said.

'Well, you know why. I would have been more than happy to keep things amicable but you couldn't seem to do that.'

It occurred to Gilly that he'd got married in the first place so he'd have someone constantly on hand to blame things on. Nothing was ever his fault, it was always hers, however unreasonable he'd been.

'Shall we go through?' said Cressida, who seemed nervous. 'It's all ready.'

Although she knew Cressida would be perfectly prepared Gilly leaped to her feet. 'Let me give you a hand!' She followed Cressida through to the kitchen.

'I'm so sorry, Gilly,' said Cressida immediately. 'It was not my idea to invite Sebastian. I've always thought there was another side to why your marriage broke down.'

'There was, but I never wanted my children to see quite how bad things were. It was harder to keep it from Helena, who was still at home, though.'

339

Cressida nodded.

Gilly spotted an open bottle of wine. 'Do you mind if I have some of that? I'm going to need help if I'm going to get through this.'

'Of course,' said Cressida. 'You can always get a cab home.'

Gilly smiled faintly. While Cressida's back was turned she sent William a little text asking how he was. Making contact with him gave her courage.

Back in the dining room, sitting round the glass table which made you cold if you leaned on it, Cressida served out salmon and steamed vegetables. Everyone was given two little new potatoes. Martin put an inch of wine into each wine glass. The wine didn't have room to breathe, it had room to hyperventilate and faint, Gilly felt, very grateful for the extra half-glass she'd gulped down in the kitchen. She was still trembling with indignation that Martin had invited Sebastian without telling her.

Three forkfuls in, Martin said, 'So what's the big announcement, Mum? Apart from the fact that you don't want to sell your house?'

With everyone looking at her, Gilly, just for a moment, was tempted to declare she had a terminal illness, just to see their faces. And in fact this thought gave her courage. Think how much worse the whole revelation could have been!

'OK, well, it's quite simple. William, my boyfriend, is moving in with me. We'll have to get rid of some furniture and I wondered if you wanted your old desk, Martin.' She knew she'd been lucky to get such a long sentence out without being interrupted. During their marriage, even when she wasn't delivering life-changing news, Sebastian had found it very hard to let her say more than about five words at a time.

'What!' shouted Sebastian, spitting a little.

'Mum! William is your f — freakin' accountant!' said Martin.

'Gilly!' said Cressida, who had been an ally for such a brief time. 'What about Leo?'

'Leo and I were not destined to be a couple,' said Gilly, deciding not to tell Cressida that Leo was a lying fantasist with strong leanings towards embezzlement.

'You're going to let your miserable accountant move in with you?' demanded Sebastian, leaning towards her in the intimidating way he had used so often in their marriage. 'Well, let me tell you, that's not going to happen!'

'It's nothing to do with you, Sebastian.' Gilly reached out for the bottle and topped up her glass.

'Really, Mum! How can you even think of moving another man into our home!'

'I raised my children in that house — the one you insisted on keeping although I was entitled to half!' said Sebastian.

'But you didn't raise your children in it, I did; and I did keep it. It's mine, and if I want William to share it with me, it's my decision. Cressida, dear, is there more wine somewhere?'

'Getting drunk won't help!' said Martin.

'Usually, I'd agree with you,' said Gilly, her head never clearer. 'But right now, I think wine is the only answer!'

'So tell us about this William, then?' asked Sebastian.

'He's an accountant,' said Martin as if that were sufficient to damn him.

'His hobby is gliding,' said Gilly.

Sebastian laughed. 'Well, you won't be able to join in with that, will you?'

'Oh yes I will,' said Gilly quietly. 'I like gliding.' The way she said it gave the impression she'd done it more than once, but as she fully intended to go often, it wasn't really a lie.

'What?' said everyone, more or less at the same time. The general disbelief was at once patronising and rather satisfying.

'It's amazing up there. We live in such a good area for it, the scenery is so beautiful.'

'But you won't even fly in a small plane!' said Sebastian.

'A lot of things have changed since you knew me,' she said. 'I'm not the woman you left crying in a heap.' She picked up her glass. It was empty. Cressida leaned across and topped it up.

'You can't do this, you know, I won't permit it,' said Sebastian.

A memory of fear touched Gilly like a ghost. He'd been a bully and frightened her. The expression 'coercive control' hadn't been in use at the time but that was exactly what she had suffered throughout her marriage. She would give in to keep the peace, until she stopped giving in and that was when he began to get really threatening.

'You have no power to stop me doing anything,' said Gilly. 'You bullied me all through our marriage and I put up with it for the sake of our children. But they're grown up now and

342

your influence over me is finished! I have met a man who makes me happy, who loves me and who is kind. We are going to live together and there's not a thing you can do about it.'

'Oh, really? I think you'll find I can do a lot — '

She gave him a look which she hoped made him feel like dirt under her shoe. 'Now if you'll excuse me,' she said, picking up her handbag. 'I'll just pop to the loo.'

Once she was in the hall, Gilly opened the front door and let herself out.

She walked down the drive and past her car. She knew she wasn't fit to drive although she still felt very clear-headed. When she was out on the road she found her phone. She sent Cressida a quick text thanking her and explaining she had to leave unexpectedly. Then she went to 'Favourites' and called a taxi. Because she was a good customer they said they'd come immediately.

However, she knew it would take them a good fifteen minutes to reach her and she began to feel anxious in case anyone came out of the house to look for her. She walked along the road and round a bend so she would be out of sight.

While she was walking, adrenalin making her heart race, Gilly's mind focused on the failure of their marriage. In Sebastian's opinion, men were the ones to be adored, to be pandered to, appeased, obeyed. Gilly blamed his mother for making him believe this. She'd been a strong woman who never pandered to anyone, but she'd never liked Gilly, never thought she was good enough for her son. Gilly had been perversely pleased that they'd stayed married until after Sebastian's mother had died, not giving her the chance to say, 'I told you so.'

Martin shared some of his father's faults although Cressida would never be bullied, and back there she had been a little bit on Gilly's side. Although Gilly realised now she and Martin had set her up with Leo, to try to get him to persuade her to sell her house. However, she doubted if they'd intended that Leo should ask her to marry him in the bizarre way he had.

She realised these thoughts weren't calming and tried to focus on something else, but at that moment there *was* nothing else. She tried some deep breathing and that did help.

Then she heard what she'd been dreading: slamming car doors and raised voices. She stepped behind a tree, hoping she was hidden, and heard a car drive away at speed, shooting past the tree where she was sheltering. Sebastian always set off before he thought where he was going, before he'd done up his seatbelt, and, latterly, before he'd put on his glasses. Now, he'd have been better off looking for her on foot, but that wasn't his way. Thank goodness.

Although she was anxious lest the cab would arrive and the driver not be able to find her, she stayed where she was. It was possible that Martin would also go in search of his mother.

There was the sound of a second car but as far as she could tell it was going in the opposite direction. So Sebastian and Martin had both gone off in their fast cars, looking for a woman

344

who wasn't exactly a speed-walker.

There was a little park not far away from Martin and Cressida's house. Gilly had spent a lot of time in it years ago when Ismene was a toddler.

Martin would know about this park but Sebastian wouldn't. She made her way to it. If Martin found her it would be OK. Just as long as Sebastian didn't. The thought of being alone with him in a lonely place in the evening was not pleasant. She wished Helena wasn't so far away, somewhere in the hills above the Wye Valley.

She had time to wish she'd been wearing her Fitbit and that she hadn't fallen on the wine in quite such a desperate way before she had a text from her cab driver asking where she was. She told him about the park and within a very few minutes he was there and she was being driven back to Fairacres at speed. She wondered when her heart would catch up with her brain and stop beating so fast.

As the cab approached the Fairacres drive, Gilly saw William's car parked in front of the house and then William himself, waiting by the front door. She thrust a couple of notes into the cab driver's hands, ignoring his protest that it was too much money, and got out of the cab and ran towards him and into his arms. 'Oh, William! How lovely to see you! What are you doing here?'

'Your weird text told me something was wrong. I didn't know where your son lives so I came here. What's up?' He held her and stroked her back and her hair, murmuring words of comfort.

'Let's go in the house and I'll tell you.'

Now she was safe Gilly felt as if she'd panicked and knew that if she hadn't had too much wine she wouldn't have been so impetuous. But Sebastian could be frightening and Martin could be dominating.

'Well, it was my fault really. I had too much to drink.'

'Why do women always blame themselves for things? Or have you been conditioned to do that?'

William wasn't usually so blunt but it made her think. She headed towards the kitchen and he followed her. They sat opposite each other at the kitchen table.

'I probably *have* been conditioned to do that. Everything was my fault in my marriage, from the roof leaking to the weather being bad to the fact I had a difficult relationship with my mother-in-law. Although she was a very strong character, my ex, Sebastian, blamed the problems we had entirely on me.'

'So why did you feel the need to drink too much? Although you don't seem remotely drunk.'

'I'm not drunk but I've probably had too much to be legal to drive. And I did it because Martin sprung Sebastian on me. I panicked. He and Martin together can be very overbearing.'

'You haven't told me much about your marriage. When you were getting divorced you were always so careful to keep it as businesslike as you could. Although his attempts to get his hands on your house must have been devastating.'

From habit, she got up to put the kettle on. 'It

346

was. Fairacres had been my parents' house, as you know. Sebastian never contributed much to it financially and yet he made it so I had to pay him off by selling the orchard and that bit that went for a building plot.' She paused and smiled as she sat down again. 'I should have let it go by now and really, I have, but seeing him tonight and him being so awful about — ' She stopped.

'About what? Let me guess, the thought of another man going to live in what had been his home?'

'Yes, basically. He and Martin were very territorial. I suppose it's different for Martin but Sebastian has no right to be like that at all.'

'Has he married again?'

'He did, for a short while, but it didn't last.'

'Oh well, we won't invite him to our party then.' She laughed.

William picked up a pepper grinder that was on the table between them. 'You haven't changed your mind? Martin being unhappy about it hasn't made you feel you'd rather I didn't move in?'

'If I worried about what made Martin happy I'd never redecorate! Or if I did, I'd have to keep the same colours. He's always had a rather rosy view of what his father was like. But I'm sure he'll come round.'

'And if he doesn't?'

'Well, we'll still have the party! And you'll still come and live with me. And I'll still move his old desk to make room for yours.'

'But you'd be unhappy about it.' It was a statement, not a question.

'Well, of course I'd prefer it if he gave us his blessing but if he doesn't then maybe I have to live with that.' She paused. The kettle was boiling. 'Do you actually want a hot drink of any kind?'

'Not really,' he said, getting up and going round to her side of the table. 'I think we both need an early night.'

She smiled and put her arm round his waist as they went upstairs.

35

'Helly! Darling!' It was late the following morning, and Jago and Helena had just arrived back from their time away. Helena found herself enveloped in one of her mother's special hugs as Gilly intercepted them at the door. Gilly had waved William off a few moments earlier.

'Everything all right, Mum?' she asked.

'Of course! Come in. Jago! How are you? Are you hungry? What can I get you?'

Jago kissed Gilly. 'It's lovely to see you again. And as always I'm starving. Breakfast seems a long time ago and I only had toast.'

'There are few people I love more than hungry ones, especially when they are always so appreciative,' said Gilly. 'What would you like? Why don't I make you a proper B & B full English? With or without baked beans — not a fan myself. I've got some black pudding and some homemade hash brown potatoes to go with the usual things?'

'Oh my goodness,' said Jago. 'That all sounds like heaven.'

'You could go and eat in the dining room. I've opened the doors to the garden, it's such a lovely day.'

When Gilly had put plates of food down in front of them, Jago's so full she had to use a side plate for the fried bread and the hash browns, Gilly sat down at the table too.

349

'Are you sure that's enough, darling?' she said, looking at Helena's bacon and tomato on wholemeal toast.

'Yes, thank you, Mum. This is just what I fancy. And if I ate all that' — she looked at Jago's mountainous plate — 'I'd have to become a brickie to use up the calories.'

'Well,' said Gilly, apparently satisfied by this reply, 'I'm so glad you're here. I've got something I want to tell you.'

Panic ripped through Helena like a lightning bolt. 'Are you all right?'

'Yes!' said Gilly, laughing. 'I'm very all right. It's just William is going to come and live with me, here at Fairacres.'

Relief made Helena suddenly weak. 'God! Mum! Why all the drama? That's lovely news.' She got up and kissed her mother.

'Yes, it's great!' said Jago. He looked at Helena, who shook her head slightly. She wanted to hear all about her mother before telling her about how she and Jago had come back together again.

'I'm so pleased you're pleased,' said Gilly, sounding relieved and a little surprised. 'I went to see Martin and Cressida last night. He was not impressed by the thought.'

'Oh, men!' said Helena. She made a dismissive gesture with a hand that happened to be holding toast and marmalade. 'He just wants you to stay being his mum forever and not anyone else's partner.'

'He summoned your father for backup.'

'What? Dad?'

'He's only got the one father, darling. You and he have that in common.'

'But why?' demanded Helena, crunching loudly.

'For backup. Sebastian wasn't impressed either. He seemed to think he had rights to this house and could say who lived in it.'

'That's outrageous! I do hope you told him where to get off.'

Gilly seemed a little embarrassed. 'I think he got my drift.'

'So what happened? Tell all!'

'More toast, Jago?'

'Mum! Don't change the subject. You're hiding something. What went on?'

Her mother exhaled sharply. 'I had a bit too much to drink.'

'What? At Martin's house? I didn't think that was possible!'

'I went into the kitchen. Cressida had a bottle open and I had a quick glass while I was there.'

'And she allowed that?'

'She was quite sweet about it actually. She was embarrassed about Martin inviting Sebastian. We shared a moment of solidarity.'

'But what about the rest of it? And so far, you've had a glass of very dry sherry — ' Helena turned to Jago. 'Martin always gives her very dry sherry. He knows she doesn't like it. But, Mum, you couldn't have got drunk on that.'

'I didn't actually get drunk, darling. Although I did have at least two glasses of wine at the table — one of them I poured myself so it was nearly full. But too much to drive.'

'So, you got a taxi home?' said Jago. 'Do you want help picking up your car?'

'I do need help with that, Jago, although to be honest I'd forgotten about my car.'

'Did you get a taxi?' asked Helena. 'Or did Martin or Cressida run you back?'

'No. I left without telling anyone I was going.'

'So . . . you ran away?' asked Helena slowly.

'Yes. Your father was really quite angry. I was a bit . . .'

'Frightened? He frightened you! Bastard!' said Helena. 'You were worried he'd come after you?'

'Only briefly. William was here when I got back.' Ulysses the cat jumped on to her lap. 'So I had Uly and William to protect me if he had.'

'My father doesn't like cats,' Helena explained to Jago. 'We got a kitten as soon as the house was properly ours.'

'I like cats,' said Jago.

Remembering how they had met, Helena smiled. 'So do I. But, Mum, why was William here?'

Gilly seemed a bit embarrassed. 'He was passing and he just called in?'

Helena shook her head. 'Try again, Mum.'

'I'd sent him a text while I was in the kitchen at Martin and Cressida's house. Apparently it gave him the impression all was not well. He didn't know where they lived so he came here.'

'Good for him,' said Jago.

'So you really don't mind if William moves in with me?' said Gilly, who seemed to be a bit obsessed.

'No, I'm utterly delighted, Mum!' said Helena

and went back to kiss her mother again.

'And if we had a big party to tell the world what we're up to, you'd come?'

'Of course!'

'Try to keep us away!' said Jago.

Helena felt her mother had relaxed a bit as she and Jago went through the house with her looking at furniture. Gilly had already put stickers on everything she wanted to get rid of.

'Can we say yes to everything?' said Helena.

'There are some nice pieces here,' said Jago.

Gilly seemed sceptical. 'It's just a load of old junk, really, and very battered.'

'I like battered,' said Jago. 'And I'd like to restore some things.'

'But do ask Martin,' said Helena. 'I'd hate him to think we'd taken everything.'

Gilly cleared her throat. 'I'll ask him. I'm not sure any of this is his and Cressida's style though.'

'No, but you know what he's like,' said Helena. 'He'll get cross if he isn't asked.'

Gilly sighed. 'He will.'

'Are you tired, Mum? You must be. We'll do the car another time. We'll get out of your hair and let you find an *Escape to the Country* to sleep in front of.' Helena hugged her mother. 'Don't worry about Martin. He'll come round eventually.'

★　★　★

But Gilly couldn't relax. After Helena and Jago had gone, Gilly went out through the front door to deadhead her hanging baskets. She was so happy that Helena was completely relaxed about her living with William, but while Martin was upset about it, she couldn't properly relax.

She was surprised to see her car parked there. She sighed. Its presence implied that someone — probably Martin and Cressida — had delivered it without coming in to say hello.

All her happiness about living with William melted away, leaving her with a feeling of unease. She and Martin had never been as close as she and Helena for all sorts of reasons but while she didn't always like him, she did love him very much. The thought of him being upset with her was heart-breaking.

She'd gone against Martin with regard to selling her house and releasing some capital so they could upgrade. And while she hadn't liked to disappoint him, she knew she was right to stick to her guns and keep the home she loved.

But maybe inviting William into that home was going too far. Maybe it was unfair to Martin when he was so against it, and even if Martin was being unfair, she and William were quite happy as they were — or at least, happy enough. Or perhaps the elegant town house near the shops and restaurants should be considered seriously? Should she throw her lot in with William, sell her home and share out the money?

Even though she made herself think about it, she knew she couldn't do that. But nor could she do something that would make her son so unhappy.

Before she could change her mind she rang William.

'I can't do this,' she said, the moment he answered.

There was a tiny pause. 'Can you hold that thought?' he said. 'I'm coming to see you.'

'Could you do that?' Suddenly Gilly yearned for the comfort of his arms around her.

'Don't go anywhere. I'll be with you in half an hour.'

Gilly was thinking about lunch when William arrived. She couldn't decide between soup or salad or a sandwich and had half made all three, unable to focus because she was so preoccupied with Martin and his feelings about her living with William. She'd always put her children first and felt that was right. But Martin wasn't a child any more; was she crazy to put his needs above her own?

She got out her phone, tempted to ring Helena and ask her what she thought but realised it wasn't fair on her. Helena and Martin didn't always get on that well and she couldn't risk making that worse. Then her phone buzzed in her hand. It was a text from William. *Nearly there.*

Delighted, she put down her phone and ran upstairs to check her make-up and to decide if she was wearing the right thing. She ran down again when she heard his car, and was in his arms before he had a chance to get to the door. She felt her tension and anxiety begin to melt away as he held her and she knew she was in the best place in the whole world.

She let him go reluctantly. 'Can I make you lunch?'

'Have you reached a point of no return with lunch? I'd like to take you out.' He smiled a little questioningly. 'I'd like to take you gliding.'

'Oh, I'd love to go!' she said. 'And no. I can just fling everything back into the fridge. Although I'd better find a jumper.'

'You go and find a jumper and I'll fling everything back in the fridge.'

As she went back up the stairs she felt elated, knowing for certain that she wanted him in her life and her home forever. He was already well established in her heart.

William did a good job magicking away Gilly's abortive attempts at lunch. Sebastian had never learned where anything went in all the years they were married. She knew it would be very different with William.

'You look lovely!' said William and even Gilly, who never realised when she was being complimented, couldn't mistake the light of love and desire in his eyes. 'Phone!' He handed it to her. 'Now let's go gliding before we get distracted.'

∗   ∗   ∗

Gilly was still nervous about gliding but once they were up in the clouds she really did feel she'd left her problems and concerns on the ground. It was another beautiful day, and William had been able to borrow a two-seater glider at short notice. Apparently everyone needed accountants and William did the accounts for most of the gliding club. A couple of phone calls and he had acquired one for the afternoon. He'd told her all this on the way to the club, not letting her tell him he couldn't move in. They both knew the situation but William felt Gilly could make the decision better with a clear head. 'Gliding is the perfect head-clearer,' he said.

And so it proved. By the time Gilly had come back down to earth she had decided that William should move in. But there was still a place in her heart that hurt for her son.

'I wonder if Martin will come to our party,' said Gilly while William was driving her home.

'We'll ask him — and his wife and daughter, of course — and just see.'

William's calm manner added to the calm she had gathered while swooping over the landscape.

'I really hope they do decide to come,' she said, sounding positive, feeling less so. 'But we'll still have fun if they don't.'

★ ★ ★

Helena was having tea with Jago the following day when she saw an unknown number calling her. She nearly didn't answer it but then decided to risk it.

'Helena? William — your mother's friend.'

'Of course!' said Helena, relieved he wasn't likely to sell her anything.

'I wonder if I could ask your help. Could we meet for a drink this evening? I could meet you anywhere that suits you.'

After they had arranged where to meet, she turned to Jago. 'That was William. He says he wants my help.'

'Ah,' said Jago. 'I wonder if I know what it is.'

'Then tell me! I can't think.'

'I imagine it's to do with your brother being unhappy about your mother wanting to live with William in your old home.'

Now Helena understood. 'Ah. He wants me to try to talk him round.'

'I expect so. William won't want Gilly being unhappy about Martin. In theory, he's a grown-up and should just suck it up. But your mum is very maternal. She won't want to do anything that makes him unhappy.'

'You're absolutely right. But this is her time. She should have a chance of happiness!'

Jago shrugged. 'She's very caring.'

'Too caring,' said Helena, determined to insist that William did move in if that was what her mother wanted.

Sitting in a wine bar a few hours later, Helena really understood why her mother loved William. He was kind, a good listener but not too full on. He was a slow burn rather than instant conflagration and he obviously cared about Gilly very much.

'I know that however much she says she'll put up with Martin being unhappy, she will be miserable,' William said. 'However unreasonable Martin is being she's still affected by it. I'd love to start organising this party with her knowing she has the blessing of both her children.'

'She does hate it if we fall out and I know she'll be miserable if she thinks Martin is unhappy about anything she does.'

'Exactly.'

'And you want me to try to talk Martin round?'

He had a very endearing smile. 'Do you think you can?'

Helena shrugged. 'I'll certainly try. I think you're absolutely right about Mum. This should be a very happy time for her. I know she likes you, William. She should be allowed to enjoy that and stop being a mum all the time.'

'Thank you for being so understanding. You see far more of Gilly than Martin does. Don't you mind about it?'

Helena shook her head. 'I was with Mum during the divorce. And before that, I saw how vile my dad could be to her. Martin never saw it. I think maybe Dad behaved a bit better when he was around. Whatever, Martin and Dad are quite close. I don't really have much to do with my dad.'

'Are you sad about that?'

'I'm sad my dad wasn't different but I seem to manage OK without one.'

'I won't ever be a father to you,' said William. 'But if you ever need help with anything — anything you need advice about — I'd be more than happy to give it a go.'

'That's very kind.'

'Only please don't ask me anything that involves being fatherly. But I'm good on tax, not too bad on cars, and can find my way round a computer if I have to.'

Helena smiled. 'I'll bear that in mind. It's a very nice offer.'

'Not at all. I know how much Gilly values your

opinion. It's important for me to get on your good side.'

Now she laughed. 'You're already on my good side. And I'll see what I can do about Martin.'

'There are some things you may not know. Martin and Cressida tried to set Gilly up with a man — '

'Leo. Yes, I know. What they didn't know — nor did Mum — was that he was the man who nearly killed me and Mum in a car when I was a teenager.' She fiddled with her hair for a second or two. Then she flung her plait over her shoulder. 'I don't know if Mum's told you, but I have this weird thing — I can recognise people and remember who they are. I can also do it if only a bit of them is on show, like in a photograph.' She sighed. 'It's not always a great talent to have, to be honest.'

'Gilly did mention it. Which makes Martin's dislike of me a bit ironic.'

'I know! And they were dead set on Mum selling her house so she could move into a nasty little annexe and look after their daughter. Outrageous!'

William nodded. 'Just to be clear, I have a house of my own. I have absolutely no interest in your mother's property. I showed her my house, which is nice and in the very best area . . . ' He smiled. 'She obviously liked it but I could tell she didn't want to live there. But if she wanted, I would sell it and buy somewhere more rural we could live in together.'

'But she didn't want that either?'

'Not really.'

'But if you sold both properties you could buy a mansion!' said Helena.

'Martin would really love that,' said William. 'Us having exactly the sort of property he wanted . . . ' He paused. 'And I don't think Gilly would.'

'No, she wouldn't,' said Helena. 'And you don't mind her having the B & B?'

'Not if it makes her happy, no.'

For William it was obviously as simple as that.

36

Helena arranged to meet Martin near his office after work the next day. It had taken a little persuasion to get him to see her and he was late. Helena tried not to be annoyed but he always had thought his time was more precious than hers. But she smiled and got up and kissed him when he appeared. He accepted her hug but he didn't return it. Helena realised he probably knew why she was there and wasn't happy about it.

'I think I can guess what this is about,' said Martin.

'Oh?'

'Mum sent you to try to convince me that it's OK to have another man moving in with her. But it's not OK.'

'First, Mum didn't send me. I don't suppose she knows we're meeting and, second, I'm not trying to convince you of anything.' This was a small untruth but she allowed it. Martin wasn't going to change his mind easily, if at all.

'Oh?'

Helena flirted with the idea of telling him this meeting was all her idea but decided life was complicated enough without lying. 'Well, actually, I am going to try to talk you round to the idea of Mum and William living in the house together. And William asked me.'

'The snake! Trying to get you to do his dirty work!'

'It's not dirty work! They want to be together; William wants you to be happy about it. That's perfectly reasonable and he's not a snake. He really loves Mum.'

'Mum? Or her very expensive real estate?'

Helena swallowed hard, shocked that he should mention 'real estate'. After all, he and Cressida had set Gilly up with a man who had tried to persuade her to sell her house. She wondered what kind of kickback they'd offered him? And had they thought through the implications of Leo inviting Gilly to live with him? Bang went their free nanny-cum-gardener! Maybe they'd reckoned his property was so fantastic that Gilly would happily move into it, having sold hers and given them the money, which would at least have got them their new mansion. Although of course Gilly didn't want to sell and he didn't actually own his property. Gilly had explained all this to her. They probably hadn't bargained on him wanting to live in Fairacres when he couldn't convince her to sell — that scuppered *all* their plans. And would Martin have been happy for Leo to live in his old family home?

But now wasn't the time to ask him. She forced down her fury at the way he and Cressida had behaved. She was here as a peacemaker and it wouldn't help to rake up those things. 'William has a very nice house of his own. He doesn't need Mum's house; he just wants to live with her. And she wants to live with him.'

'I'm surprised at you, Helena. You're the sentimental one. Aren't you bothered about

363

there being another man in Dad's place? What about respecting the memories?'

'What memories, Martin?' asked Helena softly. 'Were there many good ones?'

'Of course there were good ones! Christmas! When we were little and all the cousins came to stay. It was brilliant.'

'But more recently, I remember some really awful times — '

'Like what?' Martin came back quick as a flash.

'Sunday lunches when nothing Mum did was right . . . ' Helena quailed as she thought about it. 'He was on at her all the time. Had her jumping up and down to fetch this, that and the other. Never letting her finish a sentence, interrupting her . . . '

'Oh, for goodness' sake, all couples bicker.'

'It wasn't bickering, Martin, it was bullying.'

'Not as I remember it.'

Martin had inherited some of his father's characteristics; Helena had only come to realise this fact as she grew up, although they had got on well when they were small.

'Anyway,' she said. 'We're all grown up now. We have relationships of our own. And Mum wants another chance of happiness. Is that so wrong?'

'Yes! I'm not having another man in Dad's place at home.'

Helena opened her mouth to tell him how ridiculous he was being but remembered again that she was not here to have a row with Martin, she was here to make life happier for her mother.

'Well, just think about it, Martin. Mum's a relatively young woman — '

'She's a grandmother. She should just concentrate on doing what she does well and not mess about like this. Our family home should be for her family, not for any Tom, Dick or Harry.'

'William isn't any of those,' said Helena in a desperate attempt to stop her brother being so angry.

'Oh, don't be ridiculous!' Martin was shouting now. 'Why can't Mum just be a grandmother and stop all this nonsense? She'd have been perfectly happy and fulfilled if she'd agreed to our plan.'

'OK,' said Helena quietly. 'I'm sorry you feel like this but I don't think I can do anything about it.'

★ ★ ★

'How did you get on?' asked Jago when she got home, handing her a glass of wine.

'Utter failure. He's in complete denial about Mum. He thinks she should just be a grandmother and not have a life of her own. So unfair!' She pulled out a chair at the kitchen table, watching him stir something on the stove.

'You might feel differently about it when you have children yourself,' said Jago.

'You think?'

He nodded. 'Yup. I think when you've got a little one you'll be forever running over to Gilly with your baby.' He tasted something and then threw down the spoon. 'I won't be able to be

365

around all the time during the day. You'll need your Mum.'

'I'm sure I will, but I hope I won't expect her to sacrifice her entire life for me and my babies.'

Jago smiled in a way Helena thought was distinctly soppy. 'You want to have lots of babies?'

She was feeling fairly soppy herself just then. 'Think so. I'd see how it went after the first.'

'So we'd better get a move on. Get married. It's not essential to be married to have children, of course, but I think your mum might prefer it.'

Helena wasn't sure her mother would particularly care, but she was keen on the getting married idea. She nodded.

'So, we'd better go ring shopping!'

'What a good idea!'

'Would tomorrow be too soon?' said Jago. 'Tell me if you feel rushed.'

'Tomorrow would be perfect.' She smiled. 'This is a lovely ending to a rather medium day!'

★   ★   ★

'It's so kind of you to come over and help with the puddings,' said Gilly the following week.

Helena hugged her. 'It's a tradition, us making puddings together. What are we doing?' Helena had been delighted when Gilly had asked for her help with the 'announcement' lunch she and William were giving.

'We'll start with the amaretti cheesecake. Do take your ring off!'

Helena looked at her left hand with a

sentimental smile. Her fourth finger was adorned with an antique topaz and diamond ring which she thought was the most beautiful ring ever. 'I will. But I'll put it in my bra so I don't forget it.'

'It is a lovely ring,' said Gilly.

'Jago wanted to buy me a socking great diamond it would take years to pay for. His previous fiancée had insisted on one of those. He was surprised and pleased when I just wanted something that I really loved and didn't cost a fortune.'

Gilly, who obviously wanted to go on chatting about Helena's love life, was on a mission to get the puddings done too. She handed her daughter an apron. 'He had a bad time with her, then?'

'Yes. When the whole scandal about the fire blew up she completely lost interest in him. Although to be fair it must have been horrible being doorstepped and having your picture all over the papers.' Helena reached for a packet of digestive biscuits. 'Do you want these blitzed or shall I just bash them?'

'Bash, please. I want the food processor for the amaretti. They're a bit harder.'

'How many are we catering for?' said Helena a little later.

'About fifty, I think. You never quite know, do you?'

Helena knew she was thinking about Martin and Cressida and hoping they'd come although there had been no communication between them since that awful evening. 'So that's ten puddings? Five to a pud?'

'Yes, I'm doing five kinds of pudding but doubling up.'

367

'You're not over-catering are you, Mum?' This was said with a wry smile because Helena knew the answer.

'Probably but you know what it's like, if people don't see much food they don't dare eat it. Then there are leftovers, and your classic under-caterer gives even less the next time till it's one nibble per person.'

Helena laughed. Her mother was very good at justifying her tendency to have too much food but she did agree that everyone enjoyed having at least two helpings of something sweet and creamy.

Helena was folding mashed raspberries and strawberries into whipped cream when Gilly said, 'Have you thought about your wedding, Helly?'

'Yes. You can't help it when you're engaged, I've discovered.'

'So what do you fancy?'

Helena looked at her mother. 'What I'd really love — but only if you're absolutely OK with it . . . '

'Yes?'

Helena knew that her mother knew what she was going to say. 'I'd love to have it here — in a marquee in the garden. Simple, not too expensive, flowers in jam jars, fairy lights in the trees.'

'It sounds lovely! And I'd be thrilled to have it here. I'd be offended if you tried to have it anywhere else — but the fact is, the garden is a bit small.'

'I'm sure it's big enough. Jago hasn't many

relatives he still talks to and not so many friends.'
She paused. 'Although I suppose there may be
some he'd like to get back in touch with, now all
the scandal and disruption is well over.'

'What about his parents? Where do they stand
in all this?'

'Well, his dad took his brother's side. That's
the wicked uncle, so he and Jago don't speak.
His mother lives in Australia, I think. She moved
as far away as she could from everything. There's
his sister of course. She's a bit bossy, I gather,
but they are close.'

'Poor Jago,' said Gilly. 'Yet he seems to
manage without having parents.' She became
thoughtful again and Helena knew she was
thinking about Martin.

Helena brought the subject back to the
wedding. 'But you're not doing the catering for
my wedding. Not even the puddings. I want you
— you and William — to enjoy the wedding and
not have to work.'

'Oh, darling. How sweet of you.' Gilly
suddenly seemed a bit tearful. Helena couldn't
tell if this was normal 'my little girl is getting
married' stuff or because of her wretched
brother. 'But could you restrict your guest list to
fifty? That's how many we're having tomorrow.
We had to leave out lots of people we'd have
liked to invite.'

'But you're probably inviting all sorts of
friends and family of William's we wouldn't have
for the wedding.'

'True,' Gilly acknowledged. 'But I do have a
lot of cousins — people I know and am fond of.'

Helena nodded. This extended family had been very kind and supportive during the divorce. She could see Gilly wouldn't like to leave them off a guest list. But still, the wedding was all a long way off. It was far too early in the proceedings to think about whom they would ask.

'It's such a shame I had to sell the orchard as well as the building plot,' Gilly said.

'It works OK, doesn't it?' said Helena. The orchard had gone to neighbours who had grazed their children's ponies in it.

'It did,' said Gilly, 'but the other day I met Natasha at the Farmers' Market and she said her son was coming home for a bit and wanted to put yurts on there and offer glamping.'

'Oh!' Helena tried to imagine the view outside her old bedroom window including yurts.

'And apparently several of the trees are really old now so he wants to take them down to make room for the yurts. Natasha seemed a bit embarrassed about it and asked if it would affect my bed and breakfast business.'

'What did you say?'

'She was being served then so I didn't say anything. But I don't think my normal clients would fancy sleeping in a yurt.' Gilly paused. 'I don't think I can complain, can I? Yurts aren't permanent structures. I don't suppose they need planning permission.'

Helena resolved to find out. Jago would know.

'So what's the next pudding?' she said.

'Would you mind chopping nuts for brownies?'

'No, but you could make another recipe — one that doesn't involve nuts? Less work?'

'I think it's better to make the recipe I know best,' said Gilly.

Then Helena remembered — her mother used to make those brownies to send to Martin at university. He loved them. She concentrated on her chopping for a while and then suggested they put on some music. There was so much unsaid between them, it would be good to fill the silence.

After lunch, they went to look at the marquee.

'It looks amazing!' said Helena. 'So big! We could have a wedding here easily, surely.'

Gilly shook her head. 'No, I promise you, this only takes fifty. You'd need something bigger unless you leave off most of your relations and half your friends.'

'Couldn't you fit a bigger one in here?' asked Helena.

'Not really,' said Gilly.

Helena sighed. 'Well, we don't need to worry about my wedding just yet.'

'No,' Gilly agreed. 'But this marquee definitely needs flowers. A few big arrangements, I think, and then tomorrow I'll put posies on the tables. Let's get cutting.'

As they clipped and snipped in the garden, getting enough material to fill the big stone crocks Gilly wanted to stand in the empty spaces, Gilly said, 'Do you remember when me and other parents got together to turn the school hall into a summery bower for a play?'

'Oh yes! A cut-down version of *A Midsummer Night's Dream* — I was Titania because I had the longest hair.'

'You looked lovely!'

'And so did the hall.'

'It did involve hacking down whole branches of leaves and every flower in the garden — in every garden in the village practically.' Gilly smiled, obviously thinking back to her days as a young mother with fondness. 'Of course we had the orchard then so I had extra trees I could use, but it still wasn't enough, so a group of us mums went into the churchyard and started raiding that! We were terrified someone would come along and tell us off. But it looked so pretty!'

'There are photos somewhere,' said Helena. 'I remember.'

'We carried lots of it into the church afterwards so as not to waste all that work and because we felt guilty about the churchyard ivy being torn off in strips. I was worried about decorating the church at Christmas without it. But it grew back OK and the churchyard always had wonderful holly.' Gilly fell silent.

'OK, Mum,' said Helena, thinking her mother's reminiscence had gone on just a bit too long. 'Let's finish up here. I want to see your outfit for tomorrow. Did you buy a hat? Or just a dress?'

'Oh, I didn't buy anything new. I've got lots of clothes.'

'Mum! This is a party that your lovely new man is giving so his family can meet you properly — and so our lot can meet him — and you haven't bought something new to wear?' She glanced at her watch.

'It's too late now!'

'We could always pop down to the supermarket,' said Gilly. 'Get something from there?'

Helena tutted and shook her head before putting her arm round her mother and leading her into the house.

★ ★ ★

'You look lovely in this,' said Helena, pulling out a dress that brought out the colour of her mother's eyes.

'Yes, but I wore it when I went out with Leo. It reminds me of him. In fact, I'll have to move it on.'

'Oh. Seems a shame.' But Helena did understand. 'Maybe keep it but just not wear it tomorrow.'

'OK, I'll keep it. So what else have we got? What about this?'

Helena shook her head and tried to pick her words. 'No . . . too mumsy.'

'OK. Definitely get rid of that then.'

'Shall I find a bag?'

'Look in the top shelf. I keep them there.'

Eventually they created an outfit they both liked and which didn't have any bad connotations. It was a long, finely pleated skirt that Gilly had bought in a charity shop years ago because she loved it and had now come back into fashion, and a fitted wrap top that, Helena declared, made her waist look tiny.

'And your big locket on the black velvet ribbon,' said Helena. 'Now, let's arrange a wash and blowdry.'

373

'Too short notice,' said Gilly, running her fingers through her hair out of sight of the mirror.

'I'm going to ring Debbie. I know she'll sort you out; she never lets you down.'

'It's not really fair — '

'I'll ring her,' said Helena firmly. 'She'll probably fit you in really early tomorrow so you'll have plenty of time to get ready. And what about your makeup?'

'I'll do my own make-up!' Gilly seemed a bit panicked at the thought of someone else putting make-up on her. 'You know what those make-up artists are like. They always want you to look natural — the last thing I want!'

Helena laughed. 'I do remember that time we went to the health farm and everyone had makeovers.'

'They all looked amazing and I looked awful,' said Gilly. 'I couldn't understand why it didn't work on me.'

'They looked natural,' said Helena.

'So did 1,' said Gilly, 'which was why I hated it. Now, glass of wine? Supper? Why don't you ring Jago and ask him to join us?'

'Actually, I've got a few things I must do, but I'll come early tomorrow. At about eleven? Just to help you with the flowers for the tables and anything else you may be panicking about.'

'Which will be everything! Supposing William doesn't turn up!'

'He'll turn up. He adores you.'

When Helena was driving away she reflected it wasn't William not turning up that was worrying her mum, it was Martin. And he wouldn't turn up, not if he was still feeling angry and resentful. She had a few phone calls to make, she realised, before she could relax and sort out what she was wearing for the lunch the following day.

37

'It's so kind of you to see me so early,' said Gilly to her hairdresser as she was handed a cup of tea. 'I should have sorted it out sooner but I got distracted.'

'That's OK,' said Debbie. 'I don't mind an early start. Working from home means I'm here. Aren't you lucky with the weather!'

'I know! We had made provision for it being cold and rainy but I don't think we'll need the heaters.'

'These days all the seasons are unpredictable,' said Debbie. 'So, just a wash and blow-dry?'

'Please.' Gilly settled back to enjoy the blissful experience of having her hair washed. 'I couldn't drop off last night and of course went into a deep sleep at about five thirty.'

'Oh, I hate that! But you feel all right now?'

Gilly nodded as Debbie's skilful hands rubbed away her tension. 'I'm fine.'

'You know, when people say 'fine' they always mean the exact opposite.'

Gilly laughed. 'No! I really am fine!' She crossed her fingers under her robe. While she longed to confide in Debbie and knew she'd be wise and nonjudgemental, she felt that not talking about Martin's refusal to accept William made it less real. Besides, there was nothing she could do about it today.

'So, tell me about William then,' said Debbie,

when Gilly had moved from the washbasin and was in front of the mirror.

'He's lovely. Sort of quiet but exciting enough for me.'

'What do you mean? Or shouldn't I ask?'

Gilly was perfecting her 'I'm totally happy' laugh and executed one now. 'I mean, he took me gliding and I loved it!'

Debbie was suitably impressed. 'Wow, Gilly!' She hesitated. 'Should I just take a bit off the back? It seems a bit heavy . . .'

Gilly liked the effect her new enthusiasm for gliding had on people. She briefly considered buying a set of motorbike leathers and telling everyone she had a Harley. Her reputation as a 'nice lady' would finally be in pieces.

Feeling better for having her hair done, when Gilly arrived home she went out to meet the caterers who had arrived while she'd been away.

Franco from the Italian wine bar near William's house, who was in charge, was delightfully Italian, full of compliments and charming comments on the surroundings. Once she had been reassured that everything that should be served hot would be, and the cold things would be cold and not room temperature, she allowed herself to be taken to see the contents of Franco's special van.

There were platters of charcuterie, so finely cut you could probably read through it. Plates of stuffed artichokes like little roses, finely sliced courgettes formed into cylinders and filled with (Franco told her) pine nuts and breadcrumbs, parmesan and thyme. Salvers of stuffed courgette flowers, almost too pretty to eat, and comforting troughs of aubergine parmigiana, lasagne and something Gilly couldn't identify but looked delicious.

'Everything will be served just as it should be,' said Franco. 'Our waiters will fill glasses, provide water and soft drinks; everything will be perfect.'

'I'm so happy,' said Gilly.

'We are doing our best for William,' said Franco. 'He is good man.' There were also bowls of salad and piles of roasted asparagus: enough vegan and healthy options to please even Cressida (should she happen to come).

'It all looks amazing,' Gilly said. 'Thank you so much.'

'As I said, it is for William. He once helped us when we were in trouble. And now he has a beautiful companion, we want to do our best for her, too.' He took this opportunity to kiss her hand.

As she went back into the house she was blushing and chiding herself for being flattered. Franco probably said that to all the girls, she told herself.

Now to see to the flowers for the tables.

As she went round her garden, secateurs and bucket of water in hand, followed by Ulysses who was grumpy because he'd been thrown out of the catering van several times, she realised she was excited.

Mostly she was looking forward to seeing William. He had rung her while she was in bed and it had been lovely talking to him. Sadly one of the things he had said was that he wouldn't be able to get to the house until just before the party, but that was OK as she was used to dealing with these things on her own.

As she went round, snipping and stripping off excess leaves, she fought the cold little bit of her heart that reminded her Martin was unhappy. But she wouldn't have behaved differently, she realised, she was just as entitled to happiness as he was. He would get over it. He was an adult and he would eventually realise she was allowed to be happy with another man.

She left the flowers in her favourite dark shed to soak up as much water as they could (she was aware she should have picked them the previous evening) and then went up to have a shower. She would get ready after Helena had come and helped her arrange the flowers.

A shower using her favourite honey-scented soap cheered her and she pulled on some old and comfortable clothes which were also soothing. The outfit she and Helena had chosen the previous day was hanging outside the wardrobe. She didn't dare look at it too closely in case she changed her mind and had to go through the whole process again.

She remembered Helena's surprise that she hadn't wanted to buy anything new. This made her laugh — Helena was notoriously reluctant to buy new clothes herself.

She had finished doing her make-up when Helena arrived.

'Are you up there! I'm here to do the flowers!' She ran up the stairs. 'Oh! Jeans and an old linen shirt — I thought we'd sorted out your outfit

379

yesterday? Your hair's looking good though.'

'Thanks! But I'm not going to do the flowers in my glad rags. Let's have a cup of coffee and get these flowers done. Time is moving on!'

When there were flowers on every table and the large arrangements had been tweaked (not everything looked as perky as it should have done) Helena and Gilly looked around them.

'Oh, this is exactly what I'd love for my wedding!' said Helena.

'Yes, but it'd only work if you just want something very small,' Gilly reminded her patiently.

A split second later Helena said, 'I think something a bit bigger would be lovely as long as it can be here, like this. But we'll squash it into the garden somehow.'

When Gilly went up to dress she realised that Helena wasn't particularly bothered about having a big wedding but that she wanted her mother to have what she wanted for her daughter. She was touched and knew she was very lucky that they got on so well. They were bound together by adversity, she decided, and that was why she and Martin weren't as bonded.

As Gilly was tweaking her hair and worrying about her earrings she was aware of feeling anxious — stage fright probably — and then she heard the front door creak.

She went to the top of the stairs and listened. It could be the one bed and breakfast guest she hadn't managed to cancel, or one of Franco's staff members. It was unlikely to be a burglar but she thought she should go down and check.

She was halfway down the stairs when she saw

380

a man with his back to her looking at the visitors' book. On the bottom step she realised it wasn't a burglar, it was worse.

It was Leo.

He turned as he heard her and she realised when she saw him properly that he was very drunk. She took a breath. She would have to play this very carefully.

'I heard you were having a party,' he said.

'Yes. But I didn't invite you, Leo.'

'No! You didn't! That's because you're having it with your new fancy man!'

'His name is William,' she said calmly, lowering her voice, hoping it would encourage him to lower his.

'I know what his name is! He's your accountant. And does he know that you must have been keeping us both on a string at the same time?'

'It wasn't like that, Leo, and now could you please leave?'

'No. You may think you can have everything you want but you can't.'

'I can have who I like in my house and I don't want you in it, so please leave.'

'Is it your house though? Or is it your children's heritage?'

'You're drunk, Leo. You're not making sense.' He was giving her information about how he got to know about the party though. Martin must have told him for some reason. Possibly spite.

'Oh, I am making sense! I'm just not quite as clever about life as you are, am I? You saw the main chance and you took it. You decided shacking up with your boring accountant was a

381

better bet than I was. Women don't reject me, sweetheart, I reject them!' He started to walk towards her.

Gilly was beginning to feel really frightened now. It was early, no one who was likely to come into the house was due yet and William said he might not be able to arrive until just before the guests were due. Leo was so menacing, angry, resentful. The thought that he might try to rape her crossed her mind. She didn't let it linger. She was a relatively fit woman and she could either fight him off or escape. She backed away, edging towards the sittingroom door. The French windows were open; if she got into the sitting room she could get outside.

'You're a little slut, do you know that?' he said, still walking towards her.

His hand shot out just before she reached the door and his fingers gripped her shoulder. She shut her eyes, not wanting to see his face approaching hers. Her mouth went dry, and her brain stopped functioning.

Then suddenly he was pulled away; there was a crunching noise and a crash. Her eyes flew open to see Leo sprawling on his back on the floor.

'Now get out,' said William. He went to Leo and helped him get up from the floor. 'Oh God, he's drunk. He can't drive.'

'I'll ring Helena,' said Gilly. 'I'm sure Jago will help if he can. Taxis aren't keen on taking drunk people.'

'I'm perfectly fine!' said Leo, furious, but clearly more in control of himself now.

'I'll make him some coffee,' said Gilly, glad to have an excuse to leave the scene.

Once in the kitchen she found her phone and called Helena. 'Darling? Is Jago there? Leo came round here and is drunk. We need to get him out of here urgently.' She paused. 'William hit him.'

'Oh my God!' said Helena, extremely impressed. 'I'll call Jago. He's just in the shower but he can come out.'

A very short time later Jago said, 'Hello? Gilly? What can I do for you?'

'You couldn't come and pick up Leo and take him home? I know William would do it but, between us, I'd rather it was someone young and fit like you. Also, it won't matter if you're a bit late to the party.'

'On my way. No worries.'

Helena came back on the phone. 'He is so kind,' said Gilly. 'I must make him a cake or something.'

'Don't worry, Mum,' said Helena. 'He loves helping people. Mind you, he also loves cake.'

Gilly made a strong cup of instant coffee and took it out to the hall. Leo was sitting in the hall chair while William stood over him.

'Here's some coffee. You'd better drink it, Leo,' she said.

'I'll take him home,' said William.

'No need,' said Gilly quickly. 'Jago is on his way.'

She suddenly felt weak and shaky. She went back to the kitchen quickly so she could sit down and breathe deeply. She realised now what a narrow escape she'd had. Thank goodness William had been earlier than he'd said he'd be. It took her a little while before she felt herself again.

At last she heard sounds that meant Jago had arrived. A few moments later, William came into the kitchen. Gilly got up and fell into his arms. 'Oh God, thank you so much for rescuing me! I felt so vulnerable!' She had a horrid feeling she was going to cry which she really didn't want to do as she'd made such a good job of her make-up.

'Darling, of course I'd rescue you! If I didn't, or couldn't, there would be no point in my being in your life,' he said, holding her and murmuring into her hair. 'I'd go through fire for you!' He paused. 'Although I must say, punching someone hurts so much more than I ever thought it could.'

Gilly instantly went into caring mode. 'Oh, William! Come with me to the downstairs loo. I've got some arnica and plasters and things.'

'I'm not sure I need a plaster.'

'If you've broken a finger I'll have to stick it to the next finger — '

'I'm sure I haven't broken anything,' said William, following Gilly.

'Let me just have a look.'

He allowed her to put arnica on it and they were still crammed together in the tiny bathroom when he said, 'Is there time for me to have a cup of coffee before the guests arrive?'

'Of course! You arrived early — thank goodness.'

'I know. I'm so glad. My errand took less time than I allowed for it.'

Gilly found her curiosity piqued. 'Was it anything exciting?'

384

'Hardly,' said William. 'I'm a boring accountant.'

She laughed, all her fear dissipated. 'Boring accountants are absolutely my favourite kind,' she said and kissed him.

Helena found them in there. 'Um, is this the party venue? Sorry, didn't get the email . . .'

Gilly laughed, beyond embarrassment. 'No, there's no room for the band in here.'

Now Helena really did look confused. 'You're having a band?'

'No! Figure of speech,' said Gilly. 'Now let's get this party started. Woo!'

'Mum?' said Helena. 'Now you're scaring me.'

'And me,' said William. 'A quick cup of coffee and we'll be ready to greet our guests.'

Gilly glanced at her watch. 'I think we need to open a bottle of something.'

'Oh, me too!' said Helena. 'I'll do it.' She took a bottle of champagne out of the fridge, one of a few Gilly had hidden in there for later. When she'd dealt with the bottle and handed everyone a glass of champagne, she said, 'I want to hear all about William decking Leo. I so wish I'd seen it!'

'I'm afraid I had my eyes shut,' Gilly admitted.

'Just as well. It was very inelegant — not at all like it is on telly,' said William. 'If Leo hadn't been drunk and off balance he'd never have fallen over.'

Gilly realised William wanted to make light of it so didn't point out that Leo had been gripping on to her very hard, so in spite of being drunk he wasn't off balance. It must have been quite a punch.

'What would you have done if he'd stayed standing, William?' asked Helena.

'Punched him again, but I'm very glad I didn't have to. My hand hurts quite enough.'

Jago walked into the kitchen. 'Has the party started without me?'

'Not really,' said Gilly, 'but thank you so much for getting rid of Leo for us.'

'It was a pleasure,' said Jago.

'Are you wearing that for the party?' asked Helena.

Jago was wearing jeans with ripped knees and a band T-shirt that he probably used for sleeping in. He looked down at himself. 'Oh, I see what you mean. Should I go home and put on my suit?'

'I think you look absolutely fine,' said Gilly firmly. 'Don't go anywhere.'

'Totes agree,' said William seriously. 'Isn't that what the young people say?'

Helena closed her eyes, shook her head and took another sip of champagne, but she was smiling.

'Oh, are we late?' said a voice.

It was Amy and she had James with her. 'I thought I was early,' Amy went on. 'I came in case you needed any help.' She pulled James forward. 'You said I could bring a plus one,' she said shyly. 'This is James.'

'How lovely,' said Gilly.

'It's so cool you're still friends!' said Helena. She gave them both a hug.

'Don't get overexcited,' said Amy, after there'd been quite a lot of hugging and arm punching.

386

'It's very early days.'

Gilly and Helena exchanged glances. They'd heard those words before.

'I think you both need a glass of champagne,' said Gilly. 'Not that we're celebrating . . .'

38

The party was due to start and Gilly and William were waiting in the marquee, welcoming smiles at the ready.

'Are you all right, Mum?' asked Helena.

'Yes, I just want to get started. I've got stage fright,' she said.

'Aunt Daphne and the others will be here any minute,' said William. 'I had a text to say they were nearly here. I almost regret teaching her texting — she can't seem to stop. It's like a sort of Tourette's.'

'It all looks great!' said Jago, looking round the marquee. 'I'd like this for our wedding, Hels — if you'd like it?'

'Just what I want,' said Helena. 'It's so good we agree.'

'Ah! Here they are!' said William.

'Oh my God,' said Jago. 'I think I'm scared.'

All William's aunts, and apparently several other people, had decided to wear hats. They looked magnificent but, Gilly thought, a bit overdressed for what was basically a buffet in a tent. There were chairs and tables for everyone to sit at but it was supposed to be a very informal occasion. This phalanx of women looked ready for Ladies' Day at Ascot, or the wedding of a minor royal.

'People love the chance to dress up,' said Gilly, moving forward. 'Daphne, how lovely to see you!

And I adore your hat.'

'Not hat, hatinator,' Daphne corrected her, kissing her cheek. 'Not to be confused with a fascinator.'

'You've obviously looked into it,' said Gilly.

'Of course!' Daphne turned her attention to Helena. 'My, you're a pretty girl, aren't you?'

Gilly looked at her daughter through a stranger's eyes. She had tonged her long hair so it came over her shoulder in ordered curls. She wore a simple dress — an old favourite — and ballet flats. She was wearing mascara and a bit of lipstick and looked, to Gilly's entirely biased eyes, beautiful. And at her side was Jago, who, although he wasn't wearing his suit, looked kind and handsome and just the man she would have chosen for her daughter (if the matter had anything to do with her). Gilly appreciated him deeply for being who he was. She'd have loved him if he'd been wearing budgie smugglers and a snorkel to her party.

Daphne patted Gilly's arm. 'Lovely young couple, darling. You're so lucky.'

'Yes I am,' said Gilly, feeling lucky until her son came into her mind and she felt just a little bit sad. 'Now, where are you going to sit?'

'Isn't there a seating plan?' Daphne was put out by this basic mistake.

'Well, no, we thought people would just — '

'Don't worry about it, darling. I'll organise it.' Daphne clapped her hands. 'People! Follow me!'

Other guests began to arrive and the enclave of hat-wearing aunties was less prominent. But they still looked like a flock of exotic parakeets on an English bird table.

William and Gilly found they couldn't go and sit down themselves for a while, so many people wanted to congratulate them, which, Gilly realised, was really a chance for one set of friends to get a look at their friend's chosen partner. Gilly was glad to see the chaps from the gliding club, whom she knew.

'You're looking very lovely, my dear,' said one. 'We're all so pleased that William has found the right girl at last. One who can join in with his hobby and not resent it. And you won't regret your choice either. Salt of the earth is our William.'

'I'm sure I won't,' said Gilly, smiling happily. 'He's perfect.'

'Not sure I'm perfect, darling,' said William, overhearing, 'I don't wash up very thoroughly.'

'It's OK,' said Gilly, preparing to greet the next guest, 'I have a dishwasher.'

★ ★ ★

People had mostly gone to the buffet and sat down again, the waiters had filled glasses, fetched water and made sure that Daphne's little crew got cups of tea. William looked at Gilly. 'Time for a quick speech?'

'Do we have to?'

'Just a very short one,' said William. 'I think we should.'

'But you haven't got any food yet!' said Jago. 'I'll get you both some. If you go, you'll never get back to your seats.'

390

Gilly didn't want William to make a speech just yet and she was glad to be presented with a plate of delicious food by Jago. It put off the moment when, basically, she had to give up hope. Although she couldn't really eat the food, she played around with it.

She had just put a pepper stuffed with goats cheese, and, it transpired, a bit of chilli, into her mouth when she saw some movement by the entrance of the marquee.

It was Martin, Cressida and Ismene. Martin was wearing a suit, Cressida was wearing a very bodycon gun-metal dress with a fascinator to match and Gilly's only granddaughter was dressed in the kind of smocked dress Gilly would have refused to wear when *she* was a child. She thought her heart would overflow with happiness. Issi waved at her. Gilly waved back.

Martin and Cressida made their way across the marquee, through the people who still hadn't sat down with their plates of food.

'Sorry we're late, Mum,' said Martin. 'There was a lot of traffic.' He only met her eyes for a second or two but that was enough. He was here. Gilly swallowed back tears of joy.

'That top looks lovely on you,' said Cressida. 'It brings out the colour of your eyes.'

'You look lovely too,' said Gilly. 'But then you always do.'

'Are there chocolate brownies, Gilly?' asked her granddaughter.

'Yes. I did them specially for you, but they're in the kitchen. In the tin. I didn't want everyone to have them.'

The little girl sighed. 'Thank you. Mummy says I can eat whatever I like today.'

'William,' said Martin, with a nod.

'Martin,' said William.

'We'd better find somewhere to sit,' said Cressida, 'and get something to eat.'

'There are some lovely salads,' said Gilly.

'I know,' said Cressida. She smiled, really quite warmly. It was like being smiled at by a glacier — a bit unnerving.

'We can do the speeches now,' said Gilly happily when she'd seen Martin and Cressida find seats. Issi had gone into the house, probably to find the chocolate brownies. Gilly had made them in the vain hope she would get to eat them. And now she was.

'Will you go first?' said William.

'Are you making a speech, Mum?' Helena sounded surprised.

Gilly hadn't planned one before but now she got to her feet. 'It's my house, I should welcome our guests.'

William tinged a glass, the conversation died away.

'Hello, everyone,' she said. 'I won't keep you long. I just want to welcome you and thank you for coming. This party is just a bit of a celebration and it's lovely to have you all here with us.' She took a sip of champagne. 'In case you're wondering what we're celebrating exactly, well — it's that gliding has become my hobby.' There were cheers from the gliding-club contingent. 'As that may seem a bit surprising to most of you, as it was a surprise to me, we

392

thought we should mark it with a party. Now I think William wants to say something.'

William got up. 'Strangely, although I am delighted Gilly has taken to gliding, I think we're here to celebrate something slightly different, although no less momentous.'

'Did we go to the church service? I can't remember,' said one of William's aunts.

'William and Gilly are very modern,' said Daphne in a stage whisper, 'I don't think they're getting married.'

'Oh, that's very sad,' said the first aunt. 'I wouldn't have worn a hat if I'd known. I bought it specially.'

William cleared his throat loudly. 'Just to set your minds at rest, beloved aunts and honorary aunts, I do have a ring in my pocket . . . '

Gilly gasped. Somehow, with everything else she had on her mind, this hadn't occurred to her.

'Although I had intended to ask Gilly if she would do me the honour of becoming my wife in private.' He leaned in and whispered in her ear. 'I'm so sorry. Just say yes now for the sake of the aunts. I'll get Daphne to explain later if you don't want to marry me.'

'It's all right, William, I do want to marry you,' Gilly whispered back, having just realised it was true.

Assuming Gilly's answer had been positive the aunts began chanting, 'Show the ring, show the ring.'

'Oh, go on, William,' said Gilly. 'Show them the ring.'

'I'll show it to you, first.'

It was a large sapphire surrounded by tiny diamonds. 'I can change it if you don't like it.'

'It's lovely,' said Gilly, holding out her ring finger. 'Put it on.'

'I've got another present but I insist on giving you that in private.'

Gilly held out her hand and everyone admired the ring.

People flocked around them, congratulating them, admiring the rock on Gilly's hand, telling William what a lucky man he was.

Martin came up. 'I'm happy for you, Mum. Cressida made me see this is *your* home now, and not the family's. And I'm sorry for trying to get you to sell it and introducing you to Leo. I didn't realise he was such bad news.'

Gilly kissed him. 'It's all right. I'm just so glad to see you.'

He patted her shoulder awkwardly and went back to his family.

'Come on,' said William. 'I can't wait to talk to you alone.'

The kitchen was full of Ismene eating chocolate brownies, and the sitting room had an aunt, lying flat out on the sofa, hat askew, snoring gently. Eventually they went into the tiny office where Ulysses had been having a nap. Now he'd been woken, he stalked off to join the party, scattering hair as he went.

Gilly was dying of curiosity and anxiety in case William had bought her something she didn't really want. Would she be brave enough to tell him so it could be sent back?

He pulled an envelope out of his inside pocket.

It was a holiday, she decided. That was OK.

He handed her the envelope. 'I've been talking to your neighbour and her son,' he said. 'They were willing to sell this.'

Bewildered, she opened it. It took her a few moments to take in what she was reading. 'The orchard,' she said a little breathlessly. 'You've bought the orchard. Oh, William! I never dreamed this could happen.'

'It's for you, it's a present.'

Gilly wasn't worried about the details, she just wanted to hug him. So she did. 'Oh, thank you so much, William! Now we can have a proper wedding!'

A COUNTRY ESCAPE

Katie Fforde

Fran has always wanted to be a farmer, so how she ended up a chef in London is anyone's guess. However, her childhood dream is about to come true. She has just moved into a beautiful — albeit very run-down — farm in the Cotswolds, currently owned by an elderly relative who has informed her that if she manages to turn the place around in a year, the farm will be hers to inherit. But Fran knows nothing about farming. She might even be afraid of cows. She's going to need a lot of help from her best friend Issi, and also from her wealthy and very eligible neighbour — who might just have his own reasons for being so supportive. Is it the farm he's interested in? Or Fran herself?

A SECRET GARDEN

Katie Fforde

Lorna is a talented gardener and Philly is a plantswoman. Together they work on the grounds of a beautiful manor house in the Cotswolds. They enjoy their jobs and are surrounded by family and friends. But for them both, the door to true love remains resolutely closed. So when Lorna is introduced to Jack at a dinner party, and Lucien catches Philly's eye at the local market, it seems that dreams really can come true and happy endings lie just around the corner. But do they? Troublesome parents, the unexpected arrival of someone from Lorna's past, and the discovery of an old and secret garden mean their lives are about to become a lot more complicated . . .